The two c... ...nants of a ...ssed column when Hellboy felt Abe's touch on his arm. He followed Abe's other hand, pointing off to their left, a spot on the nearest wall they might have overlooked because it blended so well with the rest of the destruction. Optical illusion—when you first looked at it, you didn't see it for what it really was. No, that took a few moments. At first, all you saw was a wide circular area more than halfway up the fifteen-foot wall that had been turned into a blackened cinder.

Stone, plaster, wood—whatever was there had been blowtorched into some crumbling alloy that faded into the pigments of the mural painted there centuries ago.

Look deeper, though, and then you would see it: the desiccated suggestion of a man blown off his feet and hurled high against the wall, fused *into* the wall, a charcoal man outstretched in his final agonies and joined to the architecture in bas-relief. Stand in the right place and you could picture how it probably happened: The guy's running when he catches his assailant's attention; no chance of dodging the fireball, but it's partially deflected and absorbed by the square pillar standing between them . . . the only reason there's as much left of the guy as there is, why he wasn't rendered even further down to ash.

Something like that, stuck to the wall—you don't do it just because you have to.

You do it because a part of you likes it . . .

ON EARTH AS IT IS IN HELL

BRIAN HODGE

POCKET STAR BOOKS

New York   London   Toronto   Sydney

This book is a work of fiction. Names, characters, places and incidents are products of the author's imagination or are used fictitiously. Any resemblance to actual events or locales or persons, living or dead, is entirely coincidental.

An *Original* Publication of POCKET BOOKS

A Pocket Star Book published by
POCKET BOOKS, a division of Simon & Schuster, Inc.
1230 Avenue of the Americas, New York, NY 10020

Copyright © 2005 by Mike Mignola

All rights reserved, including the right to reproduce this book or portions thereof in any form whatsoever. For information address Pocket Books, 1230 Avenue of the Americas, New York, NY 10020

ISBN-13: 978-1-4165-0782-6
ISBN-10:   1-4165-0782-5

This Pocket Books paperback edition October 2005

10 9 8 7 6 5 4 3 2 1

POCKET STAR BOOKS and colophon are registered trademarks of Simon & Schuster, Inc.

Cover art by Mike Mignola

Manufactured in the United States of America

For information regarding special discounts for bulk purchases, please contact Simon & Schuster Special Sales at 1-800-456-6798 or business@simonandschuster.com.

ACKNOWLEDGMENTS

This novel came together much more quickly than I'm used to, and thanks are due to those who helped keep it proceeding smoothly and on track: to Christopher Golden and editor Jennifer Heddle, for savvy and constructive overseeing; to Wildy Petoud and Frank Festa, for translating bits of text into languages I don't speak; and to Mike Mignola, for once again letting me poke around in his world. It's a great place to visit and, who knows, I might even enjoy living there.

Berlin,
April 30, 1924

He believed in God once. And could again, provided he found the right one, a god to replace the one that had been pounded out of him by the artillery barrages of the Battle of the Somme. The one that had bled from him into the mud of the trenches bordering No Man's Land, that had peeled away with the skin of his feet. After all, gods die easier than the need for them.

Here on the north side of Berlin's Friedrichstadt quarter, people still seemed to run from the war years after the guns had fallen silent. They just didn't know it, and most never would. Let them live long enough and perhaps a few might, if they were lucky enough to keep their wits into old age, looking back over all they had done and all they hadn't. *Yes, it makes sense from here,* they might say. *So that's what we were doing—trying desperately to prove we were still alive even though our souls were dead.*

In these years in the shadow of the Great War—the War to End All Wars—Ernst had heard Berlin called the wickedest place on earth, and he believed this was true. To look at them in the streets, in the clubs and cabarets, the theaters and brothels and dance halls, you would never know these were a beaten people. Berlin had become a crucible of the kinds of lust and abandon that must have gotten Sodom scorched from the face of the earth.

Good. Things could grow here. New things always grew from ashes and decay.

Ernst Schweiger was still a young man, born just two years before the twentieth century, but he looked older. And now he felt older when he moved. Shrapnel, bullets, bayonets . . . these could not pierce the body without altering time, injecting years or leeching them away. He'd been *born* old, too, or so his sister had told him when he'd come home from the trenches and could barely hobble from his bed to the chair by his window, to look out over the hills and steeples of Heidelberg. He never wanted it but she cried for him anyway—cried for the solemn little boy she remembered helping raise, and for the wounds and rot that had brought body and soul so much closer together.

Gerda's tears—how could he have felt such scorn for a reaction so heartfelt, so human?

But however old he was, however old he felt . . . how could he possibly explain to anyone the degree to which a man like Matthias Herzog made him feel like a child?

Go, Herzog could say. *Bring.* And there were people who would kill each other for the privilege.

Ernst hadn't had to kill. Just say yes.

Could anyone say it wasn't an honor to be so trusted?

At the Kamm-Revue, where the air was thick with sweat and smoke and lager, Ernst worked his way through a crowd that clamored its approval toward the stage where twenty women danced, half-dressed in cheap-looking Egyptian garb.

He watched the audience at their tables: officers and gentlemen and those who could never aspire to either, men who had known fighting, men who hadn't, and men who had been ruined by it, and the painted women who still found something in them that they could desire. The loud, ravenous thugs were the least of Ernst's fears; you knew where they stood and how hard they might fall. It was the self-contained ones that scared him, sitting quiet and sober and still, moving only to bring their cigarettes to their thin dry lips. They wore their scars like men who had transcended the need for dignity. Any one of them, behind his watchful eyes, might be capable of leaving a *lustmord* splayed in an alley or flayed on a roof, then sleeping well. Your gaze could meet theirs from ten, twenty paces away and you could see everything that war had taught them, beyond courage and cowardice, victory and defeat. You could see what war had taught them to *enjoy*.

At the stage door, he exchanged a few words with a stubble-headed man who guarded it with his arms crossed over his barrel chest. The money came next—he may have been expected tonight, but nothing was ever free—and the man let him through.

Backstage, Ernst wormed through the performers, some coming, others going, and into a tight network of hallways branching into offices and dressing rooms. Up a flight of splintering stairs, there was more of the same. Water stains had faded the walls to a moldy green, and clots of plaster gathered around the baseboards. When you passed some-one in the halls up here, they avoided looking you in the eye.

Room 28. He knocked, heard a voice telling him to enter.

"Fraulein Kiefer?" he asked.

She nodded as if no longer interested in what she was called. Angelika was her Christian name—he knew only that about her, and that the placard out front billed her as a chanteuse—although she looked neither Christian nor an-gelic. She too could not have been very old, but had been aged by war, if not directly, then by soldiers and depriva-tion. He could see only one eye, the other shadowed be-hind a mass of dark curls. Against a backdrop of deep blue curtains pulled across the window, she sat slumped into a wooden chair, ankles wide, her dressing gown parted over a brassiere and the slack little bulge of her belly. A garter cut into the plump skin of her thigh, as pale and soft as cheese.

"You're the one they said would be coming about, Erich?"

Ernst said he was.

"You have the money?"

He gave her the envelope of Rentenmarks. Sealed, it felt slim, not all that much inside, but at least Germany's cur-rency was worth something again. When she slit the enve-lope open with her thumbnail and counted, Angelika seemed content. She slid it under a pile of yellowed news-papers stacked on her mirrored dressing table, near an ash-tray where smoke curled from a cigarette stained with her lipstick. Beneath the smoke, the room smelled sour, like a heap of unwashed sheets.

"And the child . . . ?" Ernst said. "Where is he?"

She jerked her thumb toward a corner.

The room may have been cramped, but it was cluttered, too—he hadn't noticed the baby until now, nesting in rubbish and shoes and the ruins of old costumes. In silence, too. Erich was awake, but he'd yet to make a sound.

And now Angelika was looking at the infant with regret. "I should never have named him. It's easier to let loose of them when they have no names."

"You've done this before?" He looked at the slack skin of her belly, the full breasts sagging inside her gown. He'd told himself many times on the way here that he would resist temptation, but still . . . he wanted very much to touch them.

"No. But I've had friends." She shook her head. "I was stupid to name him." She watched Ernst stand in the same spot and stare at the baby as if it were an unexploded shell that had landed in front of him. "Well? Are you going to take it or not?"

Bright eyed, Erich watched him too. He may have been underfed, but this was no newborn. His eyes had strengthened. He could see across the room. Maybe he was accustomed to a parade of unfamiliar faces.

"When was he born?"

Angelika counted on her fingers. "A little more than five months ago."

"And his father?"

She laughed, a sound as bitter as herbs. "I was hoping you might tell me."

Ernst stooped before the quiet bundle, let the baby squeeze his fingers while he smiled down at him, made silly faces, tried to make him laugh but couldn't. He was still giving it his failed best when Angelika's foot scraped toward him across the floor, the tip of her high-heeled shoe tapping on the scuffed wood.

"When I told you I had never done this before, I didn't mean I never would again," she said, smiling at him from beneath her curls. One hand was stroking the inside of her thigh, just above the top of her garter. "We could make another, you and I. You could maybe guarantee the sale that way, and then share a little in the money."

Two fingers still clutched in the baby's fist, Ernst stared at her legs, now stretched and parted to either side of him. For a long moment he felt lured in, mesmerized by the caressing movements of her hand and the smug, satisfied way she had of touching the tip of her tongue to the corner of her mouth. Except none of it, he noticed then, seemed to touch her eyes. They may as well have been the eyes of something posed in a wax museum. His gaze returned to her hand, and to the way the skin of her thigh now seemed so loose, as though if she kept rubbing it, it might tear open over the muscle and fat.

He scooped the infant into his arms and stood, and turned for the door.

She was on her feet and at his side then, with both hands clutching at his arm, enveloping him in a miasma of tobacco and perfume.

"He'll have a good home, won't he?" she asked. "They'll place him with an officer with a home in the countryside, where the air is better, right? He'll be able to climb trees and hills there, won't he?"

Ernst didn't know the specifics of what they'd told her.

Just that she was selling her child to a broker who specialized in placing babies with war-wounded officers who had lost their ability to father children. Beyond that, they'd probably told her whatever she'd wanted to hear.

He leaned in and kissed her once on the forehead, above the furrow that had appeared between her eyes.

"He'll swim in lakes, too," Ernst said, "and have all the dogs to play with that a boy could want."

She nodded. Maybe she even believed it.

He pulled his arm from her grasp and left the room, and wondered if she might have come running into the hallway if she'd heard her baby cry even once.

That Erich didn't make a sound—just smiled up at him—made him think it really was better this way.

Even though he'd had a driver for this last leg of the journey, he'd still done too much walking tonight. He felt he might slough off the skin of his feet all over again by the time he and his bundle made it to the warehouse.

He'd been here only once, two days ago, and then not very far inside. It was a functional stop, so they could be sure he knew where to come when it mattered. Before that moment, even knowledge of this place had been denied him. Initiates of *Der Horn-Orden* met in a handful of lodges around the city, and he'd been led to believe that that was sufficient for their studies.

Did it not make sense, though, that they would require a more private place for experiments and ceremonies?

And private it was. The warehouse was a hollow giant in an eastern sector that still wore the grime belched by smokestacks of factories that had fallen silent by the end of

the war. In the light of the moon and street lamps, he could
see nothing that hadn't one way or another fed a war machine that had broken apart in the end. Ernst wondered
what it had held, this warehouse of brick and timbers. He
wondered if anything from here had found its way to him
in the trenches, to save his life or make it worse: cartridges
he'd loaded into his rifle, or shells that had whistled overhead and fallen too short, showering him with earth and
slivers. Maybe the tires on a truck that had carried him to
the front, or the ambulances that had driven him away. Or
the roll of barbed wire in which he'd become entangled
after a failed charge and for the rest of the day pretended to
be dead, wearing the rotting entrails stolen from an even
unluckier man within reach, in hopes that the British soldiers passing through would be less likely to bayonet him
where he hung.

Strange, to look upon so silent a building and know it
must have been complicit in so much death. Stranger still,
to bring to it so tender a life, rescued from squalor it would
never remember, to share in the higher glories of the only
life it would know.

Initiates who came to *Der Horn-Orden* as grown men
and women were fine, and welcome, Herzog had said. But
it was best of all to get them young, before they could accu-
mulate worldly corruption that would first have to be un-
done. It was a lesson that Herzog claimed he'd taken from
the Jesuits.

At a far corner of the warehouse, Ernst knocked on a
wooden door stout enough for a stockade. A small grill slid
back at eye level, but the opening showed only blackness.
He hesitated, having no idea if what he couldn't see recog-

nized him or not, so he held up the baby who'd been sleeping in his arms. His burden. His ticket.

The grill clacked shut again and he heard locks disengaging on the other side of the door, like the mechanism of a vast clockwork; the grind of a beam heaved from its brackets, one end thudding to the floor with a cavernous echo. The door whispered inward on hinges so carefully oiled they were nearly silent, then he stepped through into a dimness where nothing was louder than his heart . . . one of those moments made precious by how rare they were, when it seemed his whole life had led to this point.

From his side, a hand on his shoulder and someone's breath, enough garlic and schnapps to burn the nose, and it brought him down to earth again.

The man welcomed him, called him brother.

Another came from the other side, bulky shapes in the gloom—the only light came from a few scattered lanterns whose reach was feeble here—and the men had nothing else to say as they ushered him through the warehouse, footsteps swallowed by the dark. To this place even the moon was more blind than not, the skylights obscured with soot.

Again, a hand on his shoulder, holding firm this time.

"Stop," he was told. "Wait here a minute."

They moved in front of him and with his eyes growing accustomed to the gloom, Ernst was surprised he hadn't noticed it . . . a low housing set in the floor with two wide doors angled toward them, like the entrance to a storm cellar. When his escorts flung them open, he was bathed in the yellow-orange light that shone from below. A broad wooden staircase, planks as old and heavy as a ship's deck, led down . . .

. . . and behind him, above him, the doors thudded shut, and once again he heard the sound of locks.

If they were waiting for him below, they gave little sign of it—dozens, maybe even more than a hundred, who looked no different from the revelers at the cabaret. Here to learn, or here to worship, and, he suspected, some were here only because they found it the fashionable thing to do; had tasted everything else that Berlin had to offer and pronounced themselves bored with it already, so now they found themselves here. Some of them held wooden flutes, and others drums—for what, he couldn't say. His arrival, with babe in arms, seemed a minor curiosity, nothing more.

The place was lit by a thousand flickering gas lamps and candles, and he'd never been anywhere that looked so warm yet felt so chilled. Not even the amassed body heat seemed to make a difference. With its rough wooden walls and packed earthen floor, the cellar had all the charm of the trenches.

The baby had awakened again and was starting to squirm, and though Ernst had rather liked the soft, warm weight tucked against his chest, he was glad to turn it over to Herzog when the man shouldered through and appeared at his side.

"He's a puny thing," Herzog said in appraisal, holding the infant aloft, at arm's length, "but I think his heart is stout enough." Then he drew the baby close, doing it all with one arm. One was all he had to work with.

For now.

And already, as they strolled from one end of the long,

narrow cellar to the other, Ernst was forgetting whether he'd found Matthias Herzog or the man had found him . . . tonight, and in the beginning, too. He did that to you, seemed to dissolve your past simply by making your acquaintance, until you went to bed one night and stared at the shadows on the ceiling and realized that he'd always been there, always been in your life, and even if you could remember a time when you hadn't yet heard his name, you realized he was the piece of the puzzle you'd always known was out there, waiting to find you or be found. He was the one who could tell you he'd talked with things on the other side of death and you believed him, from no more than the look in his eyes. He was a big man who never tried to hide his height, with a face as sculpted by wind and rain as any mountainside rock, a face that you could recognize at once, yet never quite describe. A man who, more than any cleric in a flimsy pulpit, could make you see beyond the worst of your pain to understand that there truly could be a reason for it.

And as he spoke, so he lived. The evidence was inside his left sleeve. He'd lost the arm in France, or so he said, and whether true or not, what mattered was that Ernst had seen a photograph of him shirtless, his shoulder reduced to a raw knob of jutting bone beneath stretched and sutured flesh.

No longer, though. It was growing back, a slow but steady restoration of bone and skin and muscle that Herzog attributed to an act of will, no more and no less. He'd seen it, Ernst had, just once . . . small and pink and hairless, a child's limb still, but the fingers could flex. He could raise the arm, could make a fist.

"Don't look so nervous," Herzog told him. "You survived a losing war. The next one is yours to win."

And as they approached the far end of the cellar, the air began to warm with every step, and Ernst could see the gleaming head that rose above the heads of everyone who still stood between them and the far wall. Wordlessly they stepped aside, some bowing their heads in deference, until finally this human curtain had parted and he could see what waited.

It was bronze, he thought, rubbed to a shiny dark yellow at the top, where perched upon a set of massive shoulders, the crowned and fearsome head of a bull stared out over them all, huge mouth open wide in an eternal roar. It sat upon a throne, regal and arrogant, yet held both arms stiffly before its thick chest, human hands empty and upturned. Strangely, its color changed from the top down, the polished head and chest fading to a deeper tone that in turn became a glowing red. Its legs and the seat and enclosed base of the throne shimmered with heat, while smoke fumed from vents cut into the sides.

As Herzog stepped away from him, someone thrust a small frame drum into one of Ernst's hands, a beater into the other.

Whatever Herzog had to say next was mercifully brief, and in no language Ernst could understand. Then the man turned his back on them all as the place erupted into a cacophony of rhythmless drumming, tuneless piping. It came from everywhere at once, and was nothing any sane person would call music—volume was all that seemed to matter. One-handed, Herzog slung Erich onto the outstretched bronze hands, a natural cradle from which the baby could not roll free. Even if Ernst could no longer hear the infant he'd carried so far on aching feet, he could see the tiny arms flailing in fear, and then the baby began to rise, an impossible sight, both bronze arms lifting upward in jerky movements, as though ratcheting one gear tooth at a time, until the hands were at the gaping mouth . . .

And the hands were empty once more.

While the band played on, Ernst was ashamed to find himself playing along too, helplessly battering at the drum they'd given him, not daring to falter, because what if his contribution to this din was all that kept him from hearing the screams that had to be coming from inside the statue.

Even so, it still wasn't loud enough to mask the sound of a low, subterranean groan of satisfaction.

CHAPTER 1

Forty-nine hours after the inferno, he could still smell what made it unique.

Fires and their aftermath had their own signature smells. Anyone who fought them for a living could tell you as much. A forest fire? It smelled natural . . . just wood and sap, and lots of it, like a big campfire. An urban blaze was totally different—toxic with all the synthetics they put into the buildings, the furniture, the clothes on their own charred backs.

The thing was, he knew smells that few firefighters had ever encountered, and even if they had, most couldn't have recognized them for what they truly were.

Hellfire? He knew the smell, all right. Brimstone and bitumen and something like the roasting of marrow-rotted bones that might blacken but never fully burn. Sometimes he felt the smell was never far from his nostrils, something he just *knew,* a birthright he carried in his blood.

This smell, though? Here, in this wreckage and ruin? It was a first for him.

Although that didn't mean he had no idea what it was.

Divine fire, holy fire, fire from Heaven, to clear and cleanse . . . it left a lingering scent in the ash, mixed in with the stink of immolation and meltdown, a subtle but jarringly incongruous fragrance, like blossoms in a midsummer field, only more astringent. Sniff it in too great a concentration, and he imagined that it would sear the nostrils. He suspected that it bore some relation to the phenomenon known as the Odor of Sanctity, the sweet fragrances that were sometimes reported accompanying the appearances of saints and manifestations of the divine.

That such a smell could linger in a place of so much devastation seemed more than a little like mockery.

He'd never smelled it before but was surprised to find that he knew it so readily, as surely as he knew its opposite. Another birthright, maybe, innate knowledge of an enemy he'd been conceived to fight but never had, never would, because he'd chosen differently. Hell's enemies were not his own. Hell's enemies were his allies—the enemy of my enemy is my friend.

Or so he'd always believed.

Divine fire, holy fire, fire from Heaven, to clear and cleanse . . .

The last place he'd expected to come across it was the Vatican.

BUREAU FOR PARANORMAL RESEARCH AND DEFENSE
Field Report EU-000394-59

Date: October 16, 1996
Compiled by: Dr. Kate Corrigan
Classification: Open Access

Interview Subject: Father Rogier Artaud (assistant curator, Vatican Secret Archives; specialist in Palestinian antiquities)

The incident under investigation occurred at approximately 10:30 pm on Monday, October 14, as Fr. Artaud was working in the private research area on the fourth floor of the Archives.

[Before I continue, I should clarify a possible misperception for the benefit of anyone in the BPRD who may refer to this file in the future. It was, I admit, news to me: The Vatican Secret Archives aren't nearly as covert as the name implies. They were founded in 1612 by Pope Paul V as a repository for papal records, correspondence, official files, etc. . . . comprising, at present, a whopping 25 miles of shelf space. The "secret" designation lies in the archaic definition of the word: private, rather than deliberately withheld. They're open to any scholars who obtain permission for admittance. As of this writing, all papal archives up to the late 1920s are available for study. An approximate seven-decade restriction prevents access to the modern era . . . roughly comparable to the lifetime of a living pope, or, in the case of the longer-lived pontiffs, his adult life and career. That said, there are also numerous historical documents in the Archives that have secular origins, or otherwise fall outside of official Church business. Fr. Artaud cites a

love letter penned by King Henry VIII to Anne
Boleyn in which he pledges his heart to her . . .
ironic, considering the eventual fate of her head.]

At approximately 10:10 pm, Fr. Artaud removed
Document s/00183/1966 from its drawer in a
temperature- and humidity-controlled vault used
for storing and protecting particularly fragile artifacts. [Re: Document s/00183/1966, see Field
Report Supplement EU-000394-59supA.] Permission for its removal had been requested by Fr.
Artaud nine days earlier, and granted the afternoon of October 11. The circumstances leading
up to its necessity are still not fully understood,
but at this point, what we know is this:

In the earliest days of October, Fr. Artaud wished
to compare high-resolution scans of Document
s/00183/1966 (which exist to facilitate document
analysis without need of handling the original)
with various points raised in an article about to
be published in a journal of the *Ecole Biblique*, a
Jerusalem archaeological school operated by
French Dominicans, which has exercised considerable influence over the Dead Sea Scrolls since
their 1947 discovery. The article in Fr. Artaud's
possession concerned paleography: the study of
handwriting in ancient manuscripts—in this particular case, manuscripts from first-century Palestine. However, for reasons as yet unknown, the
two physical copies of the document's scans had

evidently been misplaced and the computerized version corrupted and thus inaccessible. In retrospect, this is extremely suspicious, but initially it appeared to be a mere unfortunate coincidence of sloppiness and bad luck.

Note: That so few copies of these scans existed is a reflection of the highly sensitive nature of Document s/00183/1966, rather than the inadequacies of the Archives' data backup policy. Although, if I may be indulged another personal observation, while I wouldn't be so presumptuous as to pass judgment on the integrity of their physical recordkeeping, which I'm sure is ordinarily above reproach . . . they trusted a single electronic copy to Windows 95???

At a minute or two before 10:30 pm, as Fr. Artaud was rescanning the document in preparation for his study, he became aware of two anomalies: flickering and dimming in the electricity, and an abrupt drop in the air temperature in his work area. This was no minor chill passing through, and well beyond the capabilities of a malfunction in the A/C system, which was not in operation at the time anyway. Fr. Artaud estimates the temperature drop to have been at least 50° F in a minute's time. As it was cold enough for him to see his own breath, this was far below the outside temperature as well. According to local meteorology reports, routine measurements near the Vati-

can at 10:30 pm on the night of October 12 put
the temperature at 64° F/17° C. Fr. Artaud also
noticed that the cold was unmistakably descending from above.

I'm tempted to say this is the weird part, but
then, it's all weird. According to Fr. Artaud's testimony, over the weekend, while he was riding
his bicycle in a large market area near the Vatican called the Borgo, he was stopped by a young
man who warned him, with the kind of deadly
seriousness that only a street lunatic can muster,
to "run when the ceiling turns to ice." Naturally
Artaud dismissed the encounter and went on his
way.

And, just as naturally, it came back to him during this abnormal temperature drop. But at this
point, his concern was primarily for the integrity of Document s/00183/1966. Like all fragile documents, it's best protected from shifts
in temperature and humidity. Because the low
temperatures appeared to be originating overhead and the power supply appeared unstable,
and because Artaud was now a bit unnerved by
the warning, he placed the five separate sheets
of Document s/00183/1966 in their storage
drawer and sought lower ground. He didn't
linger to talk with any of the handful of other
Archivists working at this late hour, among

whom the drop in temperature was the obvious topic of conversation.

This undoubtedly saved both Fr. Artaud's life and the document. As he reached a staff-only stairwell, he heard the shattering of glass and looked back long enough to witness two figures entering through a tall outside window. He also reports hearing the breaking of at least one other window, out of view, leading to the conclusion that the intruders numbered at least four to six.

What he saw he describes as humanoid, if not strictly human. At first he thought they were some sort of commando team. But then, "They changed from shadow to light in only a moment or two. I don't mean they moved from one to the next, like stepping out of a dark room. I mean this is what they were made of. In one moment, like a cloak of dark rags. In the next, so white they seemed to glow, like the filament of a light bulb."

Fr. Artaud didn't pause for more than a brief glance. It was at this point that the arrivals began spewing fire. Exactly how they went about this is unknown, as there are no other witnesses, but the attached photos of the damage inflicted upon that section of the Archives is testament to their efficiency.

One observation: The process by which these entities created fire from their own bodies is, by all available evidence, different from that shown by the BPRD's resident pyrokinetic, Liz Sherman. Although Ms. Sherman's abilities are still not fully understood, she appears to be the fire's conduit, rather than its creator.

On the other hand, the beings at the Vatican Archives appear, to some extent, to be subject to the laws of physics and thermodynamics. They evidently did not generate their flames out of nothing, but instead, immediately prior to their attack, drew the required energy from the air temperature in the vicinity and from the power grid.

Because I'm preaching to the converted here, I shouldn't have to remind you of the oft-reported phenomenon that certain spiritual manifestations are sometimes accompanied by temperature drops and electrical disturbances. The most widely accepted rationale for this occurrence is that the spirit entity requires energy to make itself visible, and uses the process of convection to obtain that energy from the nearest sources: warm air, electricity, etc.

A similar phenomenon appears to have happened at the Vatican Archives, only the siphoned energy was weaponized. The expended energy had to have been far greater than what was drawn from the local environment, leading one of our physics consultants to speculate—at the risk of making an obvious paranormal event sound overly mechanical—that the attackers also functioned as their own transformers.

Completion pending conclusion of on-site investigation . . .

CHAPTER 2

Hellboy got as much of the background from Kate
Corrigan as seemed relevant—he would skim the
reports later, maybe—then decided to push on and inspect
the wreckage for himself.

Stone columns and archways, fluted ceiling joists, old
oak cabinets and tables . . . most of it had probably
looked much the same for centuries, and the only way he
could tell it had once been beautiful was by context, the
hallways and the rooms he and Abe had passed through
to get here. There was nothing beautiful about it now; it
was like the inside of a kiln that had been used too many
times without cleaning. They'd be scraping this place out
for weeks. Even the lighting was harsh now, most of the
normal fixtures destroyed and, for the time being, replaced with cable-fed portables with the same harsh glare
as a mechanic's garage.

"How hot would you say it got in here?" he asked.

"You can cremate a body in half an hour at 1300 degrees or so," Abe said. "So in excess of that. Because these
look more like flash fires. They don't seem to have burned
for long. They cooked everything in their path, but . . ."
With a gray-green hand mostly concealed within the

sleeve of his topcoat, he pointed to the ceiling, the floor.
"They didn't spread beyond this section of the Archives.
Those kinds of temperatures, for any duration . . . this
could've been worse."

As they walked along a row of oak cabinets charred
down to kindling, Hellboy felt, heard things grind underfoot. They could be walking on bones, or what remained of
them, and never know.

"Spontaneous human combustion," he said. "That's
what it reminds me of. I've seen it twice. Not while it was
happening, but after. There's some freaky selectivity in that
kind of fire. One guy burned so hot it melted candles in
their stands across the room, but the easy chair he was sitting in . . . give it a good cleaning and you might've been
able to use it again."

"What it reminds me of is gang warfare," Abe said.
"An assassination, except they were using fire instead of
bullets. And weren't a bit concerned who got caught up
in it."

Hellboy nodded. Some of that, yeah, he thought . . . but
part spree killing, too. Like the guy who walks into the
place where he used to work and starts unloading, and it no
longer matters who he does and doesn't have grudges
against. If it catches his eye, it's a target.

You could follow the paths of some of the flames,
trenches dug and melted into the patterned tiles of the
floor, as though concentrated bursts had generated on the
spot, then coursed after their targets. Most of the paths
were straight, like third-degree burns that slashed across
rooms, down hallways, along ceilings. But a couple of them
had altered course . . . one curving in a broad arc, the other

hooking a sharp left after twenty or so feet and reducing a display case to a pile of slag.

No concern for who got caught in the crossfire, Abe had said. Hellboy didn't doubt he was bothered greatly by the human loss—seven casualties was the estimate so far, and the number would've been a lot higher had this attack occurred during the day instead of late at night—but Abe would be mourning more than life. This place had been called a decanting of history, and Abe Sapien would be mourning that, too. He wasn't strictly human, Abe wasn't—or not entirely—but he read more than just about any five other living souls that Hellboy knew. If Abe had been in some other kind of skin, this might have been the sort of place he would've ended up, and happily so, tending to the past so that it would continue to live and speak.

They were just things, that's all, someone might have said. Just books, just papers, just manuscripts and ornaments and trinkets. Nothing when compared to the value of a human life. They'd never drawn breath, all these inanimate things. They didn't scream as they burned. But *things* often survived the people who owned them, then outlived everyone who'd remembered their owners, until the day came when *things* were all that were left to speak for lives long gone.

The two of them were stepping around the crusted remnants of a large, square, frescoed column when Hellboy felt Abe's touch on his arm. He followed Abe's other hand, pointing off to their left, a spot on the nearest wall they might have overlooked because it blended so well with the rest of the destruction.

Optical illusion—when you first looked at it, you didn't

see it for what it really was. No, that took a few moments. At first, all you saw was a wide circular area more than halfway up the fifteen-foot wall that had been turned into a blackened cinder. Stone, plaster, wood—whatever was there had been blowtorched into some crumbling alloy that faded into the pigments of the mural painted there centuries ago.

Look deeper, though, and then you would see it: the desiccated suggestion of a man blown off his feet and hurled high against the wall—fused *into* the wall, a charcoal man outstretched in his final agonies and joined to the architecture in bas-relief. Stand in the right place and you could picture how it probably happened: The guy's running when he catches his assailant's attention; no chance of dodging the fireball, but it's partially deflected and absorbed by the square pillar standing between them . . . the only reason there's as much left of the guy as there is, why he wasn't rendered even further down to ash.

Something like that, stuck to the wall, you don't do it just because you have to.

You don't do it out of a sense of duty.

You do it because a part of you likes it, the sport of it.

"Hellboy . . . ?" said Abe. "What can *do* this?"

"There's Liz, for starters. But she's on the other side of the ocean right now, and it's not her style anyway, so we can rule her out," he said. "Other than that, plus what my nose tells me? My guess is seraphim."

Abe had one of those faces that could be hard to read a lot of the time. Not his fault. He didn't have the full set of features that helped with all the nonverbal cues. Like eyebrows. Or a brow ridge, for that matter. Still, he sometimes had this way of looking at you, and you just knew how much he hated what he was hearing.

"Seraphim," Abe said flatly. "And here I thought that, of all places, this one was on the side of the angels."

"If there's any truth to the old stories, seraphim are a breed apart. I've heard them called Heaven's stormtroopers. Never saw one, but I've always gotten the idea they do what they're told without a lot of questions. Not that it's going to make you feel any better, but the last I'm aware of them unleashing this kind of firepower was in Sodom and Gomorrah."

And the question hung in the air unasked, because neither of them had to: What could possibly have come along, after upwards of 3500 years, to pose enough of a threat that would warrant this level of response?

"Dresden." Kate's voice, behind them. He hadn't seen her rejoin them. "You forgot Dresden, Germany. Near the end of World War Two."

"That's just a rumor. Not even a convincing one," Hellboy said. "One Allied phosphorous bomb for every two people? You don't need seraphim with that kind of payload raining down."

"You're looking at it wrong. If it's true, Dresden wasn't cause-and-effect. It was opportunity seized," Kate said. "Where better to blend in and cover their tracks?"

On this one, at least, they could agree to disagree. Kate Corrigan definitely knew her business . . . and if it was weird, well, then it was her business. A fortyish woman with a tousled bob of sandy hair, she'd been consulting for the bureau for the past dozen years, when she wasn't teaching history classes at N.Y.U. Or hunched over a keyboard.

The woman wrote books almost as fast as Abe could read them—sixteen at last count, her own ever-growing shelf in the folklore and occult section.

She'd beaten him and Abe here by a full day. Had been on some unspecified sabbatical at the Paulvé Institute in Avignon, France, when the summons came in that the Vatican, of all places, was asking for a discreet outside opinion.

"It's taken awhile, but I'm finally getting somewhere with these guys," she said. "You know, I'd hoped that maybe, just *maybe*, this place would've been different . . . but no, you show up and it's the same as any other bureaucracy. They beg for your help, they tell you how glad they are you're here . . . and then it practically takes a case of whiskey and a pound of laxatives to get the relevant truth out of them."

"A lovely image," Abe said.

And Kate was beaming. She didn't do that often. She frowned, she scowled, she had a whole closetful of thoughtful looks, but she hardly ever *beamed*. Especially in places like this, where death was still so fresh.

"What's going on here, Kate?" he asked.

"The confirmation of a legend," she said. "They just gave up what that hit squad must have been after: the Masada Scroll."

BUREAU FOR PARANORMAL RESEARCH AND DEFENSE
Field Report Supplement EU-000394-59supA

Date: October 16, 1996
Compiled by: Dr. Kate Corrigan

Classification: Restricted Access—Need To Know
Subject: Vatican Secret Archives Document
s/00183/1966

Although the Masada Scroll has for the past
thirty years been a quiet but persistent rumor,
impossible to substantiate, its existence has finally been verified by a physical artifact. At this
early stage the BPRD cannot take a position one
way or another on its authenticity, only cite the
claims made about it.

Background: According to the only known con-
temporaneous first-century source (*The Jewish
War*, by Josephus Flavius), Herod the Great, King
of Judea, built the fortress known as Masada in
the fourth decade B.C.E. Installed as a puppet
ruler by the Romans, Herod was reviled by the
Jewish populace, and thus intended Masada to be
a personal refuge in the event of an uprising.

For strategic purposes, the location was well
chosen. Herod utilized the natural features of a
remote mesa and cliff structure located at the
western end of the Judean Desert. The eastern
side plunges hundreds of meters straight into
the Dead Sea. At the western side, the plateau is
still roughly a hundred meters above the desert
floor. The pathways up were few, openly ex-
posed, precarious to navigate, and thus could be
easily defended by a relatively small group.

Nevertheless, in the year 66 C.E., during the Jewish Revolt, a group of rebels defeated the Roman garrison at Masada and took control of the site. After another four years of conflict, following the fall of Jerusalem and the destruction of the Temple, Masada became a final stronghold for hundreds of militant Zealots who left Jerusalem with their families. For two years they used Masada as a base from which to launch incursions against the Romans.

All that came to an end in 73 C.E., when Roman governor Flavius Silva besieged Masada with the Tenth Legion and additional units. After establishing camps and closing off the immediate area with a wall, they began a mind-boggling feat of engineering: using thousands of tons of stone and packed earth to build an enormous ramp from the desert floor up to Masada's western side. After it was completed in the spring of 74 C.E., they wheeled a battering ram up the ramp and broke through the fortress wall.

However, the Roman victory was Pyrrhic at best. They were met not with further resistance, but by the corpses of 900 to 1000 men, women, and children. Rather than be taken alive, Masada's defenders opted for death at the hands of their family members and compatriots, until the last man alive committed suicide. They also burned everything but the food supplies, to make certain the Romans knew that they hadn't been driven to their deaths by starvation. Josephus Flavius' account of Masada's last hours was allegedly based on testimony taken by him from the only known survivors: two women who hid to escape the carnage.

While Masada's location was verified in the modern era as far back as 1842, it wasn't until the mid-1960s that international teams of archaeologists undertook a serious excavation of the site. It was during one of these digs that the purported Masada Scroll was unearthed by a joint British-Israeli team, although it has never been a part of any official inventory of artifacts from the site, much less offered up for public study, like the Shroud of Turin. It has, for all intents and purposes, been a phantom find, the archaeological equivalent of an urban legend . . . spoken of by various sources, but its existence uncorroborated by any scholar connected with the Masada excavations.

[Note: Fr. Rogier Artaud's informal checks into the background of the scroll, as detailed in the Vatican Archives documentation (see attachment Field Report Supplement EU-000394-59supB), have without exception led to dead ends, all traces of the personages involved seeming to end by no later than 1968. Because Artaud's resources are limited, I recommend that the BPRD conduct a more thorough follow-up, although it's difficult to avoid drawing conclusions from Artaud's lack of results, however informal his efforts.]

The Masada Scroll: According to the aforementioned copy of Vatican Archives documentation, the scroll was found in the floor under the remains of a structure that has come to be known as the Administrative Building, from its Herodian origins. It had been secured inside two clay jars, one nested inside the other and cushioned by an inner layer of soil, with the opening of the larger jar sealed over with pitch. These jars had in turn been buried .8 meter down in a natural hollow of rock, the remainder of the space filled in with additional earth that had been tamped into sufficient compactness to blend it with the natural floor. Thus protected, it survived the conflagration that burned directly above it, and the 1890 years that followed. Both of the jars and the outer seal remained intact until after their discovery.

The scroll itself consists of five inconsistently sized sheets of parchment, which had been rolled and bound with a leather thong. The state of preservation of all materials was regarded as remarkable—although the same could be said of many finds at Masada—due to two primary factors: the site's remoteness and inaccessibility, and the dry climate.

The text's authorship is, in the salutation, attributed to Yeshua (Jesus) the Nazarene. Its intended audience, also established in the salutation, is a group in Ephesus, on the western coast of what is now Turkey. A full translation of the text will follow, pending approval by Fr. Vittorio Ranzi, Artaud's immediate superior, but according to Fr. Artaud, it is not an earlier document brought to Masada, but was written at the site, with clear references to the Roman siege. It appears to have been begun relatively early in the siege, with hopes expressed that the Romans would fail in their endeavor. A current of pessimism enters later and the letter remains unfinished, as its author appears resigned to the fact that it will never be delivered or read by its intended audience . . . although the author, or someone else, obviously had optimism that it might be discovered later.

The majority of the text, according to Fr. Artaud, portrays the bittersweet reflections of a Jesus knowing he is at the end of a long and painful life . . . not specifically denying his divinity, but coming to the understanding that he is just "one of many sons of God." He also hopes to refute what he clearly considers distorted and divisive interpretations of his original message by Paul (né Saul of Tarsus), and reconcile the schisms that were, even in his lifetime, starting to violently oppose one another.

That Jesus could have survived crucifixion and lived into old age is considered possible by medical science, with various theoretical scenarios citing biblical as well as forensic details. And, while most often condemned as heresy, the premise that Jesus lived into old age appears in different forms, including one legend that he and Mary Magdalene and other followers fled Palestine and eventually settled in the British Isles, with his descendants alive today in Western Europe. However, the "Masada theory" is thus far the only one that comes with potential physical proof.

The Vatican takes no official position on the scroll's authenticity—or even a consistent unofficial position, for that matter—preferring to instead quietly relegate it to permanent exile in archival storage like any other historical artifact. However, they have, in strict secrecy, subjected it to analysis by various scientific tests that have emerged since its discovery (after, it bears noting, the as-yet unknown and undocumented means by which the document came under Vatican control).

Paleography, spore analysis, and radio carbon dating of the leather binding have all indicated that the document does indeed date to the first century, and thus is unlikely to have been buried at Masada at some later date. However, its authorship—certainly a deeper and more vital authenticity—cannot be proved, only disproved . . . and thus, with the scroll certified as a first century relic, its custodians have arrived at a stalemate.

CHAPTER 3

Hellboy and Abe kept to the trees while they waited. Behind the scenes, some sort of mid- to high-level meeting was going on, archivists and a few Church officials haggling over what to do next.

Hellboy hoped they weren't *too* high level. He'd met plenty of priests over the years and felt only fondness for most of them . . . but then, they'd nearly always been the grunts, never the glorified, the guys who dutifully put on their collars and took care of their parishes without much of anybody to take care of them. Start giving them pageantry, power, and positions to protect, though, and the distinctions between holy men and politicians started to become a lot less clear.

As dawn came, Vatican City started to awaken around them, lights winking on in buildings near and far . . . although nothing was truly far away here. Enclosed by a wall like a medieval city, all but the opening to St. Peter's Square, this was the world's smallest sovereign state—the beating heart of Rome, yet a world unto itself. Most of its buildings were clustered along the eastern side, and much of the interior was like a park, full of trees and gardens and green lawns. Here Hellboy and Abe lingered, facing the long, castle-like western wall of the museum complex that housed the Archives, the Apostolic Library, and art beyond price and artifacts beyond numbers. As the sky lightened, he could see the blackened scorch marks on the stone above several windows in the middle. To the south loomed the enormous gray dome of St. Peter's. No getting away from that one. It rose over all and saw everything.

A discreet fifteen paces away stood the member of the Swiss Guard that had been assigned to them. Invited into Vatican City or not, you didn't just stroll around the grounds like a tourist. An escort was mandatory, so whenever they weren't in the company of priests, a corporal by the name of Bertrand took over, stoic enough about this all-night duty but still seeming embarrassed about the formality. The Swiss Guard was a token unit, the last remainder of the papal armies of centuries past. Even in this day and age, they carried halberds.

Hellboy nudged Abe and kept his voice low. "Is this guy freaking you out a little?"

"Me? No," Abe said. "Maybe it's the uniform."

Strangest uniform Hellboy had ever seen. No camouflage here. You could see these guys coming a mile away. Their uniforms had big, bold, vertical stripes of saffron and maroon, with puffy sleeves and legs, and were topped off with a dark beret. The effect was like a cross between a soldier and a harlequin.

"He makes me nervous," Hellboy said. "He's like the guy that follows you around in the store because he's afraid you're gonna break something."

Abe just looked at him. "When was the last time *you* were shopping, anyway?"

Footsteps along a nearby path—as a man in a black cassock drew closer, Hellboy saw that it was Father Artaud, the Palestinian antiquities specialist who'd saved the scroll. He was Belgian, Kate had said earlier, and looked to be in his late thirties, early forties, and all that bike-pedaling must have paid off. A less athletic man may not have cleared the attack area in time.

"Come with me," the priest said. "Hurry."

They followed as he led them back into the museum complex . . . down palatial hallways, through further doors, up a flight of stairs. Then, along a deserted second floor corridor he stopped before what appeared to be just one more muraled panel in the wall, until he stooped and his fingers found pressure points in the lower corners. The panel ground open to reveal the rough stone blocks of an inner corridor.

"Not you guys too," Hellboy said.

Artaud motioned them inside. "The Vatican is honeycombed with them. These places were built in a more dangerous time. Who knew when these passages might be needed? And today . . . ?" He almost smiled. "To waste them would be a sin."

Down again, as the panel ground closed after them, and Artaud led the way with a penlight.

By the time they stopped, they must have been well below ground level, in a plain stone-block chamber the size of a small chapel, lit with nothing more modern than a dozen candles. A hole bored into the floor of one corner might once have served as a crude toilet, mercifully unused in a very long time. Too inconvenient for storage, too dry for a dungeon, too unadorned for a ritual space, the place would once have been good only for hiding away from an invading army. Or, today, making sure that something spoken in secret remained that way.

At their arrival, all heads turned, and Artaud closed a thick wooden door that fit as tightly as a cork in a bottle.

"Why, Kate Corrigan," said Hellboy. "Tell me you're not down here corrupting an entire roomful of priests."

"If anything's getting corrupted, it's my lungs," she said quietly, and flicked her gaze toward a pair who stood along one wall conversing over cigarettes, taking rapid pulls off them as if in an agitated race to see who could finish first. If there was any means of circulation, Hellboy couldn't spot it, and the air was turning hazy.

Artaud included, there were six men in black down here—four in cassocks and two in suits. None of them appeared to have enjoyed a restful night, with bleary eyes and stubbled faces all around. A rotund fellow sat repeatedly nodding off in his chair; his heavy jowls would squash outward with every sharp droop of his head, then he'd bob upright again and blink. A thin man with a balding skull and the prize for the room's darkest shadow of whiskers was pouring himself coffee, black as oil, from a silver thermos. Artaud introduced him as Vittorio Ranzi, his superior in the Archives.

"I'm not much for ceremony, so it doesn't bother me," Hellboy said, "but if this is the best conference room you can come up with, it leads me to believe that whatever comes out of here won't have an official stamp of approval."

"Official can mean many things," Ranzi told him. "Whatever comes of this will have the support of many hundreds more than you see here. For now, it is best if that support is quiet. Away from eyes and ears that would be better off blind and deaf to it."

"Spoken like a true conspirator," Hellboy said. "Let me tell you something, just so we're clear on it: I *hate* doing other peoples' dirty work. And I hate it when people twist the truth to try and get me to *do* their dirty work."

Kate put her hand on his arm. "Hey. You're getting a little ahead of yourself. Hear them out."

The plump man in the chair, introduced as Archbishop Bellini, had jolted awake for good and struggled upright. "This place, this Church—if you know anything about her, then you know that no matter how tranquil she seems on the outside, underneath she always has some unrest. Always some struggle going on beneath her surface." He shook his head. "Dirty work? No, no, no. Where the Church is concerned, we here speak of evolution."

"I don't believe I've ever heard that word spoken in positive terms by the clergy," Abe said.

"And the reasons for that, the attitudes . . . " Bellini said. "Would you be the one to see them continue on, unchallenged? You especially, of all beings."

No secrets here. They knew what Abe Sapien was, all right, or near enough. He may have taken care, on a trip like this, to conceal himself in a high-collared topcoat, under a hat, and behind glasses, but there was only so much normality he could project. Come to a place like this, where so many spent so much time dwelling on higher things—on the Creator of the world and their place in it, convinced they knew the answers to everything that mattered—and you had to wonder what they *really* thought of their visitors. Of someone as unique as Abe. *Or,* Hellboy thought, *someone like me.*

He figured the reactions split along a pair of likely polarities.

One: *God indeed works in mysterious ways, and must surely love infinite variety.*

The other: *A pity it's not four hundred years earlier, when we might have killed these things with impunity and the thanks of a grateful city.*

Bellini spoke of evolution? One look at an unconcealed Abe Sapien left you with the thought that Darwin had definitely been onto something. Abe had been found in the mid-'70s in Washington, D. C., deep in the basements beneath St. Trinian's Hospital. A plumbing crew had broken through a sealed door and happened upon a large room that not only predated anyone's living memory, but had also evaded replication on any known blueprints. Floating inside a tall, circular glass tank tipped back and resting at an angle, its base sunk into stagnant ooze, there he was: a long-slumbering fellow, humanoid in appearance, hairless and sleekly muscled, but with finned forearms and a neck that bristled with gills. The only clue to his origins—and scant evidence at that—was a note, penned by what appeared to have been an ornate Victorian hand and curled like parchment, affixed to a piece of the corroded and broken-down machinery near the tank.

Icthyo Sapien, it read. *April 14 1865.*

The same day President Lincoln had died.

For an uncommonly intelligent entity thus far denied understanding of where he'd come from, Abraham Sapien was as good a name as any. Although he had on occasion been known to get testy with people who called him a fish-man. Strictly speaking, he was amphibious, as at home on dry land as in water.

And Hellboy himself? No trench coat could hide his nonconformities either—if anything, it was even more of a lost cause than with Abe—but he wore one anyway. Had to wear something. The clothes make the man, it was said, to which he might have amended that the clothes *un*make the demon. No matter what else the rest of the world saw when they looked at him—built like a linebacker, tough skin as red as a lobster, prehensile tail, ground-down stumps where horns should've been, and a huge stonelike right hand that could crush bricks like beer cans—they saw the coat and, well, it just looked so *normal* it was downright disarming. Sometimes that was all that was needed to work past the prejudice.

Here, though, at ground zero of the Roman Catholic world, there was a two-millennium legacy of thinking long and hard about abominations and what to do with them. He'd answered their appeal, and maybe they really even needed him. But for some of them—not necessarily in this room, but surely somewhere on the grounds—he knew how he must be regarded, first and foremost: a living, breathing validation of everything they'd devoted their lives to opposing.

Except for one little problem: How he had ended up on their side.

Father Ranzi poured himself another coffee. "You understand about the scroll, what it is, yes?"

"Katie briefed me."

"You recognize the danger it poses."

"Contradiction of two thousand years of dogma—yeah, I get the picture."

"So then you understand why it was . . . shall we say . . . targeted."

"Now that's where I'm having some trouble," Hellboy said. "It doesn't add up. I've seen what happened, and it seems clear to me what did it. But why here, why now? If your tests are right, that scroll's been around for over 1900 years, whether or not it's what it claims to be. The fact that it drew this kind of attention and cost seven lives, that seems to give it *some* kind of legitimacy . . .

"But here's the red flag: For all but the last few decades, it was buried on a high plateau in the middle of a desert. Where it had already survived one inferno. Then it's discovered, it's transported, it's studied, it's stored away—thirty more years of that. And I'm supposed to believe these seraphim are only now taking notice? They had all the time in the world to burn that thing out of existence and no one would've ever known. But they didn't. Until a few nights ago. So no—I *don't* understand why it was targeted. But I bet somebody down here does."

The six churchmen exchanged glances, and finally one of them stepped forward from the background. One of the two who'd been smoking earlier, he wore a sober but well-tailored black suit over a charcoal gray turtleneck sweater. He had a tautly lined face and graying hair clipped just a little longer than stubble. Long, slender hands, like the hands of a pianist. Monsignor Burke, Artaud had called him earlier.

"A few minutes ago, I'm sure the well-fed Archbishop

here didn't tell you anything you didn't already know," he said, the only American accent among the six. Upper East Coast, it sounded like. Not New York. Boston, maybe, and he'd spent a lot of time trying to get rid of it. "Something's always seething under the surface of the Vatican. But right now, there are undercurrents of some of the biggest divisions the Church has seen in decades. Now, the Church is slow to change, you know that . . . "

Hellboy was eyeing Ranzi's coffee. "Millions of its members *like* that about it. In a world that's always changing, here's this one anchor in their lives that's resistant to change."

And temptation got the better of him. He reached toward the thermos with his left hand, the normal one, and made a tipping motion. Ranzi looked as though he didn't dare refuse. Didn't pour, just gave it to him thermos and all. Hellboy guzzled straight from its mouth and nearly swooned. Have to find out where he got this and see if the person wanted a job in the States.

"Resistance to change isn't an automatic virtue," Burke said. "Forget about the Inquisition, episodes like that. Those are easy criticisms, and just as easy to distance ourselves from, because they were centuries ago. No, let's look at our own lifetime. In Ireland, the Church ran a network of what were called the Magdalene Asylums. Basically, slave labor prisons where families would send young women for perceived moral infractions. Like getting pregnant out of wedlock. Or being too interesting to the boys. Terrible places, physically and morally appalling . . . the ruin of countless lives. And the last of them wasn't closed until earlier this year."

"I'm not saying the Church *shouldn't* change, ever. Just

playing the Devil's advocate." Hellboy looked at the other smoker, who looked to be the youngest of the lot, and who'd been hanging back the farthest the whole time and showed no inclination to step any closer. "Hey. You knew I had to sooner or later."

"If the Church is to survive the coming century as anything more than a folk religion and a museum relic, change is essential. Especially throughout Europe, where people have very long memories of its history of intellectual repression, and still see us as a force for irrationality," the monsignor said. "That's finally being admitted, and in unexpected places, too. Many prominent cardinals. They see what's happening and they know it can't continue. Not everyone is comfortable with the way I choose to put it, but we're rotting from the inside. In America, even non-Catholics can see the obvious . . . that we're not adequately replacing the priests we lose to retirement and death, and as a result, parishes are being consolidated and churches are closing. Plus we're just now starting to see the tip of another coming iceberg: lawsuits against the Church caused by a few priests who couldn't keep their hands off children, and bishops who were too cowardly to do anything other than shuffle the offenders off to other parishes and hope they'd stop. The only places the Church is really growing right now are Latin America and Africa."

"And that's not where the money is," Hellboy said.

Burke looked as though blood had been drawn. But he didn't refute it. "Nobody can say how much longer His Holiness will remain in office. But only a hopeful few can see many more years ahead of him. When that throne is vacant again, and the next conclave is convened to choose a successor, there's a very good chance that the more progressive factions within the Church will prevail. And set the stage for the most comprehensive set of modernizations since John the Twenty-Third called the Second Vatican Council more than thirty years ago."

Whether the monsignor knew it or not, and there was no reason he should've, it was the right thing to say. Of the five popes who'd held the office during Hellboy's lifetime, John XXIII was the one he'd always wished he could have met. Down to earth, with the easy touch of a parish priest, and downright impish at times—a pope as imagined by the lighter side of Charles Dickens. Somebody had once asked the man how many people worked in the Vatican. *About half of them* was his answer. You had to love a guy like that.

"Assuming your side maneuvers into position," Hellboy said, "what then? What's up your sleeve?"

"Nothing radical. There are certain hot-button issues that we still would never touch, and those should be obvious. But, for starters, more defensible positions on birth control. And permitting priests to marry. There's no reason they shouldn't, other than tradition. It wasn't a mandate until halfway through the Church's existence, and even then it was a power play . . . more to do with property and potential heirs than moral authority. So let them marry if they wish. There are many more men who would answer the calling to the priesthood if it didn't mean a choice between a flock and a family. God knows it hasn't been the downfall of the Anglicans."

"How about the ordination of women?" Kate asked.

"You've got women who feel the calling too. That hasn't been the downfall of the Anglicans, either."

"Still under discussion," Burke said, a little too quickly.

"So far it doesn't seem to call for a fire-from-heaven kind of response. What else is on the agenda?" Hellboy wanted to know. "Anything to do with the Masada Scroll?"

"We plan on making it public, possibly available for outside study. Not endorsing it, of course, but not refuting it, either . . . mainly putting it out as a historical relic, much the same as all the additional gospels and other texts that weren't chosen for inclusion in the Bible. If it proves to be another way of expanding the faith, or broadening the permissible concepts of Jesus and enhancing the sense of his humanity, then so much the better."

"And what happened upstairs the other night," Hellboy said, "you didn't take that as a sign from above to rethink your plans?"

"No," said a man who, until now, had been content to listen. Father Laurenti, they'd called him. "The attack on the Archives may have come from above . . . but it was not the work of Heaven."

Like the monsignor, Laurenti too wore a black suit instead of a cassock, but in contrast, his looked old and worn, mended a few too many times. His olive face had a weary gauntness that came from more than just a sleepless night or two, and his hair was a tall shock of loose, unruly curls, very black.

"You may think of angels in their work as being dispatched, and they can be," he said. "But these that came for the scroll . . . they were not dispatched, but *summoned*. There is a difference. The decree came not from God, I believe, but from somewhere within the Church itself."

"Who's got that kind of pull?"

Laurenti shook his head. "Even if I could tell you—or any of us could—I would not. For now, it is enough to recognize that nobody who seeks change can bring it about without making enemies. Even enemies of those they believed to be their brothers. But this is not your struggle. It is ours."

"Then let me be the first to ask the obvious," Abe said. "What *are* we doing here?"

Hellboy had been thinking the same thing. The reasons for the bureau's existence were explicit in its name: Paranormal. Research. Defense. But they already seemed to know what they were up against here, and wanted no help ferreting out the individual or the cabal that had done the summoning.

"Take the scroll," said Father Artaud, with the quiet desperation of a parent asking someone to whisk his child out of a war zone. "Its value may be inestimable. So take it with you. Please."

Ranzi nodded. "I understand that you can protect it better than we are able."

Hellboy glanced over at Kate, ticked his brow upward in question.

"I told them about the containment facility that the bureau had built for Liz when she was a girl," Kate said. "She hasn't needed it for more than ten years, so it's sitting there idle. But: If it could keep that kind of fire *inside*, then it should be able to withstand the same kind of fire from the *outside*, too."

"And I understand that you will treat this scroll as the important relic it is," Ranzi went on, "and that no matter what may happen here in Rome, your group's neutrality will not be compromised."

He was right on that count. The BPRD's most overtly political days were in the beginning, when the bureau was founded during World War II, a countermeasure to the Third Reich's attempts to use the occult to turn the tide of battle. Since then, the bureau had largely stayed out of affairs of state. The things they encountered most often neither knew nor respected national boundaries.

The monsignor took another step forward, like a sales-man trying to close a deal. "You came here to investigate an attack, and your reputation precedes you. I know you're very good at what you do, and that if something gets on your bad side, it usually doesn't last long. But I have to question whether or not these particular assailants are something you could ever defeat."

"Now you're just being insulting."

"Using your usual approach, then," Burke amended. "But in our case, I don't think that's what's called for. Re-move the object of the attack, and you remove the likeli-hood of further attacks."

"Attacks here, you mean," Hellboy said. "If I take your scroll home, it's like taking a lightning rod back to the place and people that mean the most to me."

The shabby Father Laurenti raised a conciliatory hand. "It's true, you may run that risk. But these seraphim, they are not all-knowing. They go where they are sent and do what they are told. As long as this knowledge is kept from those who would control them, then the risks to you may be not so great after all."

Hellboy gave it a few moments of thought, and finally agreed.

"A courier run, that's really all we're talking about here," he said. "Point A to Point B . . . how hard can *that* be?"

CHAPTER 4

Liz pushed the whistle across the tabletop and let the young man stare at it a few moments, bolstering his nerve with a few deep breaths. Most people, all they'd see would be a silver whistle, the kind you'd find hanging around the neck of any coach worth his jock strap or her sports bra. It was all Liz saw, for that matter.

But Campbell Holt wasn't most people. Much like Liz wasn't most people. They just weren't like most people in very different ways.

In a sparely furnished room whose walls still smelled of their fresh coat of cerulean blue paint—the color Campbell found most relaxing—he reached for the whistle as though about to touch a skillet that may or may not have been hot. Resting one finger on it, two fingers . . . then he had it in his palm . . . and finally his hand closed around it. He let his eyes drift shut and the magic—or whatever it was—happen.

"Oh, okay, I know him. This belongs to . . . Agent Garrett?" Campbell said.

Liz shrugged. "You tell me."

His head tipped downward, chin toward chest, as he seemed to fall into the whistle, deeper and deeper, following its curves and filling its hollow.

"Yeah . . . definitely Agent Garrett. He coaches his son's peewee football team. He . . . he's a good coach. No yelling at the kids. I mean, he *yells*, he just doesn't insult them. Like he knows exactly how tough he can be with each kid and where the line is between motivation and bullying. For each one of them. And he's careful to never cross it."

Campbell was doing well. Relaxed, into it, letting it flow, no agitation. Although she wouldn't expect any psychic turbulence to come from anything belonging to Dion Garrett. The man was a career bureau agent—fairly low-level abilities, your basic garden-variety empath, although it gave him awesome people skills—and as devoted a family man as she'd ever known.

Campbell's brow furrowed. Not deep, and it didn't spread to the rest of his face; just enough to let her know that he'd hit something that made him wince a bit.

"He wanted to play pro and probably would've. Only . . . he blew out his knee in college. So that was that. Losing his chance, it still bothers him sometimes when he's watching the boys play. He tries . . . but he can't stop himself from having all those what-if thoughts."

"I never knew that about him," Liz said, and maybe shouldn't have, but it was out before she could reconsider. She was supposed to be in charge of this session, *all* of it; couldn't afford to have Cam thinking she was ignorant about the items she was shoving at him. That she might accidentally give him more than he was ready for.

"No reason you should've," he said, and didn't appear to hold it against her. "He keeps all that to himself."

Campbell returned the whistle to the tabletop, pushed it back to her with a nod.

"That was really good," she said. Next, from the box on the chair at her side, she selected a handbell that had spent decades in the tranquil grasp of a Tibetan Buddhist monk who sometimes came to visit. "Now try this one."

Psychometry, it was called. The ability to hold an object and see into the life of the person who possessed it. Cam wasn't sure how it worked, and certainly Liz didn't know, any more than she could give a logical explanation of how her own so-called gift worked. Nobody could, really. It was like trying to tell somebody how to balance on a bicycle. His gift, hers . . . they defied rational explanation, which was just as well, because if they were explainable, then sure as hell somebody somewhere would develop an agenda to engineer them in people lucky enough to have been born normal.

Neither she nor Campbell had been so fortunate. And yet sometimes people who found out—blissfully ignorant *normal* people—envied them: *Wow, I'd love to have that. Love to be able to do what you can do. Nobody would mess with me then. Nobody'd get away with anything around me.* Blah blah blah. These so-called gifts only looked good on paper. Living with them, waking up with them, walking around with them like parasitic lovers who only demanded and rarely gave . . .

This was the existence that nobody ever stopped to imagine.

She'd been working with Campbell for the past six weeks, ever since his discharge from an Omaha hospital at summer's sultry end. Liz had paid him a visit several days earlier, Cam still plugged into the intravenous tubes reversing his dehydration and malnutrition, and his left forearm swathed in a fat muffler of gauze. The day before that, he'd turned up as a promising blip on the radar—the low-key, informal human resources network that the BPRD maintained with reliable members of various law enforcement agencies and the medical community.

"Hey. I'm Liz," she said. "Liz Sherman. I flew here from a place in Fairfield, Connecticut, to see you. It's . . . kinda hard to describe, but I guess you could call it a sort of institute."

"Psychiatric?" he muttered, as if already convinced it couldn't be anything else.

"You wish. No, it's a place where you might actually have to work instead of sitting around the dayroom watching TV and waiting for your meds."

Maybe four degrees warmer in interest: "What kind of work?"

"That depends on your area of expertise."

She took a couple of steps closer and leaned on the chrome rail of his hospital bed. Blood loss and trauma and other maladies aside, he appeared much the same as he did in the pictures she'd reviewed, his sandy hair clipped ascetically short, as though he couldn't bear to risk catching it in something he wouldn't want to tangle with. Underneath his sheet, he looked as if when standing he would be tall and thin, lots of angles; that he'd never filled out the way young men often do when they make the transition from their teens into their early twenties.

"Look, I know why you're here," she said. "Not the obvious medical reasons. Those are just symptoms. I mean the *big* why . . . *your* area of expertise. Don't pretend you don't

know what I'm talking about. Because I've got one too."
She glanced around the room. "Not using an oxygen tank
in here that I haven't spotted, are you?"

He shook his head no, so she raised her hand from her
side, gave a gentle flex to the indefinable, immaterial thing
that hovered somewhere in the vicinity of her solar plexus,
and let a tongue of blue-orange flame lick the air above her
palm. Then reined it back in to snuff it.

He looked wildly unimpressed. "You do magic tricks,
big deal. What's next—doves are gonna fly out of your ass?"

"Do you see me wearing a clown suit here? Do I look
like I'm stopping in every room to entertain the kids?"
Then she flashed a quick rope of fire across the room that
might've toasted the windowsill had she let it live long
enough.

And *now* she had his attention.

His story came in fits and starts, from his hospital bed as
well as during their talks after he'd accepted the invitation
to come to Connecticut . . .

While most adolescents grow up plagued by the no-
tion that they're not like everybody else, in all the wrong
ways, for Campbell Holt it was a stark reality that first
manifested when he was fourteen. No dramatics, nothing
remotely like Liz's involuntary and apocalyptic initiation.
It was, in fact, sweetly innocent and benignly kinky. One
Saturday morning, while home alone, he'd picked a pair
of his older sister's panties off the bathroom floor, given
them an experimental fondle . . . and suddenly found
himself bowled over by the delirious sensation of some
other guy's fumbling hands tugging them down her
thighs the night before. A quick spiral into all possible ex-

planations of what had just happened: *I'm an incestuous pervert, I'm going insane, I'm gay, I'm a transvestite, I'm gay AND a transvestite.*

Further episodes were quick to follow, never predictable, rarely welcome. At sixteen, he'd narrowly avoided a head-on collision while driving a friend's car and finding himself helplessly plunged into intimate knowledge of what her father had for years been doing to her after witching-hour drinking.

And it wasn't always personal possessions, either. It may have been rare, but public property could also pose a risk, objects tainted by recent essences so negative their power was akin to contamination. In a restaurant, a ketchup bottle might be merely glass . . . but then again, it might flood him with a toxic distillation of hatred left by a misanthropic hand that had clutched the bottle before him. This helped explain his spare frame, too: He'd once nearly dropped a barbell onto his neck after tapping into a psychic whiff of some steroidal date-rape predator who'd preceded him on the weights, who'd felt he *owned* the barbell.

By seventeen it was becoming a party game, guaranteed to freak out his classmates and humiliate the more insufferable ones into keeping their distance . . . not an unwelcome development, maybe even deliberate, since he was getting a reputation as a resident headcase based on his increasingly cavern-eyed appearance.

By nineteen, the police knew about him. Not for crimes he'd committed, but by reputation. Word-of-mouth, fellow graduate tells fiancée who mentions it to her uncle in the department, who scoffs until the next questionable death. A visit to the home Cam still shared with his parents, except by now he'd moved to the basement and wasn't going out much, and even the crappy McJobs never lasted long, and the drop-in was strictly unofficial, understand, but still: *So anyway, Campbell, suppose I let you hang onto this gun for a minute. You could maybe tell me if the scene it came from was a murder or a suicide, right?*

He could. So why would they stop there?

Umm, Campbell, got this pair of shoes here. The girl who owns them, her parents really miss her, and . . . did she just walk off and leave 'em sitting on the riverbank because she didn't want 'em anymore . . . ?

No. No, she hadn't.

Sorry, son, but think you might be able to tell me a little something about the person who used this hacksaw?

Soon after that he took a running leap into self-medication, giving the extrasensory impressions plenty of fogs and tides to work against, which worked well enough that there wasn't much point in going home at all anymore, not when the worst blocks of Leavenworth Street offered all the neon-smeared dives he would ever need to keep him distracted, places that Bukowski at his worst would've been proud to patronize. That and a pair of gloves did wonders, except sometimes he lost them in the summer and they were stolen in the winter. Mostly he was just relieved to be away from home these days; all those trinkets of his parents just lying around waiting to be touched, to rub his nose in the worry and fear and peculiar loathing they had begun to feel for him.

Good to be on his own.

A couple years of that and one night he made it back to

the old neighborhood anyway, not that anyone was awake at that hour. It had been a week since he'd last had a pair of gloves, and his hands felt raw with the accumulated weight of ten thousand souls, some of whom he'd met but most of them strangers, their violence and their sorrows coagulating in him like oil from a tanker that had broken apart on a reef.

To pass the rest of the August night, its air as thick as boiled blankets, he broke into the neighbor's storage shed, shoved the lawn mower out of the way so he'd have enough room to stretch out. While lying on cool concrete he looked up at a blue square of moonlight on the wall, cross-hatched by the windowpane, and in a moment of epiphany he saw the hatchet hanging from a pair of pegs.

He fumbled it down from the pegboard and ran a finger along the honed silver edge of the blade. It told him nothing, except for how much it wanted to meet the flesh and bone of his wrist.

After she'd run him through the whistle and the prayer bell and a half-dozen other items, Cam looked visibly tired and Liz decided that was enough for one session. All of this was as new to her as it was to him. She was going mostly on instinct here, but Director Manning had professed nothing but faith in her, kept telling her, *"You'll do great, you'll do great."* She wasn't convinced his blind faith in her was warranted, but one thing was sure: She damn well *needed* to do great.

The program she'd put together for Campbell was an extrapolation from aversion therapy, with a side helping of creative visualization. Under controlled, serene circum-

stances, within the cerulean walls, she would present him
with a series of objects—early on, items whose backgrounds
and owners could be fully accounted for, to minimize the
risk of nasty surprises—and while holding them in his remaining hand he would "read" them at his leisure. Little by
little, she would teach him to build filters inside, between
his perceptions and the external impressions that sought to
impinge on them. They would be like membranes, never
more permeable than he wished them to be.

He could be in control; he *had* to know that. If the reading was pleasant, non-threatening, then fine; let it in. If ab-
horrent, then close the filters, thicken the membranes, stop
the assault . . . and eventually he could explore whatever
was there without letting it ruin him.

But they were at the easy part now. Whistles, prayer
bells, old hairbrushes. What would be rough was when she
had to take him back to the ugly stuff, bringing in items
like the firearms and hacksaws that had put him on his
downward spiral. Because he had to be able to handle it all,
whatever the world and its darker corners might drop in his
path.

"Question?" he said as she was boxing things up.

"Sure."

"What was it like with you? How'd it start?" he asked. "I
mean, I overheard a couple of things, something about an
accident, but . . . "

"Yeah. An accident. A really *bad* accident." And she
wanted a cigarette, a really *big* cigarette, as she usually did
when this subject came up. "Why not just leave it at that?"

"Because you've got just about the saddest eyes I've ever
seen, and I'd like to know what made them that way, is all."

She snickered. "It might help get you somewhere if that didn't sound like the world's lamest pickup line."

He blushed, actually blushed. "I'll know sooner or later, you have to realize that. You'll leave a pen around, or your lighter, or something, and then I'll have it. Or I'll ask somebody else. I just thought it would be more upfront to ask *you*."

"Can't fault you there," she said, and reached for the Tibetan prayer bell, let it toll in the room, so delicate, like air condensed to a chiming note. Nothing at all like the clanging of fire bells. "I was eleven years old when it started. I was just playing in our yard and minding my own business. Then the neighbor boy came over from next door. He was a hateful little turd whose mission in life was making other people miserable. It's been more than twenty years and I should probably stop speaking about him that way, and if he was the only one who'd gotten hurt that day, then yeah, I'd probably be eulogizing him by now. But he wasn't the only one, so to me he's still a hateful little turd, because I haven't been able to forgive him for what he goaded out of me that day."

She set the prayer bell down, too sharply, metal on wood.

"I had my hair in ponytails, and he seemed to think that was the funniest thing he'd ever seen. He told me I looked like the ass-end of two horses. He started yanking on one and wouldn't stop. And I was *so mad*, you know? Something stupid like that, as an adult, it's just an annoyance— you tell the guy to piss off, you throw a drink in his face. But when you're eleven, all that anger and humiliation . . . they're so pure. So consuming. It feels like your world's coming to an end. So I guess what must've happened is, on some level, I decided to take the rest of the world with me . . .

"He started to burn," Liz went on, and could still hear the kid screaming, a climbing note, up up up, until it could've ruptured the eardrums of dogs. "It only took a couple of seconds before he was engulfed. Then he was running. A couple of seconds later his front door started to burn . . . then the rest of their house . . . and then *my* family's house . . . and it just kept going. I was standing in the middle of all this chaos and didn't know what to do, because no matter which way I turned, the chaos spread that direction, too. It was feeding on itself by that point. Because of me, the entire block looked like a jet crashed into it. Thirty-two people were dead before it was over. Twenty-five neighbors, three firemen . . . plus my mom and dad and brother. And one hateful little turd, too, I guess we have to count him."

She gauged the look on Cam's face, pale on his best days and now somewhere near the color of a mild cheese.

"Sorry you asked?"

He shook his head and mouthed the word no.

"Good. Don't be. And another thing: Understanding is fine out of someone, I *appreciate* understanding. But no pity. That's another thing you can eat up when you're eleven or twelve, but it's been a long time since pity does anything other than bug me."

"You don't have to worry," he said, and stuttered out a laugh. "I haven't quite gotten over the *self*-pity part yet, so it's not like I've got any to spare right now."

He really could be an asset here. A lot of potential, and

it seemed almost irrationally important that she play a role in helping him realize it. For most of the twenty-three years since her childhood went up in flames, keeping her own head straight had been a full-time job. It felt good to be directing those intentions elsewhere for a change, toward someone who needed the same kind of salvage operation. You didn't have to be a firestarter to self-immolate.

"Is that wrong?" he asked then.

"Feeling sorry for yourself? Sometimes no, sometimes yes. I can't tell you when the transition should happen. The things inside us that make us so different, they take an adjustment period, and that can last years, because it seems like we never start out in a place that's conducive to it. But just going from personal experience . . . ? If you're at a point where it even occurs to you to ask if it's wrong to feel sorry for yourself, then, yeah, maybe now it is."

He was resting both forearms on the table. Two arms, two wrists, one hand. She tried to imagine the resolve it must have taken to line up the hatchet in that space between the bones and perform the amputation—it had required more than one blow. And she wondered how it felt to him after the point of no return, when he saw that his orphaned hand and his bleeding stump had parted company at last. If it felt as though half a curse had been lifted.

The most hopeful thing about it, which no one seemed to have recognized? Before making the cut, he'd improvised a tourniquet out of a canvas strap from a leaf bagger, and used it to cinch off his forearm. *He'd wanted to live.* He joked about it later, saying that if he hadn't been so drunk, he would've held out for a table saw so he could've sliced off both hands. But still, even at his lowest, he had wanted to live.

"Used to be, I was the only freak I knew," he said. "In a weird way, that was convenient. It meant I had an excuse for just about anything I did to try to get away from it, and whenever I told somebody that they didn't understand, that they *couldn't* understand, I really got to mean it. Then I come here . . . "

"And it's a freak factory, right?" Liz finished for him.

He nodded. "So all the old excuses, they don't cut it anymore. Especially after I hear a story like yours. Or if I see somebody like Hellboy, or Abe, because then I start wondering what it must be like to look so obviously different—the two of them, they can't hide it for a second. It makes me feel selfish. Like, 'Okay, maybe life's been a bitch, but at least *that* didn't happen to me.' "

"Whenever my knack would get the better of me, it could be a genuine danger to anyone around me," she said, and thought of the year-plus spent shuffled among foster homes before the BPRD had found her, taken her in, helped her get control. The flare-ups under strange roofs, the bad dreams that could set the quilts aflame. Never an episode as serious as the first time—no one ever died—but enough to get her branded as a jailbait pyromaniac. "When yours gets the better of you, you're the only one that suffers. I don't think you could say one's any more isolating than the other. Bottom line? Okay, maybe somebody has a worse story than yours, but so what? You're the one that's got to live your own, and it's the first time you've done it, and most of the time you have to make it up as you go. I won't tell you it's easy, but if it couldn't be done, I wouldn't be here now."

And since he'd brought them up, what of Hellboy, of Abe? She too had often wondered what it was like to exist in such a different body. Although a breed apart, she was human, no different to the eye or in behavior than most any other woman. She had a smile that often left men wondering what she was thinking, and enjoyed that subtle control; had a habit of wearing a velvet choker and cross even though she wasn't a bona fide believer; had her periods with almost calendrical regularity. She could pass for normal any day of the week.

Not so, her closest friends.

But maybe, in some respects, it was easier that way. They had no footsteps to walk in, no molds to fill. They were strange pioneers, not so much defying expectations as writing the book on what those expectations could be, and if they were not strictly human, they could nevertheless give lessons on *being* human to those who were, yet who fell so very short of its ideals.

There was a soft knock at the door then, and she called for whoever was there to enter. The door opened just wide enough for a head to poke through, a big smooth dome that shone under the fluorescents like burnished walnut.

"You got a call. It's our man in Rome."

She wrapped up the pep talk with Campbell, then stepped out into the hallway.

"Here's your whistle back," she told Agent Garrett, and put it into his hand. "Thanks."

Dion grinned. "So now he knows all my shameful secrets, huh?"

"Yep. And he expects that first check by the end of the

day," Liz said, then winked. "Take care of that knee, by the way . . ."

Down the hallway, she ducked into the wing's main office and picked up the waiting landline.

"H.B.? That you?"

"Pack a bag. You're on the next flight to Rome," he said, in that *basso profundo* voice that could soothe infants or rattle windows, depending on his mood. "And don't forget to bring your sea legs."

CHAPTER 5

Coming up with a secure way to transport the Masada Scroll halfway around the world . . . that was the *easy* part.

It wasn't as though Hellboy had never transported sensitive documents before. Several years ago, prior to the fall of the Berlin Wall, he'd played the role of courier to get a crumbling fourteenth-century alchemical text out of East Germany and into the southwest of England. In the port city of Bristol, at the site of a mass burial pit—six centuries old but newly discovered—members of the British Paranormal Society had used the text to stop a virulent incursion of plague-spreading revenants.

If not for the Vatican's initial reluctance to fully admit what the situation was here, that an ancient manuscript was involved, he could have shown up prepared for the same kind of duty.

The custom-made case he had used before was right where he'd left it after the Bristol run: back at BPRD headquarters in Connecticut. Liz would be bringing it, but she was no errand girl. She was going to be every bit as important as the case in transporting the scroll safely.

"I'd rather be moving," Hellboy said. "I hate sitting here

waiting to see if the same thing's gonna happen all over again."

Although, as Abe pointed out, while they may not have been on the move, they were hardly hunkering down in hiding. There was boldness, honor, and more than a little recklessness in that, wasn't there?

At the moment they were keeping a vigil at the very pinnacle of the Vatican, strolling around the railed parapet of the lantern tower that crowned the enormous dome of St. Peter's. It would prove to be either the cleverest of their limited options or go up in flames as a fool's gambit: They had the scroll up here with them, locked in a steel storage drawer, similar to a bank's safe deposit box, and resting on the floor of the tower. Nearby stood Bertrand, their everpresent Swiss Guard, doing a yeoman's job of trying not to look worried that he could be just feet away from an incendiary time bomb.

Not an ideal solution, but it would suffice for the hours it was taking Liz to cross the Atlantic, and it was born of need: no more hiding for the scroll. By now they had to assume that, with the confusion of the fire having died down, the scroll's would-be destroyers knew it had survived. Stashing it in the museum complex, or even in the hideaways and passages that honeycombed the old thick walls, could be an invitation to another inferno. No hiding place, however short-term, could be entirely safe, because you never knew who might be a spy.

Instead, they had chosen to hide it in plain sight—Abe's idea, a chess-player's stratagem. The first fire had been publicly explained as an explosion from improperly stored chemicals used in the cleaning and restoration of artifacts.

A tragic accident, and easy enough to accept at face value. Conceivably, though, whoever had summoned the fires of Heaven, in defense of Church tradition, might feel bold enough to try it once more, so long as the fire was again confined inside the walls.

But would they go so far as to instigate the destruction of the top of St. Peter's Basilica? In front of Rome and the world?

For Hellboy and Abe, it was defense by bluff: *They wouldn't dare.*

Although once the scroll left this place, all bets were off. Maybe all restraint, too.

"You don't think she'll change her mind, do you?" Hellboy said.

"Liz?" Abe sounded incredulous that he would even ask. "Of course not. She's never left in the middle of anything before."

"But she does leave. That's the point." Standing at the railing, he tipped his chin, jutting and spotted with a patch of beard, at the city that sprawled below. At the vibrant streets and the red-tile roofs and the winding murky ribbon of the Tiber. "That's Rome down there. These people know how to live. Suppose she just decides to get lost in the crowd."

Again, he almost said, but didn't, because they both knew that if Liz walked, it wouldn't be the first time. Twenty-two years with the bureau—her entire adult life and adolescence, plus a big chunk of childhood too—and in that span, she had quit twelve times. On average, once every year and ten months. She always came back into the fold, and made the best of it once she had. Always committed, always competent. Yet she always seemed to come back not because she really wanted to, but because the world wasn't as welcoming as she'd hoped, or she didn't fit, or normality was either an illusion or just plain not all it was cracked up to be.

But one day it might be. *It might be.* After so many false starts, the restlessness inside could finally drive her in the right direction so that the pieces of her life's puzzle might one day click, and that would be it—no coming back.

Hellboy supposed he could conquer any fear but that one.

How could he presume to tell her she belonged in only one place?

"She'll *be* here," Abe said. "She wouldn't let either of us down."

Hellboy shrugged. "For all she knows, she's just delivering a souped-up briefcase. She could've changed her mind and sent somebody else."

"Ah," said Abe. "You didn't tell her about the rest?"

"That she'd be our secret weapon in case we need to fight fire with fire? I thought I'd cover that once she was here." He looked sideways at Abe. "Mistake?"

Abe thrust out his chin. " 'Oh, by the way—I may need you to flambé some angels, if they don't fry you first'? I think she might've appreciated an earlier heads-up than she'll be getting."

Hellboy scowled. "Been meaning to tell you. Of all you guys who do imitations of me? Yours is the worst."

Abe looked unfazed. With his features, it took a lot for him to look any other way. "Bad as it was, what about the rest?"

"I'll make it up to her, all right?"

And he couldn't have the opportunity to do so any too soon. Most times, a job was a job, and that was about it. Some bit of percolating weirdness needed a looking into by someone who understood the terrain better than most? He did it. And if, in the course of events, something rude needed squashing? He did that too. It kept life interesting, and left him feeling that he was earning his keep in a world that would otherwise have no place for him.

Most times, whatever came up, he rolled with it. A job took as long as it took, and he spared little thought for how long that might be. He had time, and reserves of energy—plenty of both.

But this one . . . this one was an affront on so many levels.

He had no illusions about where he was. Not even the most fawning apologist could deny that the Church's history had its share of dark, dark episodes. They were a small minority, to be sure, but there had lived popes who'd been among history's most wicked men. They'd raised armies, they'd waged wars, they'd robbed and cheated, they'd condemned the innocent for the sake of expediency and made allies of tyrants for the sake of power.

But not lately.

And through it all, faith had endured. Somewhere, out in those streets, there were people who in the name of the Church and its Christ were at this moment bringing food and clothing and comfort, hoping for no more than that they be accepted in the same loving spirit in which they were delivered.

Because the faith had endured. Look at them all down

there, walking upon the stones of St. Peter's Square. Even on the most secular day, they couldn't all be tourists. Embraced by the great curving arms of Bernini's colonnade, the piazza was big enough to hold the population of a good-sized city, and even though there was nowhere near that this afternoon, it would fill again soon enough.

For the faith had endured. He respected that about this place above all, more than its longevity, and in spite of the terrible plots that had sometimes been hatched under its gilded ceilings. It gave strength, that faith, and if it wasn't the whole picture—which he knew from experiences both bitter and sweet—it was plenty big enough for those who needed it to make their way in a world that seemed to do everything it could to crush them. It kindled warmth here on the fragile side of the void.

How dare someone hide inside its walls, summoning down a fire that burned as deadly as any that Hell had to offer.

As they'd been scanning the sky, they'd been keeping an eye on things below, as well, Hellboy sweeping a pair of Carl Zeiss binoculars over the grounds, and especially the piazza of St. Peter's Square. When a familiar shape caught his eye, he slapped Abe on the shoulder and pointed, handed over the binoculars.

"Who's that look like down there to you?"

"Where?" said Abe. "There's a lot of *there* down there."

"This side and to the right of the obelisk," he said, referring to the ancient stone spire that had been brought over from Egypt when it was still freshly carved. "Firing up a cigarette."

Abe gave it a game try but shook his head. "Sorry. I'm still not finding . . ."

Hellboy took another peek. Maybe it was his imagination, but he could swear the man was staring straight up at the lantern tower.

"Well, *I* see somebody I'd like to have a talk with," he said, and gave the railing an experimental shove with his normal hand, to see how much weight it might hold.

"Hellboy, *no,*" Abe said. "Don't do this . . ."

On the dangerous side of the railing, the great gray dome of St. Peter's swelled outward and sloped sharply down and away from them, like a waterfall of stone. At even intervals, it was braced by vaulted ribs that helped support the immense weight of Michelangelo's design, and centered between them, small portals let the light of day stream inside the cupola like rays from a benevolent Heaven.

He braced his hand on the railing and flexed his legs.

"No—we're supposed to be keeping a low profile," Abe tried.

Hellboy glanced behind them, past the twinned pairs of columns that held up the tower's roof, and gave a wave to their guard. Poor guy, standing there with his halberd and knowing there was nothing he could do.

"Sorry, Bertrand," Hellboy called out with a wave of his big right hand. "I'll put in a good word for you, tell them you did a great job."

With that, he shoved up and over, vaulting the railing in one fluid move, clearing the platform and landing astride the nearest rib. At first he took it like a playground sliding board, guided by the indentation of the shallow trough down the middle of the rib. But the slope quickly turned so sharp it was almost like a freefall, the air whistling up past his face and the back of his coat skimming along the stone beneath him, as the striated junctures of the dome's individual sections whizzed past in a blur.

He braced for the landing, touching down for a moment atop a small platform at the bottom of the rib and springing forward, in true freefall now as he hit first one elevated section of roof, then bounded onto the main flat roof over the basilica's long central nave, absorbing the shock of each landing with a flexing of his legs. Had to give it up for Baroque architecture. You could *never* do this with today's glass and steel towers.

He sprinted along the roof toward one end of the portico, its front edge lined with statues of Jesus and his disciples carrying crosses and swords. From here Hellboy launched out over the roof of Bernini's colonnade. One final bounce and touchdown later and he was standing on the stones of the piazza, ignoring the murmuring of onlookers and the rapid-fire click of camera shutters. Mostly he wished Abe could've been up there timing him with a stopwatch. He'd just put the world's express elevators to shame.

He crossed the rest of the distance at a leisurely jog until he reached the man in the smartly tailored black suit, who'd barely had time to smoke enough of his cigarette so that you'd notice.

"Monsignor," Hellboy said.

From beneath the wide brim of his hat, Burke, the sole American who had been at this morning's subterranean council, gave him a tight smile. "I've heard you have a knack for flamboyant entrances."

"Me?" Hellboy demurred. "Most of the time I creep around on cat feet."

"Really. Which I might even believe if cats' feet were"— with an arch glance downward—"cloven."

Hellboy still wasn't sure if he liked this guy. He just couldn't imagine Burke, with his cropped steel gray hair and ice blue eyes and chiseled skull, bringing *comfort* to people. Personal prejudice, probably, that priests should be these doughy guys with marshmallow hands and eyes that twinkled. He could imagine Burke boxing in his younger days, and even now running marathons, and above all, shrewdly holding his own at the conference table in a boardroom. But hearing confession, sending the person off motivated to go and sin no more? Restoring peace to an anxious deathbed? No. He couldn't picture it.

Still, Hellboy supposed he could forgive Burke all that. Like it or not, the Church needed men like this too. Mystics, on the whole, made lousy administrators.

"I heard you were up there on top of the world," Burke said. "And I'm glad you spotted me. Saves me the trouble of tracking you down. Although . . . I would've thought you'd be looking after the scroll now."

"It's in good hands."

"In transit?"

"Something like this, it's not like you can just take it to FedEx, now, is it?" Hellboy said. "I've done what I can for now. It'll be a few more hours before all the pieces are in place."

"Dare I ask how?" Burke and his tight smile again. "Speaking informally, of course."

Earlier, his colleagues had made it clear that they hadn't wanted to know much about how the scroll would be making the trek from the Vatican to Connecticut. Ignorance could be more than bliss. Sometimes there was security in it, too, and this was one of those occasions.

"By sea," Hellboy said, and left it at that. "But if you really thought about it, you probably could've figured that out for yourself."

"I suspected as much. What better protection against fire than all that water?" Burke took a long, smoldering pull on his cigarette. "You seemed in a hurry to reach me. Maybe you have something on your mind too?"

"Some unfinished business from this morning. I just didn't think I'd get very far pressing the matter down in the hidey-hole."

"That matter being . . . ?"

"Whoever it is you guys suspect of calling down the attack dogs," Hellboy said. "Father Laurenti, wasn't he the one looked like he'd dug his suit out of the charity bin? He seemed set on keeping the information close to the vest, and everybody else seemed content enough to follow his lead."

"And you have a problem with that?"

"It felt like it was getting treated as a need-to-know item, except we had two different opinions on who might need to know. If I have people putting their lives on the line because of this conflict you've got brewing under the surface here, then I'd say I've got a need to know."

"So why come to me, if we presented a unified front earlier?"

"Because you seem like more of a pragmatist than the other five put together."

Burke's grin was looser now. "I believe if you wanted to, you wouldn't have to strain yourself at all to make that sound like an insult."

"I just have that kind of face."

"And you may have just come to the right pragmatist, too. As fate would have it, you and I are on the same wavelength. Do you have an hour or two to spare before you take off?"

Hellboy thought of Abe in the tower, babysitting the scroll and bluffing out the possibility of Armageddon, and Bertrand up there, babysitting them both. He hoped Abe was in a forgiving mood.

"Because if you do," Burke said, "there's something you need to see."

CHAPTER 6

They took a taxi—easily the most harrowing experience of this trip so far, careening along streets tight as clogged arteries, mere inches from brown brick walls, and engaging in swerving showdowns with candy-colored motorscooters whose riders, if not suicidal, gave a heart-stopping impression of it.

The ride ended in east Rome, in a neighborhood where the buildings started to thin out, a place of abandonment and obsolescence. As the light of day began to seep from the sky to leave behind a firmament of rose-stained clouds, Burke pointed out to their driver where he should stop. It was a rounded, ramshackle turret of a place, three floors tall, and looked as though it might have begun life as some wealthy Renaissance scholar's idea of an observatory . . . and had then been left to deteriorate at some point in the past century or two.

Burke paid the driver for the fare, plus a bonus for him to return in forty-five minutes. They watched his taillights shoot down the street. Only when he was gone did Burke turn to a nearby building, half a block away and in marginally better repair, and lift his hand in a subtle greeting to someone unseen. It wasn't a simple wave, but rather some quick gesture that may have been an all-clear signal that he was in no trouble.

"We're being watched?" Hellboy asked.

"Not us so much as the *osservatorio*."

"By other priests?"

Burke gave him the tight smile. "How about we just call them believers."

Hellboy got the general drift. Over the centuries, even priests sometimes needed things done that required a harsher set of skills.

They paced up the walkway, past a small garden that had run riot, then died in a choked heap. Now the breeze rustled through brittle veins of dead ivy, and the husks of fallen leaves swirled at their feet.

Though bristling with splinters, the building's door, broadly curved at the top, still looked durable. The face-level slit, ringed with iron plating and sealed with a small door, seemed to be a later addition. Burke produced a key and let them inside.

It took a moment for Hellboy's eyes to adjust to the gloom, but when they did, what he could see of the place was what anyone might expect from the outside: peeling walls and unswept floors, old frescos cancerous with mildew. More rooms remained to be seen, but there was no reason to expect them to look any better. Near one wall was a hulking wooden staircase, twisting upward not in a smooth spiral, but in cruder, squared-off segments.

"Don't worry," said Burke. "It's sturdier than it looks."

They took it up past the second floor, where a glance around showed only more dirt and emptiness, then on to the third floor. It was brighter up here, the last of the day

straining through tall windows, then Burke let in more
light by turning an old iron crank. This forced a set of
gears into groaning motion as they pulled toward opposite sides the overlapping series of panels that comprised
the roof. These, at least, must have been scrupulously
maintained over the years. When closed, they looked to
fit together as snugly as the hull planks of a Viking long-
ship.

One slow 360-degree look around at the top floor, now
open to the sky, and there was only one thing to ask:
"What *is* this place?"

"As of the past few days? Abandoned, I think," Burke
said. "Men like Father Laurenti, who made it clear he didn't
want you sticking your nose in these matters . . . ? It's been
forever that his kind has been trying to root out the group
that used this place. But, whoever they are, they seem to
have been warned off just in time. Spies, remember."

Up here, it was all one capacious circular room perched
upon the living quarters underneath. Hellboy had no trouble imagining the man of money and learning who might
have built it centuries ago . . . losing himself up here, a
stranger to his family, having meals sent up as he spent his
days poring over charts and Copernicus, and his nights
studying the stars.

The cupola was braced inside by a network of rough-
hewn beams, although to Hellboy's eye, part of it had been
ripped out some time in the past to keep the central floor
space open and unobstructed. In the rafters were the remnants of a pulley system, although there was no longer any
sign of the observation platform it must have hoisted from
the floor up to the apex of the roof.

No, this place had long since been converted to other purposes.

He'd felt it even before he had seen it clearly . . . the accumulated weight of ritual and intent. Such things left echoes when repeated over time. Just as any old building might absorb the essences of the goings-on inside it, so this place had soaked up a resonance of mystery and dread.

It was more than just the things that hung on the walls and from the beams, although certainly they were part of it: archaic tools of torture and punishment, of recantation and forced conversions. Countless sets of manacles dangled from their chains. From pegs and hooks hung leg-irons and larger frame-like restraints designed to freeze the body into unnatural positions that would cause agonizing muscle cramps. From one overhead beam hung a mobile made of more than a dozen sets of thumbscrews. Elsewhere, high-tensile iron collars—some smooth for use as garrotes, others lined with spikes that would bite into the neck or skull—had been looped together into a giant chain. Fitted along one rounded vertical beam was a display of iron mutes, each with a band that clamped around the back of the head and a jawplate that filled the mouth with a gag. On the walls were innumerable scourges and flails, pokers and brands, pincers and tongs. Tools that poked and tools that ripped. An oak framework threaded with bolt-shafts and lined with sharp spikes for crushing knees and elbows.

They didn't appear to have been used for generations, the metal dull and often corroded, the stains left by long-ago victims faded to shadows, unrejuvenated by fresher blood. Instead, they hung as though displayed like museum pieces.

Or objects of power.

Hellboy stepped over to one of the smaller devices and snatched it off the wall, turned it in his hand: a thick leather strap with a primitive buckle for fitting around someone's neck and, in the middle, a short metal bar tipped at both ends with a pair of points. One end to jam under the chin, the other to bite into the hollow above the breast-bone. A heretic's fork, it was called, and this one was engraved with the word its users wanted most to hear: *Abiuro*.

I recant.

He hurled the fork at the ceiling, where it stuck into a rafter. "Seems clear enough who these used to belong to."

"Yes," Burke said. "They're exactly what they appear to be. Their *history* is exactly what it appears to be."

"But that doesn't explain the rest."

Because over decades, maybe centuries, a bewilderingly complex array of symbols had been chalked and painted on the floor and walls and beams. Many of them he was already familiar with. The heart of it all was the circle in the middle of the floor, large enough to hold over a dozen men without crowding, and its edges inscribed with such meticulous patience it seemed inhuman. Some sections held Hebraic words; others were rimmed with lettering from other alphabets . . . Theban, whose letters curled like scimitars, and the simpler Malachim, like twigs tipped with dots. The great circle was made even more intricate with an internal arrangement of seals and talismans, which had come from such sources as the *Clavicula Salomonis*—the Key of Solomon.

Underfoot and overhead were pictograms and sigils of ancient origin, plus refinements and inventions both medieval and Elizabethan, as well as things he'd *never* seen. The place was like an archaeological dig, cross-sectioned with layer upon layer from various eras and schools of ceremonial magic.

"What you see here," Burke said, "is a classic case of fanatics becoming the very thing they were trying to stamp out."

"The Inquisition," said Hellboy. "We're talking about the Inquisition here."

"Speaking bureaucratically—not in practice, thank God—the Inquisition never actually went away. It just got renamed. You knew this, right?"

Hellboy said he did. The department in the Papal Curia that, for the past thirty or so years, had worn the benign name of the Congregation for the Doctrine of the Faith had been born in the 1200s as the Holy Inquisition. Three centuries later, it became the Holy Office, although it had taken more than the name change to abolish its more barbaric practices.

"How does a thing like this *happen*, Burke?"

The monsignor seemed amused that he would ask. "Proximity . . . exposure . . . those are as good an explanation as any. On an entirely different level, the same thing happened during the Crusades when the armies of Western Europe encountered a level of civilization they hadn't expected: 'These Saracens may be infidels, but they're way ahead of us in science and medicine.' "

Hellboy finished for him: " 'So even though we're here to kill them, let's not let all that go to waste.' "

"And thus the exchange of ideas and technologies proceeds. There was a time when war was good for promoting that kind of cross-pollination." Burke waved at the grim relics on the walls. "Now, most of the poor unfortunates these things were used on hundreds of years ago truly were innocents. They simply had different beliefs, or had basically the right beliefs but expressed them in the wrong way . . . or, as it sometimes happened, they did everything right but had the misfortune to run afoul of a neighbor in a secular matter . . . and the good neighbor decided that Inquisitors were more likely than impartial judges to bring about the preferred outcome. A lot of land got stolen that way."

But sometimes, according to Burke, in their prosecution of those who deviated from acceptable beliefs, these long-ago defenders of the faith encountered practices that existed on an entirely different plane from folk remedies and other pagan traditions. Trafficking in spirits of the dead and entities that had never been cloaked in flesh at all . . . these, along with denial of the faith, deserved the most savage punishments of the body and cleansings of the soul. Yet, over time, the lesson was too stark to have been lost on even the most fiercely intolerant men: Here were techniques and methodologies that were *working*. Perhaps not enough to save the heretics from an agonizing fate at sanctified hands, but working nonetheless.

The dead could be interrogated, demons forced to reveal their secrets . . .

For a certain mindset, the temptations must have been insidiously subtle at first, and ultimately overpowering. After all, what did sorcerers desire that such zealous churchmen did not? Knowledge, power, the carrying out of their will . . .

"So they thought they could justify its use on their own terms," Hellboy said. "Adopting the enemy's ways to stamp him out, except in their own hands, it becomes something pure, right?"

"Right. The ends justify the means. It's not like we have signed confessions and records of their meetings, but from the bits and pieces we've put together, a picture emerges. They'd interrogate the dead for some of the same reasons the Inquisition would interrogate the living . . . to get them to incriminate other people. Or just reveal things they could use as leverage one way or another. And if they came upon a genuine adept of sorcery, or just an unconventional healer who understood herbs, they might summon demons and turn them loose on the person and his family. Their version of poetic justice, and probably an object lesson to the victim's neighbors on the perils of straying from the true path. They saw themselves as fighting a war against the forces of darkness, and I imagine they regarded what they did as no different than a soldier picking up an enemy's weapon on the battlefield and killing him with it. And God be praised." For a prelate, Burke could do snide awfully well. "Remember, though, we're talking about only a select few, who banded together into their own society that could *never* have gained sanction by the Church."

"If they turned into heretics themselves," Hellboy said, "why didn't they ever get stamped out along with the rest?"

"Two theories, and the reality was probably a combination of both." Burke fumbled in his pockets; seemed to have gone without a cigarette long enough. "One holds that even though the Inquisition had no reservations about going after rank-and-file priests thought to be bewitching nuns and female parishioners, they were less eager to purge their own ranks. Because to do that, they'd have to admit they were susceptible to corruption."

"You believe that?"

"I suppose it would depend on the individual Inquisitors. For the true believers, it probably wouldn't have made any difference. But we have to assume that their line of work also attracted men who may have preached a good game, but were first and foremost sadists . . . deeply disturbed men who found an accepted outlet for their worst perversions. Naturally they're going to focus their attentions on the most helpless."

"And what's the other theory?"

"That they were extremely effective at maintaining their status as a secret society. They wouldn't have been the kind of group you could infiltrate, while having another agenda, or gain information about from outsiders. Supposedly their initiation rites contained activities that someone uncommitted to this unorthodox path would never have been able to bring himself to commit. Not that *they* regarded it as devil worship, by any means . . . but that's the only way it could've been regarded by someone who didn't share their views."

"And no guilty consciences within the ranks? Nobody broke down and ratted out the others?"

"I'd be surprised if there weren't feelings of guilt in some of them. But it seems that new recruits were indoctrinated to indulge those feelings with self-mortification of the flesh. Hair shirts, that kind of thing."

Burke wandered amid the free-hanging tools, the group's grim reminders of who they were, where they'd come from.

He gave a flick to the collection of thumbscrews and watched them spin, clicking together with a disconcerting sense of dormant purpose.

"So they survived. Replenished their order from generation to generation . . ."

"And by the looks of it," Hellboy said, "survived for centuries after torture was abolished."

"They were never about torture in the first place. Not that they were any different from the rest about it in the early days . . . but if that's all they'd been about, there never would've been a secret society, because they *already* had torture at their disposal. No, these weren't the perverts. And their ultimate objectives don't seem to have varied over the centuries. They may have trafficked with lesser spirits, even evil spirits, but their highest aim has always been embodied in their name: *Opus Angelorum* . . . 'The Work of Angels.' "

"And they don't seem to lean toward the cuddly image."

"No. None of that saccharine New Age pabulum. Avengers and slayers all the way. Divine wrath, that's what they're *really* after. The outlook is primordial."

"So were the results, based on what I saw at the Archives," Hellboy said. "Have they ever pulled off this kind of thing before?"

"Not that I know of. But this was a very high profile success. They're obviously antagonized by the implications of giving the Masada Scroll any kind of credence at all. Regardless of what it was called at any given time, the Inquisition was put in place to defend doctrines. These men tolerated no rivals to the Church, not even in thought. Is it reasonable to assume that those kind of hardliners are extinct?"

"Probably not."

"The *Opus Angelorum* is just the last remnant of those type of extremists. And after all this time, they finally let something drive them aboveground."

"Intentionally?" Hellboy asked. "Or did somebody slip up?"

Burke didn't answer, but his expression seemed to favor the latter.

"So why are we here? Why are you showing me this?"

"To introduce this group to you in a way that words alone could never depict. You've already seen their handiwork. Now take a look around at their soul. Because *somebody* needs to stamp them out. But I'm afraid that men like Father Laurenti, however much they may be opposed to the *Opus Angelorum,* are neither equipped nor prepared to do it in the way it needs to be done. And I think you know what I mean."

Hellboy was sure he'd seen shrewder looking men, but at the moment, he couldn't think of any.

"I know you don't want to meddle in Church business—fine, fine. But I don't see this as Church business. This is a Church aberration." He stepped closer, put his hand on Hellboy's shoulder. "What you need to understand about this group is that until the past few days, it was never much more than a legend. A few whispers, a handful of references in some old journals and correspondence that turned up over the centuries. That's the only way the rest of us got any insight at all into what they were. Even so, it only shed light on the past. Never anything contemporary."

"Until the past few days, you say. What happened then?"

"A close encounter of the third kind," Burke said. "We caught one of them."

CHAPTER 7

She'd napped on the plane, but Liz was still feeling groggy and dislocated when she reached the Vatican. Start factoring in the time zones and her body really started to rebel. Here, late diners might still be tipping wine glasses and demitasse cups, but back home, she would have been in bed for hours.

A local BPRD agent had met her at Da Vinci Airport and driven her to Vatican City's North Gate, the breach in the wall that admitted visitors to the museum complex. At this time of night, it was closed to the public, but after a few minutes of identification checks and confirmation, a pair of Swiss Guards admitted her. One of them radioed someone to relay the news that she was here.

They then escorted her inside the museum's lobby, where she discovered that the fabled opulence of the Vatican extended even to places where they sold tickets. And here, not unwelcome, was a familiar face already, Kate Corrigan coming over to greet her with a quick hug.

"Are you coming with us?" Liz asked.

Kate shook her head no. "I'll be flying instead, to get to the safehouse ahead of you and help with the logistics from there. In case you haven't guessed, we're still making this up as we go."

"And the other end is . . . where? Pretend I'm ignorant, because I really am. H.B. wasn't big on details when he called."

Kate rolled her eyes. "Maybe I should just let him fill you in once he's down."

"Down from where?"

"You know the lantern tower on top of St. Peter's?" Kate leaned in, voice dropping to a whisper. "Looks like a nipple on a breast, but maybe that's just me." She drew back again. "Hellboy and Abe have been up there with the scroll for hours. Abe anyway. Hellboy disappeared for a while just before sunset, but he's back now. They've been waiting it out up there because they thought it was the place least likely to draw another attack like the other night."

Liz had always liked Kate, who was a decade older, give or take, and seemed a good deal looser than her academician's demeanor and no-nonsense bob of hair led many to believe. She had a definite thing for witches, historically speaking, and it was Liz's intuitive but deeply entrenched suspicion that nobody went to that much trouble to research the lives of the witches of Old Europe and New England—with neither dismissal nor judgment—unless she was a bit of a wild lass herself inside, who would very much like to command the wind.

Just the same, for a long time Liz had also found something a bit sad about Kate. Never got the sense that there was somebody special in her life—at best, just a series of not-so-special anybodies who filled the rare temporal gaps between the demands of the bureau and her books and her university position. You could see it in her eyes, though— in lieu of the wind, a longing for some kind of anchor.

Spending time around her often left Liz thinking of the future: *As much as I like her, as much as I admire her and everything she's done . . . I do not want to end up like her . . . and I'm afraid time is running out on that.*

Kate then steered her to a broad-shouldered man in a black cassock, who warmly shook her free hand. Kate introduced him as Father Rogier Artaud, the survivor of the other night's attack on the Archives.

"Any relation to Antonin?" she asked.

Eyes blanking, he turned his palms up and opened his mouth as if something more should come out than a terse croak.

"French poet, dramatist?" she prompted. "He pioneered something called the theater of cruelty . . . ?"

"Ahhh . . . I was born in Belgium," he said, as if that explained everything.

"I'll take that as an inconclusive no," she said.

A nice looking guy, this Rogier Artaud: one of those men who could lose half his hair across the top and look all the better for it—stronger, somehow. A nicely shaped head and a prominent pair of cheekbones went a long way.

He pointed down to the case she was holding. She'd also brought an overnight bag with essentials for what she'd gathered would be a longer return trip, but had set it aside on entering the lobby; unless plans had changed, they would also be leaving from the North Gate. This case, though, hadn't left her sight since leaving the BPRD. Even when she'd napped, she'd locked it to her leg. Overkill, probably—how far away was it going to sneak on a Boeing 767?—but paranoia dies hard.

"So that's what we all have been waiting for?" Artaud asked.

"Yup," she said. "You can take it as long as you can pry it from Hellboy's cold, dead fingers."

What she'd brought, which H.B. had first used to transport a delicate German alchemical manuscript, was a steroidal version of the attaché cases that had been in use for decades to ensure that documents got from Point A to Point B without theft, loss, or pilfering. But unlike a standard case, the outside of this one was made from two layers of titanium alloy sandwiching a layer of Kevlar, and was impervious to just about anything short of an artillery shell. The inside was triple-lined and could be hermetically sealed, with a built-in power source and regulatory system able to maintain up to two weeks' worth of consistent internal temperature and humidity, without which fragile old documents could deteriorate.

And, like the cases it mimicked, this one was equipped with a handcuff. The difference was, there was only one wrist in the world that this particular cuff fit: on Hellboy's right forearm, which was as big around as a gallon can of paint and made of some rocklike substance that had been stymieing scientists since before she'd been born. Plenty of similar cases, carried by everyone from diamond merchants to cocaine dealers, had been stolen by thieves who had no qualms about hacking through the arm it was chained to. Assuming someone could manage to restrain Hellboy in the first place, they were welcome to try. Take a chainsaw to his wrist and the most they'd manage would be breaking its teeth.

When he and Abe made it down from the tower, the only way she could tell they probably hadn't had any sleep since they'd gotten here was Abe's eyes. Hellboy? Forget it. He could probably lose most of his blood and would *still* walk into a room like a four-star general fresh from calisthenics. Abe, though . . . his eyes were a dark aqua color and normally shiny and bright, but they lost some luster when he was weary. As far as she was aware, he never realized that she'd picked up on this, and she was content to let it lie. Maybe he didn't even realize it about himself.

They all kept one another's secrets well. Who else was going to?

They'd shown up with another Swiss Guard, who was toting what looked like a stainless steel storage drawer. Abe came over to greet her, then took the case, seeming to want to waste no time. Artaud excused himself, and he and Abe joined the Guard, and they busied themselves transferring something from the steel bin to the case.

"Thanks for coming," Hellboy said. Was there just the slightest touch of relief in his voice? Yes. There was. "Short notice, I know."

She shrugged it off. "Kinda goes with the paycheck and the room and board."

His brow, that fearsome brow, crinkled. "We need to talk."

"I figured as much. Anybody could've brought you that case. There must be a reason it had to be me."

"Yeah," he said, and once he'd told her, well, at least that explained why every few seconds he glanced up. Up the nearest stairway, up at the high windows, up at the ceiling itself. Just up. And there was a lot of *up* around here to keep track of. Hellboy, nervous? She'd yet to decide whether that was a good thing or a bad thing; whether he was better served by a dose of caution or by the blithe self-confidence that had gotten him this far, against so many odds.

"You're really putting us in the line of fire this time," she said. "Literally."

"Are you going to be okay with that?"

"Like I'd tell you even if I wasn't?"

"You know I'd want you to. You've got to know that."

She reached up and rested her hand along the side of his face. Even apart from the whiskers that bristled down the side like a half-hearted attempt at muttonchops, his face felt like no one else's that she had ever touched. It felt alive, of course, although it didn't quite feel like normal skin, either human or animal. The closest thing she could compare it to was the fibrous bark on the giant redwoods of Northern California. When she'd visited the forests in her late teens, on one of her earlier aimless sprints away from the bureau, she'd been surprised and delighted by the way these trees felt. Massive, yet strangely warm and softly yielding. You just knew these things breathed and were aware of you, in their own way.

Appropriate, then, that they would remind her of Hellboy. Because what was he if not like some big sequoia, red and towering, and likely to be standing long after everyone else in the forest had returned to dust.

"I just have to wonder if I'd do any good if they come back," she said. "Seraphim . . . we're in uncharted territory with this one. Are they even vulnerable to fire?"

"I don't know." At least he didn't lie. But then, he wasn't very good at it. Not around her, anyway. "I do know if those things hit us, you've got a better chance of blowing them out of the sky than I do. They throw fire, you throw fire. I'm just going by what they left behind upstairs, but yours, when you're on full-burn . . . ? I think it's hotter, more forceful. I don't claim to know the thermodynamics of it, but I'm betting you could consume their fire with your own. Block it."

"If you're wrong, it's your barbecue. Mine too, probably."

"My guess is you'd be okay," he said. "Don't think I didn't spend some time mulling this over. But if you were to square off with one of these things, I think you'd be okay."

Maybe he was right. Obviously, whenever she torched up—accidentally or on purpose—she remained unharmed, immune to the effects of the blaze emanating from her being. The bureau had studied her relentlessly throughout her teens, dotted her with so many electrodes it was like having a rash, and one constant they'd found was that even during episodes hot enough to smelt iron ore, her skin temperature never elevated by more than a couple of degrees—no worse than a mild fever.

As near as she could discern, even in the midst of a full-body detonation, she was surrounded by a cocoon of sorts, an insulating layer of *something* that stood between flesh and fire. One of the researchers had called it an etheric version of the protective gel that movie stuntmen slathered over themselves when they did pyro stunts—staggering out of a flaming car wreck, gags like that—only far more effective. It not only kept her from burning herself, but also shielded her from external fires; they'd tested her with everything from candles to propane torches.

Holy fire was something else entirely, a complete unknown, but Liz figured her chances of surviving it had to be better than even. Just the same, she hoped she wouldn't have to find out.

One of the priests who'd been milling about inside the North Gate when she'd arrived now stepped into the museum lobby and reported that the armored car was on its way, heading down the Viale Vaticano from where it had been parked in waiting.

"Armored car?" she asked.

"Yeah," Hellboy said, as Abe brought over the attaché case, sealed now. "One of the cardinals pulled a few strings with a security company that works for the Banca di Roma."

She looked up, just as Hellboy had moments ago, an instinctive impulse now that she knew the next couple of minutes might turn into a kill-or-be-killed situation. Fry-or-be-fried.

Abe latched the enormous cuff over Hellboy's wrist.

As they started for the exit, she took one last look behind her, not without regret. It had nothing to do with the danger. *Join the BPRD, travel the world, visit interesting places,* she thought. *And bug out again before you've actually had a chance to see them.*

Hellboy was through the doors first, ready to absorb the brunt of another attack in case the seraphs were lying in wait, perched outside on the roof like gargoyles ready to swoop in for the kill. Tough gig, walking point under these circumstances. Fire wouldn't kill him, only hurt like a bitch for a long time. He stood in the open for several moments, tensed and ready for a fight, seeming to dare them to come for him. With his left hand he'd drawn the massive revolver he carried on his hip and, aiming it upward, extended his arm back toward them like a traffic cop's: *Wait, just waaaait* . . .

Lingering near the doorway, Liz wondered—in that way one's mind can lock onto small things during tense moments—if he ever broke sweat. She'd known him since late childhood and couldn't think of a single time that she'd seen him sweat.

All clear? So it seemed. Hellboy gave the gun barrel a couple of twitches and the rest of them were on the move, she and Abe rushing out the museum doors—Abe, ever the gentleman, lugging her suitcase—and flanked by a pair of Swiss Guards who stepped up the pace to beat them to the outer gate. Hellboy threw his gun arm around her shoulders and she felt herself yanked off her feet, puppet girl, boot tips skimming the ground in abnormally long strides as though she were on the surface of the moon.

The North Gate swung open before them and they dashed through onto the sidewalk along the Viale Vaticano—into another land, literally, the traffic and tumult of Rome so much louder now that they were on the other side of the wall. On the street sat the armored car, rumbling and grumbling like a small tank. They made straight for the back end, where a dark-skinned security guard stood in a uniform and jacket and beret, a machine pistol slung from a shoulder strap. He swung the doors open and motioned them in.

The skies were clear in the chilly autumn night, and she found it hard to look away. If they came, she feared they would come not like doves but like missiles.

She was inside the armored car then, a cross between an ambulance and a bank vault, Hellboy practically tossing her in the way men in cartoons pitch noisy cats out the door in the middle of the night, and then Abe was right behind her, with H.B. bringing up the rear, the titanium case bouncing at the end of its chain as if it were no more to him than a trinket on a charm bracelet, and the guard was pushing the doors closed and Hellboy turned and pulled them the rest of the way, two bone-rattling impacts and a sequence of sharp metallic clacks as he engaged the locks.

And they were in. Safe.

He stood framed by the doorway, staring at her peering behind him.

"What are you looking at?" he asked.

"Just making sure you cleared your tail," she said, and burst into laughter that was more relief than anything. "Because if you didn't, I don't think you'd even realize."

A moment later they heard and felt the slam of the front side door as the guard jumped back in the cab, and the armored car surged forward into traffic they couldn't see.

"So what's the plan here?" she asked once they were settled into the seats. "I feel like I'm in a hazing. You guys have grabbed me up but I don't know where I'm going."

While they'd been waiting in the museum lobby, Kate Corrigan had already filled her in on the Masada Scroll, so she'd been apprised of that much. And that the end goal—until opposing factions in the Vatican had no more reason to antagonize each other—was to get it back to BPRD headquarters, where the scroll could be safely stored inside the old fireproof bunker where she'd spent so many long days and nights weathering the turmoil of adolescence. The prison of her own making, she'd thought it on good days; on bad days, it was just the dungeon. Burn up enough bedrooms during accidents and bad dreams, and you get a reputation.

But for traveling back to the States, Hellboy had decided that flying was out of the question. They had to cover all that distance under the assumption that they might be attacked with the same ferocity that had befallen the Vatican Archives, by assailants to whom altitude apparently meant nothing. On the ground, they might have a fighting chance—it was, after all, the reason she was here—but in the sky they would be vulnerable to the point of suicide. After fireballs at 36,000 feet, and the inevitable crash, there wouldn't be enough of the team left to scrape up with a shovel.

Surface travel it would have to be, then. With the main objective getting the scroll out of Rome and, for its first way station, to a BPRD safehouse in England. Once there, on secure ground, they could work out a method for moving it across the ocean.

Even so, Rome to England wouldn't be an easy jaunt. A few months earlier, they might have motored north out of Italy and into France, then headed for the western coast and taken the English Channel Tunnel. Not now, though. It was mid-October, with snow already falling in the Alps, and they could ill afford to risk getting stranded on a mountain pass in the north of Italy or the south of France.

Under the circumstances, the best way out of Rome lay

at the end of a twenty-mile drive southwest from the Vatican: the Mediterranean. Earlier in the day, Hellboy had arranged for a charter yacht that would be waiting for them on the other end of this armored car ride, at the docks of Ostia. It would take them west across the sea, out the Straits of Gibraltar, then up past Portugal and the tip of Spain, and ultimately to the harbor of Falmouth, on England's southwest coast. From there, they could motor to the BPRD safehouse near Bodmin, in the middle of Cornwall. Here the scroll should be secure enough for the time being in the basements, while they finalized the rest of the journey . . . which, with luck, Kate and the British team would already have arranged by the time they arrived.

It would take longer than flying, but posed no risk of a fiery crash. And if the worst happened and they were attacked, the saving grace along most of the journey would lie beneath them: all that water. The seraphim were going to boil an ocean dry? Not likely, Hellboy said.

"They wouldn't have to," she told him. "Just enough to turn the immediate area into a saucepan."

"I'll make sure they focus on me. I may look like a lobster, but I don't cook up like one."

She pinched the scruff of his chin between her thumb and forefinger. "Level with me, okay? If these things went blasting through the Vatican, of all places, what's to stop them from coming after us whenever and wherever they want?"

"They have their limitations. They're not all-seeing."

Now Abe stepped in: "It seems they do what they're summoned to do. No more and, judging by the other night's failure, sometimes less. As long as the men who arranged for the attack on the Archives don't know our travel route, the farther away we get, the better off we should be."

"So why not just get away from Rome and catch a flight someplace where they wouldn't know about it?"

"Because what if I'm wrong?" Hellboy said. "I'd rather be just plain wrong than wrong and stupid."

Then his mood lightened. He didn't smile, exactly, and in fact rarely did—truth be told, whenever he tried to smile like a normal person the effect was fairly ghastly—but he had this way of cocking his head to the side that was down-right endearing.

"Make you a bet," he said. "If we make it as far as the yacht and shove off without trouble, then it's smooth sailing the rest of the way. A leisurely cruise. And if I'm wrong, then I owe you one."

"What are we betting here?" she asked, wary.

"Loser gives the winner backrubs for a week."

Liz barked a derisive laugh. "Some incentive. Your back's three times as wide as mine. And let's not even talk about the difference in hand size."

Hellboy looked at Abe with a stage-managed sigh. "Well, I tried bribery . . . "

As the ride went on, Liz tried to judge how far they'd gone. Not easy to do, with no windows to look out and the frequent start-and-stops of city traffic. They must have at least gotten far enough south to clear the main congestion of central Rome, because they seemed to be rolling more smoothly now.

Then she noticed Abe, and the way he seemed to be tensing with the realization that something was wrong, pins and needles growing under the skin. His gills suddenly fanned out and rippled.

"Abe?" she said, and now Hellboy had snapped to as well. "What is it?"

"We're going the wrong way," he said. "That last turn . . . we're going east."

"Yeah, so?" Hellboy said. "The streets here have to work around the Tiber. It's the most screwed-up street layout I've ever seen."

Except Abe wasn't having it, shaking his head no, no, no. "We're going the wrong way now . . . "

And when Abe started talking navigation, you tended to believe him. It was more than a knack, like her father's keen directional sense when childhood vacations took the family to unfamiliar towns in which he hardly ever got lost. No, with Abe it seemed to go much deeper . . . a fundamental part of him, maybe on some level aware of polarities and magnetic fields. Something to do with the *Icthyo* part of his makeup, she suspected, rather than the *Sapien*. Like the way salmon could abandon the ocean to return to the same river where they'd been spawned.

"We're heading *away* from the sea."

And that's when Hellboy and Abe's radio beepers started to go off.

CHAPTER 8

He'd hardly used it at all this trip, but it was sure squawking now: standard bureau issue, a cross between a walkie-talkie and a mobile phone. Everybody carried them on investigations for occasions when they might separate on-site. Sync up on frequency and encryption code before arrival, and they'd be good to wander apart. Transmissions could be sent to an entire group or to just one agent. Hellboy's unit had spent most of the time in Rome being ignored.

He plucked it from its leather sleeve on his belt, Abe slower on the draw.

"Yeah?" he said, but even before he heard her voice, he knew it could only be Kate.

Except she wasn't coming through clearly. He didn't know how many miles they'd ridden, and could never remember the effective range of these things, but they must have been on the ragged edge of it right now. The thick steel walls of the armored car probably weren't helping, either.

"You're breaking up," he said. "Make it quick."

Choppy, frazzing into bursts of static, whatever Kate was trying to tell him was coming in as though her words were being run through a broken fan. She must've realized it, though. Sounded like she'd boiled her message down to its essence and was repeating it over and over . . .

Bodies, he picked out.

— *guard* —

— *found* —

— *street* —

Under the circumstances, that was about all anyone needed to hear. He switched the radio on standby again and stuffed it back into its sleeve.

"I think we've been hijacked and didn't even know it," he whispered, and with Liz and Abe looking at him, he touched a finger to his lips: *Shhhh.*

He stood, moved to the front of the compartment. Undid the lock on the sliding metal plate that, when opened, would reveal a small grilled window into the driver's cab. He gave it three jaunty taps, then slid it aside. Couldn't see much. There was the back of someone's head directly in front of the window. A beret over mouse-brown hair that looked like it could use a good washing. Didn't look like it was the same guard with the machine gun who had opened the back door for them— the skin at the neck was too pale, too . . . sallow. It wasn't the driver, either; he was too close to the middle for that. Whoever it was, he wasn't moving.

And that blood-threaded gobbet on the back of his collar? Hellboy swore it was brain matter.

He leaned to the side, enough of an angle on the slot that he could see past the back of the middle guy's head and get a profile on the driver. The man was keeping his eyes on the road like his life depended on it.

"*Scusatemi,*" Hellboy said. About the only Italian he knew. "How much longer before we get to the docks?"

And wouldn't you think that the driver of an armored car, especially with two other guys in the cab with him, had better things to do than answer his own questions? A thick-jowled man with a blue sheen of beard, he looked back over his shoulder.

"Twenty minutes, about," he said.

Three words, three seconds—you can communicate a lot with that, if you're frightened half out of your mind. Very subtle . . . the driver didn't betray so much as a tic or flinch, but he held his gaze just long enough to convey everything he could not say aloud. Hellboy had seen plenty of fear in people's eyes. Sometimes fear of him, but more often, fear of something beyond their control. He'd encountered enough of both to tell the difference.

"Thanks," he said, keeping his voice light. He pointed at the guy sitting in front of the grill and gave a suspicious look.

The driver dipped his chin with an almost imperceptible nod, then turned back to the road. Hellboy waited a beat to see if he tried to communicate anything more.

"Yeah, a shame about the beach at Ostia," Hellboy went on, just to have something chatty to say, and angled his view enough to watch the driver's hands. "I hear they've got a real sewage problem. Not just their own crap, but all the crap washing down the Tiber out of Rome . . . "

He prattled on as the driver's left hand drifted toward the door, to the joystick that controlled the outside mirror on the other side of the bulletproof glass. Hellboy shifted again for a better perspective, watching as the mirror angled inward with a changing view of traffic, then the side length of the armored car, and finally the inside of the cab. He caught a reflection of the driver's face, eyes darting, and then he had it: a look at the guard in the middle. No wonder he hadn't turned, hadn't wanted to be seen.

Because this was no guard. He may have been wearing the uniform, but that bit of brain tissue on the collar said he'd taken it by force. And the face—cut with deep lines, the flesh tight against the skull—a junkie's face, or worse. In a sweep of headlights from oncoming traffic, the eyes gave a malevolent flash like quicksilver.

This may have been a man once, but the man had been gone a long time. The body was a shell for something else now. And it didn't belong *here*.

"See you guys at the docks," Hellboy said, and slid the metal plate closed again.

For a moment he stood unmoving, leaning against the wall, his eyes closed and the flat fronts of his stunted horns pressed into the steel. You just knew that the poor guy behind the wheel had a family . . . a big one, everybody waiting for him to come home after this late job. He'd always come home before.

"H.B.?" Liz said, her voice almost as soft as the touch of her hand on his arm.

"Something's wrong up there. The driver's in as much trouble as we're supposed to be."

He dug into another of the pouches on his belt for the key to the enormous cuff on his wrist.

"Get back, away from the front," he told her as he unlatched the cuff. Not exactly the plan, taking it off only minutes after this journey had gotten underway, but he didn't want to be flailing the thing around for the next few minutes.

"You too," he told Abe, with a nod toward the back, then gave him the case. "And hang onto this."

"H.B.?" Liz said again, with more alarm. "We're still moving. Shouldn't you wait until . . . ?"

"Until they get us where they want us? I don't like the sound of that."

As the armored car wove through the curving streets of south Rome, Hellboy braced into a wide stance before the sliding metal plate. He drew his revolver, one of several custom .50-caliber handguns the BPRD made for him, big-bored things that could drop a rhino.

"Cover your ears," he whispered over his shoulder. "This is gonna be loud."

With his right hand he slammed the metal plate aside, and with his left jammed the muzzle of the revolver against the grill, hesitating a fraction of a second to ascertain that it was still the same head before pulling the trigger. And it *was* loud, a thunderclap in an oil drum, numbing even his ears for a moment, but he still fared better than the thing in front of him. The head snapped forward, and through the slot Hellboy saw a cascade of meat and bone and blood slap the inside of the windshield after ejecting from the exit wound that had been the face.

And to his credit, the driver held it steady.

Hellboy waited a moment, let the remaining two up front decide what happened next. He had no doubts about the driver's legitimacy. The third one—who'd helped load them into the back outside the North Gate—he wasn't sure about. Gut instinct told him something wasn't right there either. After all, the man had been armed. But maybe he'd been coerced. Family held hostage, something like—

Jesus! As sudden as a cobra strike, the snout of the guard's machine pistol thrust into the hole in the grill left by Hellboy's bullet. One squeeze of the trigger and their compartment back here would turn into a bloody whirlwind of ricochets.

Hellboy slapped his right hand over the slot, knocking the muzzle back out of the hole just as the guard opened fire. He felt a burst of rounds pound into his palm, but they didn't penetrate, *couldn't* penetrate. That was the wonder of his mysterious hand. It was flexible and he sacrificed nothing in dexterity, but it felt no pain and was seemingly indestructible. Bullets? They might as well have been bees, and went spraying back into the cab.

He waited until the guard quit firing, then slammed the panel into place and locked it. Could feel the armored car swerving now, impacts jolting through as it sideswiped whatever had the misfortune to be nearby.

And he *had* to get up front.

He started for the back doors, but quickly thought better of it. Sure, he could open them, swing onto the roof, go up and over to the cab . . . or try, at least. The trouble was, he hadn't seen any handholds when they were running toward it at the North Gate. Slick surface, nothing to grab onto. And with the erratic way this thing was moving now, he stood a good chance of getting thrown to the pavement. It wasn't the impact that worried him, but whether or not he could chase the vehicle down on foot. Not likely. He was built more for durability than raw speed.

If you couldn't go *over* an obstacle, that left going *through* it.

He looked at Abe and Liz, both taking cover on the floor.

"Hang on," he said. "This is gonna get a lot bumpier before it's over."

Hellboy returned to the slot and ripped the panel away, let it clang to the floor. The hole made a natural weak spot—maybe not for human hands, but it definitely gave *his* a place to start. He let the battering ram of his right fist fly, punching directly into the slot. The edges curled away, into the cab.

Again he punched it, and again, and again . . . all along, careful to keep his body in line with the widening hole. If there was more shooting, he would weather the bullets that got through better than Liz and Abe.

He rained blows around the gap, like wielding a fistful of sledgehammers. He had to pause a couple of times and swat the roving gun barrel out of the way; tried to get his hand around it, but no luck. Soon enough, though. *He was going through that hole,* wasn't going to stop until it was big enough to let him. He'd made rubble of plenty of architecture this way. An armored car should only take a little longer . . . and after a few more poundings the entire reinforced partition started to buckle.

With the hole as wide as a serving platter now, he could see what he couldn't before: through the bloodied windshield, a backseat view of the street, pavement pouring under the front end, headlights sweeping from side to side as the armored car careened along, mowing down signs one moment, crossing lanes the next. He recognized where they were, enough sights and landmarks—there, an exit for the Catacombs, and there, the Basilica of Saint Sebastian—to tell him that they were on the Via Appia Antica, the Old Appian Way, the ancient road that served Rome even today.

And right in front of his eyes, the cab was a charnel house in miniature. The body of the first hijacker was slumped forward with half of his ruined head across the windshield, the other half dripping onto the floor. The driver was dead or dying; it looked as though he'd caught several rounds, probably from that first thwarted salvo that had sprayed back into the cab. The gunman too had been hit by his own fire, but his wounds clearly hadn't been fatal. He'd attempted to yank the driver away from the wheel and take control but was only half successful, all three of them up front now a tangle of limbs and blood, the living and the dead, trying to keep the vehicle on the road.

Hellboy seized the edge of the hole and gave a bellow, as much frustration as fury, and wrenched at the ragged metal. It groaned, then gave, inch by tortured inch, like ripping his way out of a giant can, and he was almost there, almost there . . .

The surviving guard abandoned the wheel to snatch up his machine pistol again. He tried to aim but the grip was slippery with his blood, or the blood of the driver, maybe both, and the one fumble was all Hellboy needed. He'd already begun to squirm through the hole, his head and his right shoulder—far enough to put a stop to this attack once and for all.

A frozen moment as he came face to face with the guard: Under his beret and a flawless brown forehead, the man's face was distinctly African, cheekbones high and round, so sculpted he could have modeled for statues. And something more. Again the eyes were the giveaway, although not the same as with the guard he'd shot. Hellboy could still see the *man* in these eyes, and the fear that came from someplace deep, as though he were watching Hellboy from the bottom of a pool, with something else between the two of them. His actions seemed not to be his own, the man trapped on the inside, helplessly watching his hands betray him.

A part of him seemed to plead even as the rest of him tried to aim.

"Fight it," Hellboy told him. "Whatever's in you, *fight it.*"

Maybe he tried. But he lost all the same. Hellboy caught the barrel of the gun as it tracked into his face. He gave it a twist, crumpling the stubby barrel out of commission an instant before the man's finger tightened on the trigger.

Too slow, half a second too slow—in a fair world, he would have been able to wrest the gun away before that last flex of the man's finger.

The final burst of rounds popped off with nowhere to go. The top of the gun blew apart in the hijacker's hand, the chamber and the rear of the barrel turning into pieces of whizzing shrapnel. Hellboy felt one crack off the stump of one horn, another clip through the sleeve of his coat to hack a shallow chunk out of his arm.

But the stricken guard caught the worst of it, ragged debris tearing into him in half a dozen places to finish the job the bullets had started. Hellboy gritted his teeth with a groan, hating it all . . . having just watched men die, having been forced into a situation to *cause* them to die, because someone or something had decided they were expendable.

The armored car was out of control now, off the road and shearing through a wooded area, uprooting bushes and clipping small trees off at the bumper-line.

He wrenched at the hole he'd torn, widening it enough to squeeze the rest of himself into the cab, yanking the bodies out of the way so he could fit into the driver's seat. Grappling with the wheel and stabbing for the brakes, until he finally brought the armored car slaloming to a halt.

In relief, he sat for a moment, staring out at the headlight beams as they pierced the night. A few dozen more yards and they would've met up with trees big enough to stop the vehicle dead. A few beats of silence, nothing but the rumbling of the engine, but after the past minutes, it seemed quiet as a whisper.

He took a look back through the hole, saw Liz and Abe picking themselves up off the floor.

"You two okay?" he called. "Anything worse than bumps and bruises?"

"I'm good," Liz said.

Abe nodded. "How are things up front?"

"No survivors," he said softly.

A moment later, Liz was at the hole, looking in, looking down. "God," she said. "Was all this really . . . necessary?"

He gripped the wheel with his left hand. There wasn't much in this world or any other that pained him, but hearing doubt from Liz? That was one of them. He knew he was rash sometimes, rushing headlong where angels feared to tread. It was one fault he tried to be honest about, trying even harder not to let it get the better of his judgment. But he didn't think he ever gambled needlessly with lives.

Although if he had to make the choice, he supposed he would rather gamble with the lives of strangers than the lives of those he loved. She had to know that. But she would never want the responsibility of it. The possibility that she would come out on the winning side of a judgment call, because it meant someone else had to lose.

"I'm not sure what happened here," he told her. "But I think there's a good chance these men would've been dead soon either way."

"It doesn't help," Liz said.

"I know."

"A few pieces of paper, basically. That's all we're carrying. Pieces of old paper."

"I know."

He'd just ripped through an armored car and still, right now he wanted to tear something, anything, apart in the worst way. But the best thing to do, the *smart* thing to do, would be to find a map and get back to the coast. Before they found themselves waylaid by the convergence of police cars that were sure to be minutes away.

He turned away from Liz and stared through the windshield again.

Something was moving out there, a couple of there-and-gone flickers amid the trees.

He'd opened the door before he could stop himself, leaping from the cab and hitting the ground with his revolver drawn again, sprinting in front of the armored car so its headlights burned past him, making him harder to spot while he could see everything in their beams.

He could hear them out there . . . slow, stealthy footfalls snapping twigs and crunching fallen leaves. Gut instinct told him that the armored car had traveled about as far as it was supposed to. Maybe a wilder arrival than someone had counted on, but this was the place.

Strangely enough, though, there didn't seem to be much here. The headlights burned through the thicket, until they were swallowed by the darkness that held fast between the trees. Overhead, a break in the branches, thinning out with autumn, showed the suggestion of hills just beyond the trees, stark black curves set against the starry sky.

So what was supposed to happen here, anyway? Lose the scroll—that seemed obvious enough. If destroying it were the objective, someone had gone to an awful lot of trouble to bring it to a specific location, rather than just getting the job done. So yeah, lose the scroll, that had to be the general idea . . . but into whose hands?

The trees stared back, divulging nothing. Whoever watched from the darkness, they had evidently seen enough to rethink what was supposed to have happened here.

"Hellboy." Abe's voice, behind him, from the door of the armored car. "I found three of these in the cab. I think they were meant for us."

"Three of what?"

Something thumped onto the ground beside his foot. Hellboy stooped to pick it up, brought it into the light. Found that he was holding a stun grenade. A flash-bang, commandos sometimes called them. Throw one into a confined space like a room—or the back of an armored car—and the burst of light and shock wave would scramble the circuits of whoever was close by.

"Or maybe all three were meant for you," Abe said.

Facing the darkness, knowing they were there and afraid, every muscle tensing to spring forward and catch one of them, find out what was going on here—

"Hellboy." Abe again, his voice sharper, more insistent. "Some other time. We need to go now."

No arguments there. Just a lot of thwarted impulse and the need for self-control. He gave the trees and their secrets one last baleful glare, then turned back toward the armored car.

CHAPTER 9

When dawn came, it came at their backs, and far from the sight of land.

Underfoot, the teakwood deck of the *Calista* rolled against the horizon line with slow, gentle undulations. She was a two-mast schooner, a vintage seventy-eight-foot motor sailer built more than four decades ago and immaculately maintained ever since. From her foredeck Hellboy watched the sun come up in a spreading stain of rose and orange. It set fire to the shimmering surface of the sea, a tranquil inferno whose only sound was the slapping of waves against the hull, the snap of sails filled by a tailwind steady enough that they no longer needed to run the engines.

If dawn was the only fire from above, he would count this day among the good ones.

It had been a quiet night since shoving off from the docks at Ostia, abandoning the ruined armored car and its bloody cargo. They had established a radio link from the yacht to Kate Corrigan's mobile phone, letting her know they'd made it to the coast and filling her in on what had happened . . . or as much as they could explain. She wished them a safe rest of the journey, said she would spend an extra couple of days in Rome to help sort out the mess, but that she should still be there to meet them in Cornwall.

With the cuff and case reattached to his wrist—for the duration of the trip, he vowed, tolerating no risk, however small, that it could be lost overboard—he had taken up a vigil in an extra-sturdy deck chair near the bow, ahead of the cockpit and the rotating crew of four who manned the wheel through the night. From here he watched the sky, hours spent scanning the blackened heavens for a glimpse of shapes that might betray their presence by blotting out stars. But they had never come.

And so by most standards it was a quiet night. But quiet is relative. A night can never be truly quiet when you can't forget the faces of the dead. The armored car's driver and the African guard . . . they would stay with him a long while. Even he wasn't sure why they'd died, so how could *they* have made any sense of what they'd faced in their last hour, last moments? They had died knowing only that they were under siege—one from without, one from within.

That was the thing about the dead: They could so easily haunt, whether they meant to or not.

With the new morning sky still gray in the west, Abe came up from below to join him, squatting on the deck beside Hellboy's chair. He seemed to expend no effort at all in keeping himself perfectly counterbalanced against the roll of the yacht.

"We didn't talk much about what happened last night," Abe said.

"Guess not."

"But now that the sun's rising, and it'll be easy to see whatever might be up there, maybe we should."

Hadn't wasted any time, had he? Probably kept watch at a porthole in his cabin down below.

"What happened with that crew?" Abe asked. "I saw only the bodies. You saw the *men.*"

Hellboy had been running everything through his mind for hours, and still didn't have it all worked out.

"The driver, he was okay. Scared, that's all. I vouch for him, alive or dead. He didn't seem to have any choice but to go along with what was happening," Hellboy said. "The one in the middle? The driver gave me a look at him with the door mirror. I don't know what kind of spirit was inside him, but whatever it was, it had been around long enough to wear the guy like an old glove.

"The guard that loaded us in the back, none of us noticed anything wrong about him," he went on. "Just seemed to be doing his job. Then when things got heavy, at first I thought he must've been a plant . . . a mercenary, somebody's paid soldier. Or somebody's fanatic, on a mission. Until I got a look at him. Something was inside him too, Abe. But not like the other one. It must've happened not long before. Look deep enough and you can see the difference . . . two opposing minds looking out of the same pair of eyes, and the one that doesn't belong has got the one that does squashed over into one little corner."

"But he couldn't have been in thrall to the one in the middle."

"No, because that guy was the first to die."

"So who was *he?*"

"I'm curious about that myself."

He'd given the body a quick search after they'd gotten to Ostia, although nothing of much help turned up—at least nothing to indicate who he'd been, where he'd come from, what he'd been mixed up in. He'd been wearing the same uniform as the other two guards, but his had fit poorly—too big around the waist, too short in the leg. It would've been an obvious conclusion that the uniform had been tailored for someone else even if its owner hadn't been discovered in an alley a couple of blocks from the Vatican's North Gate: one of the bodies that Kate had radioed about last night.

The only thing of interest that the man in the middle had been carrying was his sidearm, a vintage piece with sleek lines, a long thin barrel, and a distinctive enough shape to leave no doubt as to what it was. Hellboy was by no means an expert on firearms—was usually doing good just to handle the one he carried—but was pretty sure he knew a German Luger when he saw one.

Should've left it behind, maybe, for the Italian investigators. But his first impulse had been to take it along. Call it a jurisdictional dispute.

As for those two bodies in the alley . . . well, dead men could still tell tales, but sometimes you couldn't make out what they were saying, and this was one of them. With five corpses in all, three belonging to the security crew, there was nobody left who could testify to how the armored car had been taken over. It was an *armored car*, for crying out loud. All they'd had to do was stay inside the thing.

According to Kate, when they'd reached her from the *Calista*'s VHF radiophone, about fifteen minutes after they had left the Vatican's North Gate last night, someone had spotted the lights of an ambulance and a pair of police cars converging down the Viale Vaticano. Two of the priests who'd been part of the scroll's guardian group— Father Artaud and his superior, Father Ranzi—had hurried down the street to the scene. At the time, they weren't thinking that this was around the same location as where the armored car had sat waiting, out of sight, until the BPRD trio was ready to board. They'd only gone in case someone was in need of Last Rites or some other assistance.

Too late. Discovered by tourists, the pair was beyond help. One of them, a malnourished and even desiccated looking fellow—sounded like the one Hellboy had shot— was dead for no obvious reason. No wounds, no injuries, just an overall physical condition that implied he might have dropped dead of natural causes.

The other, the fresh kill, had been the third original guard from the armored car. He'd died quickly, shot through the eye, and Hellboy wondered if this had been done with the Luger he'd confiscated. Once dead, the guard had been stripped of his clothes—no doubt the ill-fitting uniform worn by the hijacker Hellboy had killed, with the bit of brain on the collar—although they'd left behind the topcoat he'd worn. From what Ranzi managed to learn at the scene, the hijackers had tried to disguise the fact that they were leaving bodies behind by posing them as though they were sleeping vagrants—not an uncommon presence in Rome. Homeless equals invisible. Couldn't manage that nearly as well with a man naked but for his underwear and socks, though, and while they'd had spare clothes from the hijacker, it would've been no easy feat to re-dress the corpse in a hurry. Just curl him up and drape him with his topcoat. The illusion might have held up longer if not for the spreading blood.

Ultimately, it was the coat that had raised the alarm with Father Ranzi, while he conferred with the police. Its breast bore a patch with the emblem of the security company whose armored car had not half an hour before rolled away carrying the Masada Scroll.

"Who they were, how they did it . . . I'm not gonna worry about that right now. If there's anything to find out, Kate'll get to the bottom of it," Hellboy said. "What I'm more worried about is who put them up to it."

"Not the *Opus Angelorum,* then?"

"Last night, none of that seemed like their style. If I had to put a word to it, that was too *earthy* for them. Too down and dirty. It was just the opposite of a cleansing fire. No purity," Hellboy reasoned. "Seems like if the *Opus* had known we were on the move, they'd've just called in the flamethrowers again."

"Instead, if they've lost their ritual site," Abe said, referring to the observatory that Monsignor Burke had revealed, "it's possible they're on the move as well. Maybe out of the picture. For now, at least."

"Yeah. A group that's been around as long as Burke says this one has, hard to believe they'd let a little thing like eviction put them out of business permanently."

"So we're looking at the likelihood of another faction whose presence has gone unknown until now."

Hellboy nodded. "Except this one doesn't want the scroll destroyed. They just want it. Period."

"But for what?"

"Most of the time I'm smarter than I look," Hellboy said. "This isn't one of them."

"If we knew who sold us out, that's one step closer to the answer."

They tossed names back and forth, everybody they were aware of who had known their logistics. It was a short list: Artaud and Ranzi, the two archivists most directly connected with the scroll. Bertrand, the Swiss Guard Corporal who'd been assigned to them all day, and could easily have overheard their travel plans being made, although when the man could've gotten that information out, Hellboy didn't know. Then there was the head of the security company who'd furnished the armored car, although that seemed the least likely possibility; he hadn't even known what the cargo was, only that it was a valuable historical document. There was also Cardinal Capezza, who'd flexed connections to line up the car in the first place—a totally unknown commodity here, someone they hadn't even met. Instead, he'd been contacted by Archbishop Bellini, the plump guy who'd been nodding off at the beginning of yesterday morning's meeting in which they'd asked the BPRD to take custody of the scroll. So add Bellini to the list, too. Then there was Monsignor Burke to consider, if only because they'd spoken at length last evening, although he too was a long shot at best; Hellboy hadn't mentioned anything other than travel by sea, and Burke hadn't been involved in the plans for getting the scroll to the coast.

Anyone else? Not that they knew of, but then, any one of the above could have violated common sense and mentioned it to someone else. Dumb, but far from impossible.

Like any bureaucracy, the Vatican thrived on gossip and power plays, and they'd already been warned of spies.

"Then again, at this point, does it even matter who sold us out?" Abe said. He reached across with one slim-muscled arm and tapped the attaché case, resting beside the deck chair under Hellboy's oversized hand. "It's safe and I'm optimistic it'll stay that way. To get at it where it's going, they'd have to have a *very* long reach."

Hellboy ticked one eyebrow upward.

"Of course I know it matters to *you*, and I know why," Abe said. "You wouldn't be you if it didn't. What I'm pointing out is now that we have this"—he tapped the case again—"our part in their affairs is over. The one priest yesterday, the one that looks like he belongs in a soup kitchen . . . "

"Father Laurenti," Hellboy said. Something spooky about that guy . . . although not in a bad way. Spooky in the same way that somebody else might have leveled the same verdict against him, or Abe, or Liz, or even Kate, for that matter.

"Laurenti, right. He couldn't have made it any plainer that they do *not* want us meddling in their affairs any more than is necessary to get the job done and keep the scroll safe."

"And Monsignor Burke couldn't have made that any murkier by taking me to the observatory."

"Yes, but your field trip notwithstanding, there's an official position, and it comes not just from a Church hierarchy, but from a sovereign state. That carries weight . . . even with a bureau like ours."

He knew Abe was right. Didn't have to like it one bit,

but there it was. Abe had always had more of the diplomatic about him.

"And according to the monsignor, they've taken at least one prisoner in this ideological conflict," Abe went on. "Prisoners, arson, deaths . . . this has gotten ugly. It was ugly before we were even a part of it. And the worst part is, we don't know which side is going to prevail. Who *should* and who *will* are two different things. We may have our sympathies, you and I, but you probably know what kind of directive is going to come down."

Here it comes, Hellboy thought. *The P-word . . .*

"Politically, we can't take an official side any more than we already have. You and I may not like it, but regardless, we *are* part of a government agency. And when our work comes into conflict with the demands of state . . ." Abe let the words hang, then shook his head.

And they were getting at the paradox of his whole existence, weren't they? Despite having spent his entire life in the care and then the employ of the government—or at least the only life he was cognizant of, given his apparent origins—he'd felt insulated from government's minutiae and dictates of policy. Face it: What they did in the BPRD, what they encountered, what they killed or were killed by . . . most senators and representatives and cabinet officials didn't even want to *know* about. True, the bureau had been founded in 1944 as a response to the Third Reich's increasingly successful occult experiments, seeking to turn the tide of the war back in their favor. Later, there'd been similar clashes with the Soviet Union. After which the bureau's political star had dimmed. This was inevitable. It had been decades since a government had harnessed such powers.

But chaos rarely served a master. It sought entry anywhere it could. And surely that was the only reason an agency like theirs remained funded, even tolerated at all. They didn't so much defend the country as they defended reality itself.

Easy, then, to forget that there was still a bureaucratic hammer over their heads, however unobtrusive it may have been most of the time.

Hellboy glanced back past the cockpit, in the direction of the companionway, the stairs leading belowdecks. "Was Liz awake when you came up?"

"Definitely not," Abe said, then stood and stretched out his long, lean body, sleek as an eel. He took a couple of steps toward the rail, gazing off across the water, a plain of gunmetal gray with a light chop starting to hurl back the highlights of the rising sun.

"Go on, you know you want to," Hellboy told him. "But I'm not giving you mouth-to-mouth if you overdo it."

Abe tossed a look of friendly scorn over his shoulder and then was gone in the snap of a finger. Even if the boat had been anchored in the middle of a glass-calm sea, Hellboy doubted that he would have heard a splash. Abe Sapien usually hit water like a knife.

Hellboy left his deck chair and stepped over to the railing, stood there awhile staring down at the surface of the sea, where Abe kept pace with the prow of the yacht as it sliced westward. Agile as a porpoise, Abe moved through the water with a speed and grace that made even Olympic medalists look like dog-paddlers.

It was moments like this in which he envied Abe a little.

What, seventy-five, eighty percent of the earth's surface was covered in water?

No wonder there were times when Abe seemed to belong in this world a lot more than he did.

Later he dug into one of the deeper pockets of his trench coat—draped now over the back of the deck chair in deference to the warming day—and pulled out the Luger he'd taken off the dead hijacker. He turned it over and over in his hand until he got tired of looking at something that he couldn't interrogate, frighten, or wheedle into giving up any secrets.

He walked it back to the cockpit, where the captain was taking another turn at the wheel. Bastiaan Karabachos was one of those men who looked as though he might as well be welded to the wheel of his ship, his veins running with the blood of mariners who, so he claimed, went all the back way to the time of Homer. Hellboy allowed him his fantasies—it was a good marketing ruse for the more naïve among his legitimate customers. Even so, with his weathered face—the skin roughened by the elements and the corners of his eyes cut deep by squinting into fifteen thousand suns—and his bush of hair that looked windblown even indoors, you could imagine Homer taking a gander at some ancestor of his, nodding, and saying, "Yes, *here* is my Odysseus."

"Hey. Bastiaan," Hellboy said. "Knowing what I do about the rest of your business, you're going to disappoint me if you don't have someone on this boat who knows as much about guns as he does rigging sails."

With a grin, Bastiaan nodded at the Luger in Hellboy's

hand. "What is this, you're traveling lighter these days? For a hand like yours, that thing isn't any more than a derringer." He laughed, then yelled over his shoulder to a younger crewman he called Nikos, who was standing at the stern rewinding a thick coil of rope they'd used to haul Abe back aboard after his morning swim.

"Don't let his face fool you," Bastiaan said. "Nikos has some expertise."

Up close, in the daylight—Hellboy hadn't seen him very clearly when they'd boarded last night—Nikos seemed not much more than a kid, with the large, dark eyes and flawless skin that gave some young Mediterranean men an almost feminine appearance. That he'd buzzed his hair down to stubble seemed like nothing so much as an attempt to look older, tougher.

But damned if he didn't know guns. A boyhood obsession, maybe, fixated on firearms instead of something healthier, like soccer. When Hellboy handed the pistol over for a look, Nikos gazed upon it the way other men might stare at Ming vases, handwritten Mozart manuscripts.

"Something interesting about this?" Hellboy asked.

"A Luger in general, no," he said. "But the age and condition of this one . . . where did you get this?"

"Nazi gun, right?"

Nikos curled one corner of his mouth. "This is possible. But just as possible not. Yes, Lugers were used then, but very early in that war the German military replaced them with Walther P-38s. Lugers were in much more common use in the First World War."

"That early, huh?"

"And this one, she was made even *before* the war. Here,

look, look at this." Nikos tilted the top of the pistol toward him and pointed to the rounded toggle lock near the back, ran his finger along a monogram—*DWM*. Hellboy had noticed it already, just hadn't thought much about it. "As good as a fingerprint. This was a private munitions company that manufactured them before the war, along with the German government. You have a real antique. I never saw one this old, not with my own eyes, only pictures. It's seen *some* use, but the condition . . . beautiful . . . it could have been in a museum most all this time."

"Not likely," Hellboy said. Giving serious thought to what the hijacker of an armored car was doing with a well-preserved firearm that was eighty-five, ninety years old.

"Maybe a time capsule, then, eh?" Nikos said, and over the next half hour offered to buy the thing four or five times before deciding his effort was futile. Unless it had something to do with Hellboy's musing aloud if it would take a good solid backhand to get him to take no for an answer.

Sometimes it could be so hard to tell.

CHAPTER 10

Liz was up at midmorning, emerging from below with both hands wrapped around a gargantuan and copiously steaming mug of coffee. She scuffed over to him, her bare feet making soft slaps across the deck and her reddish-brown hair straight as a stick and blowing loose around her shoulders.

"My god, just look at you," she said. "You've been sitting out here so long you've gotten the worst sunburn I've ever seen."

He pretended to glare but unfortunately had the kind of face that didn't show much distinction between pretend and the real thing. He thought Liz got it this time.

She had him hold her coffee and forbade him to drink it while she retrieved another deck chair from the rack along the front of the cockpit, dragged it over next to him, and settled in.

"Nice cozy little cabins down there and I bet you haven't even seen one yet."

"I don't do cozy," he said.

She tipped her head back for a long, sighing look toward the day's few clouds. "If it wasn't for the constant threat of

129

death, this really would be the life." Now a peek over at him. "Clear skies, I assume?"

"Unless you count the gull that nailed Abe. Heard him say a couple words I didn't even realize he knew."

She laughed. "Sorry I missed that. He's normally so un-flappable." Coffee next, and lots of it. "I'm glad everything's been quiet. Some secret weapon I've been since last night, huh?"

"You gotta sleep sometime. You're only human."

"Rub it in, why don't you."

She sank down deep in the chair and stretched out, legs long inside the gray sweatpants she was wearing, and kicked her feet up onto the railing. He gazed at them for a few moments, and they seemed so small, childlike al-most, and in the moment he found it hard to associate them with a person that harbored the kind of power she did, something so apocalyptically destructive. Although there were many at the BPRD—and for now Liz was one of them—who had come to believe that she was not its cause, but merely its conduit. That the fire was a living el-ement that existed, if not quite a part of her, not apart from her, either.

A fine distinction, maybe, but an important one.

"Tell me something." She glanced around at the yacht. "Am I totally off base in the feeling I've been getting that this, umm, charter operation isn't completely on the level?"

"What gave you that idea?"

"They leer," she said. "I mean *really* leer."

"At you, you mean . . . ?"

"Yes, at me. A couple of them anyway. It doesn't seem like it would be good for business if your boat is crewed by guys who can't keep their eyes in their heads. But there's something greedy about it, too. A hey-wouldn't-*she*-fetch-a-nice-price kind of leer."

He had to take a few moments to think about the right thing to say here. Offer to have a few words with Bastiaan? Not on your life. With Liz, you didn't offer to intercede on her behalf as though she were some helpless little thing in need of rescue. Because she was anything but, and would resent the hell out of him for the rest of the day and probably tomorrow. Couldn't just dismiss it, though, because then she would think he didn't care.

Then he had it.

"It would be almost worth it to see them try you," he said . . . and yes, it was just the right thing. "Anything else, or is that your sole evidence against them?"

"Plus when I was down in the galley getting ready to make coffee, I opened the wrong cabinet door and found a suspiciously large number of Rolexes."

"It really is a charter boat. The last I heard, it goes for $3700 a day during peak season," he said. "But Bastiaan has . . . sidelines, I guess you'd call them."

"I figured as much."

"You don't sound disapproving."

"Well, I really wanted that coffee something fierce." She shrugged it all off. "Underneath the spookshow trappings, what *is* the bureau, anyway, but another intelligence agency? Isn't the first rule of the intelligence business that sometimes you have to deal with some shady people?"

"I think the first rule is don't get caught, but the other probably comes in a close second."

"So how do you know these people, and how is it that

they apparently dropped everything to come to our aid as
fast as they did?"

"Bastiaan, he's the only one I know. I never met the
other guys," Hellboy said. "The boat, the business . . . the
sidelines . . . all these were things that got passed down
from father to son. Along with an obligation."

"So you two go back a long way, then."

"He was just a boy then. Really close to his old man—
Zosimo was *his* name. So the obligation, there was never
any doubt that Bastiaan would honor it. I kept in touch
with him enough over the years that he had to know I'd
hold him to it one day. I knew he was in Naples, so the
time finally came."

"You're worse than the Godfather sometimes, you
know?" she said. "What was the link?"

It all went back to a rogue archaeological dig near the
site of Catal Huyuk, in Turkey, he told her. More than
thirty years ago. Catal Huyuk dated back around 8500
years, making it one of human civilization's oldest known
cities. The BPRD knew of at least three cities that were far
older, although not by the quantifiable means that kept or-
thodox archaeologists happy.

The rogue dig had been financed by an Algerian busi-
nessman, and through means that the BPRD had never
been able to discern—after things went wrong, he'd made
himself as inaccessible as a despot—the man knew approximately *where* to dig, but not exactly what he would find.
And indeed, in less than two weeks the site had yielded one
of those items the earth periodically coughs up—artifacts
that, according to traditional learning, should not be where
they are found, or should not be at all. In this instance, it

was a statue that stood over seven feet tall, carved from a substance that was, while not identical with, every bit as mysterious as Hellboy's hand. It appeared to represent some unknown life-form, rendered in a triumphal pose that was as majestic as it was grotesque, even if it bore no resemblance to any known anatomy.

It had been crated and, in violation of the Turkish laws concerning indigenous antiquities, had been trucked to the coast, where the *Calista* awaited, Zosimo Karabachos having been hired to transport the thing to Algiers. At which point, as far as anyone knew, it would join the private collection of the man who had paid handsomely for its recovery.

Except they'd never made it. Throughout a long night in the deep waters south of Greece, the crate had been opened by hands unknown, and some of the statue's limbs—if they could accurately be called that—had *detached* from the main body to graft themselves onto the bodies of the crew. Zosimo had described seeing one of his men curled against the stern, wracked by violent spasms as parts of his body began to solidify with spreading veins of the same stonelike substance that had comprised the artifact.

Soon after, it had begun to work on reshaping his bones.

The crewman had smiled throughout, though . . . smiled with a beatific radiance and, with the ardor of a prophet, spoke of the frozen perfection of dead worlds. Until his tongue, too, turned to stone in his mouth, and so, wordlessly, he had begun to sing. The sound of it, the ferocious *joy* of it, had driven Zosimo to find first a filleting knife from the galley, and then the softer parts that still remained in his crewman's body.

He had long since locked Bastiaan, then just eleven years old, down below, where he'd been trapped after another of the crewmen grew solidified and malformed over the companionway entrance, like a misshapen latticework of unbreakable stone.

Zosimo had pushed the *Calista* as far as the southern tip of Malta, where he sought refuge in the fishing village of Birzebbuga . . . and was quickly quarantined on the beach by the normally welcoming locals once they'd gotten a look at his cargo and what remained of his crew.

And it was from here that an old colleague from England, on Malta to study the Neolithic temples of nearby Hagar Qim, had called in Professor Trevor Bruttenholm. One of the founders of the BPRD, and the man Hellboy had gladly called Father.

"It was one of the first times I'd seen him work," he told Liz. "I mean *really* work. Not just academics and research. Fieldwork, the dangerous stuff. It'd already been, what, twenty or so years since I'd come into the world and he'd taken me in . . . helped raise me, train me. But this was something new to see. This could've killed him."

There was no single word for what Professor Bruttenholm—tall and slender and in nearly all respects the quintessentially proper Englishman—had performed at the southern tip of Malta. It was a hybridized working of his own devising, equal parts exorcism, banishment ritual, and shamanic journey. It had been a spiritual combat that required days before the statue's spreading contagion had been contained and then reversed, yet even then all but one of the afflicted crewmen had perished.

But Zosimo's son Bastiaan had been spared. A debt that

the elder had vowed would not go unpaid, no matter how long it took.

"The way he was," Hellboy said, "I don't think Professor Bruttenholm ever had any intention of collecting. For him, what he learned from the experience . . . that's what he considered payment."

Two years dead now, he was. A respectful enough time to wait before calling in old markers on the favors the great man was owed.

Two years dead, and still there were days when Hellboy missed him so much he could just about feel the pain of it all the way into his big right hand.

"What happened to the statue?" Liz asked. "Is it down in the basements back in Fairfield with all the other oddities?"

When she was a kid, Liz used to joke that the bureau could hold the scariest yard sale in the world.

"Nah," Hellboy said. "There's nothing left. I don't know why . . . but it rotted. Just like a big frozen beef carcass left out in the sun."

"Yum," she said, and drained the last of her near-bucket of coffee. "Who's ready for breakfast?"

During those times when Liz decided she'd had enough of bureau life and struck out for parts unknown, he didn't know which was worse: his dread that something would happen to her, or maybe *because* of her . . . or the fact that he was once more missing out on times like this. Talking about things that the average person had never seen, never experienced, could never even relate to.

You needed that to keep yourself sane, to remind you that no matter how deep the darkness, you still shared the light with someone. Professor Bruttenholm had always been good for it. Abe too. Nothing against them. But sometimes you didn't need a surrogate father, a surrogate brother. Sometimes you needed a Liz in your life, the surrogate sister in the family you'd gathered about yourself.

No question about it: Whenever she wasn't around, while this world may still have had its wonders, its beauties, they seemed dimmed and diminished.

"With everything that's been going on since you came in last night," he said, "I didn't get much chance to ask how your project's going back in Fairfield."

"My *project?*" Liz gave him one of those looks that she sometimes turned on him whenever she found his choice of words to be less than optimal. "My *project* has a name. Campbell Holt. Remember him? He's the one whose wrists aren't as durable as yours."

"Sorry," he said. "I just forgot his name, that's all."

"He's . . . coming along well. He's getting a handle on it. Controlling it, not letting his quote-unquote gift control him. Slow steps, but he'll get there."

"Sounds like somebody else I used to know."

"Did you know they've offered—more than once—to fit him with a prosthetic for the hand he cut off? He doesn't want it. He says he'd rather look at the stump every day, because he wants a constant reminder, in the starkest possible terms, that he's got to remain in control. I admire that. It'd be like if I wore a glass locket around my neck that was filled with ashes from the neighborhood where I grew up."

She tipped her head back as though it had suddenly doubled in weight.

"I need this, H.B. I need this to work. I know what it's

like to be on his side of the desk . . . or the straitjacket . . . and realize that the person who thinks they're helping you doesn't have a *clue* what it's like to be in your skin. So when I think of the difference in the way Campbell looks now compared to the way he looked a few weeks ago when I first visited him in the hospital . . . I see that change in him and I *know* that it's something I helped to make happen. It's something I helped build instead of burn."

Liz looked across at him, eyes so open it was like he could see all the way to the bottom of a well . . . a Liz filled with renewed purpose. With a familiarity both idle and tender, she slapped her hand atop his right one. Left it there as she turned her gaze once more toward the sea and the sky.

"If I can help him get to the place he needs to be," she said, "everything I've been through . . . maybe it'll seem like it had a purpose after all."

He watched her hand. Tried to feel its touch, so light, deeper than he really could.

CHAPTER 11

The man in the cage hadn't said a word for the first three days, but finally let the wall of silence between them start to fall when Gino Laurenti sat down on freedom's side of the bars and poured them each a glass of wine. He reached between the bars and set the glass onto the rickety wooden table—peace offering, or just something to break three days' monotony of water—and was pleased to see their captive wander over and accept it, and take a long, appraising drink.

"Amarone?" he asked, his first word since they'd taken him at the *osservatorio*.

"From Veneto, yes," Laurenti said.

"Ah . . . they know how to make it there." He nodded, saying no more until he'd made it halfway through his second glass, although it was not the wine speaking. The man drank so slowly it seemed likely he could keep his wits about him indefinitely.

"You *have* lost, I want you to know this," Laurenti told him. "The scroll is out of Rome now. It will be safe for as long as it needs protection. From you. From all of you, the *Opus Angelorum*. From what you would wrongly summon down in the name of God. It is safe."

138

The man in the cage laughed, not a pleasant sound to hear, but neither was it at Laurenti's expense. "I doubt that very much. Once they are out in the world, things like this have a way of attracting attention no matter where they go."

This place where fate had brought them had been a zoo once, a private zoo for the enjoyment of a wealthy merchant some four centuries dead. Today, few knew of it at all. Laurenti stared at the stone floor where something large would have paced long ago—a lion, maybe, or a bear—and felt defiled by what he had to say.

"If you continue to refuse to say anything of those you work with, some of those *I* work with want you tortured. I condemn it, and don't want any part of it . . . but I'm afraid I would be unable to stop it."

For all the concern he showed, the man in the cage may as well have just been told it looked like rain. "Let them."

"They would not always have reacted this way," Laurenti went on. "But the fire has changed everything."

He almost sneered. "Not changed enough, if the scroll is safe."

His name was Verdi, they had learned. Domenico Verdi. He was big enough to have fought when, quickly and quietly, their men took him outside the *osservatorio*, but he had chosen not to resist. He was a tall man with broad shoulders and an even broader belly, and wide hands that would look more natural raising bruises than dispensing Holy Communion. Long-ago bouts of acne had left his meaty face with a pitted look, and his black hair, unwashed for days, bristled into ferocious tufts.

He had no parish. His ministry was with a hospital for

the poor, tending the dying and the insensible, and indeed, it was said they were the only ones who could bear his company.

From a nearby crate, Laurenti fetched a long, loosely woven garment of barbed wire loops fitted with a simple metal latch. A piety belt, some called it. Two nights ago, he had laid the ugly thing out flat on a tabletop and counted the barbs—two hundred and sixty prickly points that would turn inward when the belt was fastened about the belly.

He dangled it before the cage bars. Watched Verdi's eyes follow its sway and thought he saw a flash of yearning.

"I suspect you must be no stranger to pain," Laurenti said.

It appeared that the *Opus Angelorum* had abandoned the *osservatorio* because, after centuries of guarding their secrecy, they somehow knew that those who opposed them were closing in. Yet Verdi had risked everything to come back for this. Had been captured carrying it from their ritual space, a museum full of such ghastly devices.

Now he appeared to force his eyes away from the belt, to deny its allure. "I was a weak man."

"The ones I spoke of, the ones who intend to see you talk . . . I'm afraid their methods will be worse."

"I welcome it," said Verdi. "Let them do all those things I never had the courage to do to myself."

And it was obvious that thoughts of what could happen to him meant nothing to Verdi. Laurenti got up to put some distance between himself and the cage. There was plenty of room to wander in this decrepit hall of bars.

After all this time, did anyone with whom he worked

even remember how this place—the zoo and the estate to which it belonged—had come into their hands? But it had ever been thus in Rome, where power, politics, and papacies mixed so freely. He could not imagine a time in the Church's history when there had not been strange alliances born of shared ambitions, and property bequeathed so that one faction or another could further common goals.

One group seeks to harness the destructive power of angels and is given an observatory. Another finds their aims obscene and is left an old estate near the Tiber. Dramas to be played out long after their original players were dust in the ground. Because here they thought beyond the lifetime of any one man or woman . . . or at least they used to. What was a lifetime when you battled for the sake of eternity?

Laurenti ran his fingertips along the cracked and flaking mural painted on the wall opposite the row of cages. The old Peaceable Kingdom motif—lambs lying down with lions, and antelopes with bears. Osprey and eagle, salmon and dove.

And now that he was talking, Verdi, standing pressed against the bars, seemed intent on pursuing him. "You seem like a caring man," he called out. His voice slapped down the corridor along the stone and plastered walls. "But you do poor service to your Lord and Savior when you work so closely with those who seek to discredit Him."

Laurenti paced back toward him. "I also like to think I can serve truth, wherever it may emerge, and that the two are not enemies," he said. "Is your faith so narrow that the possibility of a little public debate over an ancient letter makes it so easy for you to kill your brothers?"

"Not brothers . . . traitors. Heretics."

"Not the seven who died in the Archives. Their only sin was being in the wrong place at the wrong time."

"Then for them the word is martyrs."

How *did* a man become so twisted? There was a time when Laurenti thought such a thing happened to a man too apart, too alone. Not anymore. Now he knew better. That it happened more easily in groups.

He returned to the front of the cage and poured more wine.

"The *Opus Angelorum* has not always worked with angels, has it?"

Glass in hand, Verdi assumed a haughty demeanor. "In the past, yes, we took the tools of the enemy—of the sorcerer, the witch, the conjurer—and turned them against him. What could be more fitting for such blasphemers?"

"In your lifetime, Domenico, have you done this?"

His thick face turned sad a moment, nostalgic for something he'd never known. He tried to hide it, but too late, had given himself away. "No. I've *seen* things, but . . . no. Our path today has been back to the angels. It was lost for a long, long time. We were intent on finding it again." Now, once more, the pride. "And we did."

"No matter. Could a group such as yours really believe itself uncorrupted by the influence of demons and evil spirits when that was all that would answer? Could your motives still be pure when you found your way back to the angels?"

Verdi insisted they could . . . but his eyes suggested that he knew better.

"You called yourselves 'The Work of Angels,' yet you

trafficked with devils. If not you personally, then your predecessors. Did none of you, in all that time, realize that this is like labeling something 'The Work of Virgins,' then delegating it to whores?"

On the other side of the bars, Verdi drew himself up into a pillar of cold disdain. "We fought the enemies of the Church with the weapons that we had . . . not those we longed for."

"And what was lacking?" Laurenti was aware that he was asking one man to speak for generations. Not fair, but he might never get this chance again. "What kind of strength could you have longed for that faith and scripture did not provide?"

Verdi's face twisted with anguish, then fury, as he gripped the bars. "God!" he shouted. "We wanted God on our side! But where was He? He was . . . silent. If He heard our prayers, then He took no notice of them. Even if He saw us at our best, then it was still not good enough for Him."

Verdi's eyes were hollow with the miseries and doubts they all encountered, but most had learned to overcome: Where was God when the oceans rose and the earth shook? When the evil prospered and the innocent suffered? If He was aware of each sparrow falling from the sky, why did He seem to take no notice when His children died by the thousands, the millions, and in the most terrible ways?

"We wanted God, we *hungered* for God," Verdi murmured. "And in His silence we took what we could get."

"I wish . . ." Laurenti said, and if he denied having thought these very things, he'd be a liar. "I wish as much as you that we lived in an age of miracles. But we don't. If you don't find God in your heart, where else can you expect to find Him?"

"I don't know." Verdi ran a hand up and down the bar, as if seeking a weakness he knew he wouldn't find. "But I know He's there somewhere. If there was only an empty void, it would not feel this cold."

Laurenti reached across to clamp his hand over Verdi's, clenched around the bar. "Do you speak for all of them? All of them today, all of them who came before you, down through the centuries? Or do you speak only for yourself?"

Verdi snorted. "There is no difference anymore."

"You're not bound to their fate . . . even though it clings to you like a wet rag." Laurenti leaned closer, imploring through the bars. "Let me *deliver* you. Let me cast this legacy off you. I've met many souls in the grip of things they thought they could control. Let me pry you out of theirs."

"Beat the devils out of me, would you?" Verdi grinned, square teeth clenched like a little ivory wall. "And until now you sounded like such a man of reason."

Would it do any good to tell Domenico Verdi that he had done such things a dozen times before? In truth, he could not say in any particular case whether what he had faced was a true demon, eons old, or a lost and angry spirit laying siege to the flesh of the weak. He'd seen many strange things, and the more of them he saw, the stranger the whole world and the axis on which it spun seemed to be . . . bearing less and less resemblance to the orderly realm he was taught in catechism.

But I helped them, every one, he thought, as if Verdi could hear him, *from strangers, to one of my own brothers in this struggle against you and what you stand for, and if you would let me, I could help you too . . .*

"I've already found my deliverers," Verdi said, snatching his hand away. "I think maybe you'll meet them soon enough."

And as Laurenti turned to leave Verdi to his solitude and his strangely muttered prayers, he felt as if he were dragging chains, and couldn't decide which weighed upon him more: the successes or the failures.

A minute or two after the priest left, giving no sign of returning any time soon, the man in the cage sank down along the back wall where, in the tiny cracks between stone and mortar, you could still find short coarse hairs where some animal had rubbed itself many ages ago.

An omen—could it be anything else? The past was never truly dead. Only dormant, waiting to be rediscovered.

He knew it well, this wall. Had searched its every inch looking for the best patch of stone for his needs: abrasive, neither too coarse nor too smooth.

On the afternoon they'd caught him, he had a thumbnail that had gone too many days without being trimmed . . . and now he understood there was a plan in even this.

With short, quick strokes, he filed the overlong nail against the wall, as though honing the edge of a blade.

CHAPTER 12

It had been a grand day for sailing and he'd seen it all, from sunup to sundown, only rarely leaving his post at the front of the *Calista*. Late in the morning they had cleared the passage between Corsica and Sardinia, and in the early afternoon, having reached the deep waters beyond the almost-kissing pair of islands, had turned toward the southwest.

Travel was not fast this way—they never broke thirty knots—but it was steady and calm, better than risking a plunge from the sky, and the farther behind they left Rome and its intrigues, the safer the journey felt. Yet the calm was not lulling. He didn't find it a struggle to remain watchful and alert, felt no complacency in the constant presence of the sun and wind and waves. To the contrary, he found them fortifying after so much time spent breathing the musty air of the danker places of the earth, and under it.

They lost the wind late in the afternoon, so the crew fired up the craft's twin diesel engines. Not as quiet, but just as steady.

Near twilight, Bastiaan came onto the foredeck and stood with him, and they gazed starboard in the direction of lands they could not yet see, smoldering under the last of an orange sunset smeared like marmalade across the blue-black horizon.

"Hey, you stay here much longer," Bastiaan told him, "we might as well tie you onto the front of my ship as a figurehead."

"Probably kill off your business, wouldn't it? Scare the tourists?"

"Or maybe attract a whole new class. Everybody else, look how fast they get out of our way."

And it was happening again: Bastiaan seeming not to want to talk with him so much as simply stand nearby and *stare* at him, without being obvious about it. It wasn't so much his otherness, Hellboy decided, as it was the fact that, after thirty years gone by, one of them had so obviously changed and the other so obviously hadn't.

He knew they were one and the same—this agreeably weathered man and the boy who'd been pulled back into the sunlight after days trapped belowdecks, frightened but with body and soul intact—yet Hellboy still found it hard to connect them. For most of these years, Bastiaan Karabachos had only been a voice on the phone, a quick note, a postcard, or, more recently, an e-mail . . . but foremost, a contact to be maintained because the marker would one day be called due. Finishing old business their fathers had begun. Bastiaan did not appear to resent it in the least.

And so Hellboy had to wonder what it was, exactly, that Bastiaan saw whenever the man looked at him with such quiet scrutiny. A link to the past that proved he had not dreamed his childhood ordeal? Maybe. A reminder of the way, in this world, Hell could seem so much closer than Heaven? Yeah, probably hard to get around that one.

Or maybe what Bastiaan saw was a force of nature, *super*nature, untouched by the decades, seemingly as impervious to age as a face carved into a mountainside. A face outside of time that couldn't help but shove a man up against the fact of his own mortality.

Except that one cut both ways, didn't it?

Hellboy had every reason to believe that he would outlive everyone on this boat, with the possible exception of Abe. They knew of no precedent for him, much less when his days might come to an end. But for everyone else here, Hellboy knew he would walk the earth **under which they** slept, or with the winds that bore their **ashes.**

He had already come to accept that; had, with Professor Bruttenholm's death, outlived everyone who had taken him in and made him a part of this world instead of its enemy. General Ricker and the others at that Air Force base in New Mexico where he had passed his accelerated version of childhood . . . gone, all gone now.

"Got any kids?" Hellboy asked Bastiaan, suddenly thinking it wrong that he didn't know.

Bastiaan nodded, but didn't dive for photographs the way most men would. Not that Hellboy would've minded.

"Twin boys," he said. "Still too young yet for this life."

"Maybe I'll meet them someday."

"You may. Yes." Bastiaan's hands curled and flexed around the railing. "But you won't take offense if I say that I hope not."

"No. No offense."

It was times like this when he wondered how many more generations might come and go before he would want no more friends at all.

He suspected he already knew whose death would seal off the world for good.

When later that night they hit a patch of fog, Bastiaan throttled back the engines and eased them down to a slow chug. The bow lights cut through the mists, wafting past in silken clouds that clung to the skin like dew and brought with them the enclosing sense that the sea had become infinitely smaller.

Instinctively, as he had done countless times since boarding last night, Hellboy turned his eyes skyward, wondering if seraphim might use fog as a cover, even *control* it . . . or if in their obedience and devotion it didn't matter whether they came openly or in stealth. The view above was unobstructed again, clear in all directions, the crew having furled the sails after the wind had died in the late afternoon. He had no blind sides they could exploit in the dark.

And looking up into the mists, he saw it.

At first he didn't even realize what he was looking at. Nothing that caught his eye because it was moving. Instead, it slowly took shape before his eyes, like an optical puzzle that has to be stared at awhile before it divulges the image hidden inside.

He could see it in the diffused light from the cockpit and cabin windows that waned overhead along the masts. Motionless, it crouched in the angle where the gaff joined to the mainmast. Translucent, it seemed not to stand out against the mist so much as to be made of it. No . . . no, that wasn't it. Not made of mist, but displacing it somehow, or repelling it, a subtle void in the shape of a crouching man, holding casually to the mainmast with one arm and staring downward, watching, just . . . watching. Under almost any other conditions, he might not have seen it at all.

And maybe hadn't, the entire time they'd been at sea.

"Abe!" he called. "Get up here!"

A moment later, Abe left his post along the stern, scrambling onto the cockpit roof and springing off toward the foredeck to land beside him with a thump. He gave Hellboy a quizzical look, seemed to be expecting something more obvious.

Hellboy pointed upward. "You see that too, don't you?"

There was, however remote—even if he didn't want to admit to it—the possibility that he'd been staring at the sky long enough to start inventing shapes out of nothing, seeing things that weren't there. The sea could do that to men, and while he liked to think of himself as immune to such frailties . . . well, a second opinion never hurt.

To his relief, Abe nodded. "Plenty of ghosts at sea. It's as haunted a place as any battlefield."

"Yeah, but what's *that* one doing there?" Hellboy asked. "Does it belong to the *Calista*? This boat's got a history."

Abe stood absolutely still for several moments, peering into the billows of fog that thickened and thinned around them.

"I don't . . ."

—lifting a finger to trace something in the air that Hellboy couldn't see—

". . . think so."

—Abe's finger following a broad path of loops and curves, starting high and dropping lower, lower—

"Uh oh," he murmured.

Maybe it was force of suggestion, or maybe Hellboy's

eyes were growing accustomed to the murk and he could make out the finer distinctions of which Abe was capable—an advantage in the part of his life spent underwater. Either way, with Abe's help he was now seeing it too: a line, a filament that seemed to be anchored in the chest of the specter looming above them, descending like an unspooled cable—

"Where did you pick *this* up, I wonder?" said Abe.

—to finally connect with some unseen point behind him.

Abe was pointing at his back.

"That thing's grafted *onto* me?" Hellboy said. "I didn't even feel a tickle."

You might try to grab the ethereal tether, but could never succeed. It was not there in any physical sense. Yet it was no less real for that. As real as the wind, and as hard to hold.

"I've been dragging that thing behind me ever since somewhere in Rome?"

"Probably." Abe looked almost apologetic. "But none of us realized until now."

"I know one thing," Hellboy said. "It didn't stick there by itself. Somebody had to *put* it on me."

The phantom stood up. It knew. It recognized their awareness. Still little more than a hole in the underlit mists, defined more by what it wasn't than what it was, supported by the gaff even though it surely didn't need to be; but then, that was the thing about spirits. So often they clung to their old familiar relationship with the world, continuing to relate to it by what was solid and what was not. Old habits, old memories, old fears of falling.

By now it had the attention of the two crewmen on

deck, and he heard one of them scrambling about down below, yelling for Bastiaan.

"What's it doing?" Nikos called from the cockpit as he stared upward.

Good question. Except an even better one—one that settled everything as far as Hellboy was concerned—was what *could* it do? About the only potency belonging to a specter like this was its presence, not its power. It was sentient, maybe a little stubborn, and not much more. A glimpse of it might give a passing fright to the uninitiated—Nikos clearly fell into that group—but as for the passengers on this boat . . . well, the pitiful thing was going to have to do a lot more than this before it put any kind of scare into them.

Still standing, it let itself tip forward and fall, looking like nothing so much as the echo of someone committing suicide. Drawn perhaps more by the memory of gravity than the pull itself, it plunged to the deck, striking silently in front of them, splattering apart in wispy bursts and tendrils of displaced fog, and then there was nothing. Not even the spectral umbilical between them anymore.

"Looks like we scared it more than it scared us," Hellboy said. "I wish it went that way more often."

"Unless . . ." said Abe, and wasn't it just the most irritating thing the way he looked anything but relieved.

"Yeah?" Hellboy gave him an impatient frown. "Unless what?"

"Unless it just now finished what it was meant to accomplish all along."

"Such as? Cut the boredom level for a couple of minutes there, but—"

It came from somewhere out in the fog, far ahead of them and to the right: the sound that might have been made if a sunken ship had filled with air and surged to the surface, then crashed back to the water in a drenching concussion of impact and spray.

"Aw, crap," Hellboy said. "Why do you always have to be right?"

A few moments later the wave hit them front and starboard, nowhere near enough to swamp the *Calista*, but easily strong enough to lift her several feet and throw them off balance, soaked by a ragged splash of brine.

"I think it was a marker," Abe said of the specter, "a beacon . . ."

"A tracking device, you mean," Hellboy said. "And we've just been found."

As the *Calista* continued to bob in the last of the wave, they could hear a distant watery blast of breath, like a whale's gust of air expelled through a blowhole as big around as a truck tire. And then a rumbling of such depth and force that it was below the audible threshold, something they heard less than felt, the sonic equivalent of an iceberg, ninety percent of it lurking beneath the surface.

Bastiaan was on deck by now, one hand gripping the wheel and the other holding fast to the cockpit rail as he craned forward to catch a glimpse of something, anything, in the lights shining from the bow. But for now, it was only more of the same gray fog and the dark, undulating murk of the sea.

"Is that a whale out there?" Bastiaan shouted.

"I wish it were," Abe murmured.

From out in the dark came another heaving splash, and

the next huff of bellows breath sounded from the port side. Once more, half a minute later, and it came from far beyond the stern.

"It's circling us!" Bastiaan warned. A moment later he thought to hit the all-round lights installed on the top of each mast; suddenly the *Calista* was sitting in the middle of an encircling pool of white light. And beyond . . . still nothing to see but an unbroken horizon of water.

Abe turned back toward Bastiaan, and this time meant to be heard. "If you have life rafts, I suggest you deploy them now."

Hellboy gripped the rail and scowled at the sea. Above, always above, his head in the clouds . . . he'd been so concerned about an attack from above that he hadn't once considered an attack from below. Angels soared; they did not swim. But again, the same as the hijacking of the armored car . . . whatever this was, it didn't feel like the work of men who summoned angels. This was of the earth and water, not air and fire.

Bastiaan had yet to shut down the engines entirely and the *Calista* was still creeping forward. The leading edge of the lights fell upon a disturbance in the surface of the sea . . . the violent swirl of a vortex just now beginning to die and fill in again. He had seen such a thing only once in his life, many years ago, standing on the bridge of a battleship and watching the wake of a diving submarine.

He looked at Abe, then tipped his chin at the waters. That other world out there, that dimension beneath waves and tides and whirlpools.

"That's more your zone than mine," he said.

From the corner of his eye he saw Liz hurrying to the

foredeck after emerging from below, hugging close to the side of the wheelhouse, and for a moment he held his breath, because what if she slipped, what if she slid into the water with whatever was out there . . .

But she kept her footing, and drew up close enough to grip the edge of his hand. Except he had his doubts that stone was the best thing to hold onto in the middle of a treacherous sea.

Back to Abe: "So do you know what it is?"

Abe looked hesitant to commit to an answer. "I can guess," he said . . . then did.

At almost any other time, Hellboy might have even felt privileged. He had hunted things of monstrous births and evil intentions, had stood between reality and the things that hungered to rip holes in its fabric. He had battled folklore's worst abominations, killed offspring spawned by human madness. After nearly half a century of this, it had become almost routine.

But if Abe was right, this . . . out there . . . was like the coming of royalty.

The Leviathan.

In all his days and travels he'd known of no one who could say for sure that it was anything more than a myth. Ancient stories, legends woven together from threads of truth and yards of imagination. Even the freshest of them was over a thousand years old. Meaning if this truly was what was circling them, it had slumbered for the last millennium, and then some.

Yet that wasn't what worried him. Worse to contemplate was that it had been roused by someone, or some*thing*, capable of reaching it in its state of dreaming death. To do that took some serious mojo, and was likely beyond the capabilities of any mortal necromancer that he was aware of.

This, he feared, was not the work of men, but of gods. Or devils. There were times when he had to confess that it was difficult to tell the difference.

Somewhere just beyond the reach of light, it emitted a bleating groan that dissolved into liquid thunder that rumbled up through the yacht's hull.

One of the crew hurried forward with three puffy orange life vests. Liz tied hers on without hesitation. Abe simply stared at the one offered to him without reaching for it; he rippled his gills, a little indignantly to Hellboy's eyes, until the guy got the message. Liz snatched it and shoved it toward Hellboy with a stern look.

"Come on, H.B.," she said. "How easy do you think it's going to be to tread water with your hand chained to that case?"

"Hey, I'm not proud," he said. "I just can't fit into that thing."

"Then improvise," she snapped, and grabbed the third vest and lashed one around each of his upper arms.

Okay, now the pride was starting to kick in. He feared he looked like a big ugly kid with inflatable water wings, ready for his first trip into the grownup pool.

As she looked past his shoulder, Liz's eyes widened and her lips parted with something she had no words for. He knew from all the years between them that she was not easily impressed. Yet now, in the span of a heartbeat, he could see that she was awed.

He turned.

It was forty yards off the port bow, and its movement

seemed familiar enough, like the graceful curving length of a whale beginning a slow dive, never seen whole, but as an evolving mound. Any resemblance ended there. It was finally in the pool of light, giving a brief glimpse of its upper back, looking like the overturned hull of something ancient and armored, dark as slate and bristling with scales the size of dinner plates. It went on and on, a rising hump that began to look less like a beast than a land mass, the profile of its back now and again showing a low, spiny fin. Just as he was beginning to think there was no end to the thing, an ouroboros spinning in place, its vast fluked tail breached the surface of the sea like twin scythes and followed it downward, and the Leviathan was gone, another vortex in its wake.

Near the port stern, one of the crew was clutching the rail. He laughed, a sound terrible in its exultation. Yet Hellboy understood. There must have been a time when men had worshipped this thing, a place where it too had been a god. Let it rise from the depths, and so would the veneration.

Moments later the *Calista* was jolted from below, her hull shuddering, then continuing to groan as the Leviathan rasped along it like a file, tipping the vessel sharply to starboard. She had just enough time to settle before it came again, harder this time, and now the collision threw everyone off their feet and to the deck. They grappled for handholds, or crawled away from the railings and toward the center . . .

Except for the crewman Hellboy had seen laughing, who hurled himself over the side.

The *Calista* gave a forward surge as Bastiaan revved the

engines, but it was a doomed effort, an eruption of foamy water cascading over the transom as the yacht was just as suddenly shoved backward into her own wake, and this time Hellboy heard the hull rupture. It was a vintage vessel, after all, her hull crafted from wood instead of fiberglass, and it gave with the splintering sound of a falling tree.

Above it all, he could hear Bastiaan's howl of grief.

Hellboy reversed direction, scrambling for the rail instead of away from it. He held on with his right hand and drew his revolver with the left, popping off three shots down into the side of the thing when a length of it flashed along just under the surface. Then he reined back his impulse to empty the gun, reload, and keep firing. To do any good, with something of this size, he would need to pick his targets more carefully.

Don't fire until you see the black of its eyes.

Maybe use those stun grenades from the armored car, too, if he could retrieve them from the locker in the cockpit where he'd stowed them. He saw Nikos over Bastiaan's shoulder, called for him to bring the flash-bangs.

He held on as the *Calista* began to tip and spin, sparing a frantic look to check on Liz and Abe. They were working their way toward the rear deck, where someone had just pulled the ripcord on a self-inflating raft.

Hellboy glared down into the water again and saw a slow-motion pass of scales just before the ship reared upward with such force it nearly threw him across the deck. It wasn't just scales this time, though. There was the angular suggestion of a head, or the plating of a hinged jaw, so he held on, aiming, waiting for something soft to shoot at. But all that appeared was the body of the crewman who'd plunged in, now impaled through the midsection on some spiny projection that looked like a spike of living obsidian.

Then he sank from view, still pinned to the thing, his limp arm seeming to wave Hellboy onward, downward, to join him.

Even when she wasn't being rammed, the *Calista* was no longer sitting level, her deck tilting toward the front as water poured in through her imploded bow. Bastiaan had called for one of the crew to start the bilge pump, but he was merely commanding out of instinct. This ship was going down, and no pump or bucket brigade was going to stop it.

Maybe the rest of them had no choice but to hold on waiting to sink . . . but Hellboy knew there had to be more *he* could do, at least.

With the sound of splitting timbers, the front end heaved skyward. As the *Calista* tipped up like a toy he saw an ocean of stars, then he rode the deck as it slapped back into the sea and seemed to keep going down, down, down. Arms and legs flailing, Nikos came hurtling over the cockpit and fell past him into the foam, all three grenades skittering across the teakwood after him.

Even the foredeck was coming apart now, boards popping loose underfoot and peeling away from one another. He holstered the revolver and grabbed for one of the loosened boards instead, wrenching it free from the deck and coming away with a long, sharp-tipped plank, an eight-foot shard that he took to the very front of the bow. Water churned white up to his knees as he gripped the makeshift spear with both hands, the titanium case banging loose against his elbow, and jabbed it into the mass of scales before him. The tip scraped across them like a stick on stone, so he shifted his stance and attacked again, trying to work the point between the scales, under them, anywhere—this creature had to have a softer hide somewhere and by god he was going to find it, then shove it full of splinters the size of saplings.

He found a brief moment to fear for everyone but himself, and another to regret the loss of this ship that hadn't just been Bastiaan's home for so much of his life, but his life itself, and the greatest link to his father. Rogues they may have been, but certainly not without honor.

Then the fury overtook him again, and the water was up to his waist. Bastiaan stumbled forward to seize his own shard of teak and join the fight, however futile, driving it at the Leviathan and bellowing vengeance as the *Calista* groaned in death from the deepest fibers of her wood.

As the water rose and the mainmast began to topple like a log, they struggled back toward the aft deck, clambering along the rail and any other handhold they could find. Although Bastiaan had given up the fight, his hands bleeding and raw from the fractured wood, Hellboy had not, and continued to jab his pike overboard, the beast alongside them now—he *had* to hit its eyes soon, *had* to find some vulnerability.

But as the ship was lost, so was his base from which to fight.

As if suffering one final spasm, the *Calista* rolled to her starboard side and hurled them into the sea, then she gave up her ghost with a surge of air trapped belowdecks. The surface of the water seemed to boil, littered under the moonlight with flotsam large and small.

Hellboy bobbed in the turbulence, kept afloat by the vests cinched around his arms, but he still retched—must have swallowed a pint of seawater and foam. Once he'd finished sputtering he glanced around, nearly at eye level with the rise and fall of the sea. So quiet now, so eerily quiet after so much uproar, worse somehow than the screaming of survivors.

"Liz!" he shouted.

"Over here!" he heard her call from behind him.

He kicked to spin around and followed the sound of her voice; saw a small, dark shape waving one arm maybe sixty feet away—Liz, hunched in the life raft. Another silhouette beside her. Abe, was it? Or one of the crew? He couldn't tell, not at this distance, in this light.

His first impulse was to start swimming for the raft. Case or no case latched to his wrist, when he held his right hand flat it was better than a canoe paddle. He'd be there in less than a minute—

But stopped after a few strokes. He had no reason to believe that the Leviathan had sunk the *Calista* for any reason other than himself, and what he carried. He could not endanger the raft so long as they shared the sea with the thing that had dumped them into it.

He still had hold of the teakwood shard, gripped it hard as he looked around for a thrashing tail, a breaching fin . . .

Nothing. For the moment, it was staying down.

Someone else was moving close by, though—Bastiaan, from the sound of the waterlogged cough. Clinging to the cushion of a deck chair, Bastiaan kicked up beside him, sodden hair hanging into his eyes.

"You see the raft over there?" Hellboy asked.

"Yes," he said.

"Can you make it?"

"I think so, yes. But I think . . . it should matter to me more than it does."

"It matters to *me*," Hellboy said. "I got a friend over there, and I want to make sure she gets back to land."

"All right. All right," Bastiaan sputtered. "What about you?"

"I'm gonna stay here a little longer, see what happens." He reached out and put his hand on Bastiaan's shoulder. "Would it do any good to tell you I'm sorry?"

Bastiaan had nothing to say to that, for good or for ill. As he clung to debris and treaded water, his heart and soul seemed to be somewhere else.

"It was all borrowed time, wasn't it?" he finally asked, no longer the captain of his ship, but once again his father's son. Thirty years younger on the southern shores of Malta.

"If you enjoyed it, what's it matter if it was borrowed?" Hellboy dropped his hand to the cushion and gave a shove toward the raft. "I think you better get away from me right now."

Hellboy waited, aware of every sloshing wave and bubble of air bursting up from the sinking wreck . . . but when *it* came, there was no mistaking it, so enormous it might send sharks fleeing like minnows. Off to his left it rose from the sea, gently this time, taking shape and form like a living island, and finally, he thought he saw the glint of its eye.

And behind that eye would be its brain.

He held his spear and shouted for it to come.

Again it dove, tidal waves churning in its wake, and moments later he was aware of something rushing beneath him with the mass of a train and the cold vicious arc of a reaper's scythe.

He'd been hit before, hundreds of times. Maybe thousands. Hit by things whose blows could demolish walls. But never quite like this. He imagined this was what it must be like for someone caught by a cyclone, that final instant of agony and awareness when struck full-on by the house that the winds have thrown.

And yet he lived.

It catapulted him from the water, and he saw stars and the moon, and the water again, and when he slapped against it its surface felt as hard as steel, and he lay floating for a moment, but only just, and then the great toothed mouth closed over him, gulping him down with the tide.

CHAPTER 13

It had been years since she'd been in a morgue, and if it was years before she set foot in another, that would suit her fine. Kate Corrigan was no stranger to death—a part of her had always longed to know the secrets people took with them to their graves—but death knew many forms, many faces.

She had been one of those peculiar children who didn't fear graveyards. Instead, they were the most peaceful places she knew. She would read the names of the dead, the too-brief engravings that memorialized their lives or crystallized the anguish over their loss; she would do the math to work out how long they'd lived, and how long ago; she would sit for hours and stare at their stones. *I'll be here too one day,* she would tell herself, but the thought held no terrors for her, only the possibility of getting answers to so many questions. At the time, she'd believed she might get to meet them all, down to the last infant. From the clues and tidbits of their inscriptions, they had seemed so much more interesting than the living.

Even as a girl she'd been fascinated by history . . . and who made history if not the dead?

As she had grown older, and her life and career had

taken their odd turns, she sometimes thought of herself—in jest usually, but not always—as a haunter of the dead. Ruined buildings, lifeless villages, forgotten customs, and, yes, the dearly and not-so-dearly departed . . . although she now understood that death and tranquility did not always go hand-in-hand. She'd explored too many places where too many terrible things had happened to believe in a truly peaceful death anywhere outside of a feather bed. But she still envied them their secrets, and probably always would. Every grave held a piece of history, a bookful of stories that deserved to be heard.

She just wasn't used to seeing the dead quite so . . . fresh.

And as she looked—not *too* closely—at the volcanic crater of meat and bone that had been the face of a stranger, Kate couldn't help but think he'd damn well better have secrets worth knowing.

He and four others, all of them lined up on rickety gurneys in a chilly room whose air hung heavy with preservatives and disinfectants—this was all that remained of the men who'd been involved in the other night's episode with the armored car. From the alleyway, as well as from the car itself. Victims, perpetrators, or something in between—they were all in the same position now, weren't they? Horizontal, and draped in dingy sheets.

Nice to have connections, at any rate. It had taken a couple of days to arrange for approval, but if she hadn't been working with people who could pull a few strings, this little trip might never have taken place at all. Now, if they could just get a fix on how all this carnage had happened.

"Are you not feeling well?"

The priest's voice slapped off tiles, metal doors and drawers, sounding even more like an accusation than it was already.

She turned back to Father Laurenti, her impromptu partner in this foray into . . . what would you call it, really? Spiritual forensics? That was as fitting as anything. She'd have to remember that one.

"Why do you ask?" she said.

"Because I have seen bad cheese that had a more healthy color than you have now."

"Careful, Gino," she told him. "Even if your side does get its way . . . ? If you don't learn to talk to women any smoother than that, you're going to be one of the guys who stays celibate."

Not that she could see him caring. It just felt good to say.

Over the years Kate had met priests who, though they'd been gentlemen who hadn't uttered one risqué word or given any indication of having broken their vows, had nonetheless come across as intensely sexual beings. They touched things—food and books, rosaries and piano keys— as if they wanted to consume them, be consumed by them. Their eyes shone with a healthy hunger for experience, even when they knew they couldn't have it.

Father Laurenti was not one of them.

Just before coming here, she had met him at a nearby café, where he'd been content with water. And on the short walk together, they had passed no less than half a dozen women so gorgeous they left Kate feeling frumpy even in the new thigh-length Piero Tucci leather jacket she'd bought while here. Had Laurenti noticed? Not a one of them, she was sure of it. He seemed to have little use for women, although it was not misogyny. He seemed to have little use for most men, either, and few creature comforts, for that matter. His insistence that she call him Gino appeared less an attempt toward familiarity than a simple distaste for standing on irrelevant ceremony.

But put him in a roomful of corpses where violent death was the rule, and just watch him come alive. He hunkered down with each of them, getting so up close and personal you might think he believed a few lives could still be saved. She suspected it wasn't the first time, either. After the morgue's pair of attendants had lined up the last of the five gurneys, they had slipped quietly away, as if they'd been through the same routine with Laurenti before.

"This one," he said, standing over a thickset man whose heavy dark stubble made his blood-drained face look that much more pallid. "How did he die?"

"It's kind of obvious, isn't it?"

Seriously. He was talking about a man with five or six entry wounds in his torso.

"Please," he said. "What is obvious does not always explain all there is to know."

He had a point. Kate double-checked the name on the toe tag and consulted her notes.

"This was the driver," she said. "Hellboy insists that his cooperation during the takeover was due to coercion. That he feared for his life, or maybe there had been some threats earlier—that's impossible to know. As for his death, there was a moment in the struggle when there were some ricochets inside the cab. Hellboy didn't witness it, but thinks that's when he was hit."

Laurenti moved to the next in the lineup, the guard who'd been the first to die. "And this one?"

"What you see is what you get. Shot through the eye, stripped of his uniform, and covered up with his topcoat against the alley wall," she said. "According to the ballistics report, the bullet exited the back of his head and was further damaged by the same wall, but they think it was a nine-millimeter Parabellum. Hellboy recovered an antique Luger from this one"—she pointed to the gurney bearing the unidentified corpse whose face had turned into an exit wound—"and that's the type of bullet it fires. We don't have any way of verifying it right now, but it seems a reasonable conclusion that he was the one who shot the guard."

"And stole his clothes to take his place."

She wished that Hellboy had left the Luger behind to at least resolve this much of the puzzle, but he could be like that sometimes, wanting to remain in control of things even when control might be better shared. But enough misgivings for now. It felt uncomfortably close to criticizing the dead.

Stop that, she ordered herself. *He is* not *dead.*

But it didn't look good. She'd gotten word late this morning. Liz and two surviving crewmen from the wreck of the *Calista* had, after floating in a raft for close to thirty hours, been picked up by another pleasure craft and taken to the nearest port: the city of Palma, on Majorca.

It was beyond doubt that Hellboy had been swallowed by some deep-sea beast far larger than even a blue whale. All three survivors had seen it happen. Although Hellboy had gone up against things that dwarfed him before, and prevailed, hope was a little harder to cling to this time—Abe was not among the witnesses. He'd neither made it to the life raft, nor been found among the wreckage. Of course, Abe had no need of the life raft, but his failure to resurface after going into the water . . . not good.

If any two friends of hers were to go missing in the middle of the sea, she would have to say that Hellboy and Abe Sapien were the ones best equipped to survive it. But that didn't make their sudden absence any easier to bear. She could hear it in Liz's wrung-out voice as she'd relayed the news—the losing struggle against grief, the guilt that could so easily take hold of a survivor's heart.

He's not dead. They're *not dead,* Kate told herself again. *It's just like Gino said. There's what's obvious, and then there's the rest of the story. So do your job . . .*

Right. The morgue. Body by body, down to the last two . . .

The other nameless mystery man, found in the alley with the guard who'd been shot through the eye, had died without a mark on him. Although if you ignored their wounds and considered their overall physical condition, he looked by far the worst of the lot. He appeared to be American or Western European, and she guessed him to be a young man, perhaps a few years past college age, despite the fact that his fair hair was so lank and stringy his scalp was visible, and he'd evidently been eating so poorly that his muscle tone had wasted to the point that his skin had begun to tighten over his bones.

Heart failure? Malnutrition could cause that. They should know soon. He was due for an autopsy later today.

Laurenti seemed to find him of particular interest. After

two or three minutes of visual inspection, he snapped on a pair of latex gloves and pried open the corpse's jaw, peeled back the upper and lower lips. Probed around the leathery flap of tongue, then pushed the mouth shut again without a word of explanation.

Then he moved on to the last of the five.

"His name was Tokunbo Ogundana," she said. "He was a Nigerian immigrant, although that was over fifteen years ago, when he was a student. According to his employers, his work record was exemplary. Which, on the surface at least, makes his betrayal of his co-workers and attempt to kill my team members even more puzzling."

Except for the man missing his face—a single devastating wound—Ogundana had been the most grievously injured, having caught several ricochets too, then being done in when his damaged weapon had exploded in his hands.

She went on, assuming that Laurenti was still listening, just doing a spectacular job of pretending to ignore her. "Hellboy's assessment was that Ogundana wasn't in complete control of his actions. That he was being controlled by someone else."

Laurenti nodded, otherwise engrossed in the man's corpse, the dark brown skin now a mottled gray peppered with ugly wounds.

"Or some*thing* else," Laurenti said, then scowled at the body. "This would be not so difficult if he were not so much of a mess."

"I'm sure he'd apologize if he could."

One corner of Laurenti's mouth ticked. What do you know, looked like he was finally warming up to her. Then he got busy again probing a particularly nasty wound, as ragged as it was deep, that had mangled Ogundana's left shoulder.

"Gino, I have a question that may sound a little naïve. Or maybe a little insulting, so please don't take it the wrong way," she said. "But . . . what *are* you?"

Hunched over the gurney, he appeared to give the question some thought before answering. Coming up with a lie? If that were what he was doing, she wouldn't expect him to be quite so obvious about it.

She'd been wondering about him all along. The other morning, during the hastily convened meeting in the room beneath the museum complex, Father Laurenti had appeared to be the sore thumb of the group, the one who stood out among his fellow priests as . . . well, as a biker might stand out against businessmen.

"I am—" He seemed to be clawing for the right word, something he probably knew perfectly well in Italian but not in English. "—an embarrassment."

"A newer suit of clothes, a barber who can see out of both eyes, I'm sure you'd clean up nicely."

Of course she hadn't really thought that was what he meant. And, personally, she'd found his disheveled motif rather charming. The old, worn clothes, the unruly hair . . . he'd reminded her of Albert Einstein, of all people, letting the outer man go while his mind was occupied with higher things.

But it took her a few moments to catch onto what he was *really* telling her about himself, and then she had it: *My god . . . he's one of us. In his own way, he's one of us.* She remembered something she'd said to Hellboy about the Church the other day, shortly after he and Abe had linked up with her at the Archives: *For all their legacy of mysticism, they don't seem particularly experienced with it, overall . . . not anymore. You can barely get them to admit they still have exorcists.*

"You're . . . an exorcist?" she asked. Somehow it suited him . . . near-pariah status as a throwback to an earlier age; maybe a living reminder of the sins the Church had committed once upon a more superstitious time.

"If I need to be, I am." He swept his arm along the row of corpses with a dismayed and resigned expression that this was how things always had been, were now, and always would be. "I look at things like this, and yes, most of the time they are the work of men. But they sometimes are crimes *against* men, *all* men, and women, and against God too. If this is what they are, I sometimes can see things most priests cannot. Or will not. But most of the time," he said, "I would prefer to read."

"Wouldn't we all." Kate pointed at Ogundana's corpse. "What are you reading into all this?"

"The Nigerian . . . he was bitten by this one." Laurenti thumped his hand on the gurney with the emaciated westerner. "The bite is hard to see now because a later wound made it worse. But if they measure that man's teeth, I believe they will find it matches a tear in this man's shoulder."

"Okay. He bit him," Kate said. Not terribly impressive in a situation where they were shooting each other. "So?"

"It was not an ordinary bite. This one . . ." Back to the malnourished young man. "He is what some call a *portatore.* Like someone with a disease, who walks around the streets, what would you call him . . . ?"

"A carrier?"

"Yes. Carrier. But no disease. What he carries is a devil, a spirit not his own . . ."

And she was going to *have* to get this man to sit down with her and her tape recorder, and go over everything one more time. Because while it dovetailed nicely with incidents and attacks she was familiar with from at least a dozen folkloric traditions, it was also unique unto itself. She smelled a new book here—a revisionist examination of spirit possession in relation to creatures of folklore—and her heart began to race in agreement.

For the time being, at least, it was almost enough to make her put aside her worst fears for Hellboy and Abe.

The *portatore,* Laurenti told her, had been host to the entity inside for quite a long time, judging by his appearance. Years, perhaps. Although not as long as the one now missing his face; judging by the condition of his remains, and the glimpse that Hellboy had gotten in the mirror, that one had likely been enslaved even longer.

Laurenti compared the experience to living with a tapeworm: The host may eat, but so too is he eaten. Not *quite* the same way a tapeworm behaved, Kate noted, but she found the analogy valid. Laurenti claimed to have twice before seen men in the advanced stages of this sort of possession, in even worse condition yet still alive, the flesh tightened over their bones as though it had been slowly sucked out of them.

"But they're still mobile?" she asked. "Even then?"

"If it pleases the parasite, yes."

And like any parasite, it regarded the body it was in as existing only to serve its own needs: discord and terror, strife and death . . . and in some instances, more specific objectives.

Demon, spirit, parasite—Laurenti did not seem comfortable with any one term. But whatever it was, it would eventually drain the host body of so much vitality and physical mass that a new body was needed if it wished to continue existence on the earthly plane. It was extremely rare, though, that disembodied entities were able to force their way into innocent victims. One's flesh and soul provided a natural barrier that was very hard to breach. Such spirits required a willing host, an invitation from one who wished to serve as a vessel.

But they could, on occasion, transfer into an unwilling body during a physical assault by the original *portatore*.

"Through a bite, you mean," Kate said.

Laurenti nodded. "The teeth pierce both bodies . . . the physical and the etheric. For a few moments, in the confusion of the attack, a path inside opens."

It was, in his opinion, the reality behind such supposed creatures as werewolves, notorious for creating more of their kind by biting the innocent. But men did not truly become wolves, or some hybrid race between species. Rather, they might be reshaped into similar forms by malevolent devils that found those forms pleasing or useful.

She wanted to throw her arms around Laurenti and kiss his rough cheek. This may not have been the definitive word on the subject, yet for Kate, it still resolved so many contradictions she had encountered in both folklore and direct experience: Two-legged man-wolves walking upright in the Balkans; four-legged changelings virtually indistinguishable from Canadian wolves born in deep forest dens. Vampires of such refined aesthetics and keen intellect that they fashioned themselves aristocrats, and others that subsisted in the basest of squalor, aware only of their hunger. If Laurenti was right, there was no consistency because there were no true species to begin with, only the whims of demons that liked to play with flesh the way children might mold monsters from clay.

They could even ride more than one to a body, invading new hosts while the first remained occupied.

Not what happened in this case, obviously. By all indications, the *portatore* sank his teeth into Ogundana's shoulder, and was then discarded as a spent husk. It seemed plain enough that the new body, and its owner's place in the armored car's crew, was more useful to some greater plan. In that respect, Laurenti noted, the *portatore* had played a role not unlike the suicide bombers that were starting to become such a deadly plague in conflicts of the Middle East.

Yet despite Laurenti's appearing convinced of the part the bite had played, he nonetheless looked nagged by other doubts.

"What is it?" Kate asked.

"*He* bit, *he* fell to the bite," Laurenti said, gesturing to each corpse in turn. "But no matter . . . this should never have happened."

"A lot of things that shouldn't happen do."

"No, no, this is not how I mean. They should have been safe, very safe. These good men were in the sanctuary of their vehicle. They had no reason to leave it. The Nigerian, he had no reason to put himself at risk."

"Maybe I can kick in a hypothesis here," Kate said. "Glamour."

Laurenti ran it through his filters and, judging by his puzzled expression, came up with the wrong sense of the word. She resented it, too: a perfectly fine old word whose meaning had been watered down by changing times into something vapid enough to suit runway models and cosmetics ads.

"Not the glamour you're thinking. The *old* kind, the original kind," she said. "The power to weave a spell or enchantment that affects someone's vision. If you're under the influence of a glamour, you might see something that's not there . . . or fail to see something that is . . . or see something as completely different from its true appearance."

"So the Nigerian, he could have been lured out in the open by some sight he trusted?" Laurenti said.

"Or all of them. Each of the guards might have looked out their windows at this pair and seen something totally unlike what the others saw." She glanced at the culprits under their sheets. Mangled and spent, they didn't look like much now, did they? "Glamour is normally associated with the Faerie folk of the British Isles, but there's no reason to think that the underlying principle couldn't have roots that are even deeper and older."

"It is a weapon against us," Laurenti said, its worst implications clear: Weapons always seemed to get into the hands of those most willing to use them, and where they could do the most harm.

And this one seemed so terribly pernicious . . . turning someone's eyes against him. She wondered what the men in the armored car had seen. Wives or mothers or children in need. Divine virgins, radiant saviors. Whatever it took to make dedicated men forget their duty and give themselves over to the teeth of the enemy.

Laurenti drew the sheets back over the corpses and made for the door, but she stayed behind awhile, waiting for the sheets to move again, wondering if she could trust her eyes that they were really, truly dead.

CHAPTER 14

Pressure . . . he was aware of that much, at least, and by now, not much else. Ever since the lights had gone out, moon and stars eclipsed by the great head that surged from the sea and descended in a roar of teeth and foam, when was he *not* aware of pressure?

From the moment he'd been washed down the Leviathan's gullet, he'd tried to fight, but it did no good. He quickly found that pounding the inner wall of its belly was like beating his hand against a wall of thick, wet rubber that might ripple and flex, but never tear. Stone, metal—these he could smash through, because they resisted. But this waterlogged cocoon of muscle *absorbed* the blows, swallowing the force of them and spreading it around until it dissipated.

He'd gone for his gun next, getting off a single shot before the Leviathan reacted. He was blind here, of course—the darkness was as total as if he'd gone deep into a cavern underground—with no clear idea of the size of the sac he'd been caught in. He could touch one slick wall and reach in the opposite direction and feel only the stew of seawater and bile in which he was submerged, jostled by the man-sized fragments of its meals. Things with fins, things with tentacles, things that sloshed and stirred as though still alive.

But once Hellboy had fired that first shot, the organ walls suddenly closed in around him and squeezed, pressing him into a bent, cramped submission in which he had no leverage, could scarcely even move. Flies in amber would feel this way before they suffocated.

Eventually he'd relented, his struggles futile, and reasoned that there had to be some greater purpose behind this. He was not being devoured, but delivered. He would deal with whoever was there to receive him.

Yet as the hours went on, he could feel himself fading into a stasis that lingered somewhere halfway to death. It would take more than this to kill him, but he needed more than he had here to feel truly alive. Everything took its toll—the unrelenting pressure, the loss of movement, the submersion in acid and brine, the lack of air. Now and again he found himself in a fleeting pocket of gas, caustic and smelling like centuries of rotting fish, and he made do with that, even if it brought him little more than the satisfaction of flexing his aching lungs before sinking back into a delirium that deepened as the hours wore on.

Or maybe days. Or weeks. Or eternity.

Time, like light, had no meaning here.

There was sound, though, and it played tricks on him, as he could hear his blood running through his veins, and the blood of the Leviathan through the miles of arteries wrapped around him, and the ocean beyond that. He thought he could hear tectonic tremors rising from the ocean floor, and the songs of whales an ocean away, and the churning of propeller screws on ships passing overhead. He listened to them until he thought he could feel the pull of tides, and began to dream that he was no longer something separate from the sea but a part of it, digested and reborn as a piece of the Leviathan itself.

Sound . . .

And pressure.

These had been constants, so steady they'd become background ambience, but now they evolved into something new, gathering force to swamp what remained of him. From all around emanated a liquid rumbling. It passed through him, vibrating his bones like tuning forks, and then the walls squeezed in as if no fate remained but to be crushed down to nothing—

But this time there was a sense of movement rather than grinding, a feeling of propulsion as the compacted mass he was part of began to rise, back in the direction he'd come from so long ago. He felt his hand skim over new surfaces. New, yet old. He had felt these before: the gray tongue he'd slid along, the teeth like crooked stakes he'd tried to grab. The bony plated roof of the Leviathan's mouth.

And in a geyser of flesh and foam, he was spewed out into another night as dark as the one he'd left.

He was hurtling aloft for a moment, arms and legs suddenly unconstricted, so loose he didn't know what to do with them. Air, too . . . it rushed at him, washed over him, cold and fresh and cleansing. Then he splashed into water so frigid it shocked the first-drawn breath back out of him.

He struggled to break surface again, let the choppy waves carry him toward shore. Finally he felt bottom, a rapidly rising slope, and as soon as he got his legs beneath him, he twisted around in time to see the last of the Leviathan's bulk sliding away from the shelf back into the deeper waters offshore, and with a sweep of its tail and a cascade of spray, it was gone.

Only now did he realize it was raining.

Legs unsteady, pushed and pulled by the breakers, he straggled inland through a slick of silvery carcasses and blubber, until he could stumble onto a rocky beach. Beaten by needles of rain from a threatening sky that grumbled with endless thunder, he had no idea where on the face of the earth he was. About all he could be sure of at this point was that it definitely wasn't the tropics.

He lurched ahead a few more painful yards, taking stock. Time for another new trench coat; this one hung from him in bleached, half-digested tatters. But the titanium case containing the scroll was still cuffed to his wrist, and appeared no worse for the wear. Afraid he couldn't say the same about himself.

The only thing going for him was how well he could see in this night, starless and with the moon cloaked behind a thick scum of clouds. His eyesight during daylight hours may have been superior to that of men and women— 20/11, he'd been measured at—but his night vision was no better. Still, after the time he'd spent beyond the reach of so much as a spark, his eyes were sensitive enough to peer through the gloom.

Inland, step by exhausted step . . .

Inland, as the pounding of waves on rock receded behind him . . .

It began to take form on the crown of a hilltop rising gently in the distance before him: several shapes standing in a row—no, a ring—some tall and thin, others squat. At first they were men to his eyes, motionlessly awaiting his arrival . . . but no. They were far too tall for that, even the shortest among them. Some other race, then? Ancient giants, towering devils?

No, not those either.

Stones. A circle of standing stones, sunk deep into the earth by ancient hands.

Only now did he begin to suspect where he was.

He had, in one sense, come home. Swallowed whole and carried by force and vomited onto its shore, he was home again.

He pushed himself toward the ring of stones, and when his legs gave out and he tumbled to the soggy, rock-strewn ground, he dragged himself along. When his arms gave out too, he collapsed and lay with his face in the muck and the shreds of his coat wrapped around him like burial rags.

And the rain beat down.

Footsteps. Two pairs—one heavy, one light. They came crunching down from the hilltop as though someone had stepped directly from the stones. Closer, louder with every step, they came for him as though they'd never doubted he would be here.

His breath bubbled into the mud around his mouth, then he raised his head to see that they towered over him like gods. Or like devils who would never be content with anything less than to reign in Hell.

He started to lift his right hand, his fighting hand, but a gnarled hoof every bit its equal stamped it back to the ground and held it there. Teeth gritted in a silent snarl, he tilted his head toward the rain again, following the bristled leg up, up, like the trunk of a lone tree twisted by winds into a shape that should not stand, but does. Up, past the pendant gut and barrel chest to the silhouette of the head, dark and arrogant against the clouds.

And if the fight had, for now, been squeezed from him, gassed from him, he at least knew his enemy. Knew him by name. Knew him by his infernal title.

The other one, smaller but just as monstrous in its way, knelt beside Hellboy's pinned hand . . . and there were worse things than death, weren't there? There was the gnawing of promises he hadn't been able to keep. There were the growing ranks of men he'd led to their deaths for what was, in the end, nothing . . .

Because there was having to watch a pair of hands, each sprouting a dozen nimble fingers long and thin as spider legs, work at the cuff latched around his wrist and open it within mere moments.

There was *failure*.

Cuff and case, both were taken, and once the restraining hoof was removed from his hand, he tried to crawl after the pair of thieves as they ascended the hill. He glared at their backs, at the insulting leisure with which they left him behind, as if he were no more bother than a roach they'd stepped on . . . and worst of all, they were still outpacing him.

His hand went for his holster and he cursed when he found it empty. Right—he'd lost the gun in the Leviathan's belly.

Then he groped at the ruins of his trench coat and found the left pocket still intact . . . and the antique Luger inside.

Would it still fire? He switched hands for a moment,

held it in his right while working the toggle with his left to jack a round into the chamber. Then, unsteady, he aimed through the rain at the larger of the two backs. Could he even hurt them? What did it matter, anyway? You had to try. You had to try.

He squeezed the trigger, and if the gun didn't have near the kick of his usual sidearm, that was okay, because it was still the most satisfying crack he'd ever heard.

He even thought he saw the big one stumble, just before the pair disappeared into the rain and mist. *Another time,* he promised them, *finish you off some other time,* then rolled onto his back and let the water sluice down his face.

After another minute or two he heard more footsteps, this time from the opposite direction. Up from the same beach where he'd come ashore. Just one pair of feet this time, and none too steady, either. He gripped the Luger, swung it upward when the footsteps crunched close enough . . . then let his hand fall back to the ground again.

"What are *you* doing here?"

"I thought . . . you might need . . . some help," Abe Sapien said, or tried to. Awfully hard to talk and suck wind at the same time.

"Don't I look like I've got everything under control?"

Abe dropped to the ground beside him, no grace, nor heed to the rocks, looking chilled and wrung out, like a runner after a marathon through a downpour. Only now did Hellboy start to comprehend the enormity of what Abe must have done: followed the Leviathan all the way here, swimming in relentless pursuit, every nautical mile between the western Mediterranean and the north of Scotland.

"You didn't," Hellboy said.

"I caught a ride sometimes," Abe told him. "There are places to grab onto that thing. Most of the time it wouldn't know I was there."

What about the times it did, he started to ask, then decided it could wait. Right now he didn't want to imagine the close calls Abe must have endured when the Leviathan tried to shake off or swat away what it must've regarded as a clinging little parasite.

"They took the scroll," he said instead.

Abe nodded down at his bare wrist. "I see."

"I *lost* the scroll." And for all the pain and fury he felt, most of it was directed straight at his own heart.

"You shot one of them, didn't you?" Abe said, then pointed in the direction of the stones. "Maybe that one's dead, maybe—"

"You don't kill *them* with one shot. I don't know if you can kill them at all."

"Hellboy . . ." Abe said, in the tone of voice you'd use with someone rambling about how the sky had turned green. "They were only men. I saw them from a distance. Just two men."

"I saw them too. They were right on top of me. They . . ."

"Maybe . . . you saw what they wanted you to see. That's not easy to do to you, I know, but in your condition . . ." Abe snatched the Luger and pushed himself upright. "I'm going after them."

He had to be running on fumes, Abe did, every muscle screaming. But off he went, every step an effort, and was soon lost to the weather and the night beyond the standing stones.

Home again? Well, yes and no. Although this was not

the place of Hellboy's birth—that had occurred many miles to the south, in England—this was where it had been facilitated: Dreich Midden, a small island off the coast of Scotland, blasted by North Atlantic winds and barren but for the Bronze Age ring of stones whose original purpose had been lost to the millennia.

That cabal of *Wehrmacht* soldiers and occultists who had gathered here on a December night more than fifty years ago . . . had they known something about this place that history had forgotten and archaeologists had never found? They must have. What else could have drawn them so far behind enemy lines in the waning days of the Second World War? Desperation, yes—Germany had exhausted itself from the inside out and was months from collapse. And *Der Führer*'s mania for an occult means to tip the momentum of the war. Hitler had long been keen on the subject; the looming specter of defeat had turned him into a true seeker.

But desperation and mania can be indulged anywhere. Why here?

The only thing that seemed certain was that all of them, from the Nazi's upper echelon down to the lowliest technician, had been exploited by the magus at the center of it all. As a mortal man, Grigori Rasputin had been known as the Mad Monk. Spared from death at the bottom of the River Neva, after as much treachery and butchery as any man had endured, he had become something else. Something worse, in thrall to powers that sought to lay waste to humankind and deliver the world to seven gods of chaos whose wrath would make the Third Reich's worst accomplishments seem like children's games.

Or something like that.

Hellboy had gleaned enough from Rasputin to understand that he was supposed to play some part in it all, but the madman's secrets had been his own, and had finally died with him a couple of years ago. Which ended it, as far as Hellboy was concerned. Ignorance may not have been bliss, but it got him through the night. He had no part to play in anyone's plans but his own.

Still, this island . . .

That he'd been brought here, spat up here, robbed here, *humiliated* here . . . it was impossible to believe there was no deeper message in it. Hell shoving his nose into his own history: *You forget who you are . . . what you are . . . whose you are.*

"I never knew," he told the earth on which he lay, and whatever else cared to listen. "So there was nothing to forget."

And Abe was back.

"They're gone," he said. "I thought I heard a boat motor fading in the distance, but couldn't see anything."

Hellboy grunted and rolled over again, pushing himself to elbows and knees. Abe helped him the rest of the way, and together they made for the standing stones. Hard to say who was holding whom up now. Pull either of them away and they'd both go down. They sought shelter at the base of the broadest, flattest menhir. Between its tilt and the sideways slant of the rain, the stone gave them as much protection from the elements as they were likely to find on this desolate hump of land.

"One observation?" Abe said. "You've smelled better."

"Hey. You're no rose on a *good* day."

Abe clasped his shoulder for a moment, gave it a shake. "The ones that took the scroll—I know what I saw. What were *you* seeing?"

"Not men, that's for sure. Maybe they were wearing the *skins* of men. But definitely not men inside."

He supposed he should've known better, that if he'd been thinking more clearly, he might have known his eyes were being deceived. Maybe that was another reason for his having been brought to this place: He was already primed to believe that anything might be possible here.

Even so, the denizens of Hell didn't just roam the earth at will, at least not in their true forms, their true bodies. His uniqueness in the world was proof of that. They could be summoned into the confines of protective circles similar to the ones he'd seen at the observatory in Rome. In many cases, whether they were truly corporeal or just an extraordinarily powerful projection was still up for grabs, although if the latter, they were no less dangerous to the conjurer for it.

Their surest path into the world was in the bodies of servants and sycophants willing, even eager, to house them. But you could forget all that business about little girls with rotating heads and a gorgeful of pea soup—these people *wanted* to be taken. And when it served Hell's purposes, its principalities might call upon beasts such as the Leviathan . . . beings so ancient, so reclusive, they could only be regarded as surviving fragments of the chaos that had stirred the primordial seas.

"The one that took the cuff off my wrist," Hellboy said, "that one's called Surgat."

Abe shook his head. "I don't know the name."

"Minor, as demons go. But he can open any man-made lock."

"And the other one?"

"Moloch. I couldn't tell you firsthand whether it's true or not, but the old texts say he's a prince of Hell. I've got no reason to doubt that. In the Middle East, in Old Testament times, there were tribes that worshipped him as a sun god."

"And now he has the Masada Scroll," Abe said. "What Heaven wants to destroy, Hell wants to possess."

"Doesn't sound good, does it?"

"But if Hell is deceit, why be so obvious about it?" Abe asked. "They let you see them. They *wanted* you to see them. They may have worn men's skins, but they didn't try to hide behind them."

"Arrogance?" he guessed. "Make sure we knew they were able to succeed where angels failed? Never underestimate the power of pride."

But it would've been personal, too, wouldn't it? Anything between Hell and himself would be personal, always. Because he was Hell's own runaway.

What an affront to them his existence must have been. Yet he couldn't say they'd ever tried outright to kill him. Meaning they must have thought they needed him. Or maybe they tolerated him because the triumph of tempting him back would eclipse the shame of having lost him, with such rejoicing that the world would writhe.

Either way, he wasn't going to give them the satisfaction.

"We really need to get off this rock," he said. "Any ideas?"

He'd already noticed that Abe was as bereft of gear as he was. Abe was bereft of *everything*. Different reasons, though, probably. What Hellboy hadn't lost during the shipwreck, the Leviathan's belly had claimed. More likely Abe had shed everything on purpose, to eliminate surface drag during his phenomenal swim. Not that their global phones would necessarily even work by now, despite being waterproof, but it would've been nice to see that the bureau's R&D guys had gotten it right.

"If I remember correctly, the Scottish mainland isn't far off," Abe said. "I could swim for help."

"Show-off."

Abe grinned. "I've caught a second wind."

"Lots of fisherman along these coasts, so watch who you trust. Last thing we need is for you to end up in a bowl of cullen skink."

Now Abe just looked affronted.

"And promise me you'll find a blanket as soon as you can. You don't want to be scaring anybody with . . . whatever that is down there."

Abe asked if he had any other advice that wasn't totally unnecessary, and when Hellboy couldn't think of any, once more vanished from sight long before he reached the water's edge.

Hellboy stretched out with his head against the stone and let the rain have him. The elements he could handle fine. It was the solitude, at all the wrong times, that he never quite got used to.

CHAPTER 15

As the days passed, Laurenti wondered if they both weren't captives here, he and the man in the cage. No progress—now on his tenth day behind bars in the old shell of a private zoo, Domenico Verdi had yet to provide any useful information on the *Opus Angelorum*. Their identities, where they might be found, what they might be scheming, attempting. If they'd ever had a contingency plan for what to do in case one of their numbers had been found out. Verdi was still without remorse, without repentance . . . and without any apparent desire to be free.

Laurenti had dwelled on his ominous words of a week ago—*I've already found my deliverers. I think maybe you'll meet them soon enough.* Dwelled on them a little too heavily, perhaps. It seemed certain that Verdi had meant the seraphim, implying that another attack was imminent.

But as each sunset came and each night gave way to another dawn with nothing happening, apprehension slowly subsided. If no retaliation had yet come from Verdi's unknown collaborators, maybe it never would. For a time, Laurenti feared that Verdi might be planning on initiating it himself. The rites that they'd successfully used to call down the seraphs were unknown to him, but Laurenti could think of no reason why one man couldn't do it instead of a group.

He'd gone to visit the *osservatorio* again, to examine the signs and sigils that had been used to accomplish the summoning. He could make little sense of them—they looked so jumbled, with layers upon layers—and he came away convinced that they were of such complexity that it seemed unlikely a man could remember them exactly, to recreate them verbatim . . . at least under these conditions. All the same, he made sure that Verdi's cell was kept free of things he could use for writing.

As well, if the stains on the old wood of the *osservatorio*'s top floor were what they appeared to be, blood was a part of these rites. Perhaps not a sacrificial death—he found it difficult to believe that even they would tread this far into the forbidden—but nonetheless, blood was life, blood was energy, and its release was known to charge many a ceremonial stage.

So, after they'd shared wine last week, no more glassware went through the bars, and Laurenti made doubly sure to keep anything else sharp out of reach as well. No razors, not even with safety blades, and Verdi sprouted a coarse beard that began to mask the pits and pocks of his face.

So too had Laurenti dwelled on Verdi's reaction to his assertion that the scroll was beyond Rome and therefore safe: *I doubt that very much,* he'd said. *Once they are out in the world, things like this have a way of attracting attention no matter where they go.*

An accurate but otherwise innocent assumption, or had he known something like this was imminent? Laurenti was inclined to believe the former, that he truly knew none of this; that, as the BPRD and nearly all his compatriots believed, the sinking of the yacht and the scroll's theft were the work of another faction entirely.

At first Laurenti saw no value in even mentioning it to their captive. Why give him a chance to gloat? Then Laurenti came to wonder if that wasn't his only reason for withholding the news—that he was motivated more by embarrassment than strategy. Perhaps some good *could* come of sharing this terrible news, if only for the chance it would give him to watch Verdi's reaction. Laurenti had looked into the eyes of all manner of liars, from those who lied to save face or spare feelings, to those who lied for power and gain. If Verdi knew something of this, regardless of his words, Laurenti felt sure he would sense it.

And when he finally told him, there was nothing in Verdi—to whom smugness and sanctimony seemed quite natural—that appeared anything other than sorrowful. None of what the Americans called *I-told-you-so*'s. He sat quietly with his hands folded in his lap, and under the fuzz of new beard, like a dark moss, his face loosened and sagged.

"Now do you see," his voice a hush, "why we would rather have it destroyed?"

Laurenti nodded. He *did* recognize this, even if he couldn't agree with their intentions, much less their methods. "And do you see that it never would have been so vulnerable if you had not first tried that, and failed?"

"Only a matter of time," Verdi said. "The wrong hands . . . they never would have stopped groping."

As they sat in the rays of light slanting through the covered portals in the roof, Laurenti stirred in his chair. Pointed back at the faded mural on the wall behind him, the Peaceable Kingdom of lions and lambs.

"Can we put aside our antagonisms for a moment?" he asked. "I have something I want to ask you."

Verdi seemed to sniff the air for duplicity, then gave a conciliatory nod.

"What are they like?"

"Who?"

"You know what I'm speaking about."

"Ahh. The angels," Verdi said, and he tipped his head back with his eyes focused on nothing. "They are . . . the purest essence of magnificence and dread. Would you ever want to see one, meet one? I bet you were just like me growing up, and dreamed of it. But be careful what you wish for. I don't think you would want it at all."

He did not seem to gloat even now.

"The air, it grows cold around you, and then they descend. Different people see them in different ways, but I have seen them descend like huge doves with skin like glass, filled with a flame they will pour out on the heads of their enemies."

Except . . .

They didn't truly descend, Verdi told him. People only thought this way because people only thought in terms of up and down. But the seraphs didn't come from above, because they didn't come from a place you could get to if you climbed a tall enough tree. They came not down from above, but rather from the outside in, entering this world where its air was thinnest.

Laurenti thought of the Archives, the charred remains

of people and property. "Do they not have any concept of mercy?"

"Why should they?" Verdi laughed. "They are . . . in-complete. Pure in what they are, but incomplete. Are there angels that are heralds, or guardians, or comforters? Maybe. Probably. But I've never seen *them.*"

"Then what are these?" Laurenti asked.

"Isn't it obvious? They are the perfect manifestation of His wrath, and nothing more," Verdi said. "And for so long, they have had nothing to do."

After the priest left, another of his captors brought the man in the cage the pair of wooden buckets filled with warm water—one sudsy, one clear—that they gave him for his daily washing, then stayed behind to make sure he behaved himself with them. They evidently did not trust him even with smooth-edged wood, or perhaps they feared he would try drowning himself in the water.

Wooden for wash water, plastic for his toilet—it was a system.

As he had done each day, Domenico Verdi carried both buckets into the corner of his cage, kept his back turned to the bars, stripped out of the loose slacks and shapeless pullover shirt they'd given him in place of his cassock, and began scrubbing himself down with the sponge floating in the soapy bucket. As he did each day, he took utmost care that his backside was all anyone could see from the other side of the bars.

They would have no reason to think it anything other than modesty.

Let them continue to think it.

His thumbnail, and what was becoming of it as it grew and he daily filed it against the stone—this he could hide easily enough, by curling his thumb behind the next two fingers.

Not so, this greater secret he wished to keep.

And as he washed, he thanked God for seeing fit to give him such a broad chest and big belly, wide enough to contain such a marvel.

CHAPTER 16

E ngland again.

It was no secret in the BPRD that he had developed a habit of retreating here after the bad ones—the cases that brought him not just face-to-face but soul-to-soul with the worst things that could happen. The worst things that could *exist*. Whether it was in the earth, air, or water, there was just something about the English countryside that got inside his head and washed it out in all the right places.

And if this business with the scroll was far from over, well, they could cut him some slack. As if anybody was going to begrudge him a day or two of recuperation after the way—and where—he'd spent the last four. And as long as he was in the neighborhood anyway.

He'd spent another eight hours on the island after Abe had left for the mainland, and then the both of them had been choppered down to the Cornwall safehouse where they'd originally been headed. Finally getting there, only late and without the scroll.

He hadn't stayed long. Everything they were getting done right now—they didn't need him for that. Kate had left Rome for Cornwall immediately after she and the priest had checked out the bodies from the armored car, and she was now up to her nose in research. Liz had gone there from Majorca and, on Hellboy's request, was now waiting for her protégé, Campbell Holt, to come over. And Abe? The last he knew, Abe had been asleep for seventeen hours straight and counting. With everybody else rejoicing in the news that rumors of their deaths had been greatly exaggerated.

Better for them all if he returned to duty with his batteries fully charged.

So for now, it was enough to sequester himself in the more out-of-the-way places of the Western Midlands and walk the once-green fields that had given way to autumn, and let them work their tonic effects. When he needed it, this whole country was like one big decompression zone.

Most of it, anyway. There were still a few hot spots.

Right here in East Bromwich, for one.

BUREAU FOR PARANORMAL RESEARCH AND DEFENSE
Field Memo UK-000164-01

Date: October 25, 1996
Issued by: Dr. Kate Corrigan
Classification: Open Access
Subject: Moloch and Moloch worship

Whether through official channels or the grapevine, by now you're all no doubt aware of Hellboy's encounter off the north coast of Scotland, some time during the late hours of Wednesday, October 23. After spending approximately

92 hours in the stomach of the mytho-historical creature known as the Leviathan, Hellboy was subjected to the Jonah-like indignity of being regurgitated onto the island colloquially known as Dreich Midden. For reasons that may only be symbolic, or that may have some thus far undetected significance, this was the same island where the ritual was conducted that directly or indirectly triggered Hellboy's appearance in East Bromwich, England (December 23, 1944). Regardless of whether the choice of Dreich Midden was symbolic or significant, one conclusion is inescapable: that the sinking of the charter vessel *Calista* was orchestrated for the purpose of bringing Hellboy there so the Masada Scroll could be taken.

It is Hellboy's belief that, although carried out by the physical forms of two unidentified men, this theft was engineered by the demonic entity known in various grimoires and other sources of arcana and history as Moloch, with the assistance of Surgat, a lesser demon infamous for opening locks.

For those of you who didn't grow up in ancient Palestine (and, the totally uncalled-for cracks about my age from you novice agents notwithstanding, neither did I), a background on Moloch should be helpful in letting everyone know what we're dealing with.

Although clearly a malevolent entity to our, ahem, enlightened sensibilities, Moloch was worshipped as a sun god in first millennium B.C.E. Palestine and beyond. You can hardly rub two historians together without generating sparks of disagreement, but Moloch has been associated variously with the Ammonite and Canaanite tribes, and biblical accounts indicate that Solomon imported the cult of Moloch worship into Israel at a location outside Jerusalem called Tophet (likely translation: "place of abomination"). Moloch worship, or something very similar, also appears to have gone on in North Africa at Carthage and elsewhere, as well as Malta, Sardinia, Sicily, and other locations around the western Mediterranean.

If we refer to later sources, although concerning events even more ancient, we find a greater consensus on Moloch's identity, disposition, and inclinations. There is a concurrence among medieval- and Renaissance-era demonologists that Moloch is a prince of Hell; according to some sixteenth-century sources, his power is greatest in December. (As we are just weeks away from December, the events we're now experiencing suggest that we should take seriously the possibility that they are proceeding according to a definite timetable.) If you recall your Milton, Moloch was one of the instigators among the host of rebel angels, as well as one of its greatest warriors, and is described in *Paradise Lost* as "besmeared with blood of human sacrifice and parents' tears . . ." A similar passage in the twelfth-century grimoire *De Vermis Mysteriis* describes him as one who "takes supreme pleasure in causing mothers to weep."

The BPRD has in the past observed that incorporeal entities can indeed be strengthened by devotion. So I—and I'm far from alone in this— consider it a possibility that Moloch was greatly empowered by his worship among various peoples of antiquity that mistakenly regarded him as a sun deity.

Their worship was invariably sacrificial in nature, and there is also little room for doubt that (a) immolation was the means of delivery, (b) when human beings were sacrificed, the chosen victims were children, and (c) the centerpiece of the sacrificial rite was a large statue, likely made of bronze. Less certain is the precise methodology of burning, as the surviving ancient writings vary.

Some rabbinical accounts describe a hollow statue having seven compartments, each of which was reserved for a specific offering—the seventh being the child—which were consumed by a fire kindled within the base of the statue. In other accounts, the child (whether alive or freshly killed by some other means) was placed on the statue's outstretched arms directly over a firepit kindled in front of the statue. Multiple accounts refer to priests and others present at the rite playing drums, tambourines, flutes, pipes, etc., in order to create a cacophony that would drown out the victim's screams.

As always, we have to allow for two considerations: regional differences in idol worship that really did occur, and the possibility that some accounts were exaggerations or complete fictions, as propaganda generated by a tribe or city-state's enemies.

Although it certainly wasn't intended as propaganda, the greatest enduring misperception about these rites does have its origins in fiction. French novelist Gustave Flaubert's 1862 novel *Salammbo* described Carthaginian Moloch worship as involving a large statue whose movable arms were rigged with chains so that the priests could raise them; a child placed upon the statue's outstretched hands was then mechanically deposited into Moloch's gaping mouth, and delivered to the flames within.

It wasn't true then. Unfortunately, it appears to be true *now*.

Although widespread, institutionalized Moloch worship died out over 2000 years ago, small cults and other pockets of devotees have been sporadically reported over the centuries. The last such group that the BPRD is aware of was active in post-World War I Germany: *Der Horn-Orden* (translation, the Order of the Horn, presumably in deference to Moloch's traditional appearance as having the head of a bull). This group thrived in the decadent atmosphere of Weimar Republic-era Berlin under the leadership of war veteran-turned-occultist Matthias Herzog, who was frequently described by the more sensationalist press of the 1920s as "the German Aleister Crowley." (Predictably, Crowley was quick to denounce him in every way possible.) The group was devoted to the typical secret society goals of knowledge, power, and influence, although they apparently went so far as to profess their chief ambition to be the ushering in of a new age of Hell on Earth.

Certainly that description could apply to much of Europe during World War II, but *Der Horn-Orden* was long gone by then. The group appears to have vanished by 1932—not merely disbanded, but completely disappeared, along with most of its initiates. Estimates put the number at over 860. Although it is possible to trace a handful of the group's members to later Nazi-era occult circles, the BPRD has found no connections to any individuals identified as being involved with the December 23, 1944, incident linked to Hellboy's appearance.

Virtually all of our knowledge about *Der Horn-Orden* comes from a book whose intimidatingly long Teutonic title translates into English as *Things Better Forgotten*. It's an uneven but generally useful history of then-contemporary German occult lodges/societies, with an expected emphasis on the Fraternitas Saturni. It was published in 1942 by a Munich press in an edition of fifty copies (only six of which are known to have survived World War II, with two in BPRD possession), and was the work of Ernst Schweiger, who was dead of an undiagnosed bacterial infection within two months, at the age of forty-four.

Schweiger was a fellow veteran of WWI who purports to have been active in *Der Horn-Orden* during its early years. He describes sacrifices to a Moloch statue that was constructed in obvious accordance with the Flaubert version, complete with raising arms, although he does not describe the use of chains, and in fact seems not to have ever learned how the illusion of motility was accomplished. Since the existence of such a statue has never been verified, even in photos, we do have to consider the possibility that Schweiger was making it up. However, there are two arguments in favor of his claims' authenticity:

(1) Although Schweiger adopts a more distant tone in his book concerning his activities with *Der Horn-Orden*, a small collection of his private

correspondence, found in 1957, professes unrelieved guilt at having helped procure sacrifices meant for the statue, most of them unwanted infants born to performers and prostitutes in Weimar Berlin. He cites his involvement as having begun on Walpurgisnacht in 1924, and goes beyond his book with the claim that Matthias Herzog was actually the father of many of the procured children, because to Moloch, these children made more acceptable sacrifices than those of strangers. In short, these children were destined for the furnace from birth.

(2) The existence of an operable Moloch idol in the early twentieth century is not the most outlandish assertion in Schweiger's book. That honor would have to go to his claims that *Der Horn-Orden* leader Matthias Herzog regenerated an arm lost at the shoulder in World War I, much like some reptiles are known to regrow a missing tail. Mere propaganda and occult cachet? Hardly. This *is* documented by verifiable evidence: a sequence of six photogravure plates from 1924/1925 that were discovered in the archives of Oskar Dorfman after his death in 1962. Though now known only to collectors of vintage smut, Dorfman was a popular pornographer during Germany's interwar years, who fit right into Berlin's licentious climate. He also happened to be rigorous in his recordkeeping. The gravure plates cover a sixteen-month span and show the

same man, shirtless, with his left arm in various stages of regrowth, from entirely missing to new-born to child to adult. Both the plates and the imagery have stood up to all BPRD analysis attempting to debunk them as some sort of optical fraud, or accomplished with a series of prosthetics. A follow-up memo will be coming out of HQ to notify you as soon as the plate sequence is ready to go up on network for general viewing, although at the moment we're still waiting for the IT department to come in after-hours.

In the meantime, here's the directive: Cross-reference the attached list of names, terms, phrases, dates, etc., with all active and dormant case files, beginning with the last five years and then working backward. All hits pertaining to Scotland or populated islands (Shetland, Orkney, Skye, the Hebrides) or Northern England should be accorded a top priority for immediate follow-up investigation. If there's anything out there relevant to the continued existence of *Der Horn-Orden* or other twentieth-century Moloch worship, it's imperative that we get a handle on it.

One's birthplace should hold a sacred relevance to his or her life, but Hellboy harbored no such affection for his own. How could anyone find something hallowed in a place that had hosted a birth that left scorch marks on the stone floor still visible more than half a century later? Though he'd tried to make good on it, to atone for the ill intent of others—the road *out* of Hell could be paved with good intentions, too—sometimes it still didn't seem enough.

The old church in East Bromwich must have been a grand sight in its heyday, but that day had darkened some 300 years ago. Now it was nothing more than a jigsaw puzzle of fragments and ruins, ever so slowly being reclaimed by the land. Here, a wall crawling with ivy, red as blood now that autumn had come. There, a vaulted window, gnawed by time and neglect down to its arched frame and the broken inner lacework of its tracery. Stand so that you could look squarely through the window's remains and you would see that the place was presided over by a broken crucifix, still standing after the centuries, its eroded life-size Christ missing its left arm to the elbow.

This church was close enough to the cities and towns of the Western Midlands that you'd think it would draw the young, the curious, the daring. But it didn't. He saw no graffiti, no empty cans. No signs of tourists tramping through with cameras. He couldn't even spot a bird's nest up in the surviving wall tops and rafters. It seemed to repel them one and all, as if they instinctively knew that this place was not picturesque, but poisoned.

He'd been here twice before, with no recollection of the first time, but then, no one he knew could remember his or her delivery room. Professor Bruttenholm had told him he'd entered the world in a huge welder's arc of flame and a shower of broken stone . . . an infant as big as a human toddler, his right hand already full-sized; he'd had to grow into it.

Cause and effect: On that cold, wet island in the north,

they'd managed to rip a hole between worlds, dimensions, whatever . . . and he'd popped out here.

Cause and effect redux: He had created his own destiny, wholly in defiance of his conjurers, simply by being himself. There may have been a BPRD without him, but it wouldn't be the same today. He had become, at the moment of his birth, the world's foremost living, breathing, concrete-chewing proof that lurking beyond the veil of everyday reality were threats that really must be dealt with. He'd managed this just by showing up.

Some good had come out of this place, at least.

He wandered until he found a spot along a surviving wall in what appeared to have been the church's nave, near the west end entrance. Right where he remembered: a shadowed suggestion of faces peering out at him from behind a ragged curtain of ivy. He brushed it aside for a better look.

There were two of them carved in the old limestone. With his imperious beard and the cross on the chest of his tunic, the male had the look of a medieval crusader. The woman at his side, her face a perpetual balance of serenity and woes, was likewise cloaked against the world. Whether they were here by coincidence or some far-reaching design, he had come to associate them with a brother and sister, priest and nun, whose souls had been ensnared here for centuries in a cold gray limbo.

He'd seen them die.

That was on his other visit, just last year.

He'd come, finally, after five decades spent ducking the place, dismissing it as irrelevant to who and what he now was. Kate had called his longstanding refusal to set foot on these unhallowed grounds again a form of denial. Liz, ever more blunt, called it chickenshit. And Professor Bruttenholm, in his fatherly wisdom? He'd never called it anything, barely acknowledging it, as if he had known that Hellboy would visit when the time was right.

Had the man ever been wrong about things that mattered?

And so he'd come last year to wander the maze of ruins, seeing it all for the first time because not a bit of it stirred a single memory. Come night, he'd slept, and soon dreamed . . .

Dreamed of a dying old woman repenting the sins of her vain and impetuous youth, and the shadow-walking demon she had worshipped, loved, bedded. Begging her children—the elder a priest, the younger a nun—to intercede on her behalf and save her soul from damnation.

Their efforts had been in vain.

Hellboy knew better than to trust dreams without question, even when they were so vivid they came to waking life around him like echoes of history. Because it was possible they were only echoes of things that *might* have been, not things that had. Still, he feared his hopes were as doomed as those poor wretches who'd been blasted apart by the claimant of their mother's soul.

The horned titan that came for his due had spoken tenderly to her of a child they'd conceived together, still growing inside her. He'd turned and looked at Hellboy and spoke of their coming son. Then skewered the woman on a chained hook and left her dangling from his steed.

Yeah, just go and try explaining that one away as indigestion. A blot of mustard, a crumb of cheese.

He touched the pair of limestone faces carved into the wall and let the curtain of ivy fall back into place.

Dreich Midden, East Bromwich . . . so linked were these two places, by the simultaneous events of 1944 if nothing else, that after having been spit out on the island again, he'd shown up here today half expecting to find . . . something.

But nothing had changed. Same old mysteries, same old questions, same old legacy of lies.

Although if he shut out everything else and listened very closely, he thought he could hear the sound of laughter.

One day he was going to come here and, with nothing more than his two hands, hit this place like a force of nature and not stop until the last two stones still joined together were wrenched apart.

But not today.

He had promises to keep, and one more stop to make along the way.

CHAPTER 17

She was on her fourth cigarette when the car was checked through the gate and appeared at the end of the long, long drive. Only then did Liz's heart start to race. Not the good race, either, the kind of quickened pulse that could pave the way for rumpled sheets and a languorous breakfast—rare enough even at her best times, but not so long in the past that she didn't remember what it was like.

No, this was more like the feeling of tipping backward in a kitchen chair and realizing you're within a millimeter of the point of no return.

From the front terrace, she watched the car roll closer, a black sedan dour against the green meadows and the golds and reds of autumn. She'd been here at the house in Bodmin, Cornwall, enough times over the years that she couldn't remember what it was like to see it through the windshield for the first time. *Safehouse*, they called it, and technically speaking that was true, but she'd always thought the term failed to do the place justice. No stables, and a wine cellar that had been converted into a reinforced bunker, but from the outside it looked like the kind of Georgian manor house where you might expect a proper foxhunt each Christmas morning.

The sedan rolled halfway through the circular drive that looped around a fountain where a group of Greco-Roman nymphs in mid-frolic had been waiting years for the water to be turned back on. They now stood in what looked like a dirty round bathtub. She'd always felt sorry for them.

Liz tossed her cigarette and ground it to death with her boot tip as the sedan's back door popped open and Campbell Holt stepped out. He wore a long dark coat that hit him at the knee, the empty left cuff flapping, flapping. He flipped her a nonchalant wave with his right hand.

"Hullo, luv!" he called out in a voice that clearly wasn't his. It took her a moment to place it as a decent Liverpudlian fake. He patted the sedan and grinned, and his voice returned to normal. "I feel like one of the Beatles, only going the opposite direction."

"Your hair's too short," she said.

His eyes performed a disappointed pan-and-scan across the terrace and grounds, empty but for her. "I really was hoping for more screaming fans."

Nice to see that one of them wasn't sweating this out.

Hellboy's idea, this was, and whether it would prove to be a good one or a bad one, they'd know soon enough. If it worked out, there would be enough credit to go around. And if it didn't? Well, put it this way: She'd never seen anyone blame H.B. for anything. Because he did so much right. Because he did so many things that nobody else could. And because he was so utterly unique. She didn't have the same star status, never would, and while she honestly didn't care about that crap while it remained on the level of shallow adulation, at times like this she felt the disparity more keenly.

If it didn't work out, Liz knew that, even if nobody said anything, they'd be looking at her as if she were the mother of this particular failure. Because Campbell Holt was *her* boy, *her* charge, the challenge she'd gone out of her way to take on—so who else to blame if he couldn't hack it in the field?

Nobody would remember her objections. Nobody had heard them except for Hellboy. He'd been discreet enough yesterday to present his idea to her while they were alone.

"I don't know, H.B.," she'd said. "I've only been working with Cam for about seven weeks. And the first month I was time-sharing him with his detox and rehab program. There's a lot of work we still have to do before he's on solid ground."

"You sounded pretty proud of him on the boat the other day," Hellboy had countered.

"I think I sounded protective of him, too," she'd said. "Yeah, he's come a long way from the guy I first saw plugged into tubes in his hospital bed. But there's a lot more progress to make before he gets his diploma."

"Liz, I don't want to come off like I'm second-guessing you on this, but this kid's got a talent we can use *now*. We don't have the time for you to bring him along slow anymore."

Was it Hellboy's fault if he had the sort of chin that made him look stubborn every moment of his life?

"I respect psychics and all that," he'd said. "It's just that they never seem to do much of the heavy lifting. So the fact that I'm asking at all should tell you how important I think this is."

More arguments, back and forth, pro and con. The two

of them could quarrel like siblings because, well, that's what they were, weren't they? She'd grown up with him, known him since she was a child, and although he'd reached his full towering height years before she'd been born, in a sense he'd grown up with her, too.

He was playing on emotion here and didn't even realize it—Hellboy surviving in the GI tract of something believed to be ancient enough to have swum the seas when the continents looked different than they did now, while she'd spent those days fearing she might have finally seen the last of him.

After the sinking of the *Calista*, she'd leaned against the low rubber wall of the life raft, the only thing between her and the hungry sea, saying little to Bastiaan and the lone surviving crewman. As she'd watched the waves and tried to ignore the growing thirst from having to ration the last of the fresh water, she'd felt hope curl inside her chest and die like a starved child. If she'd been with someone other than strangers, if Abe had been beside her, maybe he could've talked her through it . . . but for all she knew, Abe was dead too. Thirty hours in the raft, three more on a rescue ship, overnight in a spartan hotel room on Majorca, a turbulent flight to England, and during the whole interminable span, she had careened through a crash course on the stages of grief.

And now he was back, he and Abe both, and all he wanted was to send an agent out into the field. Where they all went eventually, at least the ones with talents.

Who was she to deny him?

There was more than just success and failure on the line for the bureau as a whole. There was also, even though no one had spoken of it and never would, redemption. Hellboy may have survived something that no one else could've, but he had still been bested. He'd lost what he'd been entrusted to carry.

Could anyone else see what that did to him? Could anyone who hadn't grown up with him look past the unearthly gold of his eyes and see the new imbalance there, the overturning of his natural order?

He would save himself by saving the world . . . or whatever corner of it was threatened this time. He'd been doing it all his life.

And then, in their debate yesterday, he'd put the knife in:

"Campbell will do fine, he'll *be* fine. You know how I know that?" he'd said. "He'll have you with him the whole time."

She wished she could share the same confidence.

And now that Campbell was here, she wished she could spin him around and put him in the car again and send him back across the ocean. His coat fit him and still looked too big. He looked so young, so godawful young.

I got you into this, she thought, *and maybe it really wasn't the best thing at the time, maybe you really might have been better off in some half-decent mental ward . . .*

"So the big red guy really asked for me, huh?" he said.

Campbell was alongside her now, carrying the single bag he'd packed for the trip. She wondered how difficult it was to fold clothes with one hand. If he'd walked through the airports with his left wrist in his coat pocket to conceal the stump. It's what she would do. Freak is as freak does, so don't give the normals any excuse to stare.

"That's a *good* thing, right?"

"It shows a certain level of confidence, yes," she said.

"Cool," he said, sounding genuinely pleased, before getting to the flipside. " 'Cause I know the bureau isn't without, um, casualties."

"Don't worry. You're not going in with the lions anytime soon."

"Cool." A moment later they were through the safehouse's front doors, and Campbell went back on pan-and-scan. "Is he here now? It's not like I've actually met him yet."

"No, he's a few hours north of here. Taking care of some things."

She left it unsaid that H.B. was on walkabout again, if only for a day or so. Not that he could lose himself in the forests and fields, the way he normally liked to. He had an assigned driver this time, which to her mind defeated the purpose of walkabout, but it was an essential compromise; none of them knew when something crucial might break. And if it did, what, he was going to take the trains? Only if he wanted to get bogged down somewhere signing autographs.

He'd been a public figure since the late 1950s—had even been on the cover of *Life* magazine, among others—but the novelty and the paranoia factor had worn off long ago. He'd evolved into the world's most unique celebrity: intimidating yet approachable, with no need of plastic surgery to keep him looking the same over the decades, and forever denied the ability to duck an encounter by telling people, "Sorry, you've mistaken me for someone else."

She envied him his sanity through it all.

Campbell was still taking everything in from the foyer. The place resembled a cross between a hunting lodge, a corporate retreat, and a crypt full of oddities and curios. Once he'd finished marveling over the suit of armor standing guard—she'd heard it used to move quite on its own until Professor Bruttenholm put a stop to it twenty-odd years ago—Cam began craning his neck to peer down hallways.

"Let's show you around, get you introduced—really small staff compared to Fairfield, so it won't take long," she said. "And get you something to eat if you're hungry. But don't get too settled in. We'll be off for Rome in the morning."

"We'll be staying someplace like this there, too?" he asked. Ah, such naïve hope in his voice.

"I haven't seen the place," she confessed, "but don't count on it."

They'd barely gotten into the nickel tour, and were standing in the middle of the library, when Kate interrupted. She said hello to Cam—had first met him weeks before—and pulled Liz back out into the foyer.

"This better be good," Liz said. "I was about to regale him with tales of the phantom librarian."

"Huh?" Kate's face pinched with bemusement. "There's no phantom librarian here."

"I know. I just thought it might keep things lively. What's up?"

"A few minutes ago we got an ID on one of the two John Does from the armored car attack. Fingerprints routed from the Rome *polizia* to the BPRD and from there to the FBI and NCIC database."

"So he was an American?"

"His name was Michael Clark Boddicker." Kate handed her a photo. "Here's the morgue close-up. Obviously, of the two unidentifieds, he's the one with his face still intact."

"Such as it is," Liz said. He'd obviously seen better days.

"He's the one who dropped dead on the street. According to Father Laurenti, he was used up and discarded by a malign entity. The best the autopsy could confirm was heart failure. Now: Here's a fresh printout of a photo we were just sent. It's the last known picture taken of him while he was still alive, about two weeks before he disappeared. It's a mug shot."

Liz nodded. "Yeah, I thought it had that 'I'm-screwed' vibe."

"He's twenty-two years old here. He'd been working on a master's degree in political science at the University of Illinois, and he'd just been arrested in Chicago during a violent anti-war demonstration."

"Gulf War?" Liz asked. Although she couldn't even remember any particularly violent protests staged against that one.

Kate shook her head. "Vietnam."

"No way."

"You say that even after you've seen a series of a guy growing his arm back like a salamander?" Kate laughed. "Boddicker was arrested in the riots at the 1968 Democratic Convention. He was charged with conspiracy, so he wasn't looking at just a slap on the wrist. After his parents made his bail, he apparently left for Europe. Whereabouts unknown ever since."

Liz held the photos, one in each hand, and stared back and forth.

"So he's twenty-two here," she said, and waved the mug shot. Next the morgue shot. "And he's supposed to be fifty here?"

The photos showed the same young man with longish dirty-blond hair, and even accounting for the gauntness of his face and the effects of death, you'd never guess the two photos had been taken more than two or three years apart.

"This is no dead middle-aged man. This is a dead college student who's hit the skids. Those times I ran away from the bureau when I was in my teens? I spent plenty of days and nights with kids who didn't look much better, and there were probably times I didn't either." Liz handed the pictures back. "Where's he supposed to have spent the last twenty-eight years?"

"I don't know," Kate said, "but it looks like a pattern is starting to develop. There's young Mister Boddicker here, there's the antique Luger that Hellboy recovered, there's an entire cult of *hundreds* that disappeared from Weimar-era Berlin. I'd love to get an ID on the other John Doe, just to find out where and *when* he came from. Because it sounds to me like there's a crack somewhere that people and things fell into . . . and now they're starting to fall out again."

CHAPTER 18

Hellboy had never given much thought to retirement, not seriously. For someone like him, or Abe Sapien, life with the BPRD had always seemed like life in the Mafia—something you just didn't retire from. You either got whacked in the normal course of business, or you hung on until you were doddering and senile and only *thought* you were still useful while waiting for natural causes to catch up. Neither option seemed likely to happen to him anytime soon, so even after half a century, retirement was still something that others got to look forward to.

But if he did retire, if such a thing were possible, he supposed he would want to retire to Winograd Heath. It was tucked amid the forests and fields along the sloping western edge of the Cotswolds, and like all the drowsy little villages of Gloucestershire, preserved every storybook image of pastoral Old England that still survived, from the sheep grazing its hills to its overgrown cottages built of limestone the colors of honey and ash.

It was, in his heart, everything that East Bromwich wasn't.

And they knew him here.

Today he had come down from the Midlands, through Worcestershire, and bypassed the usual benevolent haunts that never failed to put his mind right during one of his English sojourns—streamside at the old mill, fireside at the Badger's Claw Pub—and headed straight for the vicarage.

For twelve years they'd known him here. But Father Simon knew him best of all.

"Well . . . ! By the pricking of my thumbs," he first said upon opening the vicarage door, "something clumsy this way comes."

"Nice to see you too," Hellboy said. "Been working on that one long?"

It had been work—what else?—that first brought him here: the last appearance of Springheel Jack, the preternaturally acrobatic assailant who always seemed to arrive out of nowhere to terrorize some local populace. He'd been at it since early Victorian times, mostly in London, and eventually elsewhere toward the end of Jack's first fifty years, after which his sprees became more rare, sometimes with decades in between. Always to return, though . . . modern times, but still the same old Springheel Jack, ugly as sin with breath like blue flame, and bounding between streets and rooftops, and roof to roof, with the ease of children playing hopscotch. He never killed, just liked to claw and scratch, rip and tear—women and their clothes, mostly—before bounding off again.

Bad for the tourist trade, though, by the time he turned up in the Cotswolds during the summer of 1984, and Hellboy figured he'd probably come to the region for the same reasons anyone did: felt like old times here. When Jack sprang into Winograd Heath, Hellboy was already waiting . . . the first time in nearly 150 years of assaults and getaways that Jack had had to contend with a foe that could keep up with him. After an energetic chase that lasted less than half an hour, Hellboy had him bagged.

Once caught, Jack lapsed into a kind of coma from which he'd never awakened. They still had him back in Fairfield, warehoused in the sub-basements along with the talking mummies and other peculiarities. As near as anyone could tell, he was the malformed offspring of a female imp and an incubus.

Although the job had been done to near-universal gratitude, it had nonetheless earned Hellboy, if not enemies, at least a handful of grumbling critics loath to forgive his tactics. While Springheel Jack was lightfooted enough on the rooftops, Hellboy carried four times the mass. His landings had played havoc with a row of picturesque thatched roofs during the rainiest summer in a decade. And good thatchers were booked months, even years, in advance, even for the rich who settled here and paid handsomely to preserve the illusion of the past.

Something clumsy this way comes . . .

The Reverend Simon Finch had always gotten a perversely good chuckle out of the collateral damage; seemed unlikely to ever let him live it down.

Then he got serious, putting a hand to his chin as he stared from the doorway.

"You look to either be on your way to East Bromwich again, or you've just come from there," he said. "Shall I get my jacket, or do you want to come in?"

"I was there early this afternoon . . . and yeah, let's go for a walk."

Easier on Mrs. Finch, he figured. Lovely woman, but he always got the idea she worried he was going to demolish her furniture.

The vicarage was in the shadow of St. Mark's, the Anglican parish church, a gray monolith with a tall squared-faced Norman bell tower made friendlier by the carpet of green ivy growing from bottom to top. They automatically steered down the lane toward it as the daylight seeped from the sky.

Small talk for awhile—Father Simon was always a good one to expound upon various single malts from around the isles, and while Hellboy wasn't as particular when he felt like downing a shot, he found it easy enough to warm to the enthusiasms of a whisky connoisseur.

Then, as they stood on the road and he watched the last of the sun send a final flare through St. Mark's stained glass and suffuse the air with a butterscotch light, he got into it. Told Father Simon everything, from the attack on the Vatican to the business with the armored car, from the sinking of the *Calista* to his unexpected return to Dreich Midden. Told him about the Masada Scroll at the center of it all.

Father Simon didn't interrupt, didn't question. He had the patience of a man who'd been around long enough to earn it the only way you can: by letting life unfold at its own pace. He was just past sixty, Hellboy thought, or maybe just shy of it, a slender man with thick white hair and a jawline that was only now starting to soften.

"I'm having some real problems with this one," Hellboy finally said. "Most of the time I go into a situation and it's so black and white. Like twelve years ago. Springheel Jack comes to town, doing what he always does. You can't let a thing like that go on. End of debate. It's simple, it's clear, it's . . ."

"A no-brainer, I believe, is the term you're looking for."

"Exactly."

"And this one isn't."

They started to walk again—the stained glass light show was over—strolling further down the lane as glass-walled cages in the row of lampposts began to wink on.

"First thing that's been bothering me is the scroll itself," Hellboy said. "When I went into this, I went in knowing that even the Vatican couldn't say if it's genuine or not. If it's not genuine, though, why am I still caught between Heaven and Hell over it? It's drawn the attention of both sides. One side wants to destroy it. The other side kept trying to take it until they got it. Doesn't seem to me like either side would be this interested in it if it wasn't authentic."

Simon nodded. "A reasonable conclusion."

"But if it *is* genuine," Hellboy went on, "that's even worse. Because what are they still fighting for? What's the point of all this if . . . if the entire basis for the Church has been repudiated by the man it's based on."

Simon's eyebrows creaked upward and he eased out a sigh. "That's a tough one. Are you sure you shouldn't be talking to one of your Vatican pals instead of a bloke like me out here in the sticks?"

"My Vatican pals have their own agenda. You, you've got no dog in this fight."

"Well, I do wear the dog *collar* on Sundays and random occasions the rest of the week."

But they both knew what he meant. Hellboy was quite

certain that the whole creed, Anglican and Roman and Protestant alike, could collapse tomorrow and it wouldn't make a bit of difference to Father Simon. He would go on as though nothing had changed. He'd put on his collar when appropriate, he'd say Mass for whoever straggled into the pews, he'd sit for hours at a deathbed. He'd sing—rarely on key—and he would pray. Like always. It was who and what he was. *My religion is kindness,* the Dalai Lama had said, and Father Simon probably could've said it too.

"I don't believe it matters to the world and the forces it's caught between," he finally said, "whether the scroll is genuine or not."

"You're kidding, right?"

"No. As long as it's not an outright fraud or hoax . . . and if I heard you right, that's not an issue, is it?"

"It's first century, all right. There's no question about that."

"Then I would say it's immaterial whether or not it's genuine or simply a work of . . . early creative allegory, let's call it. As long as there's room for doubt, then there's room to exploit that. So its power doesn't reside in whose hand really put the ink to it. Its true power lies in what human beings—and *other* beings—choose to make of it. Things like this, they call them bombshells? Well, it all depends on where the bomb is dropped, doesn't it?"

Moloch as bombardier—not a prospect he liked to consider.

Father Simon clapped him on the shoulder. "The *first* thing bothering you, you said. What else?"

"The seraphim. They're supposed to be the good guys, aren't they? On the side of *ultimate* good? Not from what

I've seen, they're not. Priceless pieces of history, innocent lives . . . they incinerated everything with no more thought"—he sniffed the air, the autumn scent that came wafting in from one of the nearby homes—"no more thought than you'd give to burning a pile of leaves. Their tactics don't seem any different from the other side. Their body count's about even so far. Which doesn't say much for their boss, does it?"

"Got the toughie out of the way first, good for you." Simon pointed straight at him. "You're your own best answer to that one."

"How's that?"

"You're the greatest illustration of free will that I've ever seen, or ever expect to. Even if you don't know everything about yourself, or what you were intended to be . . . still, you were, by every indication, conceived in evil, then delivered in evil, by evil men with evil intents . . . and yet you've chosen the side of good."

Hellboy shrugged. "Hey, I was *raised* by the good guys."

"True enough. But when you got old enough to look inside, like any adolescent, and ask some hard questions, you still had to have made a conscious choice to defy the obvious about yourself and instead live in accordance with the way you were raised. Really, now, what could you have been afraid of if you hadn't—a spanking? They'd take your allowance away? Not snatch it back out of *that* hand, they wouldn't."

Hellboy knew exactly what he'd been afraid of: disappointing those who'd taken him in, who'd come to mean something to him over the years. Who he'd come to love, and who'd found something in him worth loving. Which pretty much proved Father Simon's point, even if he hadn't said it outright: that there was a human conscience underneath that red hide.

"So if *you* were able to make that kind of choice, and be right," Simon went on, "is it any less possible that angels could exercise free will and be wrong?"

"Stands to reason that they could, yeah. But . . ." And this just kept going, didn't it? The vicious circle at the heart of an imperfect world. "That puts God in an awfully remote position."

"Aww, and just look what you've done now. You've put us back over into the tough ones again, haven't you?"

They'd come to a curve in the lane, where a pair of yew trees flanked the road, their huge runneled trunks purple in the twilight, their branches meeting overhead to form a green archway. Father Simon stared at the left one, and when Hellboy took a closer look, he thought he saw the ghost of an old scar in the dense bark.

"Two lads hop in a car with a sackful of lagers and a few packets of crisps, and a couple of hours later, that's where the ride ends." Simon pointed at the mar on the tree. "Both mothers together at the hospital, and we're all of us waiting for the news. Then it comes, and what am I supposed to do then? Tell them 'God saved your son, but not yours'? How do you comfort anyone with words like that when His intercession seems so random? There's always the old fallback of God working in mysterious ways, but there are so many times when that's no more help than a slap in the face." Simon shook his head. "The hardest thing I have to do is decide when to give God credit for something and when not to. Because if you credit Him for making the oaks and ivy in all their beauty, and that sunset we were just now privileged to witness, then you have to give Him equal acclaim for the bubonic plague."

"You think too much for a priest, you know that?"

"Curse of my race, us tweedy Anglos," Simon confessed. "So the best I've been able to sort it all out to my satisfaction is that because chaos and destruction seem to be such an intrinsic part of the system, then God must have an unshakable faith that renewal will always follow in their wake. That's the good news, that we're worthy of that kind of faith. The bad news is that it punts the challenge down to us to minimize the destruction, and keep it from feeding on itself. To be there when it's time to build again."

Until the next violent rampage? Hellboy wondered. Until the next crashing wave, the next upheaval of the earth, or madman with a war machine?

Yeah. Until then.

And the next one, and the one after that.

It was the only way to beat Heaven at its unfathomable games.

Father Simon turned and looked him in the eye. "I don't know if God made you. I suspect not. But you still seem to fit right into His plan . . . and in such a way as to leave me feeling awfully hopeful for the way it all ends."

And again, Hellboy remembered why he always liked coming to England to clear his head.

CHAPTER 19

From the sun-dappled Cotswolds to a rain-soaked Glasgow slum . . .

What a difference a weekend could make.

With no trace of dawn in the sky yet, Hellboy and Abe bailed from the car that had delivered them from the airport, sprinted half a block along a row of battened-down shopfronts, and clambered into the back of the unmarked van. Quick hellos all around with the three-agent team pulling surveillance duty—two Scots and a British medium from just over the border in Northumberland, with scarcely a decipherable accent among them.

"Anything happen since I talked to you from the plane?" Hellboy asked.

"No' a move in the four hours we been here," one of the two Scots answered, the male of the pair. Muir, his name, and he kept watch on a pair of monitors. One screen showed the feed from a small roof-mounted camera aimed at the target's front door, the other a remote signal from a camera that appeared to be secured in an alley and trained on the exit.

"But there's *something* in there . . . ?" Hellboy said. "Not just some cranked-up loser with an antisocial attitude."

"Oh, aye." Ormston, the Brit, gave a disgusted nod and wrapped both hands tight around a mug of coffee poured fresh from one of several thermos bottles. "And the foulest thing it is that I've ever sensed from a block away."

"You got a photo on the guy yet?"

Kirsten, the other Scot on the team, said they did. She slid it from an envelope and handed it over while trying to tame her reddish hair, turned by the humidity into a bumper crop that exploded from beneath her watch cap.

Hellboy gave it a look, saw a dark-haired man in his mid-thirties with a broad, open face that might've been called friendly if not for his eyes, as cold and narrow as archers' slits in a stone tower. He handed it to Abe.

"Could that be the main guy you saw on the island the other night?"

Abe held it for a long study while rain hammered the van's roof like hailstones. Actually, they could all stare at the photo. The back of the van would have been close quarters for three, and with five now—particularly with someone of Hellboy's size—it was claustrophobic, everybody bumping knees and feeling the cloying wet air of rising body heat.

Ormston gave a suspicious sniff. "Swear I can smell roast monkey-nuts."

Hellboy grimaced. "That'd be me."

"You should've smelled him a few nights ago," Abe said, then gave the photo back to Kirsten. "Could be, yes. But 'could be' and 'was' are two different things. Sixty paces in rain and lightning . . . that was the closest look I ever had."

The man's name was Calum Gilmour, and he'd surfaced during the BPRD's last few days of database frenzy—cross-referencing names, known occult registries, odd police reports . . . anything that could be triangulated into a plausible pattern that would give them someplace to begin.

They'd already been checking leads since Friday night, around the time that he would've been having his impromptu consultation with Father Simon. But this one was made up of component bits that, when reviewed together, sent up a red flare.

Gilmour had, in the past few months, entertained at least two visits from the police following up on neighbors' complaints about a smoky smell and emanation from his apartment. Nothing came of either visit; the officers had given the place a look-see and could find nothing that would cause whatever his neighbors were blaming on him. A total non-event on the surface, but in context, and the way Hellboy's own eyes had been fooled on Dreich Midden, plus Kate's theory about a glamour being used against the armored car crew, Hellboy had to wonder if the police hadn't missed something right under their noses because they honestly couldn't see it.

Worse, the area in a three-mile radius around his home had, in that same period, experienced a slight increase in the number of children reported missing. Maybe a statistical blip, but . . . look at the big picture.

Calum Gilmour was already on the BPRD's watch-list, albeit at the lowest, most plebian classification. He had, four years ago, served a jail term of several months for a failed attempt at burglarizing a rare books dealer in Edinburgh. Just one volume, that's all he was after: Ernst Schweiger's *Things Better Forgotten*.

Word went north out of Cornwall, and in the follow-up drive-by, Ormston, the medium, had gotten such a hit off

Gilmour's place that he'd doubled over in nausea that still hadn't entirely passed.

Something seriously wrong was going on behind that door.

"What's the layout like, anybody know?" Hellboy asked.

"A basemen' fla', but iss a big'n, doon the whole lef' side o' the buildin'," Kirsten said. "No way o' seein' in. I coun' three skinny wee garden windows, but I tried to hae a keek inside earlier and couldnae. He's go' 'em all blocked o'er."

Hellboy blinked. "I'll take that as a no."

"Everything that pointed us here, it could still be coincidence," Abe said. "I'd feel better if we had one totally solid thing to go on before we start kicking down doors."

"Like his membership card from Campus Crusade for Moloch?" Hellboy said. "It's hardly ever that clear when we're talking about citizens."

He decided he was going in alone. The others could act as backup in case anything tried to slip out ahead of or behind him. He sent Abe off with Muir to cover the basement flat's rear entrance, had Kirsten and Ormston stay put in the van and continue monitoring the front. He watched the second screen until, in grainy black and white, he saw the pair of them flash past the camera, Muir pointing it out and Abe lifting a single finger: *One more minute to get into position.*

Hellboy watched the time tick down on the van's clock, then heaved himself out the back of the van. Nothing else was moving out here other than the downpour—it was raining hard enough to drown even Abe—and he paused for a better look around. Tenements and row houses, mostly, their gray walls shedding bricks that would slowly work their way loose like rotting teeth, to fall in the middle of the night.

He splashed across the street and down the block; could hear the muffled peal of a distant church bell calling whatever brave souls might care to venture out for early Sunday Mass. Normally he enjoyed the sound, but this morning it sounded funereal and forlorn, an afterthought in a world where God and Man alike had forgotten one another. Dawn seemed to be taking forever to get here, too—just latitude, lateness of the year, and the clouds, he knew, but this dismal place could use some light this morning.

He swung around an iron railing and down a three-quarter flight of stairs to the doorway of Calum Gilmour's basement flat. Beneath an old coat of green paint that was peeling away in filmy strips, the door looked thick and sturdy, as though it might stand up to the first blow from a police battering ram.

Not so, his right hand.

He drew his revolver, a replacement for the one lost to the Leviathan, fetched from the armory in the Cornwall safehouse. A flashlight next—it looked dark in there. He pushed the fractured door aside and stepped in, slid through a tight entry hall that doglegged to the left.

Hallway by hallway, room by room . . . the maze unfolded around him, a dank burrow that looked as if years of moisture and decay had taken hold all at once. The doors were half-sealed, stuck in warped frames. Wallpaper crawled with new patterns of fungus and mold, and wept trickles of water from ceiling to floor. Elsewhere, clotted plaster had sloughed away like wet scabs to reveal the rotting boards inside the walls. When he pinched one with his fingers, it came away in splinters and pulp.

And the farther back he went, the more the place seemed to flicker around him. It was not light on the walls, but the walls themselves, and the floors, the dilapidated furnishings—all of it putrefying one instant, then a feeble pulse of cleanliness and order, like an acetate overlay in a book. A glamour, he thought, coming apart as if the spell's connection to its power source were quickly eroding, weakened but struggling to maintain its illusion.

It could fool no one now . . . and with him aware of the trick, it seemed to diminish all the more.

He estimated that he had to be getting close to the rear of the flat when he wrenched open another bloated door and came upon the bathroom. Or what had once been the bathroom. The floor was a deathtrap here, its tiles slick with mildew, and its walls had been slathered with unknown substances to create a repeating pattern of symbols as old as Solomon. And when he shined the flashlight inside the hulking clawfoot tub, he saw what must have been the source of that last irate report of smoke.

The blackened tangle of small limbs, the charcoal nubs that would've once been fingers . . . Hellboy had to shut his eyes for long moments and quell the boiling of his blood. He would smash nothing. He would not bellow loud enough to drown out church bells and rain. No, this was a rage better channeled toward its most fitting end . . . and the impulses passed like a seizure.

Onward, through the rest of this fetid cistern.

The main room was just beyond, and here he found them: three bodies, graylit by the strobing glow of a television that managed to still work in the swampy air, even if it showed nothing but static. The pair from the night on Dreich Midden, and some unknown assistant? For now, as good a guess as any. They appeared quite dead, the two smaller men for sure.

One sat at rigid attention in a spot of open floor space, his head tipped upward and back as he seemed to stare at the yard's length of two-inch copper pipe protruding from his mouth. From the look of things, the pipe hadn't entered there; this was only the point of exit.

The other was a wiry fellow, slumped to one side of a sofa that smelled of rodents that now seemed to be nowhere around; even vermin were smarter than people sometimes. Something was terribly wrong with his fingers—stretched and lengthened, hardened and multiplied, like slivers of blue steel and bone. The fingers of Surgat, to whom locks were child's play . . . at least as Hellboy had seen them the other night. One hand lay palm-up at the man's side. He'd plunged the other into his throat, ramming the handful of spikes and needles in up to the malformed knuckles.

His eyes still shone with a hideous rapture.

Hellboy knew, even before he retraced his steps for a more careful search, that the case and cuff removed from his wrist were no longer here, if they'd even made it this far.

He took a moment to radio the team outside and tell them to stand down. That nothing was coming out of this place unless it was dragged or carried.

Back to the main room then, where he took a closer look at the third body. This was Calum Gilmour, no mistaking it. Wreathed in the odors of sepsis and infection, he leaned against a wall, propped into the corner atop a bloodied heap of newspapers and magazines that had been molded by seepage into a fused mound, a paper throne.

Used up, thrown away by the devils they had courted . . . he felt no pity for either of these two from the island, got no sense that the third man was in any way deserving of pity either. Maybe they hadn't known where it would lead, but they had wanted this all the same. They'd chosen, and badly.

He swept the flashlight from body to body, and when he looked at Gilmour again, saw that the eyes that had been closed moments before were now open. He shined the light directly into them and watched the pupils constrict.

Behind him, the TV died a sudden, silent death, depriving the room of its sickly gray flicker. What the flashlight didn't reveal, he could no longer see. The rest was eaten by shadow.

Gilmour's jaw dropped, strained, and after a creak of air and phlegm, out poured a guttural inundation of words never meant for human ears to hear, much less throats to speak. Calum Gilmour's throat, but not his words. Not anymore.

Hellboy wasn't having it. "You got something to say to me, say it in a language I understand."

The voice abused the throat through a series of variations, as though cycling through a sequence of dialects. Just taunting him now, a babble of blasphemies, until he huffed what sounded like a sigh of resignation. Finally:

"English, if it must be. It holds few words for what is truly important, but if they only fall on ears that refuse to hear . . ." The voice was still wrong, somehow, as though the vocal cords had been stretched and frayed beyond repair. "Have you forgotten the tongues of home, the barbarous tongues?"

"Anything that matters, I can remember that just fine."

Gilmour's eyes, or the eyes *behind* them, looked him up and down with open disdain, the poisonous gaze lingering on the stumps upon his forehead. "You seem to have forgotten yourself. If it is a reminder you need, then it is a reminder I should give you . . ."

The neck began to twist, the head to tremble, the teeth to grind in their sockets. Gilmour's mouth—although it was hard to regard it as *his* anymore—began to stretch wide, pulled down at the corners as if by hooks and wires. The eyes, like slits already, narrowed further, showing only the whites as the forehead began to break a river of sweat . . . and one to a side, protrusions began to form in the skin. They grew, thickened, lengthened, the sharp points beneath stretching the thin skin of the forehead but never breaking through, as inch by slow inch, the pair of fledgling horns sprouted from the skull. Further and further, until at last the skin, pulled taut and shiny red, began to darken, atrophying over the fresh bone into a substance like keratin and bristled hair.

"Does it remind you of anyone?" it asked.

"I may look like one of yours," Hellboy said, "but the resemblance ends there."

"Now you lie to yourself. Hell is more than skin deep." Upon its makeshift throne, the Moloch twisted as if in discomfort. Grunting, it reached around to dig into ribs, spine, something. It brought its hand back around and, with casual interest, examined the palmful of blood and suppurating tissue before slinging it spattering to the floor. "You shot me in the back. Was that an act of Christian mercy? Was it even an act of heroism?"

"You turned your back to the bullet." Hellboy felt his teeth grit. "I'd've shot you in the face if you hadn't been running away."

"Did I offend you?" The Moloch feigned an ugly parody of surprise. "That helpless red carcass on the ground that gave up his prizes so easily . . . I thought he had no more fight left in him. He struggled so weakly under this"—the Moloch jerked one leg up and peered at the boot it wore before letting it thud back to the floor—"this small bony foot I borrowed."

Hellboy decided to quit rising to the bait. "The scroll . . . why go to all that trouble to take it? You don't strike me as much of a reader."

It ignored him, tipping its head upward to sniff the air with nostrils gone grotesque, seeming to pull in one last whiff of ambrosia. Leaning in the direction of the bathroom turned charnel house.

"The fires have gone out here," it said, sounding almost wistful. "But there are others . . . always others." Now it craned its head toward the papered-over window, the streets beyond. "Can you hear it? The weeping of mothers and the splashing of their tears? They were never told their children's fate, but in their dreams they know . . ."

"*The scroll,*" Hellboy tried again. "What's it mean to you?" Because if he didn't remain focused on the job, he'd give in to temptation and tear this meat-puppet apart, lose whatever tenuous connection he had with the force behind it—probably what it wanted, another taunt. "You don't gain anything by keeping the scroll a secret. Why not let the Church have it, make it public?"

Now he had its attention. The Moloch seemed to entertain itself by pretending to muse things over.

"In *our* time and way. Not theirs," it said. Then it fixed him with its eyes, so much less than human now. "Your blindness does you shame. Do you truly not see that even as you try and fail to correct this situation, it is of your own making?"

His hand itched—his *right* hand. It had never itched before, not that he could remember. Had never wanted so badly to crush words, and the mouth that formed them.

"You belong to two worlds—the world of weakness and squalor I see before these eyes, and, though you deny it, the world of black flame behind them. You deny this because you forget you exist to open the doorway between them, so the world where you now walk may be perfected." With Gilmour's eyes, it tried a paternal look, all wisdom and good sense. "That doorway has never been closer. If I were to tell you where to find it, and how to open it, you could save so many millions of lives."

Hellboy almost laughed. But not here. "Whenever you guys start talking about doorways, they're always something that's better off staying shut."

"There are other ways of opening the door. And it *will* open. What you must do, and do soon, is decide how you will be greeted by what comes through." It leveled a warning gaze at him. "Never think yourself such a favored son that if found to be obsolete, you could not be cast into Oblivion as Hell's own Judas."

Hellboy leaned in close, closer, as if they shared secrets.

What this thing would not give him he realized he still might be able to take.

"Oblivion, yeah? How's the décor there?" he asked. "Can I get a little something to hang on my wall?"

He grabbed the left horn and ripped it from the Moloch's head. It came away with a thick cracking sound, in splinters and blackened blood. After a brief spasm—right or wrong, Hellboy wanted to think it a reaction of outrage—the demon retreated from the body, leaving only the man behind.

And Gilmour breathed. Just not very well.

Stained crimson with burst capillaries, his eyes roved, struggling to see beyond the flashlight's beam that must have seared like the noonday sun. He seemed to be taking stock of where he was. If he was yet in the Hell he must have been promised.

No, he seemed to realize, he wasn't. Worse. Much worse.

". . . what year is it . . . ?" he asked in his ruined voice.

Hellboy told him nothing, content to wait and bear witness, as long as it took, until Gilmour carried the question with him to the Hell he deserved.

CHAPTER 20

Auburn-haired woman in a glassless window, green shutters thrown wide against burnt-orange plaster—Liz had been sitting there so long that she had to figure anyone watching would think she was contemplating a jump. Sorry to disappoint. Even if she were so inclined, there were more efficient ways of offing yourself than flinging your bod from a third-floor window. At best, from this one, you'd only smash your legs on the flat-topped cobblestones of the street.

And why spoil such a perfectly fine afternoon, anyway.

How good was it? It had been hours since she'd felt much of an urge to fire up a cigarette. That good.

Liz had felt cheated on her brief stay in Rome ten days ago. A pop-in under the cover of darkness and a tumultuous ride in an armored car—that was no way to see the Eternal City. She still wasn't seeing much of it, but this would do. This would do just fine.

She and Campbell had come to a bustling neighborhood called the Borgo, in the shadow of the Vatican's eastern walls. Since the sixth century this place had catered to the needs and wants of pilgrims, priests, and penitents alike, as well as plain old secular travelers—meals and

241

lodging and souvenirs of all sizes, and always cheaper than what was charged by the merchants in St. Peter's Square.

The BPRD had quietly maintained a six-room apartment here since the first year of its founding . . . one of the easiest arrangements the bureau had ever finagled. The liberation of Rome in June of 1944—the German army retreating to the north while the Allies marched in from the south—had earned the U.S. government, even its youngest agency, tremendous capital with a populace elated to see the Nazis leave. Credit the young Trevor Bruttenholm with having the foresight to press for a low-key base that not even the Vatican was to know about.

Now that she was here, Liz had to wonder if a part of him hadn't wanted the place as a quaint little getaway spot, like a time-share condo that he'd get to use year-round. She could understand, and blessed him for it, though he was two years in the grave. Even now it felt like a bequeathal, the kind of place into which she would love to disappear and live on the cheap, spending her money mostly on coffee and oil paints; pick the sunniest room and set up an easel and see if anything that hit the canvas was worth keeping.

Although if she were going to be playing house this way with a man twelve years her junior, she would want it to be later in life, when she could *really* count it as an accomplishment.

"When's the guy going to be here, again?" Campbell asked from the kitchen, where he was getting a bottle of mineral water.

"No quicker than he was since the last time you asked," Liz said.

Antsy—who could blame him? The first time he'd be proving himself to the bureau for real, an ocean away from its cloistered walls.

Ever since they'd gotten here yesterday afternoon, she'd kept finding excuses to leave, coming back after each excursion with bread or wine, cheese or olives. Nothing to do with Campbell's company—she just loved wandering in the Borgo. Church bells pealed near and far, and on the edges, there was even something fun about watching the smelly tour buses, almost as plentiful as the pigeons, forced to contend with the chaotic, random way that modern-day Romans had of parking their cars.

But inside, in the heart of the place, where there was no such distinction as street and sidewalk . . . that's where the life was. You walked pathways and touched walls, both bright and somber, that had been walked and touched by the feet and hands of the Renaissance. On a sunny day like today, laundry dried overhead like the flags of a hundred nations, while you dodged soccer balls and motor scooters and were wise to regard them as equal dangers, and passed benches where old men sat and smoked and rued the modern age, as old men did everywhere she'd ever been. It was village life, in the middle of one of the world's oldest cities.

"You want a water?" Cam asked.

"No thanks. I've got one."

"How about an apricot? These are the best apricots I've ever had in my life."

"No, I'm good. And no bread right now either," she told him, and finally turned from the window. "Why don't you spit out what's *really* on your mind?"

He looked flustered at having been found so transparent, but when she'd first started working with him, it hadn't taken long to catch onto the pattern of his evasions, his deflections, his stalling tactics. Her own, back in the day? Or a skill that she'd honed with normal people uncomfortable around her, subsurface freak that she was? Maybe a bit of both.

"I was talking to somebody at HQ after you left," he said. "I had a few days to myself there, you know, not much to work on if I didn't feel like it . . ."

"Better watch that. An idle hand is the devil's workshop." Amputee humor; he quite liked it most of the time.

"It's just that you kept telling me how if I worked hard and applied myself to doing my visualizations and keeping a clear head that I could get a handle on my life, on my *gift*"—he spat the word with no little irony—"on everything. You said that if I'd let it, the BPRD could be my salvation."

"That's really the word I used, huh?" Liz thought she knew where this was going. Not that she'd seen it coming, but come to think of it, it would be due anytime now, Campbell away from Fairfield just about long enough for the first-time excitement to wear off and let him get back to whatever fresh misgivings he'd been nursing.

"Yeah. Salvation. That was definitely the word."

He was pacing the hardwood floor, looking angular and lost inside ancient jeans ripped through at the knee and a sweatshirt under horse-blanket flannel that flapped around his frame like a sail. The look out of Seattle that you just knew would start dying not long after Kurt Cobain had a couple of years ago, although you had to figure that the ripple effect would've been slow in getting to Nebraska. She found it endearing on him, actually.

"And you no longer believe that's true?" she asked.

"I don't know. You tell me. If it's such a salvation, then why have you left the bureau *twelve times?*"

Her first impulse was to tell him, as diplomatically as possible, that it was none of his damned business. But she bit down that one, and was glad of it. It wouldn't help a thing, and she supposed that there was no way this discovery wouldn't make her look like a hypocrite.

"Some of those bailouts, you can write them off to youthful indiscretion," she said. "I really was a kid when I first came to the bureau. Much younger than you are. I still hadn't even had my first fit of self-righteous teenage angst. I've lost my family and now I'm around all these strangers telling me what to do and trying to figure out what makes me tick? It would've been weird if I *hadn't* run away."

She popped her head out the window for another glance up and down the street. Still clear, looked like. If their visitor wasn't here in another hour, okay, maybe then it would be time to worry.

Liz pressed her hands together and frowned at them a moment, looking for the words, the *right* words.

"I don't think there's anything that describes life at the bureau any better than *family.* That's what we have there, for better or worse . . . usually for the better. I know there are lots of places a person can work where they'll tell you you're joining a family, and I suppose at some of them that's the truth, but in most of them, it's just another con job. But in the core of the bureau, it's no lie. That's what we have because we're all we've got, really.

"Hellboy, he's the big brother who's always watching out for everyone," she went on. "Abe's the cousin from that branch of the family that you're not too sure about. Kate, she's the cool aunt who'll level with you about the world in a way your parents would never dream of. And Professor Bruttenholm . . ." This was the only part that had the power to make her eyes burn, her throat catch. "Well, you missed a gem there. He was the father, or maybe the grandfather, who knew more than you thought any one person could, and who would never give up believing in your highest potential even when you'd let him down."

"I wish I could've met him," Cam said, sounding painfully sincere. He had to have heard talk about the Professor around Fairfield, *had to*, and plenty of it.

"Maybe you can, in a way." The solution was so obvious, she couldn't believe she hadn't thought of it until now. "We've all got things that belonged to him, things that he cherished. I think it'd be a good idea, after we all get back, to round them up and let you spend some time with them. With *him*."

"I'd like that," Campbell said. Then looked at her with raised eyebrows and expectation: *Your turn.*

"Right. Family. Me." Stalling tactics and evasion? Perish the thought. "I guess I'm the sister who, no matter how much she may love the rest of her family, still can't help thinking there's something better for her out there. So she has to go off and have a look, or . . ."

Great, speaking about herself in the third person now. How's that for deflection?

". . . or I'll go crazy thinking I'm missing out on something that's probably not even there for me."

Judging by the sagging appearance of his face, that last admission hadn't really helped the cause.

"Look," she said, "we've got some overlap, you and I. But some fundamental differences, too. I carry something around inside me that can hurt people, no matter how much I might love them. It's been a long time since I've had an accident, but it's there. And every so often, I've gotten this idea in my head that I can leave it behind. I don't really believe that, of course, I just act like it's true.

"You, though . . . what gradually consumed you until you almost let it kill you . . . you can impose restrictions on that in a way I never could with mine. As long as you're in a place where you can control your environment and the objects in it, then you can keep the bad shit at arm's length. Literally. You can *do* that at the bureau. Now, it's not free. They'll need your help sometimes, like we do now—hey, they'll demand it sometimes—and yeah, there'll be bad shit involved. That's the nature of the beast. But you won't be facing it alone. I *will* be there to catch you if you fall, I've always promised you that. So the BPRD . . . maybe it won't be your salvation, because that's something you'll have to find in yourself. But it *can* be your sanctuary. And that, I guarantee you."

Spoken as one who'd come crawling back to sanctuary a dozen times—was that good or bad? She didn't know, but she'd at least spoken from the heart.

"So . . . are we okay here?" she asked.

"Yeah, we're good." He shoved back the sleeves of his sweatshirt and flannel and, with a grin, held out the knobby stump of his left arm. More amputee humor. "Shake on it?"

Half an hour later she noticed Father Artaud coming up the street. The sight of a man in a black cassock riding a bicycle—she'd seen it at least a dozen times just since yesterday and it never looked any less ungainly. As Artaud dismounted, she leaned out to watch him chain the bike to a wrought iron railing on the front of the building.

"I see that!" she called down; startled, he looked up as if expecting to see the finger of God. "What kind of message does that send about your faith in your fellow man?"

As usual, he seemed to have no idea how to answer her, and she rather liked the feeling, however fleeting, of having that effect on a man. The fact that it was a priest, though . . . she couldn't decide if the whole business was playful, irreverent, or just plain pathetic on her part.

After he'd jogged up the four flights of stairs—scarcely breathing harder, okay, impressive—she got Rogier a water and introduced him to Campbell, who, she was relieved to see, refrained from offering to shake with his stump this time. Refrained from offering to shake at all, she noticed, but he was subtle about it, standing a couple of feet out of reach behind the two-sided kitchen counter. Not all of his coping skills had come from the bureau. He'd brought a few with him.

Rogier unburdened himself of a bag that he'd carried

looped over his shoulder and across his chest. He set it on the amber tiles of the countertop and spread out its contents: a ring, an ornate pen that looked made of walnut, a missal, several more items.

"Wow, good job," Liz said. "You know, if this priest thing doesn't work out, you could have a solid career as a pickpocket."

"Please . . ." He looked as though he needed an antacid. "I don't feel good about this, not a bit."

"You'll be returning them on the sly, so I think you'll be in the clear. I'm pretty sure the commandment is 'Thou shalt not steal,' not 'Thou shalt not borrow without permission,'" Liz said. "So . . . let's see if we can't find out who's been breaking 'Thou shalt not kill.'"

It was Hellboy's idea, and a calculated risk, but his gut feeling was that among all those they had dealt with, Father Artaud was the one who kept the best interests of the Masada Scroll closest to his heart. That the Belgian archivist cherished it first and foremost as an artifact that had survived two millennia, not what it might represent between opposing factions.

Hellboy trusted Artaud in a way that he wasn't now prepared to trust the others who'd been instrumental in arranging for the scroll's departure from Rome. Not that they were all corrupt, but because it appeared that one among them was not what he appeared to be. One of them was in league with forces that, rather than see the scroll destroyed, would steal it for their own purposes.

So who was it?

For Hellboy, the quickest way to the heart of this mystery was Campbell Holt. And for someone on the inside they trusted to surreptitiously round up a few personal items from the rest of the inner circle.

"However you want to do this, it's your call," she told Cam. "We're not in the blue room anymore."

"Can't spend my whole life in the blue room, can I?" He puffed out a tense sigh and stepped from behind the kitchen counter.

Liz pointed at the scattering of purloined items. "You want to take them into one of the other rooms? Or do you want the two of us to leave you alone, or . . ."

He gave the main room a once-over and decided he wanted to stay out here. Made sense. This was where they'd spent the bulk of their time, around the fireplace and the old plush furniture, most of which had seen better days but had a homey feel. He'd grown comfortable here. His only request was to pull the windows' shutters to, and the glass down, to minimize distractions from outside.

With that done, Cam settled into the biggest chair. "Just bring them to me one at a time, and I'd rather you not tell me anything about who they belong to."

"The privacy, the intrusion . . ." Rogier still seemed queasy about moral issues. "Does this process of yours reveal . . . intimate details? Things that deserve to remain personal?"

"What, you mean like how many times a day a guy might beat off?" Cam said, and she wanted to smack him. "Sorry, what's there is there."

He must have noticed the look on her face, because Cam immediately looked as though he realized this was no time to cop an attitude.

"Umm, look . . . if it makes you feel any better," he told Rogier, trying for a hasty salvage, "what I'm looking for, if it's here at all, if the guy has this whole other side to his life that none of the rest of you knows about, it should give off a pretty big hit. Whatever else is there . . . if it doesn't look and feel like the big sharp needle, I throw it back in the haystack, because it doesn't matter."

Well done, she told him with a discreet smile and tip of her head. *Nice save.* Then a reversion to stern mentor: *Now don't ever ever ever do that again.*

She brought him the ring first, silver-banded with a black stone in the middle—onyx, maybe—that was engraved with a red cross. He curled his fingers around it and let his head drift toward his chest, the usual pose he went into when it was time to work. She'd never been able to discern whether it came from concentration, or was an unconscious defensive posture he'd evolved, but didn't want to ask. It didn't seem worth calling attention to. When it came to psychics, in her experience, the least little thing that made someone self-conscious could contaminate the reading, throw it off.

"This guy could stand to lose some weight. I'm not kidding . . ." Campbell said.

Liz gave Rogier a sideways glance.

"Archbishop Bellini," he whispered with a grin. "True, he could."

". . . but he's clean." Campbell opened his eyes and returned the ring directly to Rogier. "Seriously. Have a word, dude. This guy's having chest pains and thinking he can ignore them forever, and they're probably not going to stay minor much longer."

Next she gave Campbell a white glove; it looked like the kind of dress glove a drum major might wear. She leaned in close to Rogier.

"You didn't," she whispered. "One of the, what are they called . . . ?"

"The Swiss Guard?" he said. "Yes."

"Oh, you *are* good."

Campbell held the glove crumpled in his hand for a moment longer, then gave it back with a shake of his head and a snicker, as if to ask how anyone could ever have suspected *this* guy? "He's so conscientious about duty he probably does marching drills in his sleep."

He went through a couple more, and on the fourth got something that gave his face a pained twist as he was taking it in, but he waved them off, no problem, nothing that had any bearing on their business here, and then said he wanted to give it a rest for a few minutes.

Throughout this process, Rogier had gone from mild skepticism to interest to rapt fascination. He was clearly grateful for the break, because it gave him a chance to pose the question he seemed increasingly anxious to ask, without interrupting:

"How do you *do* this?" Rogier wanted to know. "How does this *work*?"

Campbell studied the floor a moment, then looked up with an apologetic smile. "I'm not really sure. A few days ago, I learned a couple of theories from some people, but I can't say which one feels more right to me. I don't guess one has to be totally wrong for the other to be right."

"Not that either of them has to be right," Liz added.

"In one theory, the objects we own, that have a real presence in our lives and aren't just forgotten in the back of a closet somewhere," he said, "it's like they're psychic sponges. We imprint them with what happens to us, and our strongest memories, and our feelings about whatever we love and hate, the stuff that really makes an impression . . . and for some reason, I can pull all that out of them.

"The other theory," he said, then backed up a moment. "Have you ever heard of the Akashic Records?"

Rogier said he hadn't.

"Don't feel bad, it was a new one on me, too. But if you think of everything we do as expending some kind of energy . . . our actions and thoughts and emotions . . . that energy's got to go somewhere, because you can't destroy energy, it can only change form. Well, supposedly, a part of it touches this higher plane of existence and makes a permanent impression. And that's what the Akashic Records are, if you believe in it: this master record of everything that's ever happened, no matter how small. And those personal objects I was talking about? They're nothing by themselves. But they're like"—he stopped, clawing for a comparison—"links on a web page. And for someone like me, what they do is point me to their owner's record."

Rogier seemed quietly enthralled, with an obvious preference for this theory. Beneath his wide brow and balding pate, he had the look of a boy hearing about dinosaurs for the first time.

Yeah, Liz thought, *that's the one that would appeal to a librarian.*

"Except I don't have the skill to read it the way I would a book yet," Cam said. "I mostly have to take what jumps out at me. And it's usually not subtle."

After pondering this for a few moments, Rogier asked where the lavatory was. She'd really been pushing the bottled water on him. A warmish afternoon, pedaling his bike around in Rome traffic . . . go on, go on, rehydrate. Liz pointed down a hallway and told him which door, and he excused himself. She followed the progress of his footsteps, the clunk of the closing door.

Hurriedly now, she grabbed his shoulder bag off the kitchen counter and dropped it into Cam's lap. He looked up at her from the chair as though she'd given him a dead fish.

"Yeah. Him too. Don't look so surprised," she whispered.

Wide-eyed: "I thought you all *trusted* him . . ."

"And we want to keep trusting him, so do it."

With a flash of bitterness across his face, Campbell snatched the bag in his hand, opened himself to the ebb and flow . . . then tossed it back at her.

"Nothing wrong with him, either," Cam said, and wouldn't take his eyes from hers, a glare that bordered on accusation. "You want to know what his big secret is? He likes you. I mean *likes* you. And that's really eating at him because he knows he can't do a thing about it. So he's trying hard to fight it. It's filling him up with guilt that, personally, I don't think he should feel, but he does, and now I can feel it too."

They heard the toilet flush.

"Please don't ask me to blindside somebody again when

they leave the room," Cam said. "It really makes me feel like an asshole."

She nodded, and this time felt like not only was she the one chastened, but deserving of it. Not that the subterfuge wasn't necessary, but she should have warned him in advance that it was the only way to be sure.

They were both winging it here, weren't they? And Campbell knew it.

Rogier was back after a few moments, and she started getting the cleared items out of the way before they moved on to finish the rest. Putting them back in his bag and marking them off on her list, dictated from Hellboy, and checking them against Artaud's list of who owned what.

"Hey," she said. "We're missing somebody. There's one name not on your list."

"Yes, Monsignor Burke. He's since gone back to the U.S., many days ago."

Liz scowled at the paper in her hand. "I know you can't help it, but Hellboy's not going to like that. If we don't find what we're looking for in the rest of these things, the suspicion's naturally going to fall on Burke's head. Except we'll have to figure out another way of verifying it, and that's going to take time, and be that much trickier to pull off."

Nothing they could do about it now, though, and Cam still had three items to go . . .

The walnut pen, explored and returned . . . and another was cleared. She next gave him a crucifix, on the understated side rather than garish, carved from ivory and small enough to fit in the palm of the hand. A moment after it went into Cam's, he jolted, as though he'd been physically shoved back into the chair, and she was at his side in a heartbeat, her hand cool and soothing and pressed against his forehead—

I'll catch you if you fall

—because they had already rehearsed for moments like this, like breaking the emergency glass: Feel the cool of her palm, the temperature of blue, and he would be back in the blue room with its cerulean walls, his sanctuary, where he had control and nothing could reach him . . .

"Cam?" she said. "You okay?" Her other hand was poised to grab. "You want me to take it from you?"

He thrashed his head back and forth. "No . . . no, I'm on top of this . . . I've got this by the short hairs . . ." Sucking down a few deep breaths to calm himself and stabilize, and in his mind he would be cranking valves, adding filters, regulating the flow. "It's just that . . . this guy's seen and been through some *heavy* stuff."

Liz glanced back at Rogier. "Whose crucifix is that?"

"Father Laurenti. Do you know of him?"

"Anecdotally," Liz said—Kate's new friend, or at least newfound fascination. She was still talking about the man when Liz had met up with her again at the Cornwall safehouse, nearly three days after the wreck of the *Calista*. A priest who looked like a pauper and had given Kate an insight or two into spirit possession that she'd never encountered.

Campbell was easing back to a more relaxed state and hadn't once seemed willing to break the connection. She was proud of him, proud of herself for having brought him this far in just a few weeks.

"Except . . ." he said, and his brow began to furrow.

"Maybe it's not such a big deal now that you didn't get anything from that Burke guy you mentioned." Eyes still closed, head still down, he had a look of bewilderment. "Oh, this is weird . . ."

"Cam, what about this man?"

"I think . . . he's your guy. He's the one."

Now Rogier was shaking his head. "This can't be. I would believe anyone before Gino Laurenti. *Myself* before Gino Laurenti."

"It's just that . . ." Cam was stammering now, as though reading an inscription from fragments of stone he was still piecing together. "He . . . he doesn't *know* it. About himself."

"How is this possible?" Rogier asked.

Cam's hand started to twitch, as though he were developing a tic. "More than one mind here. There's . . . there are three . . ."

Liz leaned in cheek-to-cheek, let him know she was there. "Cam, does he have something inside him?"

Shaking his head slowly, as if only gradually verifying the truth, or the truth as he perceived it. "No . . . that's not it . . . but . . . ummm . . . I'm getting some threads here I don't really want to follow—"

Liz forced her nails past his clenched fingers and yanked the crucifix from his hand. "Okay, that's enough of that, this is over."

She sat beside him as his eyes opened and he looked around the room as if to reacquaint himself with it, to remember what was most real, and she stroked his forehead back toward the clipped hairline, poor guy, halfway to a monk's existence already when you knew that without this awful gift he'd be happy with his hair in his eyes and both hands attached and playing guitar in some awful band and contending with hangovers left by cheap beer instead of tainted souls.

"You kicked ass," she told him.

She helped him up from the chair and steered him toward the hallway, led him back toward the other rooms and put him to bed, fully clothed except for his shoes, old flat-soled Keds. She worked them off and by the time the second one hit the floor, he was already asleep. She pulled a quilt over him and left him in peace.

"It takes a lot out of him, does it?" Rogier said, fumbling the question out in an awkward way that told her he'd wanted to help and wasn't sure how, because he was so far out of his element.

"When it's like that, it does," Liz said. "I don't know about you, but whenever I have these dragged-out, super-emotional confrontations, it's so draining, it saps me so bad all I want to do is go to sleep. He's the same way, I guess. He told me that when it's like that, really ugly or just really challenging, he said, 'Imagine the worst, most heart-breaking fight you ever had in your life, then multiply by ten.'"

He looked her in the eye, then shyly away, then back again with a contemplative smile that suggested to her he considered himself largely exempt from such things, and that he wasn't sure if that was a good thing or not.

"What does all this mean?" he asked. "I know what I heard him say but I don't know what it means."

She had to tell him she didn't know, either, she just lived here. This world where less and less made sense to her, and very little seemed fair.

After Artaud left, with the bag of stolen items slung over his shoulder—all but the crucifix—and the task of clandestinely returning them still ahead, Liz returned to her chair by the window and watched him pedal away. And since Hellboy was not here, she decided she would be the one to watch the sky, on guard against avenging angels, but ready to extend welcome if any benevolent ones felt like winging by.

But there were only clouds, until the sky went black.

CHAPTER 21

On the way in, the old prophecies drifted through his mind, although he couldn't say why. The seven hills of Rome equating with the seven heads of the beast that would rule over the end times, trampling upon the righteous for a few years before the host of Heaven got riled enough to get down to some serious smiting. One long-ago man's view of the end of the world, and certainly open to interpretation. Live long enough on a rocky, sun-blasted Greek island, and he supposed you'd say a lot of things that were open to interpretation.

Didn't look so menacing from the air, Rome didn't.

Didn't look so menacing on the ground, either, on the ride from the airport.

Under the surface, though . . . that's where things always boiled the hottest, in the hidden places, the places that people could never see and were just as happy to forget existed at all . . . even when the portents bubbled menacing and violent.

He thought of Pompeii, hours south of here, and the day it disappeared from the face of the earth, buried in tons of ash that baked thousands in their homes and in the streets. Yet they had chosen to live in the steaming shadow of Vesuvius all the same.

It possesses craters of fire that only go out when they lack fuel, a Greek geographer had written decades earlier.

There were times when he found it too easy to imagine a Vesuvius that would cover not just a city, but the world . . . and the people who would stand by and watch it happen.

It was after dark when he and Abe reached the apartment in the Borgo. Liz told him that her protégé's readings of the nicked items had gone well, and he assured her they'd get to that soon. For now he just wanted to meet the kid she'd been working with all these weeks, whose input had so quickly become so crucial.

He'd felt bad ever since that exchange on the boat when he'd called Campbell Holt her project, as if he were sticks she was putting together with glue. He never used to do that—ignore that there was a human being, usually in pain, behind the labels that the bureaucrats slapped onto them: *Pyrokinetic. Psychometric. Suicidal.*

"How are you doing?" he said in greeting. "I'm Hellboy."

"No—really?" Campbell said. "I was expecting somebody . . . redder."

Okay . . . bit of a smartass. It went with his age, probably. Probably a stupidly obvious introduction, too.

They'd gotten here at dinnertime—Campbell's, at least. Liz was content to have a smoke by the window as the kid wolfed down a plateful of pasta that appeared to have been dumped from a large take-out carton. Four-cheese ravioli, on inquiry. Hellboy grabbed a fork from the kitchen and speared four in one go, slurped them off the tines one at a time.

"You don't mind, do you?" Because there was no way he was going to be able to stop at four, not with these gooey babies.

"Oh. I get it. Hazing the new guy, right?" Campbell said. "I finally meet the BPRD's star agent and he steals my dinner? Pardon my disillusion."

"Just keep your hand at least two feet away from his mouth at all times," Abe said from a chair near Liz. "You'd hate to end your bureau career before it really gets off the ground."

"Did you ever think of changing your name?" Campbell asked, this time in all seriousness. "You seem to have kind of . . . outgrown it. I know, Hell*man* is already taken by the mayonnaise, but still . . ."

"I think by now I'm stuck with it," he said. "What are they gonna call me—Steve?"

Liz blew a plume of smoke out the window. "It was the only thing Professor Bruttenholm would ever admit failing to plan ahead for."

They talked awhile longer—he filched only ten ravioli total, an exercise in moderation—then he got down to business, asked Campbell for a quick overview of how this wild talent of his worked.

"It's all in my dossier. Have you read that?"

"Humor me. I'm a little behind on my reading."

"Which is like saying a little water goes over Niagara Falls," Abe had to add.

Campbell was mopping up the last of some sauce with a crust of bread but set it aside and held up his hand, palm up and fingers spread. "An object goes in here, and I can read into the life of who owns it. Usually the stuff that's been uppermost on their minds lately. Or if they're dead, the important stuff at the end of their life. But if I hang with something long enough, I'm learning how to root around and dig deeper."

"What about something with multiple owners?"

Campbell nodded. "If the thing's changed hands along the line, I can usually pick up on the previous owner, or owners. They may be weaker, but they're there. It's sort of like deciding which channel to leave the TV on . . .

"The main thing is that someone's really *lived* with it. I hardly ever get a hit off public property, or something that's passed around all the time. Like coins. It happens, but not very often. So just in case"—he tapped his fork, his plate—"I try to always use the same silverware and table service. But most of the time, the object has to have been in someone's possession to build that strong of an association. They really have to have made it theirs."

Hellboy dug into one of his topcoat's big pockets and drew out the rag-wrapped bundle. Peeled away the cloth and dropped onto the table the dark gnarled horn he'd ripped from the Scotsman's skull that morning.

"You think you can tell me about what used to possess *that?*"

He was on the roof almost before he knew it.

The horn had barely hit the table when Liz came vaulting out of her chair, snatching it up and handing it off to Abe and demanding—not asking, *demanding*—that he hang onto it and not let it anywhere near Campbell. She'd grabbed his sleeve next and yanked him toward the door, up two flights of stairs and out onto a small walkway surrounded by gently sloping red clay tiles.

"Are you out of your mind?" she asked. "Because if you expose him to that, there's a good chance it'll drive Cam out of his."

This, he felt pretty sure, was called the riot act, and she was reading it to him loud and clear.

"We can't do this downstairs, like a team?" he asked.

"There's a rule of thumb in all the better families," she said. "The parents don't let the kids see them fight."

"He's not our kid, Liz."

"In our world he is. In our world he's a wet-assed babe in the woods."

She stamped off a frustrated six paces away, as far as she could get before the flat roof ran out, then turned around and stamped back. They may have been few, but there were occasions when he wondered how it was that a woman who probably didn't weigh even a third of what he did could make him feel so small.

"I read Kate's briefing on what you came across in Glasgow this morning," she said. "If that ugly thing you dropped on the table has even a *residue* of the malevolence I know has to be behind it, then, psychologically speaking, you might as well be strapping Cam into an electric chair, because I don't have any doubt that it would fry his mind."

"You don't know that. And we still don't know what's going on around us. I just know we better figure it out soon. This would be the quickest way. We can always take the horn away from him if it's too much."

"What 'if'? There's no 'if'—trust me, it *will* be."

"You didn't want to bring him to Rome in the first place, either, but he looks like he's handling it fine."

"You weren't here this afternoon when he tapped into one of the priests. He got through it, but it put him down the rest of the afternoon. If that happens to him with one of the *good* guys—supposedly good—what do you think'll happen if he starts sniffing around your—"

Abruptly, Liz clamped down on whatever she'd been about to say. But she didn't have to say it. He could finish for her, or near enough. *Your family tree. Your relatives. Your hometown.* Something like that. Not exactly a cheap shot, and nothing he would hold against her, but it was something that wasn't ever going away. Despite their similarities, and no matter how much history they shared, their births—and all that their births implied—were poles apart.

"Look, H.B.," she said. "You call the shots and there's nobody I'd rather have do that. But this is the one where you and I . . ."

She didn't want to say it. They weren't used to this, opposite sides of a divide. So he said it for her: "Lock horns?"

One corner of her mouth ticked. "We have to find another way. We may have already. But this one's non-negotiable. Promise me you'll lock that thing up in the wall safe downstairs until we can get it back home."

She was probably right. There were plenty of men and women who had, across the centuries, divined various secrets of Hell and lived to tell the tale. He'd hoped that Campbell Holt might have their kind of fortitude, their inner strengths. But there was a difference, too. The Hell that most dark mystics had encountered had been sought.

Campbell's insights would come from a Hell that would be forced on him. So maybe it wasn't the way.

"Supposedly good guy, you said a minute ago. What did you mean by that?"

"So *now* you're ready to hear about that. About time," she said. "Father Laurenti's unwitting donation to this afternoon's roundup. A crucifix. Cam got this weird hit off it."

As Liz told him what had happened in front of her and Father Artaud, she had his ears but St. Peter's had his eyes, as he gazed toward the colossal dome that still seemed to see all, dominate all, even though it was many blocks away, with a small town's worth of rooftops in between. He wondered if he would live to see a day when it too had sunk into a state of wreck and ruin, like so many of Rome's monuments to its own past—once lustrous forums and temples, the pride of empire and republic, today just a few crumbling blocks in the weeds and clusters of chipped columns.

A house divided against itself cannot stand, a president had once said about the land Hellboy now called home, but the lesson was universal.

"Okay," he said when Liz had finished. "You're right, we should check that out right away."

"Do you even know where to find Father Laurenti?" she asked.

"Matter of fact, I think I do."

CHAPTER 22

He'd had an address to go on, and a general description of the grounds. After a few passes up and down a secluded stretch on the northern fringes of Rome, the driver of their panel truck determined that the place was an unmarked estate barely visible behind rusty gates and stone walls draped with vines. Easier to have identified it by daylight, maybe, but Hellboy hadn't felt like waiting until morning.

Monsignor Burke had given him this address at the end of their trip to the observatory . . . the place where rogue churchmen had sought to punish the wicked by summoning down angels and, according to legend, calling up devils. Burke had pointed him here immediately after revealing that he and his compatriots had finally accomplished what opponents of the *Opus Angelorum* hadn't managed in centuries:

A close encounter of the third kind, Burke had said. *We caught one of them.*

"They're holding a priest by the name of Domenico Verdi," Hellboy told them. "True or not, I don't know, but Burke said they caught the guy coming back to get one of the old torture devices hanging all over the place. A piety belt. Fits around your gut like a weightlifter's belt, except it's got two or three hundred barbs poking inward."

Liz looked appalled as only she could. "I'm afraid to ask, because there's just no good answer to this, is there, but . . . ?"

"Himself," Hellboy said. "He wanted it for himself. And, according to Burke, Father Laurenti practically moved in here where they've been holding him."

Abe's eyes narrowed. "Why should Burke tell you where to find either one of them? Especially after Laurenti told us to stay out of their fight?"

"Same reason he showed me the observatory. He thinks this *Opus Angelorum* group is a plague that needs to be taken out in a way he doesn't think his own people have the stomach for. This Verdi guy . . . I figure he gave him to me either as a place to start, or a loose end to tie up."

"He does know you're not a hired killer, doesn't he?"

"Maybe he has faith in my powers of persuasion."

The four of them slipped from the panel truck and had it continue onward, find someplace to wait out the duration, out of sight but no more than a couple minutes away at the other end of the radio. In the moonlight, they moved along the wall until they came to a round-topped doorway inset into the stone, the door a heavy iron frame full of byzantine designs and sealed by a wrapped chain and padlock.

No more problem than pulling a loose thread off a shirt, really. The chain and its broken links hit the ground like a handful of coins.

Trees loomed large on the other side of the wall, and breezes rustled through a low-lying jungle of vines and creepers turned brittle by autumn. They carried the scents of water and contamination. The Tiber. They must be near one of the many bends of the Tiber.

Hellboy glanced over his shoulder at Campbell. "You doing okay back there, rookie?"

"Sure," he whispered back. "Hey . . . you're not going to hurt this guy, are you? This priest, Laurenti—whatever's up with him, Liz told you I said it's not his fault, right?"

"I got the message, yeah."

A few yards closer and the house began to take form in the night. With staggered tiers of tiled roof, and haphazard arrangements of columns here and archways there, it had the rambling look of a country villa, and may well have started out that way, built long before the spreading city eventually caught up with it.

"How are we going in?" the kid whispered. "Should I have a gun? Nobody ever issued me a gun."

"Anybody ever train you how to *use* a gun?"

"No."

"Then I'll bet you can figure out the connection there."

"Relax, Cam," Liz told him. "These people are on our side."

"Uh huh." He didn't sound convinced. "Do they know that?"

"Anyway," Hellboy said, "I figured we'd do the polite thing for a change and knock."

As expected, Laurenti wasn't the least bit happy to see them. He spent the first couple of minutes fretting over how they'd learned of this place, whose gilded edges may have been dulled by dust, but whose past splendor wasn't entirely hidden under renovations and repairs. As near as Hellboy could tell, three guards were on duty, armed with handguns and, by the looks of them, certainly not priests. Probably the outside help that Burke had alluded to.

At first Hellboy refused to name the tipster who'd sent him here, until it became clear to him that the only way they were going to get anywhere with Laurenti was full disclosure: Monsignor Burke, who'd had different ideas on what the BPRD should and shouldn't be privy to. And, while they were at it, the bureau was aware of the observatory, too, and who had used it, and for what.

"These things . . . you should not know them," Laurenti said. "He should never have told you."

"It's dirty laundry, I get that," Hellboy said. "You'd rather clean house from the inside, I get that too. But too many secrets, that's why we're in the mess we're in now. Plus we've got reason to think you have one of your own . . . that even *you* don't know about."

Laurenti didn't understand. Who would? He insisted they had to be wrong. Who wouldn't? Hellboy reached into a pouch on his belt and pulled out a little bundle of cloth. He may not have stolen it personally, but he'd ordered it done, and felt stabbed by a pang of guilt when he unwrapped it and held up the man's ivory crucifix.

"Don't ask how or who. We don't have time for that. My fault, it was my idea. We had to find out who passed on information about the route the scroll was taking." Hellboy hitched a thumb back at Campbell. "When he holds something that's important to someone, it's like a window into that person's life. If you don't want to take my word for it, he can demonstrate. But he picked up something in you. Only you."

With disheveled hair and a three-day beard, Laurenti stared for a moment in disbelief, maybe a little fear, then nodded. "I think you come here to accuse me of something. So yes. I want to see that your methods don't lie."

Hellboy handed the cross to Campbell, then faced Laurenti again. "Ask him something. That's important to you, or that stays with you, but that he couldn't know."

Laurenti didn't have to ponder this long. "What would my mother have named my sister if she had not died at birth?"

Hellboy looked at Campbell's face, then into Liz's, full of sudden pain, and he could read her thoughts because he could so easily see the evidence for himself.

He doesn't want to. Because he knows he'll feel the grief, he hasn't learned to block that yet. Because the name has grief tied around it like a bow. So he doesn't want to . . .

But he will.

"Natalia," said Campbell.

He thought he saw a tear glisten in the corner of Laurenti's eyes. Took the crucifix and put it into the hands where it belonged.

"I'm sorry," Hellboy said.

Laurenti ignored him, looking at Campbell now: "What else have you seen?"

As they tried to make sense of the impressions that Campbell had picked up this afternoon—not one mind but three, yet not something inside the priest—Hellboy got a gut feeling that Laurenti truly was innocent. It was no act, no theater. The man didn't know he was being used. But worse, none of this made any sense to him. There was nothing in what Campbell was saying that Laurenti could connect to anything else, the big picture suddenly coming into view.

Abe ticked a finger up for quiet. "Do you have incense here? Not sticks, but a larger amount. Like you'd burn in a censer?"

It caught Laurenti by surprise—Hellboy couldn't say the request made much sense to him, either—but he said, yes, they did. As he sent one of the guards to find it, Hellboy wondered if they said Mass in this place, some consecrated spot where one of them would lead the way, swinging the smoke-spewing censer at the end of a sturdy chain.

Hellboy leaned close to Abe. "What's on your mind?"

"On the *Calista* . . . remember the fogbank we entered?" Abe said. "Remember what we *saw* in the fog?"

That spectral form tethered to Hellboy's back, which they would never have seen at all if not for the mist. The eyes, maybe the ears too, of something that had been watching from afar. He'd had greater worries since then, but had never been able to figure out where the thing had come from.

But if they found a connection here . . .

Abe suggested they move to a smaller room, where closer walls would hold the smoke better. They fired up several small round charcoal bricks in an empty tomato can. When these were burning well, Laurenti dropped in a generous palmful of incense, in loose nuggets. Within seconds it began to smolder and smoke, the air filling with the fresh, sweet floral scent of Damascus Rose.

Hellboy took the can in his right hand—no pain, no

matter how hot the metal grew—and swept it around the room, especially around Laurenti, as the smoke poured out. It swirled, it billowed, it thickened the air, and soon grew denser than any fog at sea.

Abe, who seemed to have an eye for these things, fanned the smoke this way, fanned it that, and pointed.

Not obvious, seen more for what they weren't than what they were, as the smoke wafted around them rather than through them: two vaporous tendrils sunk into Laurenti's back, just inside his shoulder blades. Fan the smoke, follow the loops, the coils, blink and you miss it . . . but Abe had the eye for this in more ways than one, the protective film that let him see clearly in water now keeping the smoke from stinging.

He followed the tendrils back to their sources: human forms again, but only barely, one cringing in the near corner, the other clinging halfway up a wall. From what the smoke suggested of their faces, Hellboy wasn't sure he wanted to see them any more clearly. Whether in anguish or madness, they seemed to scream. Maybe they really needed to. Or maybe it was the last thing they remembered doing.

"My god," Laurenti whispered, after he'd turned to see what they'd found. Like anyone would, he reached both hands around his back, trying to grab hold of something his fingers could never feel. "What *are* they?"

Good question. Prior to his own encounter, this was nothing Hellboy had seen. Even so, he had a few ideas. Not souls, but *parts* of souls, stripped free of the rest, then shackled and enslaved. He wasn't convinced anyone had truly plumbed the mysteries of the human essence, although he liked the depth and sophistication of the way the ancient Teutons had seen it: a complex entity comprised of many distinct aspects, just as the body was comprised of many organs. The hidge, the hyde, the fetch, the myne . . . maybe it was one of these that they were now looking at in the smoke, retaining just enough memory of themselves to hold onto ghostly echoes of the bodies to which they'd once belonged.

And the umbilicals—so they wouldn't become separated from the unsuspecting targets they were attached to? Maybe. But maybe these tendrils also kept them alive, in their way, a means for draining away a small but steady reserve of vitality to keep them viable. Probably nothing Hellboy would have noticed . . . but a normal man or woman? You had to wonder if Laurenti had felt like himself lately.

"I want these off me," he said.

The one that had leeched onto Hellboy's back had come loose and disintegrated almost as soon as it was discovered. Cause and effect? More likely this was because, as they'd speculated, its job was done; the Leviathan had found them. This pair seemed to recognize that they'd been found out, but weren't going anywhere. They scrabbled at the ends of the tethers sunk into the middle of their chests, heaving with silent screams.

"I want these off me now."

Liz came shouldering past him and Abe, elbowing them both out of the way, her palms wreathed in flickering gloves of blue-orange fire. She homed in on one of the tendrils, a faint void in the smoke, and it seemed to writhe, wormlike, to evade her grasp. Yet she had it, catching what could not be caught, burning it to spectral ash while shoving her other hand into the center of the hazy chest, and then she was after the next one before the first had finished dissipating into the fumes.

Smoke now. Only smoke, and nothing more.

Hellboy caught her eye, watery and red in the haze. "How'd you know?"

"I didn't."

Good call, though. There was fire, and then there was fire. The combustion of a match, which burned only matter, and the searing purity of an elemental force, which usually trumped the unnatural. Little doubt which one Liz was connected to.

Laurenti was coughing now. Hellboy braced him with one hand and pulled him out of the room and into fresh air.

"Whatever those were, I had one too. Maybe I picked it up from you and maybe I didn't. But you don't just pick 'em up like brambles on your pantleg," he told Laurenti. "Now *think.*"

"I thought . . . I thought I was ill," he said. "Two months, I haven't been the same since . . ."

"Since what?"

"A deliverance. I performed a deliverance . . ."

"An exorcism, you mean?"

Laurenti shook his head. "Not the full Rite, no, but . . . you do this thing, you still are vulnerable then . . . open to influences . . ."

"What was it for?" Hellboy asked. *"Who* was it for?"

"No. No, it could not be, that was nothing like this—"

"Who was it?"

"Aidan Burke," he said. "Monsignor Burke."

• • •

They cleared out of the house onto a side patio, letting the crisp night air wash out their lungs, their eyes. Laurenti hunched over a wrought iron table and sipped a glass of wine.

"Two months ago Aidan came to me," he said. "Across an ocean, he came to me. Yes, he comes sometimes to Rome for Church business, and comes sometimes to Rome for *our* Church business, the business that's not official . . . but he said this was not for either one. This was to be between us, only us. Would I hear his confession, he asked me. I knew it must be something terrible, if he would not tell his own confessor back home . . ."

Except it hadn't been anything Burke had done—not willingly, at least—but rather something he wished to be purged of. He claimed his nights were marathons of torment, as if caught between sleep and waking, his body paralyzed while he helplessly watched his spirit rise and wander, to visit other bedrooms, to plunder other sleepers and gratify itself with their bodies. He was host to a spirit of lust, he feared; or worse, becoming one himself. If there was a term for it at all, the only one he could think of was incubus.

"There was something wrong with him," Laurenti said. "I could sense it in him."

"So you tried to help him," Hellboy said.

"Of course, yes. It's what I do. Whether or not the Church grants permission, if I become convinced there is a need . . ." He opened his hands wide, as though to say he was helpless before duties he saw, not duties as they were defined. "And Burke, of all people? He would not request this lightly. He would never *believe* this of himself lightly. A very rational man . . . maybe too rational."

And so they'd done it—prayers and recitations, banishings and holy water. Successfully? So Laurenti had believed. And very likely it had been, just not in the way he'd expected.

So think this through a minute . . .

As Laurenti had mentioned already, the rites of exorcism left the practitioner open, vulnerable. Hell, anyone who'd seen the Friedkin movie knew that much. But the risks, the underlying principles, were far older than the Church. Who were the first holy men if not shamans, primal mediators between worlds? Even now, from equatorial rain forests to the Siberian tundra, shamans took great care not to return from their trance-journeys to the Underworld with spirits holding to them.

And what was a priest but a shaman in more somber clothes?

But suppose this ordeal of deliverance they'd undergone was a sham, a ruse, not to drive something from Burke, but to attach something to Laurenti?

And why? Because the monsignor was far from what he seemed. Because he was a man whose considerable power was being directed toward hidden aims. Because he knew that something would soon transpire that would put the Masada Scroll into play . . . maybe was even helping orchestrate it. And because he was planning ahead, planting seeds that would give him—or his masters—eyes, perhaps ears, with those who would oppose him.

And knowledge, as they all knew, was power.

It put their trip to the observatory in a whole new light,

looking at it from this perspective. Burke's not-so-subtle suggestions that Hellboy should target the *Opus Angelorum*—an attempt to wipe out an enemy? Or cover his tracks? Both?

Hellboy was even looking differently at that moment when Burke put his hand on his back and let it linger. A solicitous gesture from a priest, but now it was hard to shake the feeling that it had more sinister intentions. The spot he'd touched was *exactly* where the specter had joined to Hellboy's back. Had he planted it then, the task easier than with Laurenti because Hellboy—as he'd been told just this morning—belonged to two worlds already?

Or maybe it was because they were standing in the middle of a place of fearsome power, the accumulated charge of centuries of rites and rituals. Burke had invited, and he had gone there of his own free will.

I should've been more careful . . .

"Burke's in Boston again now, right?"

"Supposed to be," Liz said, sitting with Campbell on a concrete balustrade around the patio. "According to Father Artaud."

Hellboy nodded. "We need to call Fairfield and have them scramble a takedown team. We've got to get this guy over here *now*. And we don't have time for subtlety."

CHAPTER 23

"Does the bureau do that often?" Campbell asked. "Go in, drag somebody out of his home in the middle of the night?"

Liz shook her head. "Hardly ever. The directors hate it."

"How come?"

"It has the potential for looking really bad, even blowing up in our faces. We're not the FBI, you know. And we can't exactly follow due process. What Father Laurenti told us in there? *You* try taking that before a judge to get an arrest warrant. You'd be lucky if you made it out of there without being locked up yourself." She turned her head to blow a plume of smoke away from him. "So that pretty much puts us on the same level as the Men In Black. Whoever *they* are."

"You mean you don't know?"

"Let me tell you something, Cam. This job's not much of a front-row ticket to the secrets of the universe. All these mysteries are like the hydra. Feel like we get a handle on one, and pretty soon two more come along to take its place."

They'd been greeting the dawn from the patio, with its tiles of green and cobalt blue, where the rising sun struck in pools of light that widened as the rays gained strength through the trees. Cam had slept inside earlier, and there had been his exhausted nap yesterday afternoon after reading the objects that Artaud had brought by. But Liz had been up all night on a tea and cigarettes jag, never quite able to back off the twisty feeling of apprehension while they'd awaited word that the takedown team had quietly, successfully raided Monsignor Burke's home and whisked him off to a hangar at Logan Airport and a chartered Lear jet flight.

They must be somewhere over the Atlantic right now, closer to Rome than Boston.

"I'd feel better if Hellboy was here right now," Cam said.

"Everybody does. Even if it's just a safety thing." Liz shrugged under the blanket wrapped around her shoulders, although it was getting warmer now and she could take it off soon. "But he hates to waste time. Almost as much as he hates it when stuff eludes him. This is a two-for-one run for him."

She fished for her lighter again. The patio table was littered with tea bags and its ashtray full of butts, and she thought she smelled coffee now, too, one of the guards brewing it in the kitchen. More caffeine, great—just what she needed.

But better than the smell coming from the Tiber, when the breeze was right. Abe had gone off to spend some time at the river's edge in the predawn hours, then came back sooner than she would ever have expected, and he hadn't said a word since.

"Is this one rough on you?" Cam wanted to know. "The scroll, the fight over it . . . everything?"

"No more than most. Why?"

He pointed at her throat. "The little cross on that velvet choker. You were wearing it the day you came to visit me in the hospital. And the day you met me in Bridgeport when I flew in to start training. I don't think I've seen you without it more than once or twice. I mean, I don't know what your beliefs are, but I figure if I ever wanted to know all about you, that's the thing of yours that would show me the most."

"Yeah, well, unless you want to find yourself working psychic fairs, paws off," she said, then corrected herself, "Paw, singular," and this cracked them up in that silly way you can laugh when it's dawn and you should've slept and your throat feels as raw as your eyes and you have no idea what the day might bring, just that it probably won't be good.

She brushed her fingertips along the choker, the cross. "I'll tell you what it's doing there," she said. "Where I grew up, it probably wasn't all that different from where you grew up. It was so secure. I was loved and my parents made sure I knew it. I was so protected. Then all that was gone . . .

"It's not that I've forgotten all the old Sunday School lessons. I've just seen too much to still be able to believe that the world and whatever's beyond it works the way they all said . . .

"But this reminds me of when I *could*," she said. "And that's something, isn't it?"

They'd called it the Queen of Roads, and after 2300 years since its first stones were laid, it still cut a path out of Rome. The Via Appia Antica, the Old Appian Way, was once the empire's highway to the east, and now it was lined with fragments of the ancient past—churches and tombs, sepulchers and mausoleums—and led from the city to stretches of open countryside, where farmers still tilled their fields, and clusters of pines kept their green while the land around them browned with autumn.

No question that he was in the right place. He could still see the tire ruts chewed into the ground.

For a week and a half Hellboy had wanted to come back here as soon as he had the chance: the spot where, after that careening ride through southeastern Rome and beyond, the armored car had come to rest. No time to stand and fight that night, at least not with enemies that refused to show themselves. Yet he'd sensed they were out there, watching from the darkness and the trees, holding back only because the car's hijackers had failed to deliver its passengers in peace, unsuspecting.

What was here, though, but a pastoral niche of countryside?

He'd come hours before dawn, wandering amid the trees and the fields in hopes that the unfolding darkness would reveal something wrong with this place. He'd gazed at the stars and breathed the night air. He'd sat and watched, listened and waited. He'd wandered far enough away from the queenly old road to stand upon a hillside and look down upon a farm. He'd even crept onto the farm itself, but there was nothing wrong there either, only the warm breath of sleeping animals and a family left bone-weary by bringing in the harvest.

And now that morning had come and the sun had banished night, he was doing it all over again.

The air was warm and the light strong when he found it: a place in a cluster of pines that looked, and the closer he got, felt . . .

Wrong.

Piled branches and scattered pine needles lay over the side of a gently sloping plateau of earth, an extension of a hillside where mud had run in thick rivulets, and the turf had sloughed off like a shed skin and then been replaced. Not something he would've noticed by night, or even paid much attention to on most days, but on *this* day, in this frame of mind . . .

He pitched the branches aside, then knelt and scraped through the scabbed earth and a weave of grass and vines until he found what felt like a heavy wooden door, still stout but going rotten with age.

He'd barely begun to clear it of soil when his phone went off.

"Burke's flight got in fifteen minutes ago," Abe said. "They're on their way. You better head back here."

Some other time, Abe had called to him from the armored car that night, when his impulse was to chase them down, to root them out, to find out what they were. Abe was turning into the best friend this place ever had.

"Next time finishes it," he promised the earth, as if the end of ages was at stake.

CHAPTER 24

Without his vestments, without his European tailored black suits, Aidan Burke seemed about as happy as any fiftysomething man would after he'd been seized in his pajamas, then spent the night in vans and a plane instead of his own bed. Back in Boston, his alarm clock wouldn't even have gone off yet.

Now he sat in the north of Rome, midmorning here, hands resting before him on an oak table that could've served at a small banquet.

"Do you have any idea how many laws and international regulations you must be breaking by doing this?" he said. "I don't, but I would genuinely like to know." His eyes, so blue within the bloodshot veins, tightened a millimeter. "I do intend to find out once this farce is played out."

"Go on, Monsignor. You know you want to," Hellboy told him. "Threaten to have me busted down to writing parking tickets—I dare you."

No comeback to that, but after a long, bumpy night, Burke could still pull off a simmering burn that might give rookie agents pause to wonder if they hadn't made a mistake. With his chiseled features and iron gray hair, clipped

284

too short to muss, he still looked like a man who could demand heads on platters, and get them.

"I can't say it surprises me that you look for someone nearby to blame for your own failures." He gave a slow, sweeping glance across the room. "When one's best efforts prove inadequate, or incompetent, scapegoating is a natural human tendency." His gaze settled on Hellboy and Abe, back and forth. "How about that, it must even transcend species."

Had they expected him to cooperate? Hardly.

"I would expect that your inborn nature might sometimes lead you to see your own worst potentials in others," Burke said to Hellboy. "Tell me: How many things from the outer dark will you have to kill before you're satisfied that you've killed it in yourself? Or will you *ever* get there?"

Regardless, you were honor-bound to offer a guy the chance to get ahead of it. To take that first step toward putting things right.

"And Miss Corrigan, she's not here, she's not part of this?" he said, with another look around. "I'm relieved by that." Settling on Liz now, whom he hadn't met before, even as he spoke of Kate. "I felt such *pity* for her. She hid it well, but it seemed to me she's come to that point when she's wondering if she hasn't sacrificed the better years of her life to something that can only bring her . . . emptiness."

But you could only ask him so many questions that he ignored in favor of his own soliloquies before having to resort to sterner measures.

"And *you*, Gino," he said to Laurenti, voice now taking on overtones of sorrow, like Julius Caesar to Brutus. "When did the sanctity of the confessional lose all meaning for you? I came to you for help, and you turn it into the basis for a witch-hunt?"

But what if we're wrong . . . ?

Hellboy could not condone torture. But there were other methods. Sleep and sensory deprivation. And better yet, waiting a couple of rooms away, there was Campbell Holt.

"Take off your top," Hellboy told him. "Hand it over."

Burke gave him a quizzical look, then unbuttoned the silky pajama shirt and offered it at arm's length. A pretty good build underneath, pale skin taut over muscle and bone, the only concessions to age the gray hairs on his chest.

"Be careful with it, if you would, please," he said. "It's new."

He knows, Hellboy thought. *He knows about Campbell, and why shouldn't he, because that thing on my back was there every time Liz and I talked about him on the boat.*

They tried anyway, for all the good it did, Campbell clutching the fabric in his fist and drawing a blank, nothing there, a couple faint flickers of the man's anger and resentment at being taken from his home like a criminal. Campbell shaking his head no, nothing here, no secrets to plumb—Burke had not *lived* in this garment, hadn't made it his own.

"Is that it? Has he got anything else?" Campbell asked.

Hellboy had already checked. No rings, no watch, no saints' medallions around his neck. The pajama bottom would be as new as the top. Strip him of his underwear, then? His socks? His slippers? He could see no point to it. They would all be the same. Empty of the past and unconnected to his soul.

Hellboy returned Burke's top and let him put it back on.

"If there was a purpose to *that*, I'd like to know what it was," Burke said. When he got no reply, he put his hands flat on the tabletop, as if ready to push up onto his feet. "Am I free to go?"

"Just one more thing," Hellboy said, and of course they could always send a team back into his home, his office, to scoop up a few items and ship them over. There shouldn't be any trouble finding something that would work for Campbell; it would only take more time. For now, he wanted the satisfaction of pinning this man wriggling to a lie. "There's another prisoner here. In one of the buildings out back. You know that."

"Obviously. Since I was the one who told you."

"I got the feeling you expected me to do something about that, too. Maybe not for the reasons you made it seem like. But the more I thought about it, the more it sounded to me like you were hoping I'd kill that man in his cell because of what he'd helped unleash." Hellboy planted a fist on the table and leaned in closer. "Here's your problem: Inborn or not, *that just isn't in my nature.*"

Burke nodded patiently, eagerly, like a man hoping to put a misunderstanding to rest. "And I'm very glad for that. No matter what you thought you heard, I do not advocate murder."

"The man in the cell . . . Father Verdi. I'll bet you've never seen him since he's been here." Hellboy looked at Father Laurenti. "Has he?"

"If he has, I don't know about it."

Back to Burke: "But I'll bet he'd recognize you right away, wouldn't he?"

If that little tightening of Burke's mouth told them anything, it was that he was onto something here. Because deep in his gut, Hellboy had begun to suspect that Burke wasn't only a part of this group of progressives who had rallied around the Masada Scroll; he was also with their ideological enemies. Not because he cared about the aims of either . . . only the consequences of what would happen if their conflict boiled into a conflagration.

So how had this happened? Put it together, one theory, or some variation of it:

As one of the *Opus Angelorum*, Burke pushes for the most extreme response when it looks like a foregone conclusion that the scroll would go public one day. Through whatever means—a pair of eyes here, a pair of ears there—he knows when Father Artaud is going to be studying the scroll anew, using the upcoming paleography article from the archaeological journal. He's already seen to it that existing work copies have disappeared, forcing them to bring the scroll out to make new ones.

Maybe he's played both sides for fools, too, warning each that the other is onto them, just to introduce more turmoil into the mix.

But most of all he's sabotaged the seraphim's attack. Arranged for that warning to Artaud to run when the air turns cold. Sounds like just another lunatic on the street until it actually happens. So Artaud gets away with the scroll. Because Burke never wanted it destroyed . . . only threatened.

That way, you can put it into play. That way, you can send it into transit, where it will be most vulnerable.

And we never saw Hell coming for it, he thought, *because we never even knew Hell was involved.*

"What have they promised you, Burke? More power than you already have?" he asked. "Do you even know what Hell's going to use the scroll for?"

"I don't even know what *you're* talking about. You lost me awhile back."

He took Burke by the shoulder and pulled him to his feet.

"Let's take a walk out back," Hellboy said. "Let's let Verdi get a look at you and see if we can't start cutting through the crap."

For everything a season, for everything a reason.

The man in the cage had had plenty of time to recognize the underlying order of the events that sent him here, the perfection of each set of circumstances.

He had returned to the *osservatorio* when he should not have? This had only served to put him in the midst of the enemy.

They took care to deny him anything sharp? This made no difference, because there was his untrimmed thumbnail, and what he had made of it against the rough stone of their walls.

They thought themselves decent enough to allow him modesty as he turned to the corner to wash his body each day? It only left them blind.

And they made sure he had nothing with which to write, to draw, to recreate the complex signs of summoning? Then their arrogance and ignorance were truly profound . . . because the signs were already here.

Not long after he'd first stepped into this cell, Domenico Verdi had known what he was being called to do. The only question was when. Even in the darkest hours, as the days passed and the nights grew longer, when he was in danger of succumbing to their tactics, when he was tempted to find any kind of truth in what his jailer Laurenti had to say, when faith wavered and he feared the moment might never arrive . . . he had clung to the belief that when the time had come, the signs would be unmistakable.

And so it had, and they were.

Laurenti had mourned with him that they no longer lived in an age of miracles? Verdi was honored, humbled, exalted, to live in a new age of martyrs.

The sun was high and warm outside when he heard the zoo's door open. Their footsteps clicked and echoed down the corridor, a small group this time, more than had ever come to see him together before—even this was a sign.

And for the first moment when they came into view, his heart broke. The poor monsignor.

"So they caught you too," he said.

Then, emerging from the shadows, he saw the red thing that held his brother captive. He knew what it was, of course—few churchmen wouldn't. He knew what it called itself—as if it could render itself harmless by assuming a name that evoked a child. He was not fooled. A pity that Laurenti couldn't say the same.

With them was another abomination, hairless and green, like something that had crawled from the sea after the Father of Lies told it that it was a man.

"These creatures, *these* are what you call allies now?"

Verdi shouted to Laurenti. "These are what you turned the scroll over to? And now you claim to be surprised it was lost? It was never lost . . . you made a gift of it to them!"

Laurenti stepped forward as if to justify his actions, but there was nothing further to listen to. It would only be more lies, and maybe he would even believe them himself. So let him carry them on his lips to his judgment.

"Join me, Aidan," said Verdi, and met the monsignor's eyes, only to see with his heightened clarity that deception lived there, too.

It was time.

He caressed his thumbnail and, speaking under his breath, began the recitation of summoning, the words in a tongue spoken so rarely on this plane that even to whisper them was to roar.

As far as Hellboy was concerned, it couldn't have been more obvious. They'd gotten the reaction he had expected, plain as day. If ever there was any doubt that Burke had been in place to play both sides against each other, Verdi dispelled it the moment he opened his mouth.

As for what he was doing now, though . . .

Hellboy leaned forward over Burke's shoulder. "What's he saying?"

"I don't know, I can't hear him either," Burke snapped. "But I can guess."

And now the dread, like a chilly finger on the back of the neck. "He's not . . ."

"It doesn't matter. Look at him. Right now he's no different than a schizophrenic on a streetcorner." Burke peered back over his shoulder with more condescension than he had any right to. "You saw the observatory floor. You saw the tools it takes. You don't see them anywhere in there, do you?"

No. He didn't. What he saw was a man who'd been held captive long enough to grow a woolly scruff of beard, who didn't appear to have been abused but lived in a cage meant for animals, and who now seemed possessed by a singularity of purpose that transcended every human need.

Fanatics doused in gasoline would look this way . . .

Verdi ripped open the front of his simple pullover shirt.

. . . before they struck the match.

For a moment, Hellboy could only stare. They all did. When first faced with such devotion to duty, such obsession with detail, it was all anyone could do. Forced to imagine the hours of cutting, the terrible willpower to achieve steadiness of hand. The effort and endurance, the precision and the pain.

It was all there, Hellboy feared, written in scar tissue across the broad expanse of the man's chest and belly. The ornate and dauntingly complex circle rimmed with letters, Hebraic and Theban, Malachim and more, filled with seals, sigils, and talismans. They merged and overlapped, they melded into one.

And as Verdi's voice suddenly turned from a whisper to a shout, he feared they waited for just one thing.

He shoved Burke out of the way and sprinted forward, was ripping through the cage door when Verdi took his right thumb and made a twisting slash high on his gut, between the bottom of his ribs, and the blood pulsed bright and red.

He lunged and caught Verdi's wrist, but the man's arm was unresisting, his smile beatific.

Too late. *Too late.*

He dropped Verdi and tore back out of the cage to the corridor, grabbed Burke by the shoulder. Squeeze a little harder and the collarbone would snap.

"You were a part of them too," he said. "Can you call it off?"

Burke started to laugh. "Why would you think people like that would ever have a reason to change their minds? No, you're about to be privileged to see something that few ever have."

He let Burke go and snatched the radio from his belt to call back to the house. "Liz! Stash Campbell somewhere safe, tell anybody else to take cover or run, and get over here. We're about to need you."

He sent Abe rushing off with Laurenti, anyplace out of the line of fire, then turned a withering glare on Burke.

"You wouldn't call it off even if you could, would you?"

Burke huffed a little laugh through his nose, then looked toward the floor as if it too were full of riddles. "I dream in German sometimes . . . isn't that the oddest thing?" he said. "For years now. I dream I'm growing back an arm that I lost. I doubt even you could believe the feeling of power in that." Eye to eye now. "A confused monstrosity like you will never know what it means to evolve."

"Or maybe I'm perfect just the way I am," Hellboy said, then threw an arm around Burke, hoisted him off his feet like a bag of potatoes, and started running as the air around them turned cold.

CHAPTER 25

They came in glory, if not in grace, and she did not run to meet them.

Out the doors, down from the patio, past walls where thick vines and ivy had sunk their tendrils into rock, Liz kept a measured pace across the flagstones. To run when the fire was upon her seemed not only wrong, but dangerous, as though she might run too fast, outpace the uncertain point at which they joined. She occupied the fire's center now. She belonged to it, and it was hers.

Past the arbors and through the trees—so much brown instead of green, this place like a tinderbox—and she knew they were here because the zoo was burning already. Until now, she didn't realize that a red clay roof *could* burn.

Fire'll never lose a fight, the opening line of a song she'd first heard a few years ago and liked, and thought of it now because it seemed like an epitaph, even if she didn't know for whom. Was it even in her to survive such an encounter? Hellboy had thought so, too late to second-guess now, and she could only pray his faith was not misplaced.

The zoo was a long building, like a stable of gray marble blocks, its walls veined with vines as well. At the near end, a door burst open and out came Hellboy in full sprint, someone tucked beneath his arm—Monsignor Burke, she realized. Moments later they were followed by a ball of flame that hit Hellboy from behind and exploded around him like a nimbus, the corona of fire blasting the trench coat from his back, sending it whirling away in flaming tatters. He staggered as if kicked, and the man beneath his arm simply erupted, there was no other word for it, whole one second, and in the next a squirming mass. They'd been near enough in front of her that she could feel the heat even if she couldn't feel her own, but in her zone no worse than a snap of wind on a desert summer day. It gave her a surge of hope—she *could* live through this.

Their eyes met as he fell, and she ached to see in them so much anguish, Hellboy living through the kind of damage and pain than no mortal could bear. But she couldn't think about that now. Couldn't think about the charring bundle of limbs he dropped, or the long shriek trilling from inside the zoo, or who might be making this sound.

And the work of angels sent smoke boiling to the sky.

It stepped from the darkness of the doorway ahead of her, taking shape from behind the shimmering heat-haze between them. At first it appeared indistinct to her eyes, a shadow and a sigh, but as it stepped into the sunlight it seemed to coalesce all at once, gathering its body like a forgotten thought.

But was the thought hers? Was that what they did—pick the brains of those who saw them, reflect what the witness expected to see? A basic tenet of quantum physics: The act of *observing* a phenomenon *alters* the phenomenon. Surely it had to be this. The seraph had no reason to look this way, winged and beautiful, a transcendent echo of old stories, old longings, the paintings in lesson books from twenty-five years past. It was a sight to drop shepherds to their knees.

It stood before the zoo as if barring the gates of Eden, the rest joining it by ones and twos, drifting up from the flaming ruin below to appear along the roofline, another perched overhead in a tree beside her, all of them with skin like alabaster and hair like thick spun silk—no conferring about it, they just *did* it, each one taking on this guise the way birds in a flock will wheel together in the same instant, from first to last.

One, two, three . . .

Seven in all.

Who could even stand to look at them for long, much less bring herself to kill them? Liz had to force herself to re- member: *Their appearance isn't real . . . only their fire.*

What a fool she'd been to think she could survive this.

To her right, she grew aware of a chestnut tree crinkling with ice, its leathery golden leaves withering and dropping from the branches, the spiny yellow husks following soon after. The seraph standing before her seemed to waver, then dissolve behind a ball of fire that gathered in the air before it. The roiling mass was launched, rocketing toward her, a meteor of whirling red and orange—

Her body snapped, an involuntary response as survival instincts took over, fueled by fear, *I don't want to die,* and by rage, *How dare they not be what I remembered, or what I needed,* and she felt the powerful flex in her core. It surged away from her like a circular wall, and she tried to shape it, funnel it straight ahead, no reason to let it have its catastrophic way, wiping out everything in a radius around her.

They met somewhere in the middle, fires of different origins, each as mysterious to her as the other, one a foe and the other still not truly a friend. Warm winds washed her face, and she felt the tears on her cheeks dry into a stiff salt crust . . .

Then dug even deeper and poured it on.

Could one fire consume another? No, she didn't believe it could. Instead, she thought of hurricanes meeting at sea, the weaker absorbed into the stronger to generate a new force greater than either one, and maybe this was what happened here. She knew only that when her vision cleared, she was staring at a pillar that twisted and twined like a burning oil well, then collapsed on itself in a final bloom of flames.

More tears, slower to dry. As she stared at the spot where it lay, a blackened heap rapidly cooking down beyond all recognition, there was no victory in this. Even though she knew what it was, what it did, she still wondered when she could forgive herself for having destroyed something so beautiful . . .

And if she could even begin to do it six more times in a row.

The trees were burning, the house was burning, the zoo and grass and vines were burning. As she stepped forward through the mingled scents of ash and flowers, the seraphim descended to the ground.

"Liz," said Hellboy, sprawled to her right, pushing himself to his feet again.

"Get Campbell out of here," she told him. "He didn't sign on for this."

"Liz . . ." he tried again, and she knew it wasn't a plea for her to leave, so maybe it was the best he could manage right now at goodbye.

"I mean it."

He was up and gone then, and she knew how he would hate himself for it. He never wanted to run unless it was toward something, not away; she'd at least tried to give him that much.

The seraphim faced her in a crescent, the smoldering body of their comrade lying between their position and hers. In vengeance they seemed patient, even hesitant, looking at the blackened pile before them and then up at her. She could feel the sheath of flame crawl along her arms, ever restless, but against all six she feared it wouldn't be enough. How would it come—an onslaught from all of them at once?

They faced her through the smoke and even now their beauty made her ache, made her feel like a pallid and decaying thing herself. As one of them stepped forward, she watched the air between them, alert for the shimmer of newborn fire, but the angel merely lowered itself to the heap of ash and strange blackened bones at its shining feet. It thrust a hand into this encrusted pile—she couldn't kill it now, not knowing what it was up to—and withdrew it moments later, something clenched in its perfect fist.

The seraph stood again and stepped over the body, moving with the authority of a king. As it stood directly in front of her, Liz knew she was trembling but wasn't sure why. Even the fear had gone, sublimated by a sense of wonder. She remembered her first kiss, and yes, it might have been something like this . . . the frightening thrill, the fluttering sense that she could die.

Did seraphim mourn? *Could* they? She couldn't tell. Liz sought its eyes for anything recognizable as human, as harboring feeling, yet saw nothing but base awareness and the seeds of curiosity. It looked her up and down, as though . . . studying her.

It reached out and waited until she understood its gesture, until she took the lump from its hand.

Though like none she'd ever seen, and much worse for wear, it looked like nothing so much as a heart.

They both held a hand on it for a long moment, and while the seraph spoke in no language she'd ever heard, and hoped to never hear again, she felt she understood its meaning.

No, she thought. *It can't be that.*

As she held the heart in her hand, hers alone now, the seraph stepped back to join the others.

And as one, before they left, they bowed in silent deference, so low as to scrape the tips of their wings across the smoldering ground.

CHAPTER 26

Where to go when the roof comes crashing in, to recuperate and regroup?

Familiar ground was always the best bet, and on a day like today, the apartment in the Borgo felt close enough to home. As humble as it was, in its rough-edged Old World way, there was something about this place that Professor Bruttenholm had loved, and in the quiet moments when only the walls seemed to speak, Hellboy could feel it too.

Maybe he was hoping that if he listened closely enough, he could hear the old man's voice advising him what to do next.

Their sources were dead. Before they'd fled the house near the Tiber, with the survivors accounted for and safe in the panel truck, he had gone rushing back into the flames to confirm what he already suspected, but refused to take for granted. Even with the door ripped away, Domenico Verdi had never left his cage. It would take a shovel to get him out now.

Of Burke, there was no question. The man had immolated in his arms.

A month ago, if anyone had asked him if some people

deserved to burn to death, Hellboy wouldn't have wanted to answer. But deep down, in the place where he tried to bury the worst of what he'd seen people do to one another, to the innocent, he would have been tempted to say yes. That some probably did. And that someone like Burke, responsible for more deaths than two hands could count— not peaceful deaths, either—may have been one of them. If not for what he'd done, then maybe for whatever lay ahead, that he'd sought to bring about.

Now, though—*deserve?* It was awfully hard to think in such terms now that he'd witnessed such retribution. The blinded eyes, the charred and splitting skin, the blood boiled in its veins. How limbs thrashed, then contracted as all moisture steamed away. Yet Burke had suffered no more than the others he'd condemned to the same fate, and Hellboy wondered if there had been enough time for him to regret the path he'd taken to this point.

It would be a long time before he could put this one behind him. His own taste of it would see to that, the concussive blast of fire that seared the clothing from his back and sent him tumbling to the ground and through the rest of his day with a fading sense of agony, as though his hide had been stripped to the bone.

But wait—it got worse.

There would be no more of Burke's possessions coming from Boston to put in Campbell's hand. More fires. They'd gotten word late this afternoon: Both his home and his office with the Archdiocese had been razed. According to early reports, the devastation was total, and the cause as yet undetermined.

Hellboy knew only that there would be no sweetly astringent smell of flowers in the wreckage. Maybe they'd find evidence of incendiary devices, human conspirators they could track. Or maybe, if he were there, he could walk through the site as he had the Vatican Archives, and this time smell the opposite of holy fire: brimstone and bitumen and something like the roasting of marrow-rotted bones that might blacken but never fully burn. Something he just *knew*, the birthright carried in his blood.

Comforts, though, large and small? This day was not without them.

Abe had gotten Father Laurenti out of the zoo just before the attack, using the cover of trees and brush to get them down to the Tiber, then slogging along its bank as they flanked the house and worked their way around front.

As well, they were all relieved to learn that the fire hadn't spread beyond the one estate, largely contained by the outer walls, the few outbreaks beyond quickly doused by fire-fighters.

But while he would take relief wherever he could get it today, it didn't answer the nagging question:

What now?

And then there was Liz.

She'd come through the morning without a scratch, without so much as the pink of a first-degree burn, although only a fool would fail to realize that her worst wounds were never on the surface.

There were times when he could reach her and times when he couldn't, and now he was starting to wonder if the latter wasn't really the rule, if he'd been overrating his influence all along. Twelve times she'd left them. Would she really have left twelve times if he'd been all that effective in dealing with the crises?

For now, he was content to let Father Laurenti be the one to try. Maybe Liz needed a simple priest right now as much as Laurenti needed to be one, rather than a throwback, a fighter of demons in their guises. *No priest should be a jailer,* he'd admitted earlier, and who could argue with that. He seemed drawn to Liz now the way sensitive children were drawn to broken-winged birds.

They'd been talking for hours, chairs pulled into a corner like a makeshift barrier to signify no visitors allowed, and sometimes he saw her nodding just to be polite and other times he could tell she really meant it. If the two of them held the keys to absolve at least a little of the guilt in each other, then he was happy to stay out of their way.

He knew she felt it. Liz could wear guilt the way Dickens' Marley wore his chains. She may have had no reason for it today, but just try telling her that after the way she'd capped off the morning. Annihilating something beyond age, beyond place, even beyond understanding. Then to be granted a display of obeisance by the survivors—as if they had believed it was something she was owed.

For all he knew, Liz thought she'd destroyed something beautiful beyond words.

He didn't know how she'd seen the seraphim; he'd only had the look in her eyes to guess by, certain that they could not have been seeing the same thing. And he envied whatever spectacle her eyes had made of them. He'd already decided that he would never ask what that was . . . because if he did, he would be obligated to tell her the same.

To his own eyes, they'd looked like him.

He'd seen them as versions of himself. Not as doubles, but variations, what even might be called refinements . . . proudly horned and their muscled bodies as exquisitely proportioned as Greek statues, while their faces were the worst, cruelly handsome and majestic, rather than the brutish thing he saw in the mirror. Seven avatars of ruin and destruction. He didn't know why he should find it so disturbing, what it said about him that *these* were the forms that his eyes had given them. Only time would tell if he could convince himself it was a trick, a hallucination.

But for now, there was still the vital question:

What now?

And, finally, there was Campbell.

The kid came up behind him in the kitchen when Hellboy was wedged in front of the open refrigerator going for another bottle of Moretti. Campbell stood there with his lanky frame folded into an awkward position, as if ready for a fight he didn't want to have, his face looking nine kinds of serious.

"Look," Hellboy said, "if it's about the ravioli last night . . ."

"No. It's not."

"I know." He put the bottle back, didn't want the beer anymore. "Don't ask me this, Campbell."

"It was your idea to begin with."

"And it was a lousy one."

Campbell stepped closer, leaning in to make his point while keeping his voice low. "From Glasgow to Rome, you come all this way and it's something you can't wait to ask me. Then five minutes on the roof with Liz and it's a lousy idea."

"When I saw how much it worried her, yeah, I started looking at it another way. I can be slow like that sometimes."

"If it was a lousy idea, it was only lousy when we had other options. The last I heard, we're running a little low. So how about another look at Plan A?" Campbell said. "As for Liz . . . she's not my mother."

"No, but I don't think she'd turn up her nose at big sister."

"And she thinks of you as a big brother. So what's that make you to me—big brother once removed?" He wrapped his arms around his front, standing his ground, as though a wind were going to blow him away. "The genie's already out of the bottle. So quit thinking like a big brother and start thinking like a team leader, open up the safe, and get me the horn you ripped from that thing's head."

Where to go when the roof comes crashing in, to recuperate and regroup?

Sometimes it didn't matter, because the shingles just kept coming down.

CHAPTER 27

They'd made him as comfortable as possible, but it didn't take a lot. Nice plush chair, a footstool, a couple of blankets. Soft surfaces all around. You'd think they were worried he was going to catapult straight into epileptic fits. No cerulean blue walls, but mottled umber wasn't bad either. He thought about asking Liz to go out and find a can of paint and a roller, just to see which she'd get—the goods or the joke—but decided that now wasn't the time. She looked like she was stressing plenty already.

Handling it well, though. She'd pitched a twenty second fit when she found out, during which she gave Hellboy the mother of all dirty looks, but that was it. No more objections, no more worst-case scenarios, no reminders that he didn't have to do this and could back out any time he wanted.

"Remember what I've told you," was all Liz would say now that he was in the chair, secure as an astronaut before launch. "Remember what I've told you every single time."

He pretended not to remember. "Look both ways before crossing the void?"

Tough room. Not a flicker. Just three of them standing around him like dental hygienists, three grave faces looking down at him, red, white, and green, and the priest in the background clearly unaccustomed to milling around with nothing to do.

Hellboy hunkered down beside the chair. "You ready?"

Campbell gave a terse nod. Knew what he was supposed to look for—the trick would be to try his best to isolate it and keep the rest at a distance. Get in, get what they wanted, and get out, a psychic smash-and-grab. Easier said than done? Well . . . yeah.

He peered at the horn as Hellboy held it at the ready. A familiar thing, he'd seen plenty of cattle drives in movies, yet at the same time unnatural. Ten inches long with a ragged, blood-caked base more than two inches in diameter, tapering in a gentle curve until it hooked sharply at the tip. It looked a thousand years old and loathsome, the texture dark as mummified skin and full of fissures.

He braced his hand along his thigh, palm up but tightened into a fist. Easier to keep it steady that way.

"Okay," he said. "Just . . . put it in my hand."

Hellboy moved it closer. Waiting. The thing was just inches away now. "Uh, Campbell . . . your fingers? You gotta open them . . ."

He knew that. Just wanted to keep his fist jammed against his leg for as long as he could. Damned if he would let them see his hand tremble. He sprang his fingers open like a trap and snatched the horn away before anyone could notice.

In that final moment, when he could still think of the outer world, the world he knew, the experience was like plunging a hand into a kettle of boiling water. Not in temperature but in time, that fraction of a second before the nerves get the message, the water even feeling cool at first, and then the shock, the all-consuming shock of it rocketing up the arm and into the brain that can't believe what the hand has been stupid enough to do, *GET OUT OF THERE!,* except there was no pulling out yet, it had him, as though another hand at the bottom of the pan had latched on and yanked the rest of him in, where boiling alive was just the beginning.

The man first—the horn made of Gilmour's bone after all, Gilmour's flesh, and how he'd *hated* them, their fragility, their mortality, their tendency toward weakness and dissolution. There had to be something more, and there was, he'd found it, or it had found him, the path paved with the rabbit-fast hearts and blackened bones of—

ENOUGH

Nothing to learn here, only contamination, the toxicity of a life long since given over to the theory and practice of suffering. The man was only the tool; there was still the hand that swung it. The man was but the outer skin over the layers of the horn.

And the gates of Hell creaked open.

It roared up beneath him and he tried to dodge it, as futile as dancing on the breath of dragons—a vast and towering entity with a shadowed head that blotted out the sun and moon, and horns that gored the stars—not its true form but this one served it well, a gift from ancient tribes carried on the smoke of sacrificial fires. Screams from the embers were its symphonies, and sour tears its wine, and if it had been drunk on them before, in the next age it would bathe in salted rivers.

He was in a firestorm of its hatreds and its appetites.

Nothing could demand this much, nothing could consume this much, but it did, and had, its heart a chasm that the history of human anguish had barely begun to fill. And so it wanted more, a world not destroyed but overrun and subjugated—the human race would never go extinct as long as it suffered so exquisitely. New jihads and genocides? A good start, yes, and worst of all was understanding that Moloch spoke for legions.

They clamored, their teeth like rows of spears.

No idea . . . he'd had no idea it all could be so close . . .

ENOUGH

But he was failing, the pressure too strong, valves bursting and filters rupturing, yet he knew it was here somewhere in the maelstrom, so grab a thread and hang on, follow it to its source—

No, not a thread, a hand, a hand to replace the one he'd hacked away, a reborn hand at the end of a regrown arm— who knew the longing to be whole again better than one who wasn't?

I've got you.

Vicious triumph

I've got you . . .

even if it felt

. . . and I know what you did . . .

like coming apart in a whirlwind of razors

. . . and I know where you went

and waving goodbye

. . . and I know how to find you again.

to the ribbons of your face.

Liz's voice, *Remember what I've told you,* past and present, *Remember what I've told you every single time . . .*

I'll be there to catch you if you fall.

I remember.

And even though you couldn't, please don't blame yourself, because by now you should know better, that some of us are born for the furnace, and destined to

keep

on

falling

Hellboy knew he'd be a long time wondering which was worse: the screaming or the silence; his own sense of guilt or seeing the anguish in Liz's eyes. A long time questioning whether this had been worth it.

Answers? He supposed they were there, somewhere in the babble. They'd recorded it, of course, Abe manning the microphone, and at one point, during the godawful spasms near the end, when they'd pulled Campbell from his chair and laid him out on the floor, the horn yanked from his grasp a minute earlier but apparently failing to have severed the connection, he'd made frantic motions with his hand until Liz realized he was demanding something to write with. She'd pushed a marker into his hand and slid a pad of paper under its tip. They'd all seen experiments in automatic writing, thought this might have similar results, but it soon became dismayingly obvious that no words were taking form here. They weren't even letters. Just lines, rendered in jerks and spasms. Meaningless.

Except . . .

He was doing the same thing over and over.

There was a pattern to it: straight lines and curved lines, one set overlaying the other. Let him finish one, rip away the sheet, and he would attack the next blank in the same way, page after page, until he suddenly tore his hand away from his side and started to plunge the marker toward one eye. Hellboy caught his forearm before he could do it and took the pen away from him. When he then made as if to attack his eyes with his fingers, Liz threw herself across him, pinning his shoulders and holding his arm down until Abe, having abandoned the microphone, could get back with the medic's kit and administer a shot of Thorazine.

The silence, or the screams . . . they both seemed too loud.

Later, Hellboy slipped a pair of earphones on and listened to the tape a dozen times, transcribing and taking notes, drawing arrows between fragments that seemed to belong together, but the tape was what it was: a stream of disintegrating consciousness, bursts of observation and little of it in any particular order.

Tartarus—that came up more than once, and it had been a long time since he'd heard the word, but it was not something he would forget: one of the Greeks' names for the underworld, the lowest level where the worst of humanity went after death.

As near as he could discern from the tape, even if the realm of Tartarus was just a myth before, it was real enough now, and he supposed that there were people who would speak the name with reverence.

Matthias Herzog, for one? His name had come up too. The so-called German Aleister Crowley.

If he was putting it all together correctly, the bits and pieces of what Campbell had dug into, the professed goal of *Der Horn-Orden* to usher in an era of Hell on Earth had not just been a delusional dream they'd shared before disbanding into obscurity. Instead, it was a process that was still underway.

When he could do no more with the tape, he took the cleanest of the sheets that Campbell had scribbled on and faxed it to Kate at the Cornwall safehouse. Gave her a call a few minutes later.

"Does this mean anything to you?" he asked. "Go as wild as you want. There's gotta be something here, I just don't know what it is."

He could hear the flimsy fax paper rustling over the line, then Kate asked, "How many of these did he draw?"

"Seventeen. All of them pretty much the same."

"Well, he was obviously being emphatic about it." Now he could hear her slurping at coffee, tea, something that would keep her going until the late hours. "Maybe an emblem of some kind, a sigil? A talisman?"

"That's the first thing I thought of. Except I don't get the feeling that's what he was trying to get across. Seems like if that's what it was, it's simple enough he could've said so. He could still get out a word or two at a time at this point."

"Did he say *anything?*" Kate asked, and he heard her blowing at a cup, or mug.

"Yeah. 'Steps,' is what I think it was," he said. "What are you drinking?"

"Cuppa Earl Grey. Okay, steps . . . any numbers along with that?"

"Just once, he could've said 'ninety-eight,' but I wouldn't swear to it."

"Well, it definitely doesn't look like a stairway, this drawing." A sigh, more rustling. Kate tapping a pen on her desk. "You said to go wild?"

"Absolutely."

"What if it's a diagram for a way of moving? Instead of looking at all these lines as being part of the same thing, maybe what we've got here is two *different* things: a place, and a way of walking through it."

Hellboy spun the picture this way, that way. "Okay . . . I see what you mean."

"Say the straight lines are established paths. Like hiking trails or sidewalks or something. Or if they're inside, hallways maybe. And the line that's mostly curved, and those places where it loops before going on—you'll notice that's the only unbroken line here, looks like he drew it in a single pass. Are they all like that?"

Hellboy shuffled through the stack. She could be onto something here. "Yeah. They are."

"Then maybe that's the way of moving through the space. Intent could be a part of it too, but maybe the main thing he was trying to get across was here's your path, and here's the way you walk it."

"And then you wind up . . . ?"

"Someplace else. Probably not good. Tartarus, this *new* Tartarus, if the two are connected," she said. "Again, if only for comparison, this brings us back to the Faerie realm. Like the glamour used against the armored car crew, if that's what happened there, but I can't think of a better theory. What this drawing makes me think of are accounts in Celtic folklore where you have this hapless guy walking through the countryside, minding his own business, and all of a sudden he finds himself in this new landscape—similar, maybe, but new. The people are different, the music's different, and they all seem to be in on this big joke that he's not. He's crossed over into Faerie. He didn't mean to, he just took the right path into the place where the worlds overlap. And if he gets back, he usually finds that time passed very differently there."

"Right, right," Hellboy said. "He was only there a night or two, maybe had a good time dancing, but he gets back and everybody's telling him—"

"That he's been gone for years," Kate finished.

Hellboy could feel the pieces starting to click together. "Like that kid from the armored car, dropped dead on the street. Left Chicago for Europe in 1968, nobody sees him again, and now he pops up here looking hardly any older."

"Except he's not been in Faerie, that's for sure," Kate said. "There are these types of magic, and maybe they're most often associated with the Faerie folk, who are more mischievous than malevolent, but they don't *own* them, you see. They're just principles. And if that's what this drawing of Campbell's is, then that's the principle it's using. A whole other intent behind it, sounds like, but there you have it. This diagram . . . if you think of it as an overhead view, is there anyplace it reminds you of?"

"Not exactly," he said. "But I'm pretty sure I know the place to start looking."

"Good. Send me a memo on it soon, would you? And a rough map? If we've got ourselves a thin spot, or some other kind of portal, especially into the kind of place all of this seems to be indicating, we need to get it charted." He could hear the pen tapping on her desk again. "Umm . . . how *is* Campbell, really? Is he going to be okay?"

"I wish I had an answer for you," he said. And that he was a better liar, while he was at it. "I wish it was a good one."

"What about Liz—how's she? I know she'd really bonded with him."

"I can't tell, Kate. One minute I think she hates me, and the next I think maybe she understands. Not that it was the *right* decision, necessarily, just . . . the direction things took."

"Cam threw himself on a grenade, is what it sounds like to me. That's your job, usually. But not this time. This one only he could handle," Kate said. "Liz gave him the courage to do it. Maybe she should hear that."

"No. She shouldn't." He didn't often disagree with Kate, but this was one time he did. "I can tell that much, at least."

"I was a closet kid for a while. Before the bureau, when I was living in foster homes. Did I ever tell you that? Probably not. Probably never seemed like it had much to do with anything before."

If she was repeating herself, he didn't seem to mind.

"I figured if I just stayed in the closet, with my head on my knees, that would be the safest thing for everybody. An isolation chamber . . . I may not have known what it was called then, but I had the instinct for it. So I'd crawl in all the way to the back where I'd shoved the shoes and stuff out of the way, and I'd curl up and tune everything out until I had to pee so bad I couldn't hold it anymore. All the rest of the world stopped at that closet door."

Campbell had found a corner in one of the bedrooms,

driven by some self-protective instinct that kept going even if his need for speech had gone.

"One foster family told people I was retarded. Autistic, they probably meant, but that was at a time and place when retarded pretty much covered everything."

As she looked at him pressed into the corner, holding his knees together with one hand and the knob of his other wrist, and his eyes like two pits into which she could stare without ever finding bottom, she wondered how long the Thorazine would last, and if she would even know when it wore off.

"I'm sorry I made a promise to you I couldn't keep. I really thought I could . . ."

And with her legs drawn up and her chin on her knees, Liz sat with an arm around his shoulder, hoping he knew she was there, so that if he was trapped with something else in that closet, he might at least know he wasn't all alone.

CHAPTER 28

They waited for the break of day before breaking ground.

Here in the stretch of countryside to which the Old Appian Way had led him twice before, Hellboy had no idea if anything was going to be coming up out of that hole. But if it did, this time he wanted sunlight and a clear view on their side.

As the sun gathered strength, shuttered through the pines, a fine haze rose from the hills beyond them, and he took up the shovel he'd brought. Its blade was wide and flat across, better for scraping than for ditches or postholes. He used it like a turf-cutter in the bogs of Ireland, hacking through the vines and the great scab of earth plastered with thick mud across the door he'd found underneath it yesterday morning. He and Abe and Liz . . . they peeled and pushed and pulled, until they'd cleared the site one slab of loamy soil at a time, and it was revealed from the middle outward, to the heavy plates of the hinges: a pair of doors, each three feet by five, angled across the slope of a low plateau jutting from the nearest hill.

They were moist and stained with earth, their centers bristling with bolts that implied they were braced inside

with heavy crosspieces. Absent handles, they seemed meant
to be opened only from the inside. They didn't look terribly
old, at least not what *he* thought of as old. But could they
have been there for sixty, sixty-five years—say, since the
early thirties? When *Der Horn-Orden* seemed to vanish in
Berlin? Yeah. He could see that easily enough.

He dropped to one knee before the doors and threw his
fist into the middle where they met. The wood may have
been spongy on the outside, but it was still dense underneath, and felt thick. He pounded them until the heavy
boards began to come apart and fall away from one another, clattering on what sounded like stone. When he'd
cleared enough of a hole, he could see crudely makeshift
steps descending to what appeared from above to be a corridor five feet wide.

He ripped the rest free as the stale air of ages rose past
his face.

Hellboy went first, kicking the shattered boards to either
side, stepping down, down, down to the corridor floor. It
appeared original while the stairs did not, the steps seeming
to have been added later as a way out. Stonework, all of it,
the floor as far as he could see paved with flat, irregularly
shaped pieces that had been fitted together with time and
care. How long ago? If it was much younger than 1700
years, he'd be amazed.

"What *is* this?" Liz asked, her voice in a hush, the way
you instinctively spoke in such places.

"One big grave, I think," Hellboy said. "Catacombs."

"By the look of them, unknown to the rest of the
world," Abe said, and shined his flashlight ahead.

The beam glanced along rough walls, with hollows cut

in their sides, five and six atop one another like berths on a ship. Overhead, the ceiling was arched, and even at the sides high enough to let Hellboy pass through without stooping.

Every time he had traveled out this far, they'd passed the Catacombs of Saint Callisto and others, all of them known for centuries, where every day tourists were guided down into the distant past. But these appeared to have evaded discovery by archaeologists and excavators . . . although that wasn't to say they'd escaped violation. When they reached the first rank of recesses cut into the wall, Hellboy could see that someone had smashed the thin marble slabs that had been fitted across the hollows like seals. Shards of stone littered the inside of each compartment, in fragments and dust over bones and linen wrappings so old and dry they might fall apart at a touch.

"Grave robbers?" Liz asked.

"Maybe. But I doubt it. I don't think these bodies would've been buried with much of value," Helboy said. "My guess is desecration."

"But why?"

"It's a powerful place. Some people would consider it holy ground, even today. So there's power in defiling it, too. What we've got here . . . ?" he said. "It's a mass burial site of some of the earliest Christians."

While the pagan Romans cremated their dead, Abe told her, the first Christians sought to bury theirs whole, confident of a resurrection of the same bodies that had served them in life. Because Rome forbade burying corpses within the city, the Christians went outside it, where they dug underground into soft volcanic rock, cutting elaborate networks of passages and galleries through hundreds of acres, so their dead could lie undisturbed in the walls. They buried them here, memorialized them here, and in times of persecution, they let the dead protect them here—Roman law regarded burial sites as sacred.

But in time, as happens to all such places, they were forgotten.

When the more famed catacombs were rediscovered late in the sixteenth century, after over a thousand years since they'd been lost, they were first believed to be the ruins of an ancient city.

And they were, Abe said. Just a city of the dead.

It was silent here, the close walls wrapping their footsteps and their breath tightly around them. The farther in they went, flashlight beams sweeping ahead and from side to side, the more elaborate the layout became, with other galleries branching off this one, and breaks in the burial tiers where their builders had decorated the walls with painted frescoes of patriarchs and saints.

While the dust of so many centuries may not have been thick down here, in such an airless place, you'd think it would at least lie undisturbed. But it didn't. Footprints were smudged along the floor, and as soon as Hellboy realized they were there, he took care to follow them back where they led, lest they get sidetracked and risk confusing prints that were already here with those left by their own feet.

With Liz and Abe at his shoulders, he followed the tracks past one intersection, then another, and another, then around a bend where a new gallery skewed off from the main corridor. The deeper in the tracks led, the closer the layout seemed to match what Campbell had drawn. Not all of it, certainly, but the landmarks that he'd deemed most important.

The dead and more dead, lying amid shattered stone—the tracks led past them to a chamber that opened off the new gallery like a small room, black as the night of a new moon until he shined his light within. And here the tracks simply ended, a couple of steps inside the doorway, as if whatever made them had come and gone from nowhere.

He pulled one of the drawings from a pocket and checked it against the route they'd come. It fit. As well as he could have expected, it fit. All but for the approach, the pathwalking that became its own key.

"Ninety-eight steps, walked a particular way—that's what Campbell was trying to get across, I think," he said. "Let's count off and backtrack, see where that puts us . . ."

Very near the entrance, as it turned out. Was the entrance itself the crucial point of origin? Or was some other nearby spot the designated beginning? They examined the stones of the floor a few paces in both directions, to allow for differences in stride; checked the walls, too, for markings that might have been added later. But nothing stood out. Nothing looked as though it hadn't been here since the corridors echoed with prayers for the dead.

"Maybe it doesn't matter," Liz said, "as long as there are ninety-eight."

"Gut instinct? It matters," he said. "Magic's not open-ended. There are balances. Cause, effect. You've got a definite destination? You've got to have a definite origin."

Behind him, Abe tapped his flashlight against the edge of one of the cubicula closer to the floor, on the left side of the corridor.

"This gets my vote," he said.

Hellboy and Liz squatted down for a look. The human bones had been disturbed more here than inside the other recesses they'd checked. The skull had been shattered against its bed of stone, and in its place sat the skull of a bull. However long ago, it looked to have been put in place when fresh, scraps of leathery hide shriveled back from the muzzle and over the broad ivory dome, and the rock beneath it stained with blood and decay.

"I'll go first," Hellboy said. "We don't know one thing about what's on the other end of this. Neither of you have to follow."

"You know better than that, H.B.," Liz told him.

For better or for worse, he did.

Diagram in hand, he began, *one two,* counting under his breath as he measured each pace along the way, *eighteen nineteen,* doing his best to follow the path set down by Campbell's hand. The broad curves, the tighter zigzags, *thirty-four,* the double-backs before continuing ahead. Would anyone walk this way by accident? They might, and probably had somewhere, *sixty-six,* but if intent were a part of it too, as Kate had suggested, he had this covered as well, *eighty-three,* his will focused on making the crossing and nothing else, making the turn, pacing down the branching gallery and toward the side chamber, *ninety-six*

ninety-seven

ninety . . .

. . . eight.

Considering the totality of the displacement, the moment was remarkably calm, but he supposed it helped that he'd been walking in near-darkness, confined to a small battery-thrown pool of light. He didn't find the transition itself any more disorienting than he might have if he'd kept his head down while indoors, then lifted his gaze once he was outside.

Then his eyes truly registered the *scale* of the place.

Before he took another step, he grabbed a fat stub of chalk he'd stuffed into a pocket back in the apartment, stooped, and thickly marked the point of his entrance on the rocky floor. Pulled out a handful of chemical lights and snapped them into glowing life, scattered them into a soft blue circle, then moved out of the way.

Staring, impossible to take it all in at once, and he had to admit: Nothing could have prepared him to find *this*.

Footsteps behind him. Friendly, he assumed.

"Oh my god," Liz said. "This can't be real."

"It may not be real," Abe said, "but it's here."

CHAPTER 29

This would always be the greatest power of the unknown, the unknow*able,* Liz thought: to root your feet to the ground so thoroughly that the mere idea of movement seems impossible.

With a single step she'd crossed a threshold from one realm into another, from claustrophobia to agoraphobia, but that was the least of it. There were things the mind resisted, could barely begin to process . . . and *this* was one of them. Hubris and cruelty and decadence on a magnitude that defied imagination.

A few moments in and the panic started to hit, Liz whirling to look behind and realizing there was no doorway there anymore, no corridor either, no stone walls cut into file cabinets for the dead—*How do I get back? How will I ever GET BACK?*—and she imagined being trapped here forever. Abe must have sensed her sudden alarm and grabbed her wrist.

"If we walked into this place," he told her, fixing her with his aqua eyes as calm as a summer lake, "then we can walk out again . . . and *will.*"

If you had to call it anything, you could call it a cavern, its distant rock walls gleaming with a black sheen like coal or wet obsidian . . . but no cavern this size could have existed near the undetected catacombs outside of Rome. This could have *swallowed* the catacombs, and maybe Rome too, if not for one thing: This place was not of the earth, nor in it, but *alongside* it, a few steps away in places where the borders between worlds had been rubbed thin. You couldn't fly to Heaven, you couldn't dig to Hell, and, as with Kate's oft-referred-to Faerie, the only way to get here was knowing where and how to walk.

But right now, her impulse was to run the other way.

She supposed it was large enough to contain its own weather. The roof was far enough above that it dissolved into a murky haze—not quite clouds, nor mists either—a veil over a weak source of light that cast this world into perpetual gloom.

So maybe it was a mercy that she couldn't see the Moloch any clearer.

It rose before them, above them, something a colossus could only aspire to be. It looked cut from the rock, and where rock was not enough, cast from ores that gleamed cold in the meager light. Its head was an eclipsing shadow, and the statue squatted upon the cavern floor as if poised to spring upright, so the horns might rip bleeding gashes between worlds.

And the arms. Dear god, the arms . . .

Passing between its knees and either side of the cauldron of its belly, its arms stretched down toward them, each hand resting palm-up on the cavern floor. Its right hand held a network of temples that intimidated with spikes and spires, battlements and buttresses. Its left hand . . . she couldn't tell. Whatever it held was smaller, lower, and from this distance all she knew was that they could only be a greater or lesser degree of terrible.

And so far, it all looked deserted.

"*That's* the best they could do?" Hellboy said, and whether he knew it or not, it was just the thing she needed to hear, that could pry her feet from the cavern floor.

He decided they should check out the structures built upon the left hand, since it wasn't as obvious what they were. They hadn't yet gotten there—hadn't even reached the terraced stairs at the tips of the spread fingers—when they started to find the first bodies.

Eight of them lay scattered on the cavern floor, and immediately reminded him of the armored car's hijackers, all bones and sinew, but in worse condition, much worse, as if most of the flesh and fat had been sucked out of them, to leave behind skeletal shells in a shrink-wrap of skin.

Except they still weren't dead.

They'd been on the verge of it for a very long time, and he wondered if it would ever truly arrive, even after their bodies started to fall apart, their term of servitude to the devils they'd courted never considered complete.

He knelt beside one of them, drawn by the clothing: filthy, ragged, blue-and-white remains of an old sailor shirt . . . fetish wear among certain young men in Weimar Berlin, Hellboy had learned. This one—aged hideously, unnaturally—must have been here since the very beginning.

Hellboy hauled him up by the shoulder, looked him in the face, could smell the stale dust of his breath. He looked at the hands and forearms, worn raw and callused so many times that they looked as though they'd been dipped in a yellow, cracking glaze. He looked into the eyes, red and runny and still trying to find what was right in front of them.

"Hey," Hellboy said. "Was it everything you hoped for?"

No answer. Hellboy laid him back onto the stone with more care than he probably deserved.

"I bet we're gonna find hundreds of these before we're through here," he said. "Maybe thousands."

"Even with tens of thousands—this?" Abe said, and pointed at everything that towered overhead. "They could do *this?*"

"They're slaves, Abe. They just had the whips put to them on the inside."

He thought of the Egyptians who had built the pyramids, so many of them that today their graves were like a city in the desert. Frightening to speculate on what they might have built had they been hosts to devils.

"But watch yourselves," he warned. "There must be *some* left around here in better shape than the rest. Newer ones, maybe, haven't been used up like the oldest. Those are the ones they must've thrown at us on the outside."

They pushed on, ascending the steps to the plateau of the left hand, walking the length of one finger until the structures here began to gel into context. Machinery, it all turned out to be, dark and oiled, still gleaming with the kind of newness that can only be preserved with a lack of use, and the greatest hope he could extend toward it was that it never would be. It was an open-air slaughterhouse, an abattoir turned inside-out and rebuilt in a ring around the outer edges of the palm. An elaborate network of drains and gutters had been built to channel the runoff toward the center, where it would spill over the sides and . . .

Disappear.

There *was* no center of the palm. Just a hole. No, not even that. A hole implied edges, inner walls, and this, after a certain depth, had none. Bottomless? Probably not, but who could tell? It was a well as big around as a stadium, descending into a vortex that churned and swirled with infinite shades of darkness. He could think of nothing worse than what might one day be drawn from it.

You belong to two worlds, Moloch had told him through a borrowed throat. *You exist to open the doorway between them.*

Holding onto the housing of a contraption built for a crosscut saw the length of a telephone pole, he stared out into it, like a lake of blackest storm clouds.

That doorway has never been closer . . .

He wondered if it was just his imagination . . .

There are other ways of opening the door. And it will *open.*

. . . or if Abe and Liz heard it whispering too.

What you must do, and do soon, is decide how you will be greeted by what comes through.

"With fear, I hope," he whispered back. "That'll do just fine."

He became aware of a closer voice, and turned to find Abe and Liz wearing expressions edging toward concern, as if they'd had to call him a few times to get his attention. He gave it now, full and undivided.

"What exactly have they *done* here?" Liz asked.

"I doubt we'll ever know it all," he said, "but my take? This whole place is an antechamber to Hell. A way to connect Hell and Earth, even though they're never supposed to be connected." He gestured toward the cavern. "This space and time here . . . I think it already existed. Parallel world, whatever—possible to get to from our side. They just reworked it to what it is now. . . .

"That group from Berlin wanted Hell on Earth?" He shook his head. "Hell has its own timetable, and doesn't tolerate rivals. But it wasn't above using those people to put Hell one step closer." He pointed at the vortex, surrounded by its engine of suffering. "Once they're able to put this all the way through, the rest would probably be easy. It's the back door into our world."

Not just through the catacombs that had led them here, either, Hellboy thought. He had a feeling that another passage dumped out somewhere in the heart of Rome, if only because of how quickly the hijackers had ended up at the armored car.

In fact, it wouldn't have surprised him to learn that there were several portals to and from this realm, in the hidden places beneath the surface of the earth. The sewers of Berlin and Moscow, maybe; the subways of London and New York. And if there were, it seemed reasonable to believe that they'd been swallowing the innocent, as well as those who came willingly to serve.

They found the proof of this a little later, along another section of the abattoir, where a body hung by the neck from a framework of pipes surrounding gears and grinders. An obviously new arrival, she wore jeans and a bright pullover top, and had fashioned her noose from the straps of a nylon backpack that lay near the dangling tips of her shoes.

If you'd come to surrender your soul, would you bring it in a backpack?

They took her down, even though there was no soil here to bury her. They took her down because it seemed the only thing to do, unknotting the strap from around her bruised and purple throat. With a careful fingertip, Liz pulled free the strands of hair, dyed a cheerfully unnatural red, that had caught in the corners of her mouth. She looked dead only a day or two, but that might have been an illusion, because in this place, this new Tartarus, decay seemed to come in its own interminable time.

In her backpack they found a university ID and three books, plus notebooks and pens, a portable CD player and discs and headphones, lipstick and more. Liz folded it up, pack and all, and put it in her own backpack.

And in one pocket of the girl's jeans was the last thing she must have written:

Si je suis déjà en enfer, est-ce encore un suicide?

Hellboy handed the note to Liz. "You know French, don't you? A little?"

She took it, even though she looked as if he were handing her a bouquet of thorns. She gave it a long perusal.

So much for needing intent to walk the path into this place.

" 'If I'm already in Hell, is it still suicide?' " she read aloud, and her eyes never moved, and her expression didn't change, as her hand flickered blue and orange, the paper slowly curling to brown and black, then sifting into fine gray ash.

•   •   •

They made the crossing from left hand to right, one ebony mesa to the other. To Hellboy it felt like they'd done it in less than two hours, but he allowed that time passed strangely here. At their right, the Moloch statue was a constant presence, an eternal threat. He wondered if its pendulous belly was hollow, a furnace that could burn entire forests and send flames roaring up a throat and out the mouth so far above.

More bodies? Those too, in ones and twos and by the dozen, and at their worst it became like walking through the site of a mass suicide, another Jonestown Massacre, except these sometimes twitched or tried to crawl, to reach, to bite. It was worse than if they'd been able to attack—he could *deal* with that, had been dealing with things trying to kill him all his life. Not this, though, these fields of bodies wallowing in the rags of clothing last in style before the Nazi Party came to power. Whenever he and Liz and Abe left them behind, in the unearthly quiet on echoing stone, they continued to hear the clicking of nails and teeth for a long time after, and the wheezing of desiccated lungs.

If these people, and the things that wore their skins, had succeeded in obtaining the scroll from the armored car, he had no doubts that they would have brought it back here. He couldn't think of any reason why they still wouldn't. And if he didn't yet understand what the scroll meant to them, why they wanted it so fiercely, he had a feeling he was getting closer to it with every step.

Now that they were here, the right hand held what looked to him like a city center of cathedrals run amok, architectural cancers meant to petrify instead of uplift. They wandered its streets, the bodies even more abundant here, a hellish Calcutta where they were *all* dying, eternally, sprawled in streets and propped against walls like beggars too weak to lift their hands.

It was noisier here, too. Now and again they would hear a shriek—maybe rage, maybe pain, maybe madness—and the walls and cavern kept the echoes alive forever.

Soon a new sound whispered around the corners, then rapidly began to build with a fearsome energy: footsteps, a multitude of them, on the run.

"Guns out," Hellboy said. "I've got a feeling these might be the ones that were supposed to intercept us the other night."

They stood back-to-back and triangulated, Liz at his left shoulder and Abe at his right. The way things echoed here, it was hard to tell exactly where the stampede was coming from.

"And remember," he added, in case anyone had forgotten how the armored car's crew had fallen, *"don't let these things get close enough to bite."*

Moments later a group of bottom-dwellers—there had to be at least thirty of them—poured out of the passageway between two of the baroque black walls ahead of him. They may have been lean and leathery, but there was nothing feeble about them. They looked able-bodied enough to do damage—latter-day disciples who'd arrived long after the Berliners littering the caverns and streets, or maybe those that Tartarus had ensnared and then converted.

"We've got more back here, too," Abe said.

Hellboy cursed and started to aim. Flanked from two

sides, they couldn't handle this simply by stepping back and letting Liz broil them as they came head-on. This was happening too fast, and she needed time to get control, and Abe was too close to risk it if she didn't. No, they'd have to do this the messy way.

At his shoulders, they started shooting at the attackers coming up from behind.

Abe and Liz carried nine-millimeter automatics with high-capacity magazines. In one sense Hellboy was at a disadvantage, stuck with a six-shooter after all, but then, what it lacked in capacity it made up for in firepower. It could put rounds through a cinderblock wall as though it were cardboard. Flesh and bone were no barriers at all.

He chose his shots carefully as they came, didn't fire until he could take them lined up one after another, five and six deep, then he would squeeze the trigger and drop them by the handful, blasting through the chest of the first one, the huge round tearing out his back and into the next one, and so on, like watching them fall to a reaper's scythe.

Behind him, Abe and Liz were firing more quickly, brass casings bouncing underfoot across the stone. Men, women, and dear god even children . . . without the advantages of night and surprise they had no chance, yet they kept coming no matter how many fell around them, hurled into harm's way by masters to whom they were expendable.

The gunfire rolled through the darkened canyons in overlapping echoes, and Hellboy was already feeling sick with revulsion by the time he dug into his pocket for a speedloader to feed the revolver's cylinder another six rounds. His bullets, Abe's bullets, Liz's . . . they were only finishing the work begun years ago, decades ago. Bodies crumpled and disintegrated, they came apart and splashed the streets with blood and bile. He cursed at the senselessness of it. This was Hell's idea of sport, idle amusement. Like throwing water balloons at them.

Ahead of him, the last survivors were starting to fan out—one bullet, one kill now. With his gun reloaded for the third time, he moved forward, saving his shots for the ones that looked like they might be trying to slip around and come at them from the side. The ones directly in front he let get close enough to punch or backhand, swatting them to the ground and grimacing at the feel of breaking bones.

He heard an impact and a burst of breath, caught a flash of movement from the corner of his eye. He glanced around, saw that one of the group from behind had gotten through, close enough to take Liz down with a flying tackle. She was trying to stiff-arm him up and away, the top of her pistol wedged lengthwise across his open mouth, the way you'd block an epileptic from biting his tongue.

He reached in opposite directions—fired at his nearest attacker while crushing the neck of Liz's assailant, then wrenching him off her, hurling him at two more to send them sprawling with knees shattered backwards.

"Let's get moving!" he shouted, and made sure Liz and Abe were both upright and ready to go before rushing forward. Except for a few stragglers and wounded, the path ahead was clear, if littered with bodies and parts, strewn about like the aftermath of a bombing. Step light enough, fast enough, and you could almost fool yourself into thinking they were something else underfoot.

They sprinted past black walls scored with filigree and rivets, and openings into corridors as dim as sewers. Once they'd run far enough to put these behind them, they came to a kind of open plaza, with long views all around. Back the way they'd come, the last of their pursuers had given up the chase, still milling about the middle of the street the equivalent of a block away or more, not even showing an inclination to take cover as they were picked off one by one, at leisure. Aim, fire, watch them drop. There was no triumph in it, and it had even gone beyond the point at which Hellboy could think of them as mercy killings.

Liz fired until empty and the slide of her pistol locked open, then she hunched forward with both hands braced on her knees.

"What was the *point* of all that?" she said. "It was nothing but a slaughter, and they just kept coming."

"The way you're looking right now—that *was* the point of it," he told her softly. "Just to get under your skin."

"Well, it worked," she said.

He knew how she felt, had hated every moment, being forced to render so many bodies into pulp and kindling. The kids were the worst. And there was no way to hold accountable the ones responsible for it.

But in lieu of anything better, Matthias Herzog would suffice.

They found him on a throne in a hall fit for mad kings.

If they'd wanted, they could have spent weeks in this section of Tartarus alone, exploring and mapping and charting the apparent purposes of each edifice. Most

seemed made for worship—their version of it, at least—
topped with bell towers that soared from the sanctuary
roofs on piers of malignant blue-black stone.

But to Hellboy's eye, one building looked different from
the others, as if made to serve other needs. Its appearance
was more primeval, its base flowing outward like slag, and
into its outer walls they'd cut niches for statues, hundreds of
them in apparent homage to their rulers or to themselves.
The steps were fractured slabs, as if to test the mettle of all
who dared to ascend them, and over the doors was a hollow
in which burned a sulphuric yellow flame.

"You think it's here?" Abe said. "The scroll?"

"You think this place needs bank vaults?" Hellboy said.
"If they brought it down here at all, they brought it down
to wait for something. And *this* is a place for planning wars.
Not praying for the outcome." He looked back at Liz,
who'd gone very quiet since finding the dead French girl,
and almost totally silent after they'd been forced to gun
down so many attackers. "You doing okay?"

"I don't know what I am, H.B.," she said. "I just know
I'll be better when I'm out of here."

He shoved the doors wide and in they went.

There were no bodies here but one, and he waited for
them at the far end of the hall. Half the length of a football
field to reach a throne built for something that had never
occupied it. The man in it now was a poor substitute, mortal flesh and bone, and withered almost beyond recognition, although he carried one last great joke played upon
him. His left arm, lost on a battlefield long ago and far
away, then slowly restored from infancy to manhood as a
promise of power, had continued to grow. It hung from his

misshapen shoulder like a knotty club, tipping him forever to one side—not so large he would be anchored to one spot, but a grotesque weight he would have to drag behind him. He had the festering scrapes and sores to prove it.

Hellboy, still many paces away, lifted his right hand and made a fist. "Get past a certain size, they start to turn impractical, don't they?"

Matthias Herzog said nothing. The only way Hellboy knew he was still alive was the reverberant sound of his breath, like a whisper of wind forced through dried cornhusks.

Abe, he'd noticed, had drifted toward the right side of the hall, taking Liz with him. The same yellow fires as over the entrance burned in a row along the walls as well, but smaller, in receptacles like oil lamps. Abe seemed drawn to something above them—carvings, they looked like, panels of them, but in the dancing light and shadows Hellboy couldn't make out the details.

He slowed, though, as he approached the throne, inspecting the floor ahead with care, and the ceiling too. He doubted there were traps—couldn't imagine the builders anything but secure in their invincibility—but sometimes caution was a virtue, a hard-earned lesson he still forgot sometimes.

"Hellboy," Abe said quietly, urgently, and Liz came running back over to him.

She put her hand on his shoulder and pulled, made him stoop so she could put her mouth to his ear. "Take off your coat," she whispered. "Belt too. Everything."

"How come?"

"Because if Herzog's as half-blind as the rest of the old

ones, he can't see you yet. I don't know what he can hear, or understand of English, but I don't think he's seen you yet. You can *use* that . . ."

As he left them on the floor behind him, the outer trappings of his life, Hellboy began to understand. The clothes make the man, and *un*make the demon—he'd known this for as long as he could remember. It had been his tactic, however feeble, for reassuring those who might be prone to fear him.

But here it would be a liability. Here it was better to be feared.

Better to approach the throne not as something pretending to be a man, but in the body he was born in, the fury of his color undiminished.

His hooves clicked upon the brittle floor. He squared his shoulders and let his breath rumble deep in his chest, and with every step let himself grow back into the demon.

The throne. It could've been his if he'd wanted it. He could cast off this pitiful pretender, tear apart the fragile body and decorate the hall with the pieces, then wait for the doors between worlds to open.

But that was not his nature.

Although Herzog didn't need to know this.

He shot his left hand forward and seized the wattled throat; thrust his huge right hand out flat, demanding what was his with a wordless roar. He leaned in close, almost nose to nose, eye to milky, opaque eye. Under hair like sparse gray weeds, Matthias Herzog's scalp was as yellowed as tallow, and looked just as likely to melt. Behind a beard as patchy as what remained on his skull, his mouth smelled of rot.

If he let himself, if he looked at Herzog as a man rather than a monster, Hellboy could almost feel sympathy for him, as he would for anyone in this state. But all that went away as soon as he reminded himself of what Herzog was: He'd bred babies for the fire. He'd give the whole world over to the fire. He'd led hundreds, maybe thousands, down his path.

And he smiled. Into a pitiless red face, Herzog smiled.

"Ist es Zeit?" he wheezed. Is it time?

"Ja," Hellboy answered. *"Jawohl."*

Herzog sighed with satisfaction, the pleasure of a job well done, and in a display as humanly painful as anything Hellboy had seen in years, let his ugly tree branch of an arm tumble to the floor, then dragged himself off the throne after it. He turned then, back to the throne, grunting as he heaved a section of its seat upward on unseen hinges.

In the hollow lay the titanium case, stolen from Hellboy's wrist almost a week ago. He could have grabbed it, but why bother—every movement Herzog made looked to be an excruciating effort. Let him finish what he started, even if it ground his bones to splinters.

Hellboy took the case when offered; found it unlocked but undamaged, the scroll inside looking no worse for its detours.

Leaving Herzog gasping on the floor for now, he joined Abe and Liz at the wall.

"What's over here?" he asked.

"Past and present, some of it," Abe said. "And one possible future."

In the jaundiced flickering of the flames beneath each

one, he began to see the carvings for what they were. Scenes and tableaus cut into rock, they served the same purpose as stained glass windows and cave art: telling a story that must be preserved, depicting events to come so they'll be that much more likely to happen.

Such plans they'd had for the scroll.

The first scene in which Hellboy spotted it, it was in the possession of a horned figure shown giving it to some sort of holy man who looked a bit like a pope, and then again he didn't. False pope, anti-pope, rival pope, none of the above. Maybe some figure yet to emerge, still biding his time in obscurity. His power was evident enough, if not his identity or position. Other panels followed, other holy men—by their headgear you shall know them. In their raised hands they clenched the scroll, but he couldn't tell who spoke in endorsement of it and who spoke in denunciation. Each looked as furious as the one before.

The armies came next, the rallied faithful, although it wasn't clear what they were faithful to, or if they even knew for sure. Pogroms and persecutions, jihads and crusades. The dead piled up like mountains and blood poured from the sky and the door to Hell burst its locks.

He'd heard it said before that its hinges turned most easily on hatred.

Plenty of that out there already, just waiting for a cause.

Its power doesn't reside in whose hand really put the ink to it, Father Simon had told him. *Its true power lies in what human beings—and* other *beings—choose to make of it.*

True enough.

But the devils could never pull it off without the help of all the goddamn hateful men.

He gathered up his gear and put it back on, chained the giant cuff to his wrist. And just before they left, he paid one last visit to Matthias Herzog, who lay in a rasping heap at the foot of the throne. Hellboy glared down at the man and didn't care if he could understand his words or not, just knew he could never walk out of here before delivering the worst curse he could think of.

"I hope you live another thousand years."

CHAPTER 30

They were back on the cavern floor, the houses of the unholy far behind, when they began to voice what Liz knew each of them had to have been thinking for almost the entire time they'd been here: What should they *do* now that they knew of this place? It was all well and good to have recovered the scroll, for whatever brownie points that would earn in the long run, but it didn't change the fact that Tartarus existed. Such a realm, once made, could never be safely *un*made.

On the one hand, there was so much to explore here, so many secrets it might reveal to those who could stomach the place. But would this even matter? Expeditions might be conducted safely, but in the meantime, and maybe ever after, Tartarus would lie there like a bomb waiting to go off. It existed solely as a shortcut between worlds, and she feared that one day it *would* fulfill its purpose.

As well, it might continue to swallow innocents who blundered into it in those places where the barriers were thin.

Noémi Kivits—that was the name on the student ID. Liz reached one hand around to her backpack, felt the bulge of the girl's belongings, recovered for . . . well, she

342

couldn't say why right now, only that it felt like something that had to be done.

Next to them, she felt a harder lump, the gift—if it could be called that—that she'd accepted yesterday in the middle of the blaze at the house near the Tiber. She'd brought it for no other reason than knowing from the first moment she'd touched it that she would have to carry it everywhere, until there was a reason to be rid of it.

Better sooner than later.

"We need to go back to the left hand," she said, and if Abe or Hellboy doubted this, they kept it to themselves.

They retraced their steps from the earlier crossing, ascending the rounded stairs at the tip of the nearest finger, and once they'd mounted the platform, continued toward the ring of suffering and the turbulent well it surrounded.

The closer they drew to the area where they'd last been before setting off for the statue's other hand, the more apparent it became that something was different this time. Liz knew it even before she was close enough to see the small, subtle movements, the parody of life. She knew it the same way someone walks into a room and notices the chair that's out of place, the hallway door standing open that should have been closed.

That's not the way we left her, Liz thought. *We left her lying down . . .*

And so they had. But now Noémi was sitting upright with her back against the flat edge of a girder supporting one of the infernal machines.

"Oh, that's wrong," Liz murmured to no one in particular. "That is *so* wrong."

• • •

It was the French girl's body, obviously, but Hellboy knew she was no longer the one behind those eyes. When he was close enough, he looked deeply into them and saw the same simmering magma of malevolence and scorn that he'd last seen in a basement flat in Scotland. The same midnight sneer of junkies and cutthroats.

On the one hand, Moloch had not worn her skin long enough to truly make it his own. On the other, he was halfway to home turf here, and would be all the stronger for it, that much more *present*. Hellboy could feel it, a crawling sensation in his gut, the involuntary disgust most people felt when they switched on a kitchen light and saw the floor alive with roaches.

Noémi's hands toyed with the nylon strap that they'd removed from around her throat. It was back in place, a noose again, and her hands slid the slipknot up and down . . . tightening, loosening, tightening again.

Hellboy reached back to touch Liz's hand; felt her trembling with anger that she'd been able to suppress until now. He gave her palm a slow, reassuring squeeze.

Noémi's eyes lit on the case shackled once more to his wrist. Seeming to concede the loss with the merest tic of indifference.

"Do you know why you'll still lose, in the end? Why you *have* to?" The voice was a skinned-raw croak. "It's because what you count as victories are such *small* things."

Hellboy hoisted the case, made it impossible to ignore. "Small victory, big ripples, the way I read it back in your war room."

"Big ripples, vast ocean." The Moloch cocked its head,

taunting. "You should know. You were hauled through enough of it. At my behest."

For all it would accomplish—nothing—he still wanted to smash its face in. But to do so would only play to the demon's sense of amusement. It was already defiling the girl's body by its presence. He refused to make it worse, to let himself be drawn into that game. Moloch's kind had already had their fun and the streets of Tartarus were slick with blood because of it. No more.

He could feel Liz pressed against his shoulder. "I'm going to go ahead and do what I came back here to do in the first place," she said. "I think you'll like it."

She stepped around him, stared down at Moloch inside his puppet.

"You *won't*."

She left their company for now, the good and the evil alike, needed to get off by herself for the next few minutes. This was going to be one of those things best done alone, without others, even your best friends, looking over your shoulder.

Hellboy had no choice but to stay behind, still engaged with the vile thing whose likeness loomed above them. But Abe wanted to follow, clearly uneasy with the idea of her straying too far, and she loved him for it because so few loved her the same way, like family . . . but still, she had to tell Abe to let her be. And he did, but he was such a *guy* about it, you know, shuffling where he stood and scowling in that baffled way of warriors who've been sidelined before everything's been killed or laid waste.

Liz walked along the outer ring of the abattoir, closer to

the machines than she really wanted to be—not close enough to touch them but still close enough to feel their presence, barbed with vicious potential, aware of that cold metallic smell coming off them. When she decided she'd gone far enough, for privacy's sake, she turned to put them at her back—no need to see them, anyway.

She shrugged out of her pack and set it on the stone; opened it and dug past the MRE food packets, the water bottles, the ammunition, the last worldly possessions of Noémi Kivits. From the bottom she withdrew the hard, cloth-wrapped bundle, a third again the size of her fist; unwrapped it and held the ash-streaked seraph's heart.

They would never have given it to her as a trophy, she was sure. They had no need of trophies, probably didn't even understand the concept.

But why did they have hearts at all, why bodies that could be destroyed, she had asked Father Laurenti during those long hours they'd talked, as she'd felt burdened by the weight of having killed one.

He told her he didn't know, just his own conclusions: that where they came from they may have been creatures of spirit, but when they came here as slayers, avengers, destroyers . . . this was brute work, for a world of fists and blades and searing flames. The world of flesh and bone. They had to descend to the level of their work.

He couldn't have missed how she'd taken no consolation in this, and tried to soften it for her, relating something he'd been told by the captive Father Verdi: *They are the perfect manifestation of His wrath, and nothing more. And for so long, they have had nothing to do.*

In other words, they were obsolete, Laurenti said. And

wasn't it interesting, wasn't it comforting, he asked, to recognize how this paralleled the Bible, and the way it showed
God's evolution from a god of jealousy and wrath to one of
love?

Well, okay. Maybe. But not as comforting as it could be,
as long as the wrath was still lingering in some form, waiting to be tapped.

She held the heart in her hand, touched her lips to its
greased and sooty crust. Were they hers to call now, free of
rites and blood and symbols . . . because was she *one* of
them, in their view? She couldn't think of a single other reason why they would have given this to her, then bowed, if
they hadn't expected to see her again.

I don't want this power, she thought. *I have more than
enough trouble with my own.*

But here, things were different.

She let the flame come, just a little, flickering down the
length of her arm like a glove, until it wreathed the heart as
well. The crust began to slough away and reveal the raw
pink meat beneath—none of this planned, just going by instinct and impulse, but sometimes that was where the
strongest magic hid. She had no words for them, either,
nothing to call them with other than pure, unscripted
yearning.

It was enough.

They came in glory, if not in grace, and this time she
was glad to see them.

Winged and achingly beautiful, they looked the same as
before—no reason they shouldn't, her memories and
dreams were still the same—but now there were only six.
They faced her in a semi-circle where they'd descended

onto the statue's hand, waiting, as the distant cavern walls went pale, sheathed in a rime of ice.

From the corner of her eye, she saw H.B. give Abe his coat. Abe was shivering, and Liz imagined she would be too if the fire was not upon her.

With the heart now burning in her hand, she shut her eyes and saw what she wanted most—a fever dream of devastation, this place of cruelty and hubris humbled and brought low, machines melted, cathedral walls shattered, carvings broken into rubble, and the bodies of the near-dead granted a last kiss of mercy before the pyre . . . all but one—Hellboy had spoken his wish for Herzog, and she would have it granted, along with any other wishes he might have.

She saw safe passage for herself and her friends.

After that, and *only* after, did she see the portals sealed, all of them, large and small. And if they couldn't be sealed, then guarded, like the east gate of Eden.

Could they do it? Would it be too much even for them?

Maybe. But if they had anything, the seraphim had time.

She turned her back to them and threw the heart as hard as she could, over the ring of ugly machines. She'd never thrown like a girl in her life, even her brother had said so, shaking his stinging hand in those better days before the fire. High praise—it just didn't get any better than that.

Like a shooting star, the heart fell from sight, a tiny blaze swallowed by the dark. Maybe it would tie them to this place. She could imagine worse outcomes than that.

They took to the wing then. They prepared for war.

• • •

Hellboy kept one eye on Moloch, the other cast above, where the first plumes of fire soared overhead like the crisscrossing paths of meteors. He watched them work with ambivalence, knowing too well the pain and death they'd caused, yet still finding them magnificent in their way—these strange destroyers that he continued to see as perfected versions of himself.

For now, it was enough to know that they were finally on the same side. There was Liz to thank for that, and moments later she returned with a faraway look in her downcast eyes, as though what she'd set into motion was not worth watching.

He supposed he should have been expecting it, that with a flick of the French girl's green eyes, Moloch—who had seemed no less absorbed by the spectacle of such devastation raining down—noticed Liz's return and without warning sprang toward her. Or tried, at least. Hellboy was still faster, his hand quick as a cobra as he caught the girl's upper arm and snatched her out of mid-air. As he whirled her around, her limbs flailed with a frenzy worthy of the beast inside her, and he brought her down with him to the stone floor.

Hellboy lay on his back and pinned Moloch atop himself, reaching around the girl's body from back to front to hold it immobile so that it too faced upward. And Moloch was forced to watch.

"What's the matter?" he said into its ear. "Not such a small victory this time?"

From somewhere in the abattoir came a screech of metal, then a crash as some structure sagged and toppled.

"H.B.?" Liz, hunkering nearby. "Tell them if there's any-thing you want. They'll listen to you. I asked them to."

For a moment he wondered how the seraphim were sup-posed to hear him over the searing flames, and what words he might use to make himself understood . . . but then he realized that they were with him already, on the other side of will and intention, imagination and desire.

He knew what he wanted. Easy. All he had to do was look at what was already in front of his eyes, then envision it in a new and different way.

They heard, and rose to the challenge far above.

"I can't hurt you in that body, any more than you can hurt me," Hellboy said. "But your pride has a long reach, doesn't it? So let's watch the show . . . unless you don't think you can handle it."

There were no words for Moloch's outrage, only the straining of muscle and bone that could never overpower him, and a snarl that sounded as though it were flaying the throat into strips. But he had the devil now. Pride was on the line no matter what, and would not let it retreat from this body it had claimed.

And in this way Hellboy made it witness the fall of its world.

The seraphim, Kate had guessed, drew their power from the environment around them. Again, the plunging tem-perature was proof of that, and what he first thought was ash sifting down from the murky haze of the cavern's ceiling was, instead, snow. It drifted to the cavern floor in swirling clouds, and through it, Hellboy could see that the bull's head of the great statue, looming over its domain, was growing pale. Patches of frost spread across it like white moss as the seraphim leeched it of all the warmth and energy it had to give.

Ice . . . and fire. They poured it on like ten thousand years of accumulated wrath.

At first the effects were subtle, barely seen from this distance, the statue's face webbing with fractures and fissures that released showers of small stones as they flaked away under such a rapid change in temperature. But Hellboy had faith in greater things to come, and soon enough they did.

It sounded like thunder—a sharp crack that rebounded from wall to wall, from ceiling to floor, like the splitting of the world on doomsday. He'd heard of such sounds preceding earthquakes sometimes, a huge subterranean slab of rock stressed to the breaking point, then giving all at once.

But here it was the horn, the statue's *left* horn, the same one he'd snatched away in Glasgow. Under the onslaught of fire and ice, its own weight turned against it now, and it split from the head in a cloud of dust and the rumble of a falling mountain. It plummeted in a freefall that looked absurdly slow, then smashed onto the inner elbow of the statue's outstretched arm. It broke apart, spewing boulders the size of houses that rumbled the cavern underfoot when they struck ground. Some made it as far as the opposite side of the abattoir, crushing machinery in a cacophony of grinding metal before the wreckage of stone and iron alike tumbled into the dark well. If they struck bottom, he could not hear the sound above the rest.

Within Hellboy's arms, Moloch strained in impotent fury, heedless of the body that he had stolen and was now pushing to the breaking point. Bones snapping, joints popping, ligaments and tendons tearing. It was the last weapon left to him, the final show of petulance and rage—Moloch would know that, wouldn't he, that Hellboy could never let the girl's body go while the demon still laid claim to it. And so they both would ruin her, together.

For Hellboy's part, he held on because it was the one thing he could do for her—sparing her the worse dishonor of being used to harm those who had come here to learn her fate, to set her free.

He lay on the stone and watched the snow until it was done, and the body could break no more.

When it was over, and the body of Noémi Kivits once again knew peace, Liz stepped closer, closer, until she could kneel beside the poor lost girl with the black-bruised throat and the cherry red hair.

She straightened the contorted limbs the best she could, then placed both hands upon her—one on Noémi's shoulder, another at her waist. As the destruction raged around them, Liz found a moment of calm, and knew that it would be wrong somehow to leave *this* body for the wrath and ruin of angels.

This one would be hers and hers alone . . . this girl who had blundered onto the wrong path and found herself trapped in a Hell she didn't know how to leave. So with tenderness, and with grief, Liz let the fire come and take her.

And once the body was burning, she rushed to Hellboy and Abe, and they all three ran for the cavern floor, the way out, something better.

Unlike Lot's wife fleeing Sodom, as the flames bloomed high behind them, she had no desire to look back.

CHAPTER 31

As far as Hellboy was concerned, Campbell Holt had sacrificed himself in the line of duty the same as any agent who'd fallen to violence. There were no disagreements from the bureaucrats; they were just more accustomed to patching up broken bodies.

A broken mind? It took a lot of loud arguments before they could be convinced not to send him to the mental health center up at Hartford Hospital. Campbell didn't need the company of schizophrenics. They could still get him whatever psychiatric care he might need. But for bed and board and company, the ones who'd been there when he'd fallen felt him more likely to improve under the touch of someone who could better understand what had burned him from the inside.

Maybe it was prejudice, but if Campbell could come back to his mind at all, Hellboy didn't know a more conducive, restful place to do it than the Cotswolds.

"Bring him," Father Simon Finch said. No hesitation, no wait-and-see. Just, "Bring him, and we'll do what we can."

So Hellboy and Liz took him to the vicarage at Winograd Heath and got him settled into a spare room, where he folded himself into corners or drew shaky-handed pictures or trembled where he sat, and sometimes muttered things under his breath with the urgency of incantations, and not once seemed to respond to anything said to him in a way that made sense.

But under this roof, they would try.

This one's on me, Hellboy thought. *No matter what came of it, there was probably another way to get there. So this one's on me.*

He and Liz spent a few days and nights at the vicarage, didn't want the transfer to be a simple drop-and-run, and to be honest about it, he needed a little of Father Simon's time too. On the third afternoon, while Liz was inside with Campbell, and he was out back with Simon hauling firewood, he decided the time was right.

"Bless me, Father," he said, "for I have sinned."

Simon's white eyebrows nudged upward a millimeter. "Have you, now?"

"I lied my ass off. You're only the third person who knows we got the Masada Scroll back. Everybody else? I told 'em I was pretty sure it was lost for good. The bureau, the Vatican's people, all of them."

"That's a big one, then, isn't it?"

They let the firewood go for now and wandered toward the garden, or the ghost of the garden—November, after all, with England in the bare-branched grip of wind and drizzle that turned even the beauty of the Cotswolds damp and dreary.

"Appointed yourself its guardian and keeper, have you?" Simon asked.

"More like I just don't know what to do with it. I *saw*

how the other side wanted to use it. That could still happen. Nothing we did changed that. I could give it back to the Vatican, and the guys in control of it might be the most well-meaning people in the world, and some of them are, I think . . . but all that still could happen."

"Any plans you're kicking around, then?"

"Part of me wants to burn it. The exact thing I was brought on board to prevent."

"Why don't you?"

"I don't think I've got the right to do that. Authentic or not, it's a little piece of the past that can never be replaced. Besides," and he shook his head, "Abe would never forgive me."

He supposed it would be easier to come to a decision if he knew for sure that the scroll was no more than some early bit of creative writing. Pseudepigrapha, he'd learned such things were called: work by an anonymous scribe that claims to have been written by someone with name value.

Like Liz, like Abe, like anyone with a little leap of imagination, he had wondered what Campbell would make of the scroll if given the chance to hold it. If he would've merely gotten insights into archivists, or if the link would have been strong enough to carry him back to someone nearly 2000 years ago, the original owner, the true owner, who'd daily faced his death on a besieged plateau in the Judean desert.

Place it in Campbell's hand anyway? He'd done it. Gotten nothing.

"You could always leave it here while you're giving the matter a hashing through," Simon offered.

"I don't think so. That'd be like leaving Sauron's ring at Bag End for good. It could bring you some bad trouble." Hellboy gave him a hopeful look, this trim, white-haired man who sometimes measured his words a little too carefully. Typical English understatement, or a genuine distaste for telling people how to live? Probably some of both. "Any ideas what I should do?"

"Comes down, I think, to where your allegiances lie: with the past or with the future. Which sounds like an easy one at first, but it's not. I think we owe the past a measure of respect for getting us where we are today, and the shape of the future depends on it." He laced his fingers and tapped his thumbs together. "I'm with Abe on this one, I'm afraid. You burn it, and I'll have a bugger of a time forgiving you too."

"That makes it harder. That makes things a *lot* harder."

Simon nodded. "If you wanted things easy, friend, you picked the wrong world to come to."

And the next day, when Liz quit again, for the thirteenth time, he was reminded in the starkest possible terms just how hard it all could be.

By early December, her newly rediscovered freedom had taken her to the north of France, to Reims, where no matter how hard she tried to find other diversions, Liz couldn't keep herself from making daily trips to the cathedral in the heart of the city. With its twin bell towers and all the spires bristling from the transepts and apse, this Gothic monolith could have been an uncomfortable reminder of what she'd seen in Tartarus, just how far such beauty could degenerate. Yet it was no such thing.

With bombs and shells, they'd destroyed it in the First World War, the labors of seven centuries before, but today you'd never know it. It drew her as a reaffirmation that something could rise from ruin, and in its pews she prayed for Campbell, mind and soul alike, that the pieces could find their way back together again.

She prayed for Hellboy, too, for all he was and wasn't. Over the last few years she had come to better understand her role in his life, as a sister and a friend. With so much of his origins a mystery yet, she'd wondered how he could truly know himself . . . although gradually she'd realized that maybe this didn't matter so long as she was in his life, and he might come to know himself better through *her* eyes.

By her absences, did she condemn him to forget, if only just a little?

I'm sorry, H.B., but it just doesn't work the same way for me . . .

Thirteen times. There had to be something pathologically wrong with that.

For now, though, each day she would turn loose of her prayers, and light votives in the racks for the living and the lost. She would leave the cathedral then to walk in the snow and discover another long route back to the hostel where she was staying, and in her devotion to this routine postpone for one more day the *real* reason she'd traveled to Reims.

This was where Noémi Kivits had come from, and

where her family still lived, no doubt worrying each day where she had gone. They deserved her backpack returned, at the very least, and the closure of the news that their daughter would never be coming home.

Though quit of the bureau again, she'd still gotten Kate to tap its international law enforcement agency database, found that Noémi had vanished in the spring. During her second year at the University of Strasbourg, she'd taken a weekend trip to Paris, joining friends for an illegal late-night exploration of the city's catacombs, miles and miles of tunnels that originated as Roman stone quarries. With them one minute, her friends had reported, and gone the next.

Half a dozen times now, Liz had stood on the sidewalk across the street from Noémi's parents' apartment on Rue St. Brice, wrestled with her conscience, and moved along once again. She still had no idea what to tell them. Abhorred the truth and couldn't stomach the lies she'd devised so far. She told herself that maybe the clue to something better would be in the girl's belongings, the notebooks and journals Noémi had been filling up in classrooms and cafés.

Was it wrong to want to read them, these last things a stranger had written?

She collected quotations, Noémi did, pages and pages of them, from Shakespeare to Liz Phair, and somehow the words of others that had resonated with her provided a fuller portrait of Noémi than her own, and the world seemed lesser for her absence.

Liz Sherman kept returning to one quote in particular, attributed to something called *The Book of Thirst,* which she'd never heard of but would have to seek out soon:

Nul ne sait de quoi le monde sera fait une fois passé le tour-nant de la route.

Nobody knows what the world is made of around the corner.

She hoped she could learn to like the sound of that better someday.

ABOUT THE AUTHOR

Brian Hodge is the author of nine novels spanning horror and crime-noir. He's also written close to one hundred short stories and novellas, many of which have been sentenced to life without parole in three highly acclaimed collections. Forthcoming works include a new collection to be titled *A Loving Look of Agony,* a short novel called *The Other Halves of Heaven,* and another crime novel, *Mad Dogs.*

He frequently wanders the hills around Boulder, Colorado, shoots photographs of green things and decaying things, and sequesters himself in a home studio emitting dark electronic music and other rude noises.

Not sure
what to
read next?

Visit Pocket Books online at
www.SimonSays.com

**Reading suggestions for
you and your reading group**

New release news

Author appearances

Online chats with your favorite writers

Special offers

And much, much more!

POCKET BOOKS
A Division of Simon & Schuster
A VIACOM COMPANY

**POCKET
STAR BOOKS**
A Division of Simon & Schuster
A VIACOM COMPANY

10421